THE NEW MOON WITH THE OLD

by

Dodie Smith

Magna Large Print Books
Long Preston, North Yorkshire,
BD23 4ND, England.

British Library Cataloguing in Publication Data.

Smith, Dodie
    The new moon with the old.

    A catalogue record of this book is
    available from the British Library

    ISBN   978-0-7505-3724-7

This edition published by Corsair,
an imprint of Constable & Robinson Ltd., 2012

Copyright © Dodie Smith 1963

Cover illustration © Sara Mulvanny by arrangement with
Constable & Robinson Ltd.

The moral right of the author has been asserted

Published in Large Print 2013 by arrangement with
Constable & Robinson Ltd.

Magna Large Print is an imprint of Library Magna Books Ltd.

Printed and bound in Great Britain by
T.J. (International) Ltd., Cornwall, PL28 8RW

Contents

BOOK ONE

Jane

1

Monday

She did not believe in omens but instantly knew this was a good one: the afternoon sun, coming from behind the clouds, had turned the grey of the glass dome to a shimmer of gold. Seen from this hill top where she had got out of her car to reconnoitre – and there could be no doubt that *was* Dome House – the effect was quite dazzling, and extremely cheering.

Only a moment before, her spirits had been low. The slate roof surrounding the dome was so large, the chimneys sprouting from the roof so numerous – and she had undertaken to do the house-keeping. That might prove to be a polite name for housework. One didn't mind a reasonable amount; as a resident secretary one was usually roped in for it. But with a house that size...!

Now, in this sudden sunlight – and the rain, almost continuous during her fifty-mile drive from London, had completely stopped – she reminded herself there were said to be two excellent maids. What riches, for the nineteen-sixties! And Mr Carrington would need her secretarial services only when he came home at weekends. A pity one would see so little of him, and that he would not be there today. She had never liked a prospective employer so much. Strange that such an attractive man should have remained a widower for so many years...

Well, better take the plunge now. As usual before starting a new job, she was nervous – and very silly, it was, for one always got on well and Rupert Carrington had made his family sound delightful. And it would be pleasant to live in the country after three years in a dull London suburb working for a dull author and his even duller wife. All around her now were stubble fields, meadows, and woods already hinting at autumn, very beautiful in the mellow afternoon light. One hadn't realized how unspoilt the Suffolk country-side was or how pretty the villages were. No doubt the village she could see half a mile or so beyond Dome House would be as charming as those she had driven through.

Then the sun went behind the clouds again and the smile faded from the landscape. She shivered slightly; it was cold up on this high ground. Surely that large glass dome would make the house very cold in winter – and hot in summer? And wouldn't it be a gloomy house, with so many trees around it? One really ought to make a home for oneself, some cheerful place to return to every night. But she'd never felt capable of it, since selling up the house after her mother's death. And one could save more if one took resident jobs. Her little car was an extravagance (but gave her such a feeling of freedom) and she did like good clothes – nothing showy, but nothing cheap. Still, someday perhaps, a small flat...

'Jane Minton, you always think that, on your way to a new job,' she told herself, getting back into the car to tidy her dark hair and repair her discreet make-up. She then pulled on her leather gloves; good gloves always gave her confidence. Now for it! Really, that dome looked almost sinister, without the sun on it. A good thing one didn't believe in omens.

She drove down the hill, past the still-dripping chestnuts which screened Dome House from the road, and in through the open gate. The gravel drive curved through a plantation of trees and then through a shrubbery. This at last gave way to lawns and the house sprang into view. She did not much care for its mottled grey brick but this toned well with all the pale green woodwork – window frames, slatted shutters, a pillared porch, and an unusual scalloped border just under the edge of the roof. The general effect was pleasing and she had never seen a house look so noticeably clean. The windows positively sparkled, particularly the two very tall ones which flanked the front door; through them she could see the flicker of firelight.

As she got out of her car, a fair, pretty girl came from the house, followed by a slight, sandy-haired young man. The girl spoke first but looked and sounded diffident.

'I'm Clare Carrington and this is my brother, Drew. He'll take your suitcase and your typewriter.'

'And then, if I may, I'll put your car in the

9

garage,' said Drew. 'I'm a very gentle driver.'

His voice was more striking than his appearance; it was deep, with a curious break in it. Jane set great store by voices. As a rule she disliked letting anyone but herself drive her car but she had no hesitation in trusting Drew. And her nervousness vanished. She chatted easily about her journey as the three of them went into the house.

Indoors, she got a quick impression of a large square hall, rather too much upholstered furniture, and firelight reflected by white panelling. Then they were on their way up the wide staircase, to a gallery which ran round three sides of the hall and from which the bedrooms opened. High above, lighting both gallery and hall, was the glass dome.

She was shown into a back bedroom. Drew set her suitcase down, then went to garage her car.

'Flowers! How nice!' she said, enthusiastically and automatically. There always *were* flowers and she always praised them, while her practised eye noticed inadequacies as regards furniture. Here there were no inadequacies. She saw there was plenty of drawer and cupboard space, a desk, a dressing-table in a good light, a comfortable armchair, an electric fire already on. And miracle of miracles, a fitted wash basin! She praised it warmly.

'There's one in every bedroom,' said Clare. 'My grandmother had them put in. They're ugly but useful. The bathroom's just next door – you share it with my sister and me; the boys use Father's. I suppose you don't happen to prefer your bath at night?'

'Any time at all,' said Jane, who had lived in houses where it was hard to come by two baths a week. 'Night suits me perfectly.'

'Oh, marvellous – because my sister and I like ours in the morning. Now I'll leave you to un-pack. You've half an hour before tea. I'll let you know when it's ready.'

The door closed behind her. Jane, having bounced on the bed and found it satisfactory, looked around gloatingly. Such comfort! Not that she admired the massive Victorian furniture. But she was, admittedly, a snob about furniture, only caring for valuable antiques – perhaps because she owed so much to the few good pieces she'd inherited, the sale of which had seen her right through her secretarial training.

If anything, this room was too hot. She then discovered the radiator – all this and central heat-ing too! Blithely she turned off the electric fire and began to unpack.

She had cleared her suitcase and was shaking out dresses from her trunk, sent on in advance, when there came a knock on the door. Jane called 'Come in' and a tall, brown-haired girl entered. In spite of her height, Jane took her to be only in her early teens.

'I'm Merry,' she announced. 'That's short for Meriella. Unusual name, isn't it? Mother got it off a tombstone.'

'Charming as well as unusual,' said Jane, smil-ingly. This child wasn't as pretty as the elder sister but her lively intelligent face was most attractive.

11

'I only get called it at school but I may use it when I go on the stage. Have you been to any theatres lately?'

Jane was glad she could say she'd been to several. Merry at once extracted brief information about them, then said, 'You must meet my friend Betty and give us full details. She's going on the stage too, though her fat legs may hold her back. She's pretty fat all over really, and terribly busty. My bust's a bit late on its cue but it's started at last. What a good figure you have, slim but not bony. And you're much younger than I expected. Father thought late thirties.'

'Very late,' said Jane. 'In fact–' She was pleased to be interrupted.

'Really? I'd have said thirty-four. You still look quite girlish. Oh, is that rude? Do you mind personal remarks?'

'Not when they're as complimentary as that,' said Jane.

'You look a bit sad, too – in an interesting way. Rather Chekhovian. Betty and I are working on Chekhov at present. Are you ready for tea? If you want to pop in next door I'll wait for you.'

Jane availed herself of this kind suggestion and was then taken by the arm and steered towards the stairs, to the accompaniment of: 'What a lovely soft sweater! Real cashmere, isn't it? Oh, don't grab the handrail – that looks awful when a staircase has two and is right out in the middle of a hall. You must sail down as if the audience was over the front door.'

'But I shall fall,' said Jane, wobbling.

'Well, the carpet's very soft. I fell twice when I

was learning to run down full tilt without looking at my feet. Would you like to see me roll from top to bottom as if I'd been shot? It's just a knack – I could teach you.'

They reached the foot of the stairs safely, to Jane's relief. Drew came to meet them and Merry went on without interruption. 'Very unusual looking, isn't she, Drew? Such a pale, clear skin. But don't you think she should use a darker lipstick? Her face needs a clove carnation gash. It's all right, she doesn't mind personal remarks.'

Drew, settling Jane by the fire, said: 'You may find Merry a bit overpowering but I believe she's right about a darker lipstick.'

'I'll get one,' said Jane.

'It's such a bore I can't use make-up myself except in private,' said Merry. 'I can look almost glamorous – and years older. And I do some good character make-ups. My best is the young vampire, with blood running down her chin.'

'Not at tea, Merry,' said Clare, who was already pouring out.

'Why not? Vampires have blood for tea. They can't help it. I do think people are unfair to vampires.'

Clare asked Jane how she liked her tea and Drew brought it to her.

'Shall I go and get Richard?' said Merry.

'My elder brother,' Drew explained to Jane. 'He has a music room out in the barn and is apt to forget his meals when genius burns. It's all right, Merry; I can hear him.'

A tall, very dark young man came in. Jane thought him handsome but his pale, classically

13

featured face struck her as austere. And though he spoke to her politely enough, both his manner and his voice seemed to her a little aloof. After a few conventional civilities, he dropped out of the conversation.

Drew, having waited on everyone, sat down beside her, bringing a three-decker brass cakestand with him.

'Oh, a curate's aid!' she said. 'That takes me back to my grandmother's At Home days.'

'I bid for it at a sale *my* grandmother took me to,' said Drew. 'I was ten years old and already knew I was fated to be the family hander-rounder; Richard never did bestir himself. I'd quite like to be a curate – as regards the social side. I couldn't stand the church work.'

The whole tea, as well as the curate's aid, reminded Jane of her childhood. Never since then had she seen such a spread of toast and jam, hot scones, and thickly marzipanned fruit cake. Yet, they're all so slim, she thought, watching the young Carringtons steadily munching. Conversation continued easily but with no help from Richard. He seemed oblivious of them all and had to be asked three times if he wanted a second cup of tea.

'His head's like the island in *The Tempest*,' Merry told Jane. '"Full of noises, sounds and sweet airs" – well, perhaps not sweet airs; he doesn't often compose a tune.'

'The lot of a young composer's so hard,' said Drew. 'If his music is understandable it's probably old-fashioned; and if it isn't, one needs so much faith.'

14

'What's your special instrument?' Jane asked Richard politely.

But he had taken his tea and was already pre-occupied again. Merry answered for him. 'He can play four instruments but he very seldom does. Did you know composers can work without so much as striking a note? It's all in their minds. Well, perhaps it's only like writing a play without saying the words aloud. I've written two plays. Writing's my second string – and Drew's first. He's planning a novel. His second string is piano playing.'

'Only a little gentle Chopin,' said Drew. 'And I make it sound too gentle even for Chopin.'

'Rubbish,' said Richard, suddenly, returning to the conversation. 'You play admirably – far better than I do. Would you excuse me now, Miss Winton?'

'Minton,' said Clare. But he was already on his way.

'He's often more normal by dinner time,' said Merry. 'Have you got us all straight now? I act and write. Drew writes and plays the piano. Richard only composes and Clare only paints.'

'I don't really paint,' said Clare.

'Oh, you do, Clare darling.' Merry turned to Jane. 'She does lovely flower studies with all the stamens and things. They were always being pinned up in the studio at school. Is there anything else you'd like to know? Perhaps our ages. Richard's twenty-three, Clare's twenty-one, Drew's nineteen and I'm fourteen and almost six months.'

'Thank you, that's very helpful,' said Jane,

slightly dazed. 'Well, you're certainly a talented family.'

'That remains to be proved,' said Drew. 'At present it's just a belief our doting grandmother fostered – probably to keep us occupied on long wet afternoons. She brought us up here; our mother was always in London with Father. I rather think they were laying us down, like wine, to enjoy in middle age, but poor Mother didn't live long enough. She died not long after Merry was born.'

'Nearly a year after – and I was in no way to blame,' said Merry. 'Well, I must go and work now.'

'Homework?' Jane inquired.

'No, school doesn't start till next week. I'm memorizing Nina in *The Seagull*. Oh, you could come and hear me.'

'Not now,' said Clare. 'I want her to meet Cook and Edith.'

'Do you really have a cook who's called Cook?' said Jane.

'Isn't it archaic? But they were my grand-mother's maids.' Clare rose and picked up the cakestand. 'It'll save Edith a trip if we carry something.'

A door at the back of the hall opened into the flagged passage which led to the kitchen. Jane, following Clare in, saw two elderly, white-over-alled women sitting in front of a fire burning in an old-fashioned kitchen range. They rose, as did an elderly Golden Labrador sitting between them.

Cook was short and stout, with red hair well on its way to white. Edith was tall, gaunt and grey-

16

haired. Jane set down the scone dish and shook hands, conscious that her grandmother would have thought this incorrect; she hoped Cook and Edith didn't. They greeted her pleasantly and then encouraged the dog to offer a paw.

'He can do it if he tries,' said Edith.

Jane doubted it. Could such a stout dog support himself on only three legs? 'I'll take the will for the deed,' she said; he was wagging his tail very civilly. 'What's his name?'

'Burly,' said Cook. 'Suits him, doesn't it? Did even when he was a pup. He's too stout. They say it shortens their lives, but he's not in bad shape for fifteen. He was born just a few days after we came.'

'Never guess we were sisters, would you?' said Edith. 'I call us the long and the short of it. Nice kitchen, isn't it?'

Jane heartily agreed. It reminded her of a 'before and after' advertisement, with 'before' and 'after' neatly joined. The sink, electric cooker and refrigerator were modern but the tall dresser was old; and the wicker armchairs, half filled with cushions, looked as comfortable as Burly's rug-lined basket.

'My word, we've been glad Mrs Carrington didn't let them take away the old range,' said Cook. 'Oh, I'm grateful for central heating but you can see a fire.'

And also see the bills for coal, thought Jane, before remarking sycophantically: 'What's smelling so good?'

'Steak-and-kidney pudding,' said Cook. 'Been on since this morning. I always say they need seven hours – well, six if you're rushed. Better get the tea tray now, Edith, or we'll be behind hand.' She turned to Jane and spoke with an official respectfulness which was also slightly formidable. 'We must have a nice talk about the housekeeping when Miss Clare hands it over. I think you'll find Edith and me easy to work with.'

'I'm sure I shall,' said Jane fervently, feeling a slight tremor. She had never had to handle any Cooks or Ediths and thought it likely that they, not she, would be doing the handling.

Clare opened the kitchen door for her and said tentatively, 'I wonder – as Cook's mentioned the housekeeping – if I could have a talk with you about it? Or do you want to go on unpacking?'

'Plenty of time for that,' said Jane, only too anxious to know what was expected of her.

They found the hall deserted except for Edith, who was plumping up cushions. Like a maid in some old play, Jane thought amusedly. And now she came to think of it the whole hall resembled stage sets seen in her childhood. The many bedroom doors above suggested a French farce; guests at a party could be received at the top of the stairs. She must remember to say this to Merry.

Edith went. Clare put more wood on the fire and offered Jane a cigarette. They agreed it was a good thing neither of them smoked.

'Well, now,' said Jane encouragingly. She could see Clare was very nervous.

'It's just that... I suppose it is all right? Father did explain? If I do decide to go to this art school...'

'But he said it was settled.'

'Not yet. I felt I must see you first. I was so afraid you might be like Father's Aunt Winifred – she came to look after us when our grandmother died six years ago and we had the most awful year. Cook and Edith gave notice.'

'What did she do to annoy them?' asked Jane, hoping to avoid pitfalls.

'Just fussed terribly. And nothing was ever quite right for her – that's so depressing. In the end Father had to ask her to go, because we couldn't run this great, awkward house without Cook and Edith and of course we could never replace them. I just took over though I was still at school then – there's a good school near here so Merry and I haven't had to go to a boarding school. I shall never be really domesticated but I've managed ... somehow.'

'I only hope I can manage as well,' said Jane.

'Oh, you will – far better. And Cook and Edith are splendid. It's just that someone has to plan the meals and do the shopping and pay the bills – it's a full time job; anyway, it is for me because I'm bad at it. And doing the flowers takes such ages.'

'Then let me do them. I love arranging flowers.'

'Really? I loathe it so much that it stops me from wanting to paint them. And they're the only things I can paint, and not very well at that. I'm not clever, like the others are. But Father thinks I should go to an art school – and I must admit I don't want to spend the whole of my life just running this house.'

You won't, thought Jane. You'll marry and run

your own house. Why should such a very pretty girl be bothered to have a career? Aloud, she said: 'Well, you hand everything over to me. I ought to have plenty of time unless your father leaves me a lot of work.'

'I don't think he'll leave you any – and he doesn't come home every weekend. He's mainly counting on your releasing me. You see, as well as going to this art school he wants me to stay with him sometimes and meet people. Oh, dear, has he got you under false pretences? He felt a secretary would fit in better than a housekeeper, though he did see some housekeepers. He just went on seeing people until he found someone he thought we'd all like.'

Jane flushed with pleasure. 'I hope he thought right.'

'Indeed he did. Drew and I took to you at once and you can see Merry has. And Richard will. Of course you may not take to us.'

'I have already,' said Jane. 'I can truly say I never started any job with such high hopes of being happy.' She found it hard to believe that, less than two hours before, she had gazed down on Dome House, chilled by apprehension. Remembering, she looked up at the dome, now a pale circle of twilight.

'Oh, I am glad,' said Clare. 'Let's have some sherry, to celebrate.'

'Heavens, I'm still full of tea!' But Clare was already on her way to get the sherry. Jane noted how small and slight she was and how young she looked, years younger than twenty-one; though her figure was that of a miniature woman and not at all childish.

'There! You can drink it while you unpack. Let me know when you want the boys to move your trunk to the boxroom. Dinner's at seven-thirty. Edith will bang the gong at seven – this family has to be warned to stop working – not that we dress for dinner. Oh, Merry and I sometimes change but only into any old dress. You just suit yourself. I'll be in my room – that's the second door beyond the bathroom – and please, please come and ask if there's anything you need.' Having opened Jane's door for her, Clare sped along the gallery.

Jane wondered what more anyone could need, beyond this comfortable bedroom, this warmly welcoming household. Though there was one tiny fly in her ointment: it was a pity Rupert Carrington did not come home every weekend.

She went to the window and stood looking down on the large back garden with its wide herbaceous borders. At the far end was a small thatched barn with a window in the gable end; Richard's music room, no doubt. Beyond the garden she could see a narrow lane, then a patchwork of meadowland and stubble under a vast, pale sunset. She sighed happily and turned to her trunk.

By the time the gong sounded she had unpacked all she wished to unpack. Her summer clothes, cleaned and packed in tissue paper, could be left at the bottom of the trunk. She imagined shaking them out, next year, then mentally touched wood, but she had no serious qualms. Never yet had she lost a job; she merely left jobs when she tired of them, and it would be a long, long time before she tired of this job. At the moment she would cheerfully have signed on for life.

Now the quiet house was coming to life. She heard doors opening and closing, voices, a radio – no, it was television; she recognized the programme. Quickly she changed into the newest of her three dark crepe dresses – dark crepe got one tactfully through most evening meals, whether dinner, supper or high-tea. Then she went downstairs.

Drew and Merry were in the hall, watching television. Jane found herself accepting another glass of sherry. Clare came from the kitchen with a plate of cheese straws. At twenty-five past seven, Richard raced through the hall and upstairs, saying: 'I'm late – I know! But I'll be ready.' He came down just as dinner was served, looking even more handsome than Jane had remembered.

'Such a bore, leaving television for meals,' said Merry. 'I'd like them on trays but Cook won't hear of it.'

Richard now seemed less preoccupied; indeed, Jane found his manners very good. He settled her on his right and talked to her most politely, once he had served the truly magnificent steak-and-kidney pudding. She noticed that helpings went to the kitchen for Cook and Edith. 'We do that so that they can get finished and join us for television,' he explained.

Jane asked him the history of Dome House and learned that it had been built in 1820. His grandmother had found it in the late nineteen-thirties, much dilapidated, and been able to get a long lease at a very low rental on condition that she did the repairs. They had barely been finished before the war began.

'I can just remember the war here,' said Clare. 'The dome had to be boarded up. And Grand – that's what we called our grandmother – took in a lot of refugees as well as Richard and me, and then Drew as a baby. You can't imagine how cold the house was when we couldn't heat it properly.'

'Still, I always liked it,' said Richard. 'And the village. But not the people who live in the village. It's full of old ladies.'

'Very nice old ladies,' said Drew.

'Drew collects them,' Merry explained. 'Goes to tea with them and tries to get period details for his novel. It's to be set in the Edwardian era.'

Jane asked what had made him choose that.

'My grandmother was an inveterate frequenter of sales at country houses,' said Drew. 'That's why this house is full of large, valueless furniture which no one else wanted. She also bought books, including a collection of little red ones known, around fifty years ago, as Nelson's Sevenpennys. Clare cherished the historical romances and I wallowed in the society novels and fell in love with the Edwardians. If she and I are quaint old-world characters it's entirely due to Nelson's Red Sevenpennys.'

'Oh, is Clare interested in history?' asked Jane.

'Not real history,' said Drew. 'Just little red heels tapping the Pump Room floor and swords drawn in a flash to defend a lady's honour. And kings' mistresses – most of them charming girls even if they hadn't any honour to defend.'

'There were lovely Ruritanian novels, too,' said Clare. 'But I like Dumas best of all. He didn't come in Nelson's Sevenpennys. Grand said you could get him for sixpence in those days but I've had to pay seven shillings or more for mine.'

Jane was able to say she'd read *The Three Musketeers*. Clare offered to lend her all the sequels but was cut short by Merry. 'Miss Minton's much too modern to bother about your frowsty old Dumas. Now will everyone stop talking and concentrate on eating or we shall be late for that serial Edith likes.'

Having accepted a second helping of steak-and-kidney pudding, Jane was thankful when it was followed only by fruit salad – and cheese for anyone who wanted it; nobody did.

'Then off we go,' said Merry.

The Carringtons rose *en masse*. Richard and Drew put away place mats and napkins. Clare and Merry carried plates and glasses to the kitchen. Jane, following with the fruit-salad bowl, found Edith half-way through the washing up, Cook making coffee and Burly finishing the steak-and-kidney pudding. In a matter of minutes the entire kitchen party was *en route* for the hall, where Drew was making up the fire while Richard adjusted the television. Cook and Edith were settled on the sofa and handed coffee and pepper-mint creams. Jane began to understand why the Carringtons had kept their maids for fifteen years.

Burly was given warm milk in a saucer on the hearthstone, then boosted on to the sofa beside Cook. After accepting a peppermint cream he went to sleep.

Richard put the lights out. The serial began, prefaced by ominous music.

'Creepy,' said Edith.

Drew, sitting between the maids, insisted on holding their hands.

'I don't know what Miss Minton will think of you,' said Cook, complacently.

It dawned on Jane that the maids had Nanny status.

She had never particularly enjoyed television which she had usually watched with employers who, she felt, might prefer to be on their own; often she had excused herself and gone to her room to read. And she could not, now, follow the serial, already in its fifth instalment. But she found so much enjoyment that she asked herself the reason. Partly, of course, it was due to relief. A new job had started more than well; she had been kindly received and was now well-fed, warm and comfortable. But there was more to it than that. She was conscious of a happiness in which one could positively luxuriate. Who had created such an atmosphere? Four young people, two maids and a portly dog? She did not feel that Rupert Carrington could have had a share in it. Much as she liked him, he had seemed to her lacking in the serenity she now felt around her.

Did any of his children resemble him? She scanned their faces, lit by the flicker of television: Richard's darkly handsome, Clare's delicately pretty. Drew and Merry, alike in their small, neat features, had very different expressions; Drew's was reflective, Merry's vivacious. Only Clare had a look of her father and that was mainly due to their similar fairness. For an instant Jane saw his face vividly. How different his streamlined city offices were from this old family house. Such a very charming man... The serial ended to a repeat of the ominous music. Reverie retreated.

The next programme dealt with world affairs and was said by Drew to be 'too earnest affairs'. And the alternative was a Western which nobody wanted; Merry said she hated seeing horses fall, and Cook said gunfire disturbed Burly. So the sound was turned down and the little figures gesticulated silently about world affairs.

Drew said: 'I think one reason we like television is that we can control it. Those people in the box are our slaves. We can summon them when we want them and there's no doubt we get quite fond of them; but we still remain ruthless and powerful, capable of turning them into silent darkness.'

Merry was watching the screen. 'I'd rather turn them right off than keep them on and silent. Just look at them, *pleading* to be heard.'

Richard said: 'It doesn't make much difference to me what programme's on. I just like the miracle of the thing – it stirs my imagination. Oh, let the poor devils have their say.'

So world affairs had an innings and Jane thought Richard, Drew and Merry made well-informed comments on them. Cook and Edith also let fall several shrewd remarks. Only Clare remained completely uninterested. When the programme ended she said, 'I know I'm a half-wit but that kind of thing makes me *ache* with boredom. And now it's the dreary old News.'

'Our Clare doesn't much care for real life,' Drew told Jane. 'What she needs is to live in a book, the kind that no longer gets written.'

The News was followed by a play which was generally liked, but Jane still found her own thoughts more interesting and was glad when it ended. Cook then hoisted herself and Burly from the sofa and solicited orders for hot drinks. Nobody wanted any but Jane was glad to accept the suggestion of a hot-water bottle; she had a theory that first nights in a new bed were abnormally cold, though that might not be the case in this most comfortable house. She went up for her bottle and dropped it over the gallery to Edith. Clare came up to press bath essence on her and say that Edith would call her at eight-fifteen for breakfast at nine – 'If that's all right?' Richard, Drew and Merry said friendly good nights, Merry adding: 'We all think you're terribly nice.'

'And I you,' said Jane, whole-heartedly.

She had, in the course of her numerous resident jobs, lived in the same house with many young people and usually got on well with them. But she had often found them gauche, untidy and even dirty. Never before had she run into beautifully groomed, beautifully mannered youth, reminding her of friends known in her childhood. She felt as if in some pleasant pocket of the past, but one which had full access to the present; for she could not feel that the young Carringtons, with the possible exception of Clare, were old-fashioned. The others struck her as completely up to date, in spite of Drew's reference to himself as a quaint, old-world character. And if Claire was old-fashioned it was in a very off-key way, seeing that she was uninterested in domesticity and loathed arranging flowers.

'It's just that the whole household's unique in my experience,' thought Jane with satisfaction, lying in her scented bath.

She was not given to lolling in baths, seldom having achieved baths worth lolling in. The water so often ran cold, bathroom doors were so often rattled impatiently. But she was reluctant to leave this bath and lay listening to someone's bedside radio; only when the music stopped did she get out. She left the bathroom feeling boiled, guiltily sybaritic and extremely happy. The house was silent now, and dark except for the dull glow from the dying fire below.

What should she think of, on her way to sleep? Her interview with charming Rupert Carrington or her evening with his charming children? Rupert Carrington won by a head. How very comfortable this bed was! Everything was wonderful ... too, too wonderful...

2

Tuesday

She could not remember ever before being brought early-morning tea and biscuits and rather feared they had spoilt her appetite for breakfast; after tea and dinner at Dome House she had begun to take more interest in food than she usually did. She wasn't at all hungry as she opened her door to go downstairs. Then the smell of coffee and bacon was wafted up to her and she was instantly very hungry indeed.

Seeing Merry in the hall, she resisted her desire to clutch the handrail of the staircase.

'Splendid,' said Merry. 'You sailed down like a duchess.' Drew rose to ask if she had slept well; Clare said, 'How punctual you are!' and rang the gong for Richard. He came down and looked at Jane with faint surprise but greeted her pleasantly.

Sunlight flooded in through the hall's tall windows and into the dining-room. Breakfast was as lavish as she had expected; fruit and cereals were followed by bacon and eggs, though there was not – as, with nostalgic memories of country-house plays, she had faintly hoped – a dish of kidneys kept warm by a spirit lamp.

Drew made her toast on his electric toaster. There was a toaster in front of each young Carrington.

'Father bought them as a family Christmas present,' said Clare, 'because we were always fussing about really hot toast. Of course the wires are a nuisance; so's the noise.'

'One should think of it as *musique concrète*,' said Jane, and felt proud of herself when Richard smiled and said he'd consider a quartet for toasters. While finishing up with toast and marmalade she asked herself if she could manage such a breakfast every day and strongly suspected she could.

'I must tell you the order of the day,' said Clare. 'Cook and Edith are going out. They have to take their time off mid-week in case Father comes home at the weekend. We always give them lunch at the Swan, in the village. The food's rather good and Burly's allowed in the dining-room. Then we drive them to stay with their married sister till tomorrow night. They leave us sandwiches for this evening and we get our own meals tomorrow – or go to the Swan again.'

'I can cook a bit,' said Jane.

'How lovely! I'm hopeless at it. This afternoon Richard and I want to shop in our market town. You could come with us but there'll be a squash in the car until we've delivered Cook and Edith and Burly – he goes with them. If you don't come, you'll be on your own here as Drew's going to tea with one of his old ladies and Merry's spending the afternoon with a friend.'

'With Betty. I told you about her. You could come too, and talk about theatres.'

Jane would have been glad to, or to go with the others; but even more, she fancied being alone at

Dome House. She told Clare she wanted to plan the flowers before they next needed doing. 'Planning's half the battle – knowing which vase should go where and what flowers should go in it...'

'How brilliant of you,' said Clare. 'I just fill vases and wander round finding homes for them. What bliss it'll be to look at flowers I haven't arranged.'

After breakfast Clare and Merry made the beds so that Edith could help with the sandwich cutting. Jane went round with the girls, dusting. She was fascinated to see how the young Carringtons' bedrooms reflected their personalities, and looked forward to a closer inspection when planning the flowers; only Richard's room was without any. She asked if he did not care to have them.

'Well, he does if they're absolutely fresh,' said Clare. 'He must have chucked his out yesterday because they weren't. That reminds me, he needs some in his music room – in the big jar on the floor; never on his piano or his work table.'

'Won't he mind my going in?'

'Only when he's there. He hates being disturbed.'

The last room they came to was Clare's own. Jane saw water-colour paints set out and a half-finished drawing pinned to a drawing-board. She went towards it but Clare whisked the board away and turned its face to a wall. 'Not now, please,' she said, flushing. 'There isn't time. Would you mind getting ready? Merry and I want to show you the village before we meet the others at the Swan.'

'Oh, do let her see, Clare,' said Merry. 'It won't take a minute.'

But Jane, having noticed Clare's flush, was already on her way to her room.

The girls were waiting for her when she went downstairs. 'Look at her lovely suede gloves,' said Merry. 'You don't really need them in the village but they'll increase our prestige. Are they your best?'

'Well, I do have a longer pair.'

'You must show me some time. I'm passionate about long gloves.'

Jane enjoyed the walk to the village, which seemed even prettier than those she had driven through. She had seen them at their dullest, veiled by rain. She was seeing this one in autumn sunshine – and could it, even in spring, look better? Autumn seemed the ideal season for these mellow houses tightly packed along a curving street. Tudor, Queen Anne, Georgian ... even the row of Victorian cottages was attractive. And the council houses, though not exactly handsome, were all on their own in a pleasant little close.

'I like the Queen Anne houses best,' Jane finally decided.

'All inhabited by Drew's old ladies,' Merry told her.

'Don't exagerate, he only knows three,' said Clare. 'But it's certainly an elderly village. So many retired people.'

Jane was surprised at the number of shops, three of which sold the same things: groceries combined with green groceries, hardware, stationery and even cosmetics.

'But no baker,' said Clare sadly. 'We had one who baked the most lovely bread, but he got

32

bought up by the Co-op.'

Jane's new dark lipstick was bought.

'Let me put it on for you,' said Merry. 'I want to make your mouth a bit wider.'

'Oh, not here!' Jane protested.

'Well, I'll do it when we show you the church. That'll be nice and private.'

Jane found the ancient church very beautiful.

'Yes, it's all right when it's empty,' said Clare. 'I just can't stand services. Oh, dear, perhaps you go to church?'

Jane shook her head. She had given up church-going when it became difficult to leave her in-valid mother and had never renewed the habit.

'Oh, good,' said Clare. 'I'm afraid we're a very irreligious family.'

'But look, Merry's praying,' Jane whispered.

'She always does, before she leaves. There's a notice in the porch asking one to. She says it's a courtesy, like clapping after a play even if you haven't much liked it.'

'I'll follow her example,' said Jane.

'I just couldn't. I'd feel a hypocrite.'

Decidedly not an *ordinary* old-fashioned girl...

It was now time to go to the Swan, which they reached as Cook, Edith and Burly were being helped out of the car. Edith was in blue; Cook in green. Both of them were hatted and gloved. Jane had already decided against gloves in the village and put hers in her handbag.

'Doesn't Burly look gorgeous?' said Merry.

As his red-gold hair, white round the muzzle, matched Cook's, so his collar now matched her emerald hat.

33

'The smartest dog in Suffolk,' said the manager, coming forward to welcome the party.

The Swan Inn – no inn now but a flourishing hotel – had presented many faces to the world during its four hundred years. Recently it had been returned to its Tudor period, so thoroughly that it looked a fake – and largely was, as regards its façade; but the interior still retained its beams and some panelling, and the Victorian furniture in the dining-room had not yet been replaced by Tudor reproductions. The Carrington party was escorted to a table for seven where an elderly waitress, who had been to school with Cook and Edith, gave advice about ordering lunch. Everyone drank sherry except Burly, who lapped water and then went to the kitchen for a meal of stewed steak.

'A proper helping, none of your scraps,' Cook insisted.

Jane, as hungry as if she had missed breakfast, greatly enjoyed the meal. But, even more, she enjoyed the company; she found the relationship between the Carringtons and their maids so pleasant to watch. Cook and Edith, while still retaining their slightly bossy Nanny status, had been turned into honoured guests.

Lunch ended and Drew persuaded them to join him in a liqueur. Jane refused one but was quite glad when it got ordered for her by accident. This outing was going to cost Rupert Carrington a pretty penny, she reflected, as Richard signed the bill.

'And don't forget the tip,' Merry reminded him.

'See you again next week,' said the elderly

waitress, as the party filed out.

After the car containing Richard, Clare, the maids and Burly had driven off, Drew remembered Jane had no key to Dome House and gave her his.

'We'll all be home soon after six,' Merry told her. 'You won't be nervous, will you, alone in the house?'

Jane reassured her and started her walk back feeling cheerful. She was looking forward to exploring Dome House and thinking about the Carringtons. Still, as she entered the drive, she did wish some of them would be in for tea. Absurd, but she was already missing them – she who, as a rule, was so grateful for a few hours to herself. She heard the church clock strike three. Well, the afternoon would soon pass.

Having let herself in, she tested her knowledge of the house's geography. As she faced the stairs, the dining-room was on her right, with the kitchen at the back of it. The drawing-room, no doubt, would be on her left. She opened a door and found a formal, tidy room – neglected, she guessed, in favour of the hall. At the back, a door led into a study, presumably Rupert Carrington's. The vast desk did not look as if much work was done at it; the housekeeping books and various bills were on a smaller desk, with her typewriter beside it. Sitting for a moment at the big desk, wondering what flowers she would put on it, she noticed the photograph of a beautiful, dark young woman. This must be the late Mrs Rupert Carrington; her eyes resembled Richard's and her mouth, delicately sensuous, was very like Clare's.

35

Sad that she had known her children so little.

Returning to the hall, Jane investigated a room at the back of it which had French windows on to the garden. To judge by the pictures and books, this had been a cross between a nursery and a schoolroom; she visualized those long wet afternoons when, according to Drew, the older Mrs Carrington had fostered a belief in her grandchildren's talents. A family photograph showed her as a heavy, intellectual-looking woman who managed to combine a resemblance to her handsome son with personal plainness. This room seemed as little used as the drawing-room, except as a store for garden furniture.

Now for the bedrooms. Rupert Carrington's, she knew, was over the drawing-room; Clare had shown it to her that morning but allowed no time for inspection. She went in now but found little to inspect – nothing suggesting the vital personality of the man who had engaged her. This felt like a spare room.

Next door was a bathroom and, next to that, Drew's room – extremely like him, combining tidiness with cosiness. Many photographs, pictures, books ... that long row of little red ones would be 'Nelson's Sevenpennys'. She studied the faded spines; some of the authors' names were vaguely familiar but she had read none of the books. A strange collection for a present-day young man to cherish. On his desk a bound volume of *Punch* for the year 1905 lay open, with a pile of neatly written notes beside it. He was obviously doing the most careful research as to clothes, furniture and the idiom of the period.

What flower arrangement would suit Drew's interest in Edwardiana? She must think about it.

Richard's room was as tidy as Drew's but very far from cosy. Like the whole house it was comfortably, if unbeautifully, furnished. But its owner had added no personal touches at all. And it was as cold as it was bare, with the central heating turned off and the window wide open. Flowers would cheer things up; she remembered Richard was said to like them very fresh. Typical, no doubt – but of what? She found him so much less forthcoming than the others.

At the back of the house there was a spare room, a box room and her own room. She skipped these and turned the corner of the gallery. Passing the bathroom she shared with the girls she went into Merry's room, the walls of which were hung with portraits of dramatists, actors and actresses. Jane inspected these only cursorily, deciding that she'd ask Merry to take her on a guided tour. Really, the child's collection of plays was impressive – one wouldn't have expected her to understand some of them; indeed, as regards a few of the very modern ones, Jane hadn't understood them herself.

Now only Clare's room remained, the large front one that corresponded to Rupert Carrington's on the far side of the gallery. Entering, Jane wondered if she could permit herself to look at the flower painting that had been whisked away from her. One had every right, as a housekeeper and flower arranger, to enter rooms and look at pictures and books, but one would never, never read anyone's letter or even a postcard; that would be spying. Would inspection of Clare's work come into the same category? She was arguing this out with herself when she noticed that the drawing-board was back on the worktable again. One could hardly avoid seeing it.

What she saw was a watercolour drawing of roses, painstakingly careful but nothing more. No wonder Clare had said she didn't really paint! Sending her to an art school must just be a way of launching her into the world. Jane tried to detect even the faintest hint of talent but the more one looked, the more feeble the drawing seemed. Well, never now would she question poor Clare about her work. And she should be given a very special flower arrangement: something formal and in keeping with the pictures, which were mainly Watteau reproductions and small portraits of historical personages. Obviously the girl was extremely romantic – except that she hadn't yet struck Jane as extremely anything.

Well, that concluded the tour of the bedrooms; except for the maids' rooms, no doubt up a back staircase. One wouldn't dream of invading any maid's room. That – though she didn't quite know why – would definitely be spying.

A clock below chimed four. She would gather some flowers now. As she went downstairs she thought the hall, in spite of its white paint, bright chintzes and colourful Turkey carpet, looked cheerless now the sun was off it and the fire unlit. She looked up at the dome and decided she didn't really like it. Somehow it was ... too un-intimate for a private house; it suggested an institution. And the daylight it admitted absurd,

38

but it didn't seem like present-day daylight.

After she'd gathered some flowers she'd make herself some tea. That would be cheering – though it was idiotic that one should need cheering.

She found scissors in the kitchen and went out. The sun was now on the back garden and it was very pleasant strolling along beside a still-brilliant herbaceous border, though autumn gardens were always a little melancholy. She remembered this from her girlhood when her father had retired to the country and, so shortly, died; and soon her mother had begun her long illness... Jane sighed, and then concentrated on the flowers. Michaelmas daisies, such lovely colours, some of them new to her ... and, yes, that was nicotiana. Surely that used to close up in the daytime? This variety was wide open and starry-eyed, and there were so many shades; she particularly liked the yellow that was almost green. There were still some summer flowers but they were a little ragged. She would concentrate on tall flowers now and take them along to Richard's music room, which she had not yet seen. How indescribable the scent of autumn flowers was – barely a scent at all, really; just a faint, strange smell, pleasant but sad. Could a smell be sad or was it just the association with the dying summer?

She had now reached the end of the garden and was close to the barn. She carried her armful of flowers up the outside staircase and opened the door of the music room.

Later she decided it was then that her vague sadness changed to a premonition of disaster, though at the moment she merely felt the room was extremely depressing. The lofty roof, with all its timbers revealed, sloped down to within a few feet of the floor, and the window in the gable-end which faced the house was overhung by a tree. It was as if she had walked from mid-afternoon into late twilight.

Now she understood why there were no personal possessions in Richard's bedroom: they were all here. Books, scores, gramophone records, musical instruments – she found it odd that personal possessions could look so impersonal. His work in hand was set out with the most formal precision, each pile of manuscript under a glass paper-weight. Nowhere could she see so much as a book out of place and the large grand piano looked as if it was never even opened.

She had just located the big jar Clare had mentioned when she heard the sound of a car drawing up in the lane at the back of the garden. Some tradesman, perhaps. She stepped out onto the staircase in time to see a man get out of the car and hurry towards the garden gate.

She stared in astonishment. Surely the man was Rupert Carrington? But why was he approaching his house from the back, where the gate was not wide enough to admit a car? And why had he come mid-week and without warning?

He was opening the gate now. She saw him give a swift glance up and down the lane before entering. Then he came towards the barn, reached the foot of the stairs and looked up at her – with astonishment followed by dismay. She gazed down on him across her armful of flowers. Recognition dawned in his eyes.

'Miss Minton, isn't it? I'd forgotten... Is my son up there?'

'He's out – they all are,' said Jane. 'I'm expecting them back about six.'

'Six? I can't wait that long. Good lord...' He broke off, frowning worriedly.

Jane said: 'Drew and Merry are with friends in the village. Perhaps you could find them.'

He dismissed the idea. 'No. I must think. I'll come up.' She went back into the room as he ran up the stairs. At the top he gave another glance up and down the lane, then followed her in and closed the door. With it shut, the room became so dim that she looked round for a light-switch but he said quickly: 'Don't put the lights on. Excuse me for a moment,' then sank onto the divan and sat staring in front of him.

Something must be very wrong. Shaken by apprehension, she watched him silently. He was very pale and his eyes, almost as blue as Clare's, showed extreme tiredness.

After a few seconds, he ran a hand through his greying fair hair and said: 'Sit down, please. I can't think why it never occurred to me Richard might be out. Are the maids in?'

'It's their day off. There's no one – not even a gardener seems to be about.'

'We're without one, I think – if so, it's just as well. You'll have guessed from my furtive behaviour that I don't want to be seen.'

'Is there anything in the world I can do?'

He looked at her closely. 'Forgive me – I have to relearn you. I liked you so much when you came to my office but, frankly, I'd forgotten your

41

existence. When was it I saw you?'

'Just over a month ago. I had to work out my notice.'

'This trouble's boiled up in the last couple of weeks – and believe me, I'd never have engaged you if I'd known it was ahead. I'm so very sorry to involve you.'

She said steadily: 'I don't mind being involved if I can help – even in the smallest way.'

'Does the word "police" terrify you?'

It did, but her tone remained steady. 'Not particularly. Anyway, I promise not to panic whatever you tell me.'

He was silent so long that she gently urged him. 'Please, Mr Carrington...'

'Oh, I'm going to take you at your word – I must; I can't go without leaving some message for my children. I was wondering what's the minimum I can tell you – for your own sake. You may find yourself in a difficult position.' He rose and walked away from her; then turned and spoke with impersonal deliberation. 'I am about to leave England, possibly for good – that is, I hope I am about to leave; if I'm prevented I'm likely to spend an unpleasantly long period in jail, for fraud. How admirable of you not to say anything, not even to gasp!'

The last words were said with a touch of grim humour. Then he went on almost casually, moving restlessly round the room. 'Of course I should have foreseen this disaster and made better arrangements than I've been able to – for myself as well as for my family. I'm a very inadequate crook, completely amateur. Are you stunned or merely exerting extreme self-control?'

'I'm just waiting to hear how I can help,' said Jane.

'Thank you.' His tone acknowledged the sincerity of hers. 'Well, now: will you break the news to my children and give them my love and abject apologies – and this?' He took a bulging envelope from his pocket. 'It contains three hundred pounds – a ludicrously small amount to leave them, but it may tide them over until some of them can start earning. I'd like Cook and Edith to have two months' salary. Not much of a reward for all their years of service but please tell them I've treated them generously in my will; I shall leave nothing but debts but they'll appreciate the gesture. You, of course, must have a month's salary.'

'No,' said Jane. 'I haven't begun to work for you.'

'But you're going to – both take the money and work for me. Will you stay a month and advise my children as best you can?'

'I'll stay as long as I can help.' No point in arguing about the salary. 'Will you be writing to them?'

'Not for the present, anyway. It will be better for them – and safer for me – if they don't even know what country I'm in. Extradition laws are treacherous; apt to turn and rend the poor criminal.'

She said: 'I don't believe you're a criminal. Are you sure you shouldn't stay and establish your innocence?'

He gave her a swift smile. 'You must have a built-in sense of loyalty. It operates before it's been earned. Yes, I'm quite sure I shouldn't stay

43

in England – or here, now.' He looked at his watch. 'As a law-abiding woman, do you feel you must notify the police as soon as I've gone? Frankly, I hope you won't as it might enable them to intercept me. But if your conscience insists...'

'It doesn't. Anyway, I've only your word that the police would be interested.'

Again he smiled. 'And you've already decided my word's not to be trusted. Do you know, I'm rather truthful? One can combine truthfulness in one's private life with dishonesty in one's business.'

'I still don't believe you're dishonest,' she said stubbornly.

'Well, I grant I'm no more dishonest than hundreds of men who pass for honest. But they're luckier – or shrewder than I've been. Now listen: if you don't notify the police you've seen me, you'd better not admit it, later, for your own sake. There shouldn't be any need to. I'm pretty sure no one saw me come here. I haven't been into the village. I'm driving a hired car – I sold mine to raise some more cash – and I've been wearing an atrocious and disguising cap, well pulled down over the eyes. In any case, I might have slipped in and out without your knowing.'

'But your children will know – if I'm to tell them. Suppose the police question them?'

His manner had become brisker; now it was strained again. 'I'm sorry – I can't think clearly. You must work it out for yourselves, without considering me. Anyway, you're not likely to be questioned before tomorrow, by which time I shall be out of the country – or have been

44

stopped getting out. In either case it won't matter to me what you all say, so suit yourselves. Now I must go. Thank you for your kindness. If we'd worked together for twenty years you couldn't have been more loyal.'

She said: 'I'm quite sure my loyalty's justified.'

'Not a bit of it. You're a generous creature taken in by a shady character. You'll learn that soon enough. Keep your eyes on the newspapers – oh, not the front pages; I'm quite insignificant but there should be something somewhere. Anyway, there will be if I'm arrested. If you don't learn of that by tomorrow I shall have got away. Oh, lord, there are so many things I meant to tell Richard. About Merry: he'd better let her try the stage as soon as she can; she's the only one whose talent I'm sure of. Not that I know any of them well. You must think me a hell of a father.'

'I'm sure you've been a kind and generous one.'

'There's more to the job than that. My wife and I cared too much for each other to care enough for our children. My mother was wonderful with them, but I should have done more these last years since she died.' He opened the door. 'Goodbye, dear Miss Minton – Jane Minton, isn't it?'

She nodded and said firmly: 'You'll come back. Everything will come right.'

'I doubt that – really.' He made sure the lane was deserted, then ran down the stairs.

'Goodbye! Good luck!' she called after him.

He reached the car, turned it, then leaned out and waved to her. She waved in return. The car shot forward. She watched until it disappeared round the bend of the lane.

3

Tuesday–Wednesday

Sitting on the divan in the dim music room, she asked herself how she could best break the news to the young Carringtons, how best advise them, help them; but again and again she failed to concentrate and, instead, found herself reliving Rupert Carrington's visit, and trying to understand her own astonishing reactions.

During her fifteen years as a secretary she had several times been attracted by her employers and some of them had been attracted by her, but the attractions had never coincided and, on her side certainly, had been so mild that she had merely chaffed herself about them – lacking the woman friend who by rights should have done the chaffing. Never had she really fallen in love and she had begun to think she never would. But now–

Time after time she pulled herself up. One couldn't fall in love with a man one had only met twice, anyway a woman of her type and age couldn't. It must simply be that she was attracted – as she had been, even at their first meeting – and now the unusual circumstances, her sympathy for him, his appeal for her help, all were combining to heighten her emotions. She mustn't let this ... this absurd sense of exhilaration have its head. She must calm down, be practical, and above all remember that Rupert Carrington had relied on her.

She heard the church clock strike six. The family would be home any minute. Picking up her armful of flowers, she hurried down the stairs and through the garden. Indoors, she filled the pantry sink and left the flowers there, then ran into the hall and lit the fire.

Soon she heard the car coming up the drive and being driven to the garage. Then Richard entered, alone. He said Clare had gone to call for Merry.

Jane had imagined telling them all together – silly of her, she now saw, for she could hardly wait until they all arrived. She rather wished she could have talked to Drew first, then remembered that all Rupert's messages had been for Richard, who would now have to act as the head of the family. As he came towards the fire she said: 'I'm so very sorry. I have to break bad news.'

It was easier than she had expected. Richard, after one horrified 'Good God!' took it very calmly, simply eliciting from her all the information he could – which amounted to less than she had foreseen because she found she could not bring herself to repeat some things Rupert had said. She cut his kind references to herself, his reflection on himself as a father and his description of himself as a crook. But she did make it clear that he had tacitly admitted his guilt.

Richard accepted this. 'Oh, yes, otherwise I'm sure he wouldn't have bolted. Well, I hope he makes it – I suppose he may get caught at some port or airport. He gave you no idea how he hoped to get out of England?'

She shook her head, then handed over the envelope of notes. 'He sent apologies that it wasn't more.'

'It would have been if he could have managed it. I don't see why he doesn't want to write to us. Surely the police can't intercept letters – or can they, if they can tap telephone calls? Perhaps he just wants to get away from us, as well as the police – and I wouldn't blame him; this household must cost a fortune. But he insisted that things should go on as in my grandmother's day, that we should live here just cultivating the talents she credited us with. What are we going to do?'

'People do earn their livings,' said Jane. 'We must think of things.'

'I'm glad you're going to stay with us for a bit.'

She had told him his father wanted her to, but she'd made no mention of her salary.

'I'll advise you in any way I can. Oh, I've remembered something else he said–' She relayed Rupert's wishes about Merry but censored his remark that hers was the only talent he was sure of. 'Not that she can legally leave school until she's fifteen – and that's far too early, really.'

'I wonder if her school fees are paid,' said Richard. 'And where can she live while she's at school if we others get jobs and close this house?'

'Perhaps you can get local jobs.'

'Well, there's always a shortage of domestic help in the village. I might go out as a male char.'

She heard voices outside and went to a window. 'They're all back. I think you should tell them on your own. Shall I make some tea?'

48

'They'll have had it. Perhaps you'd start preparations for supper – Cook leaves us things. Not that I'm exactly hungry.'

'Nor I,' said Jane. 'Still, food can be a help at times like this.'

As she reached the kitchen she heard the front door open and a cheerful babble. After that, with the kitchen door closed, she could hear no more. She looked around her dazedly – how lost one felt in an unfamiliar kitchen! Well, that was obviously soup on the stove, waiting to be heated, and sandwiches had been mentioned that morning. She located them in the refrigerator, found plates and soup cups and then began preparations for coffee. Still no sound from the hall. Would Merry cry and need to be comforted? A few minutes later the kitchen door was flung open and Merry rushed at her saying, 'Poor darling Miss Minton, what a thing to happen when you were all alone – and in that gloomy music room! But how wonderful for poor father to have someone like you to talk to!' Jane then dissolved into tears and found herself being comforted by Merry, after which she was tenderly escorted to the hall to be treated, by both Merry and Drew, as a cross between an invalid and a heroine.

Clare finished getting supper, and shortly everyone was sitting round the fire eating. Richard, Jane noted, ate less than anyone. She might have thought it callous of the younger Carringtons to eat so much when their beloved father was a fugitive from justice had she not, in spite of her great anxiety for him, suddenly felt so ravenous herself.

But *was* Rupert Carrington a beloved father? His three younger children, discussing his chances of getting away, sounded boisterously cheerful; and even Richard, though quieter, expressed no concern. Almost as if he had read her thoughts, Drew said: 'Are you thinking we mind very little – on Father's account? I'm sure we're all very sorry for him. You must blame our seeming callousness on the resilience of youth. We seem to have rather a lot of it.'

'Speak for yourself,' said Richard.

'Poor Father!' said Clare. 'But we shall need all the resilience we can work up. How people in the village will gloat over us now! They think we're spoilt and lazy.'

'I deny lazy,' said Drew. 'And it's hardly our fault we've not been trained to earn. Anyway, we shall soon find some way to.'

'I shan't,' said Clare. 'I feel worse equipped than a Victorian girl. She could always be a governess. But what can I do?'

Merry said: 'Clare, darling, you really are wet. If I wasn't going on the stage I can think of lots of jobs I could do. Serving in a shop, being a waitress – or going into a factory; that's jolly well paid.'

'A factory? I should wreck the machinery.'

'I must say I can't see her in a factory,' said Jane. 'Is there no job you ever fancied, Clare?'

Clare shook her head gloomily.

'You once said you'd like to be a king's mistress,' said Merry. 'But there's such a shortage of kings now. Could you marry somebody? Not that I can think of anyone. All the well-to-do unmarried men in the village are over sev

'There's one good thing. I needn't go to school now – I never really wanted to. And that goodness Father hasn't paid the fees yet. Oh, dear, there are dozens of bills waiting to be paid. He hasn't been here to sign cheques for nearly a month.'

'I wonder if they can make him bankrupt while he's out of the country – if he gets out,' said Richard. 'We'd better listen to the News. It just might mention him; there was quite a lot about City scandals yesterday.' He turned on the television.

A play was finishing – with the arrest of the criminal.

'Plain-clothes men,' said Merry. 'I wonder if we shall get some here, looking for Father.' She watched absorbedly until the play ended, then said regretfully, 'We seem to have missed something good.'

The News began. Jane, remembering Rupert had spoken of himself as insignificant, thought it unlikely there would be any reference to him. But her heart began to beat wildly when, after dealing with the arrest of a financier whose name had been in the news for days, the newscaster began reading a list of firms whose books had been taken over by the police. She heard the words 'also those of Rupert Carrington...' A moment later the newscaster, allowing himself a flicker of a smile, concluded with a little story about a recaptured monkey.

'Well, they haven't captured Father, anyway!' said Merry.

Jane found herself faintly proud that Rupert had been mentioned. Even as a crook, she did not care to think of him as insignificant.

'Has anyone the vaguest idea what he's really done?' asked Clare.

'I think it's known as fraudulent conversion,' said Richard. 'You finance a company and then use the money for yourself and to pay dividends on the next company you finance, and then go on financing more and more companies. It's all right – until you get stopped. And when a big fish gets caught, smaller fish get into the net too.'

The telephone rang. Richard went to the study to answer it.

'Probably Father, wanting to be bailed out,' said Merry.

Jane wondered if her entire savings would be enough. She doubted it – for a man mentioned in the same breath as one alleged to have fraudulently converted two million.

Richard returned to say Cook and Edith had also been listening to the News and wanted to be assured that 'it didn't mean your father'. On hearing it did, they had wanted Richard to come and get them at once so that they could 'help'. He'd promised to come in the morning. 'They sent their love and said it would all come right in the end and they and we must stick together – which we obviously can't but I didn't mention that.'

'We might,' said Merry. 'Suppose we turned this house into a guest house?'

The idea was welcomed by everyone except Richard who said it was out of the question.

'But why, Richard?' asked Drew. 'If you and I share a room and the girls shared, there'd be quite a few free bedrooms.'

'And surely there must be attics?' said Jane. 'Are they usable?'

'Only the nice ones Cook and Edith have as bedroom and bathroom,' said Clare. 'The others are just garrets with skylights.'

'Still, even without the attics...' Drew began to plan eagerly, backed up by Merry and Jane. It took Richard a long time to convince them that a guest house would need capital – and guests, who would certainly not be available in the winter when the Swan could never fill its bedrooms.

'And though I hate to mention it,' said Jane, 'it's just struck me that if your father's made bankrupt all your furniture will belong to his creditors, surely?'

'It's a mercy he doesn't own the house,' said Richard. 'I wonder if the lease will count as one of his assets? We can only hang on and hope for the best. Luckily the rent's very low.'

'But there are rates,' said Clare. 'And the up-keep's so high. Do any of you realize what even the heating costs?'

By the time Clare had finished a dissertation on the house-keeping in general, Jane saw that Dome House would swallow three hundred pounds in no time at all. It could only be kept going – even with the most rigid economies – if the three elder Carringtons got jobs immediately. As for Merry's education... But she wasn't bringing that topic up now.

They listened to the final News broadcast but

the City's affairs were omitted. Richard then said he could neither think nor talk any more and was going to bed.

'Me, too,' said Drew. 'I find the resilience of youth is wearing off.'

Clare began collecting the supper plates. 'We'll wash these up with the breakfast things. You have your bath, Miss Minton.'

Drew said: 'As you're such a friend now, could we stop calling you Miss Minton? Perhaps "Minty" – no, I'm sure you'd hate that.'

Jane had often suffered Minty but never willingly. She said now: 'I'd prefer Jane. It'll make me feel younger.'

'I wish something would make me feel *older*,' said Drew. 'Catastrophe's obviously thrusting maturity on you, Richard, but I'm beginning to feel like a fatherless child. Not that I've depended on Father for anything but material comforts. To be honest, I've never felt I knew him at all well.'

'I doubt if any of us have,' said Richard.

'He hasn't really given us the chance to,' said Merry. 'Still, when we *have* seen him he's always been terribly nice. And I wish him good luck with all my heart.'

She spoke cheerfully and without a trace of sentiment. Jane tried to think it a good thing that Rupert's children were not stricken emotionally as well as financially, but she found it hard to understand. Later, lying in bed, she told herself she was more callous than they were. Why, if she really had fallen in love with Rupert, wasn't she miserable? Why did she find life so interesting, exciting, full of hope? She tried to harrow herself by thinking of him flying from the law through the night – or already in a prison cell. But she went on feeling interested, excited and hopeful. Well, at least she would keep vigil for him, lie awake...

She slept eight hours and only got downstairs when breakfast was ready.

'Just toast and marmalade,' said Clare. 'I thought we'd better start economizing.'

'Perhaps we can sell the toasters,' said Drew, as the *musique concrète* began.

After breakfast, Richard and Drew drove off to call for Cook and Edith. Jane, Clare and Merry did the bedrooms.

They were in Clare's room when they heard a car arrive.

Merry, looking out of the window, said: 'Two men getting out – probably from Scotland Yard. Leave this to me.'

'Ought we to?' said Jane.

But Merry had already gone, closing the door behind her.

'Why not, if she fancies it?' said Clare. 'I certainly don't.'

Neither did Jane. She had decided she would not tell the police of Rupert's visit but was none too sure she might not, if questioned, end by giving it away – in which case would she not become an accessory or a conniver or something else illegal?

'Let's keep dead quiet,' said Clare.

They strained their ears but could only hear a murmur of voices. At last Clare opened the door a few inches. Merry could now be clearly heard, speaking in a voice choked by emotion.

'What right have you to accuse my father when he's not here to defend himself?'

'She's overdoing it,' Clare whispered to Jane.

Jane, too, detected a histrionic note but Merry's visitors obviously didn't. Two male voices attempted to soothe her.

'No one's accusing him of anything yet, miss.'

'We're simply inquiring if he's here.'

'Well, I've told you he isn't but you probably don't believe me. Have you a search warrant?'

'No, miss – and we do believe you.'

'That's right, miss. No need to get so upset.' Merry now changed her tactics. Her voice, though pitifully shaken, became controlled by exquisite breeding.

'Forgive me. Of course you have to do what's expected of you. And my father would wish me to treat you with every courtesy. May I offer you some refreshment?'

'Maddening of her,' whispered Clare, closing the door. 'We may have to stay up here for ages.'

But the men presumably declined Merry's kind offer and very soon left. Jane and Clare, hurrying downstairs, found her mopping her eyes.

'Oh, you poor darling, you've really been crying,' said Jane.

'I should hope so – any actress worth her salt can cry to order. But there was an awful moment when I nearly laughed. One of them asked me: "When did you last see your father?" and I thought of that picture of the little Cavalier boy surrounded by Roundheads. Oh, dear!' She laughed now, with happy reminiscence.

There was a loud knock at the door.

'It's only the papers,' said Clare. 'The boy always knocks like that. Let's see what we can find in them.'

'Do you take six daily papers?' said Jane, as the pile was brought in.

'Well, it's only one for each of us and the picture papers for Cook and Edith,' said Clare. 'But I suppose we must give some of them up, and all the magazines.'

'We can't give up any newspapers while Father's in the news,' said Merry, searching eagerly.

Jane was pleased to find Rupert had under-estimated his news value. He had made most of the front pages, if only in a small way. There was one bit of information that hadn't been on television. His whereabouts were said to be unknown.

'Sounds as if he's got clean away,' said Merry. 'Still, we'll keep our fingers crossed for him a bit longer.'

The telephone rang. Clare returned from answering it to say one of Drew's old ladies had wanted to comfort him.

'She's sure it's all a mistake. I hope a lot of people won't ring up – though if they don't, I shall think they're unfeeling.'

The telephone rang again. 'I'll go this time,' said Merry. It proved to be the Vicar, asking if he could help in any way and undertaking to pray for them all.

'Nice of him,' said Clare. 'Considering we never go near his church when he's doing anything in it.'

Again the telephone rang. This time it was their village grocer, wanting Clare to come in and have a word with him. 'And I can guess why,' she said, when Merry brought the message. 'Let's go and see how much we owe him.'

They went into the study and ended by going through all the unpaid bills. Only the previous month's were outstanding but Jane was staggered by what they amounted to, as they were not only for the very lavish household expenditure but also for clothes, books, gramophone records...

'Did none of you have allowances?' she asked.

'Well, we've always had spending money,' said Clare. 'And quite a bit of it. But Father paid for most things – and we could order what we liked, within reason. What a lot we owe for meals at the Swan. And Merry's school fees aren't paid.'

'Just as well, as I don't intend to go back.'

'Even if you didn't, we'd owe a term's fees in lieu of notice. And you must go to *some* school.'

'Must I? You just wait and see.'

'But it's the law, Merry.' Clare turned to Jane for support.

'Here's the car back,' said Merry.

They all went to greet Cook, Edith and Burly, who had been driven back by Drew, Richard having gone to London to see his father's solicitor.

'And one or two other people who needed seeing,' said Drew, while the maids embraced Clare and Merry with lugubrious affection.

'No doubt you have relatives who can advise you,' said Jane.

'We've no relatives at all but Father's Aunt Winifred, and no one could hanker for her advice,' said Clare. 'Oh, heavens, Drew, I've just remembered Father gave her an allowance.'

'It was only to make up for sending her away. She's got plenty without it.'

'We've enough on our minds without thinking of her,' said Cook. 'Do you know my worst nightmare? It's when I dream she's back here again. Well, Miss Minton, this is a sad day for us all. But no doubt it'll turn out for the best.'

'A door never shuts but another opens,' said Edith.

'So one's always in a draught,' said Drew, *sotto voce*, as Cook, Edith and Burly proceeded to the kitchen. 'They're being absolute heroines, Clare. They swear they won't take a penny of their wages and they're full of plans for keeping the old home going but I promised not to tell you.'

Merry collected the newspapers. 'They'll want to see Father's name in these.'

'They will indeed,' said Drew. 'But what they want most is to hear him mentioned on television again. Well, they've done me a power of good. I was feeling a mite embarrassed about our situation but now I see disgrace is swallowed up by drama – and not only for Cook and Edith. You never saw such bright smiles as we drove through the village. People practically blew kisses.'

'How kind of them,' said Clare. 'Especially considering we've never been popular.'

'Ah, but our stock's gone up now. I don't deny the kindness but I think it's combined with enjoyment – nice to know someone whose name's in the news, for whatever reason. Well, we must learn to bask in reflected publicity.'

Merry returned from the kitchen to say that Cook and Edith were hurrying on a marvellous

59

lunch, to include pancakes.

'Like Shrove Tuesday, before Lent starts,' said Drew.

After lunch, the maids announced that they wished to go out for an hour or so. No, they did not want to be driven anywhere. And they would be back in time to get tea. Jane noted that they now wore unrelieved black.

'Those are the outfits they wear for funerals,' said Drew, watching them walk down the drive. 'Even Burly's wearing his old black collar.'

'Perhaps they're in mourning for Father's reputation,' said Merry. She then went off to see her friend Betty, who had telephoned most sympathetically.

'It may be unfeeling of me but I'm going to watch television,' said Clare.

'If the telephone will let you,' said Drew, who had already declined three telephoned invitations to tea.

Jane, arranging the flowers she had brought in the previous day, found herself depressed. She still felt emotional about Rupert, but exhilaration seemed to have gone off duty. She had intended the flowers for the music room, but now disliked the thought of revisiting it, so she took them to the hall. Being with Drew and Clare cheered her, until she reminded herself that only for a few weeks could she stay at Dome House. Eventually she must lose Rupert's children as well as Rupert.

Soon after four, Cook and Edith returned to say they had got work at the Swan, where the manager had welcomed them with open arms.

'Ever so pleased he was that we'd given him the

first refusal of us,' said Cook. 'We're going five days a week, starting Monday. We'll get our lunch free, and Burly will too; we bargained for that. We're to be paid by the hour – my word, that's the way to coin money. And we'll be home in plenty of time to give you dinner. Of course we'll pay for our share of the food and we'll rent our room from you.'

'But darlings, we couldn't let you pay us,' Clare protested. 'You'll be working for us.'

'Oh, no, we won't,' said Edith, firmly. 'We'll be working at the Swan. You'll let us cook our dinner in your kitchen and it'll be no trouble to cook enough for you. And if we want to clean the house a bit at weekends, that's our affair.'

'And it's no use arguing,' said Cook. 'Because we couldn't face your grandmother in heaven if we walked out on you now.'

'We wouldn't even *get* to heaven,' said Edith.

A discussion then began as to how much they would pay for their room but Jane listened with only half an ear. It had delightfully dawned on her that she, too, might get local work and contribute to the household expenses. But she did not speak of this as she felt Cook and Edith were entitled to the unshared glory of their generosity.

'Sounds as if we *are* starting a guest house,' said Drew, when the maids had gone to get tea. 'With the guests paying for the privilege of running it.'

After tea, Merry returned to say she had changed her mind about leaving school. 'Betty thinks I might get given a scholarship by Weary Willy – that's our head mistress, Jane; her real name's Vera Willy. She gave one to a girl who lost both parents in an accident. And she had it for years; I'd only need mine till I'm fifteen. It'll save trouble with the law if I don't leave at once, and I can write and ask managers to see me in the Christmas play.'

'"But will they come when you do call for them?"' Drew quoted.

'They might, in my pathetic circumstances. So if someone would give Weary Willy a hint–'

'Don't look at me,' said Clare. 'I'm still terrified of her.'

Merry turned to Drew. '*You* tackle her. You're always a success with old ladles.'

'But she's barely middle-aged – *much* too young for me. No, Merry, really.'

Jane said: 'Could I talk to her?'

Merry beamed. 'Oh, would you, Jane? She'd be terribly impressed by you, especially if you went in your car. Could you go tomorrow? The term starts on Monday.'

'Ought I to telephone for an appointment?'

Merry thought not. 'She might ask what you wanted and it'd be easier for her to refuse by telephone. You just pop in on her. I do think you're kind. Oh, Clare, before I forget, Betty's mother says that if Cook and Edith need a job–'

'They've got one,' said Clare.

Merry, on hearing the details, was ecstatic. 'How adorable of them! It makes me want to cry. Only it's terribly funny too.' She stifled giggles. 'I mean, it's like some Victorian children's book, all robins and snow – except that they're being paid by the hour and raking in lovely money. I must go and hug them.'

'And bring them back for the six o'clock News,' said Clare. But the News contained no reference to Rupert Carrington, nor did it when they listened again after dinner.

'Poor Father's just a has-been already,' said Drew. 'Well, let's see if Richard brings any news about the forgotten man.'

He drove off to meet Richard's train.

Jane, wondering why Drew's flippancies did not jar on her, decided that the deep, almost caressing quality of his voice took the edge off them. And there was a basic gentleness in him which neutralized any suspicion of unkindness. Nor did she find Merry's continual high spirits unsympathetic. These two were her favourites. Clare interested her far less. As for Richard... Really, it was unfair to think him depressing simply because he was taking the family trouble seriously. And if she did not feel she knew him as well as she knew the others, that might mean he was all the more worth while knowing.

He arrived back from London looking pale and tired, and had little to tell. The solicitor he had gone to see had not been helpful.

'He said he only dealt with our family affairs, thank God. It seems the solicitor who copes with Father's business has vanished just as Father has. The only advice I could get was to carry on as best we can and see what happens.'

'Did you go to your father's office?' Jane asked.

'Yes, and found it closed. I didn't go to his flat because it's an expensive service flat and he may have left money owing. Really, the less we know about his affairs, the better. We must live from day to day – and get jobs as soon as we can. Which reminds me–'

He turned to thank Cook and Edith, Drew having told him of their plans. Cook said it was the least they could do – looking, Jane thought, a trifle smug. Then both maids bustled off to get him some supper.

'I want to wash now; we'll talk some more afterwards,' he said to Clare, exchanging a quick glance with her.

Jane guessed that something private would be disclosed later.

'Let's decide what you're going to wear when you see Weary Willy tomorrow,' said Merry, putting her arm through Jane's and steering her upstairs. 'Your tweeds, of course, and one of your lovely cashmere sweaters. And may I see your best gloves?'

'And then go to bed, Merry, darling,' Clare called after them. 'It's nearly eleven.'

Merry approved of Jane's gloves. 'Perhaps they're a mite long for tweeds but not if you wear them all wrinkled and nonchalant. I bet you'll see Weary Willy eyeing them. Now, shoes...'

Eventually Jane's entire outfit was decided on; then Merry went to bed. Jane intended to go downstairs again but as she opened her door she heard Richard talking in the hall.

'She was terribly upset, Clare. Father didn't even say goodbye to her.'

'Oh, poor Violet!'

'I asked if the rent of her flat was paid...'

Jane stepped back into her room and quietly closed the door. So Richard had been to see some woman friend of his father's – though 'friend', presumably, was hardly the right word ... perhaps one ought to be shocked but one wasn't. And one felt sorry for the woman – how dreadful not to have been said goodbye to! Surely if Rupert cared seriously...?

Tempted to open the door again and listen, she firmly switched her thoughts to the coming interview with Miss Willy. The shoes she meant to wear could do with a polish.

He had asked her to help his children. Well, tomorrow she would do her best for Merry.

4

Thursday

The next morning, Merry suggested she should accompany Jane. 'I could sit outside in the car and you could call me in to thank Weary Willy if everythings all right – as I'm sure it will be; she was really very kind to that girl who lost both parents. And then I could take you round the school and the grounds and show you the darling ponies.'

But Jane said it would make her nervous if Merry waited almost on the doorstep; also it would be unfair to Miss Willy.

'You mean it would make it harder for her to refuse? Well, we want to, don't we? Still, if you'd rather I didn't come...'

Jane got ready and was carefully inspected.

'You look marvellous – what she calls beautifully groomed. Just wrinkle your gloves a bit more.'

They went out into the sunny autumn morning and Jane started her car. Merry issued last instructions.

'Park a bit to the right of the front door; then Weary Willy can see the car from her window. You can't miss the school. It's less than half a mile beyond the village – a big Queen Anne house with lots of additions. It used to be the Hall. If

66

you get nervous, try not to let her see it. Be a bit grand.'

Jane already felt nervous and became even more so when she sighted the school across its large grounds. It was so impressive that she feared she would not be seen without an appointment. But after sending her name in by the smartly uniformed maid she was kept waiting only a moment and Miss Willy, rising to shake hands, seemed pleased to see her.

The head mistress was willowy, long-necked and very fair, her flaxen hair slightly greyed. In Pre-Raphaelite days she might have passed for a beauty. In her strictly tailored suit she looked somehow wrong. Still, Jane eyed the suit's cut with respect. She accepted the indicated chair, facing the light, thanked Miss Willy for seeing her and began to introduce herself.

Miss Willy interrupted, her languid voice curiously at variance with the shrewdness of her glance. 'Oh, I know who you are. In this village, everyone knows everything, though facts frequently get garbled in transit. Which reminds me, is it true, the Carringtons' maids have been snapped up by the Swan? If not, I should be delighted–'

'You're too late,' said Jane, with satisfaction; she had taken an instant dislike to Miss Willy.

'Ah, well... Now tell me about yourself. Could you start work at once?'

'Work?' said Jane, astonished.

'You do know I'm in need of a secretary?'

'I certainly didn't,' said Jane. 'I've come about Merry.'

'Oh, is that it? I suppose Clare funked seeing me. Well, you can tell them I've no intention of suing anyone for my unpaid fees. It wouldn't be any use if Rupert Carrington's got out of England, as I quite hope he has. Such a charming man, if a criminally unwise one – and I don't mean as regards his present débâcle. The way he's spoilt those children! But you've seen for yourself.'

Jane's nervousness was now replaced by annoyance. 'I've found them all charming and intelligent,' she said truculently.

'Drew certainly is. Surely no one could call Clare intelligent or Richard charming, though I'll admit he's handsome. As for Meriella...' Miss Willy paused and appeared to be considering the matter dispassionately. 'No, I'd never describe her as charming and intelligent. The words are inadequate. She is undoubtedly the most brilliant child I've ever had in my school.'

Jane smiled with relief. Everything would be all right. But the languid voice was continuing.

'Not that I shan't be more than happy to lose her as a pupil. How does she propose to finish her education?'

Jane's smile froze and her nervousness returned. 'We hoped... I believe you do sometimes award scholarships?'

'A scholarship? To Meriella?' Miss Willy looked astounded. 'Is this her own idea?'

'I think her friend Betty suggested–'

'That poor girl! She was doing well at both lessons and games until Meriella infected her with a desire to act – which, believe me, was not

68

God's plan for her; she has a marked resemblance to a suet pudding, in figure as well as face. Well, I may yet salvage her if I can get her away from Meriella. No, Miss Minton, I can award no scholarship.'

'Not even for two terms – until Merry's fifteen?'

'I find that an outrageous suggestion. This is hardly a school for pupils who finish their education at fifteen. My scholarship girls stay till they're eighteen and usually go on to college.'

'I'd hoped, if you were willing to have her, that I could persuade Merry to stay until she was – well, say, seventeen.'

'Oh, I wouldn't persuade her to do that, whatever school she goes to.' Miss Willy now sounded less severe. 'As a matter of fact, I advised her father to let her finish with school as soon as she legally can.'

'Did you want to get rid of her so much?' Jane asked coldly.

Miss Willy's quick glance showed that the coldness had been noted. She was silent for a moment. Then she said: 'I must defend myself a little. I've told you I think Meriella brilliant. The trouble is, she's slanted her brilliance in only one direction: acting. Ordinary lessons bore her and she refuses to play any game. What's more, she can be embarrassingly precocious. Let me tell you what happened at our Midsummer theatricals – always rather a feature with us. This year we decided on scenes from Shakespeare, and Meriella and Betty wanted to do the balcony scene from *Romeo and Juliet*. They gave me quite a charming audition – Meriella was exquisite – but I said, frankly, that Betty wasn't the right shape for Romeo. They assured me she would be tactfully draped in a cloak and the scene would be dimly lit, so I gave in. Well, I had to be away at a conference during the last days of rehearsals and when I retuned, on the day of the performance, I heard the balcony scene had proved impracticable on our little stage and Meriella and Betty were substituting the farewell scene. Unfortunately, I didn't remember the implications of that scene. You recall it?'

'I think so... "Wilt thou be gone? It is not yet near day." – isn't that how it begins?'

'It is indeed. Of course our drama mistress should never have allowed it but she was flurried by the last-minute change and let Meriella take charge. Imagine my horror when, before a packed audience, the curtain rose to reveal a large mattress where Meriella and Betty were reclining among dishevelled bedclothes. Meriella was wearing a red wig she'd hired; and by means of make-up and sheer acting ability was managing to look fully adult – helped by the fact that she'd padded the bust of her white silk nightgown to quite Hollywood proportions. Betty, whose bust needs restraining, not amplifying, was wearing a thin, open-necked shirt and very fully-filled black tights. The two of them proceeded to throw themselves about on the mattress, Betty a very female, amorous dumpling of fourteen, and Meriella a voluptuous woman of at least twenty-five – if anything, too mature for Juliet. You can imagine the impression they gave.'

'Did people laugh?'

'Not at first – I assure you, it was too shocking to laugh at. Then, mercifully, one side of Meriella's false bust slipped round under one arm. She tried to hitch it back and, for a moment, her mask of maturity dropped and she looked just a painted child. The audience roared and I can only hope the previous impression was forgotten in laughter – in spite of which, and though the Capulets had only the haziest notion of their parts, Meriella ended by being deeply moving, even though her false bust was still under one arm. Oh, dear, I still laugh when I think of it.'

Jane, too, laughed. Then she said: 'But, Miss Willy, you said Merry was embarrassingly precocious. Surely such an incident proves just the opposite? Only a very innocent girl...'

'Quite true,' said Miss Willy. 'I ought to have said she can appear to be precocious. It only happens when she's acting – through some miracle of intuition. At other times she often strikes me as unusually innocent for her age. And she's not, by the way, sentimental. She has no sentimental attachment to Betty, nor has she ever shown one for any of her teachers, thank heaven. Me, she definitely dislikes. But I don't dislike her and when I advised her father to let her leave my school it was because I believed it had no more to offer her. She has an absolutely first-class brain, but she'll work at nothing not connected with her acting, so she should concentrate on it as soon as she's legally free to.'

'But that's not for six months,' said Jane, beginning to respect Miss Willy. 'And you do so well understand her. Would you allow me to pay her fees here?'

'Do you know what our fees are?' Miss Willy's tone was ominous.

'Tell me, please.'

'I warn you they're high, particularly for day girls as we don't care to have many. This is mainly a boarding school.'

Jane was staggered by the sum named – but she could afford it, for two terms. Without hesitation she said: 'That would be quite satisfactory.'

'You're a very generous woman,' said Miss Willy.

'Then we'll consider the matter settled.'

Slowly the head mistress shook her head. 'This isn't a question of money. And I'm not going to pretend I'm only doing what seems to be best for Meriella. No doubt it would be a convenience for her to stay here until she's fifteen. But it wouldn't be good for my school. I told you she wasn't sentimental – but others are sentimental about her. There's quite a Meriella cult and it would increase now. And think of all the publicity if Rupert Carrington gets hauled to trial. I'm sorry but I just don't want her here.'

Jane's tone became frigid. 'Then there's no more to be said.'

'Oh, yes, there is. I'll post you a list of – well, fairly good schools in nearby towns, all of which would cost you far less than you're prepared to pay me. You could, of course, just let matters drift for six months but some village busybody might inform the authorities. As soon as she's fifteen, let her try for a scholarship at some London drama school. Some scholarships include maintenance allowances.'

'But she couldn't live in London, alone,' said Jane. 'She's just a child, Miss Willy, and to me she seems a normal child.'

'Which Meriella have you been treated to? The pert, voluble one?'

'Voluble, certainly–'

'Well, that's somewhere near the real Meriella, except that she dramatizes the normality. You should see her when she's working on Shakespearean tragedy and speaks mainly in blank verse – yes, really; it's very bad blank verse but it scans. My least favourite times are when she's studying what she calls character parts and uses phrases like "Pardon" and "Thanks ever so". Oh, don't worry about her, just drag her through the next six months as best you can – not that I see why you should be involved with the Carrington problems. Now let's talk about you. I do need a secretary. Would you like to work for me?'

Jane doubted it. But it would mean she could remain part of the Carrington household, unless she would be expected to live at the school; she inquired about this.

'No, indeed,' said Miss Willy. 'We're full to overflowing. How much was Rupert Carrington paying you – or should one say, owing you?'

Jane named the figure hoping it would impress Miss Willy as much as she herself had been impressed by the school fees.

'Well, it's enough,' said Miss Willy. 'But you're probably worth it. Having your own car's an advantage and I like the way you dress.'

'Merry said you would,' said Jane; then regretted it.

But Miss Willy took it in good part. 'Shrewd of her. And a compliment to both of us, if you think it out. I've an idea we should get on tolerably well. Of course I expect hard work, just as I expect it of myself.'

And thrive on it, thought Jane. Weary Willy, in spite of her nickname and languid voice, was certainly not weary. Aloud, she said: 'Oh, I fancy I could stand up to the job – if I'm able to accept it.'

'You can't decide now? My temporary help is hopeless and the new term starts on Monday. Well, when *can* you let me know?'

'Not for two or three days,' said Jane firmly. Standing up to the job would really mean standing up to Miss Willy and one would get off to a bad start if one accepted too eagerly; anyway, the matter needed thought, and the Carringtons would have to be consulted.

'You probably have other irons in the fire. Well, join me if you can. Now I must let you go as I'm expecting a parent.' She rose and escorted Jane to the front door. 'I'm sorry I haven't time to show you over the school. We're rather proud of our new swimming pool. By the way, it will be best if you just tell Meriella I never award scholarships to girls who aren't prepared to stay on until they're eighteen.'

'But suppose she agrees to that?'

'She won't,' said Miss Willy.

They exchanged civil goodbyes and Jane drove away, wondering why Merry so disliked the head

74

mistress, who had obviously treated her with forbearance. Perhaps the star quality in Merry warred with the star quality in Miss Willy – of which Jane had been fully conscious. One could be amused by such a quality in a brilliant child but one was wary of it in a mature woman; and though Jane's own dislike had decreased, she guessed it would never be replaced by any feeling of warmth.

What worried her now was that all cheaper schools would be a come-down after this one. How much was Merry going to mind?

She came running from the house while Jane was garaging her car.

'Was it all right? How did you get on?'

Jane was thankful to have the explanation Miss Willy had suggested. Merry accepted it at once.

'I ought to have guessed that. Scholarship holders are always expected to work for the glory of the school. I'd never do that. Funny, I've always wanted to leave and get started on the stage but now ... well, I wish I'd known last term that it *was* my last term and sort of said goodbye.'

As they walked to the house Jane spoke of the list of schools Miss Willy was sending.

'But they'll be private schools, Jane. We'd have to pay.'

Jane said tentatively, 'I wondered if you'd allow me to help, Merry. I could easily afford it.'

'Darling Jane! I wouldn't dream of letting you spend money on me. And, anyway, if one can't go to a first-rate private school, which Weary Willy's really is, why not go tootling off to school with the village children?' Merry's tone was gay but distinctly histrionic. 'I can pick up a real teenage vocabulary – that's so frowned on at Miss Willy's, inhibited little squares that we are; I mean "were" as regards me – it's like having to change the tense when someone dies. But I do thank you for such a superb offer – and you've only known me four days. Seems longer, doesn't it?'

'It does, indeed,' said Jane. 'Well, let's talk again when the list of schools comes.'

Merry, after a moment's silence, agreed cheerfully. 'All right. Now I must go and tell Betty. She'll probably ask me to lunch. I'll just get my coat.' She sped indoors and upstairs, then called down: 'Jane, are you *sure* I need to go to *any* school?'

'Quite, quite sure.'

'Ah, well...' Still appearing to be extremely cheerful, Merry went into her room.

Already the house felt different. It was colder. The hall fire had not been lit, and economizing on central heating had begun. Through the drawing-room door Cook and Edith could be seen spreading dust-sheets over the furniture.

'Got to cut down on the housework,' said Cook, as Jane joined them. 'So we'll put this room right out of action.'

'And of course we've closed Mr Carringron's bedroom,' said Edith. 'That was a sad task.'

'Like as not he'll never sleep in his bed again,' said Cook. 'Well, we'd better scrape a bit of lunch together.'

The lunch was adequate, Jane told herself; but the cold meat seemed noticeably cold in the cold dining-room.

After the meal, Drew said he would work in his room. 'I shall wrap myself in a blanket and pretend I'm a shivering genius in an attic.'

'God knows what this house will be like in real winter,' said Richard. 'This is merely a brisk autumn day.'

He went to the study, accompanied by Jane and Clare, to decide which bills should be paid. Clare had got the village tradesmen to agree that their accounts should stand over, provided they were, from now on, paid in cash.

In the middle of the afternoon the police called again. Richard interviewed them in the hall and was soon able to report that they had gone. 'They asked if I knew where Father was and I said I didn't. Then they said I must let them know if I heard from him. I said "quite" which means nothing at all.'

Drew, coming down to tea, said he had opened his door to listen. 'Not very impressive, the Law, was it? They order these things better on television.'

The glory that had once been tea at Dome House was a thing of the past, Jane noted, eating bread and margarine.

'Austerity's set in with a vengeance,' said Drew. 'Cook and Edith have even dug out our thick old nursery cups.'

Soon after tea, Merry returned. Jane had told the others of Miss Willy's adverse decision but not of her own plans for Merry (or of Miss Willy's offer to herself; no point in mentioning that until she'd made up her own mind about it). Richard had merely said they must find out which school Merry was entitled to attend. He referred to this on seeing her but she said airily, 'Tomorrow, tomorrow,' and ran up to her room, coming down only in time for dinner. This, though only a stew of leftovers, was quite good, but when Cook and Edith came in for television, they brought no coffee. Drew protested gently.

'Coffee's expensive,' said Cook. 'And you've got to learn to do without things. People are saying you've been spoilt–'

'Then it's damned impertinent of them,' said Richard. 'And I've heard you say coffee doesn't keep. We'll have ours while it's still fresh, thank you, Cook.'

'Very good, *sir!*' Cook glared, but a slight break in her voice on the 'sir' turned the speech into a reproach. She stalked out, followed by Edith.

Drew said: 'Richard, how could you, when they're being such angels? I'd soon have coaxed coffee out of them.'

'We're too old to coax them.'

Jane doubted if Drew would ever be, or if Richard had ever been young enough. And at the moment her sympathies were with Richard. Much as she liked the maids she suspected that circumstances might turn them into tyrants. So she was a little sorry when Richard went on, 'Oh, I'd better go and make my peace. God knows I'm grateful to them.'

He returned from the kitchen with a mollified Cook and Edith. A compromise had been reached: tea was served instead of coffee.

Burly, offered cold milk instead of warm, showed displeasure. 'Have to warm it for him tomorrow,' said Cook. She helped him on to the sofa and gave him the last peppermint cream. 'We'll get a few more of these and keep them just for him. Can't explain to a dog, can you?'

Drew sat between the maids, just as on her first evening, Jane remembered. Indeed, everything looked much the same as then. The fire had been lit and burned as brightly...

But gone was that sense of happiness she had luxuriated in. Well, she'd thought of it as a group product, and now no member of the group could be contributing to it, except the slumbering Burly and perhaps the maids were sustained by their noble intentions.

After the News, which again failed to mention Rupert Carrington, Merry announced she was going to work on her journal. 'It doesn't yet know about Father. Please don't disturb me, anyone. Good night.'

They all responded affectionately as she ran upstairs.

'I've never known her so quiet,' said Richard, once her door had closed. 'It's hell for her having to change schools just when she needs all her friends around her. Oh, blast Weary Willy!'

A few moments later, some small sound caused Jane to look upwards. Merry had come out of her room and was leaning on the gallery railing, looking down. Their eyes met. Jane smiled. Merry smiled in return, very sweetly; then she gave a little valedictory wave of her hand and went back into her room.

BOOK TWO

Merry

1

According to Plan

She had completed the plan on the previous day, having begun work on it as soon as she knew her school fees were not paid. Then she had shelved the whole idea, convinced by Betty that a scholarship could be had for the asking. On hearing that it couldn't, she had made her decision within seconds: forward with the plan!

Not a word about it had been said to Betty. The less Betty knew, the better; she was loyal but no liar. Merry had simply told her there would be no scholarship, accepted sympathy plus a good lunch, and then departed – turning to give her friend a beautiful and memorable smile.

The afternoon had been spent in shopping, after a cross-country walk to a village where she had never shopped before and was unlikely to be recognized. Thoroughness in covering tracks was part of the plan.

And now she was alone in her bedroom with the night stretching before her – a night when, for the first time in her life, she would not lie down to sleep. She had just taken her last look at the group below, murmuring to herself Juliet's words: 'Farewell! – God knows when we shall meet again!' She was glad Jane had looked up. Now Jane, as well as Betty, would have a smile to remember.

So much to be done – and so little she could safely do until the household settled for the night, as someone might ignore her request that she shouldn't be disturbed. She could write her farewell note but felt it would be unlucky to do that before she was ready to leave. It would be best to pass the time by making an entry in her journal, particularly as she had said she was going to; even the shortest entry would turn that lie into the truth. She disapproved of lying and even of 'acting a lie'. But she sometimes gave herself a dispensation by feeling she was 'playing a part'. She would have to play a continuous part for the next six months.

She unlocked the drawer where she kept the journal, settled at her desk, and wrote:

'I am not in the mood for journal writing so I will only say that this is the most important night of my whole life. Soon, when the house is sleeping–'

She broke off. The mood for journal writing had come on with such a rush that she knew she would write, for hours if she let it have its head. She therefore concluded:

'But no more now. When – and where – shall I next take up my pen? What a cliché! I apologize, Posterity!'

Posterity, frequently addressed, had become for her a composite creation made up of herself when old and famous, biographers of her famous self, the British Museum, and some critic who would one day write: 'Publication of the journal proves she was as great a writer as she was an actress.' But she never visualized this composite Posterity without rebuking herself for conceit which she already recognized, if only occasionally, as her most menacing sin.

Posterity, anyway, was located in the far-away future. She would be outraged if anyone but herself read the journal now. Suppose her family searched for it, even broke open her drawer, in the hope of finding clues to where she'd gone? Could she take the journal with her? Well, hardly; not twenty-two exercise books.

Inspiration descended. At one time she'd had a passion for sealing her letters. Yes, she still had her sealing-wax set complete with matches and a fat red candle. (What a child one had been at twelve!) She also had some string. After tying the exercise books together, she sealed the string at the knot and every criss-cross; then wrote a note in red ink:

'There is nothing in this journal which will help anyone to trace me. Please respect my privacy. I have complete confidence that I shall find the seals unbroken on my return. Thank you.'

That, she felt sure, would prove a potent message.

By the time she had put the journal back in its

drawer, the party below was breaking up. She waited a full half-hour, then tip-toed onto the gallery. No light could be seen under any door. The real business of her night could begin.

First, she got out one of her recent purchases, a bright blue packet on which was the picture of a Titian-haired beauty. According to the instructions, you first washed your hair and then poured over it a jug of water into which part of the contents of the packet had been stirred. 'Enough for three rinses, unless a very deep shade is required.' She did require a deep shade, the rich auburn of the wig she had worn as Juliet, so she would use the whole packet.

Thanking God and her grandmother for her fitted wash basin, she began washing her hair. But even this part of the operation did not prove easy. Usually Clare did the job for her, while she held a towel to her face. Now the soap got into her eyes and she kept banging her head on the taps. The tinting was still more difficult; so much of the mixture went into her ears or down her back. And her hair emerged merely looking dark instead of mousy – but one couldn't really judge until it was dry. She pinned up some curls, put on a setting net and hoped for the best.

Now she would pack. This would need the most careful consideration as all clothes taken should be suitable for adult wear. She feared that few things would pass the test with flying colours except her one pair of high-heeled shoes and her superb running-away outfit which she had tried on before dinner.

In the spring Clare had misguidedly bought a

thick white polo-necked sweater, a boldly checked black-and-white skirt, and a very full black coat. The neck of the sweater made her head look too small, Drew insisted the skirt was a stolen horse-blanket, and the coat was generally held to in-dicate imminent motherhood. Clare's Folly – swiftly so named – had soon been relegated to the box-room cupboard, where clothes intended for rummage sales were kept. Before dinner, while surreptitiously getting her suitcase, Merry had abstracted Clare's Folly, replacing it with her school uniform.

It was pleasant to reflect that if any search was made for her it would be for a mousy, uniformed schoolgirl, not for a Titian-haired adult in dashing clothes. And the clothes, Merry was sure, would suit her splendidly as she was tall enough to carry them, nearly four inches taller than Clare. True, the skirt would be short but not so very as it had been too long for Clare. Anyway, short skirts were dashing – and only grown-ups wore them; schoolgirls wore their skirts drearily long.

After spending over an hour going through her clothes, Merry found their juvenility so depress-ing that she took a long look at Clare's Folly just to cheer herself up. It really was splendidly mature. But she must not only look mature; she must feel it – and a first step towards that would be to sound it. She would now decide what voice to use.

It must be more sophisticated than her normal voice, and she must be more than usually careful to speak what she believed Drama Schools called Accepted Southern English – not to be confused with what she and Betty called Affected Southern English, as spoken by many radio announcers. Merry had once mimicked this by saying: 'In this perm, the pert speaks of his longing for herm.'

An inner monologue in mature Accepted Southern English now began, while she packed the least-juvenile of her clothes and selected stockings, handkerchiefs and many small possessions. The monologue became so interesting when she heard herself coping with various imagined situations – such as the amorous intentions of admiring theatrical managers – that she sat entranced, just listening to herself. This would never do. The night was passing. Sternly she concentrated on packing. What books should she allow herself? Only Shakespeare. It was agony to leave all her other plays but the suitcase was already overflowing.

Now to assemble her money – from three boxes: spending money in the first box, savings towards Christmas presents in the second, savings towards theatre visits in the third. Grand total: nearly twelve pounds. She would also take the diamond brooch which had been her share of her mother's jewellery, though she hoped she would have no need to part with it. She was confident she would find a job before her money was used up.

Her hair would certainly be dry by now. She removed the net in front of her looking glass, then gasped in dismay. The colour reminded her of badly polished mahogany and combing did nothing to improve it. Had she time to wash it again? No – and what would be the use? The tinting was said to remain for several shampoos. Perhaps a hairdresser could help her but for the present she was stuck with this horrible thatch and could only hide it with a head scarf.

To cheer herself up she put on her new brassiere. This was no make-shift bust such as had let her down when she played Juliet. She had told the astonished shop-assistant it must be earthquake proof and it certainly seemed so. Now for the checked skirt and polo-necked sweater! Magnificent effect! A soft white woollen prow jutted in front of her. Unfortunately it only *looked* soft; it felt just a bit like a birdcage.

If only her hair wasn't spoiling everything! But wait – might it not be turned to advantage? Might it not be just the hair to escape in, a far more effective disguise than the one she had planned? But she must dress up to it – or rather, down to it. Off came the white sweater, on went an old pink blouse. She would pin a wilted rose to the black coat and – yes, she had some blue earrings from a cracker. She now looked superbly common, a word she had always been discouraged from using but exactly right for her present appearance. And as well as common, she was common-place; no one would give her a second glance.

What sort of voice should she use now? At that instant, a girl called Mavis was born. She spoke sloppily, called everyone 'dear', very frequently said 'honestly and 'definitely'. From now on Merry's inner monologue was mainly spoken by Mavis. Accepted Southern English was in abeyance.

Mavis required make-up. Out of the suitcase came Merry's newly acquired cosmetics. Blue shadow on the eyelids; orange lipstick; too much pink powder. Merry was enchanted by her skill but shocked that she could look so awful.

Creative effort had given her an appetite. She ate some of the chocolate and biscuits she had bought that afternoon; then brushed her teeth. Mavis remarked: 'Fussy, aren't we, dear?' Merry said: 'God's given me good teeth and I intend to keep them.' Mavis then said: 'Well, get a move on, ducky. And take the envelope that had the hair stuff in it. We don't want anyone to know what we've been up to.' Merry was glad to find Mavis was no fool; they would get on well, sharing a mind and a body.

She glanced at her clock. Heavens, how fast the night had gone! It was time to begin her farewell letter. (A job for Merry; Mavis went off duty.) She wrote:

Dear Richard,

When you read this I shall be far away. I refuse to waste dear Jane's money – or my own time – on any school. Don't worry about me. I shall be absolutely all right. I am older, in myself, than any of you know.

If you want a good explanation for my absence, say I have gone to stay with an aunt. Not Aunt Winifred – no one would believe I'd go to stay with her. Just say I'm with an aunt of mother's. She never had one. I think Betty's conscience will allow her to pretend she believes the aunt story. Give her my love and tell her I only kept my plans from her because I felt knowing them would make it difficult for her if you questioned her.

I implore you not to ask the police to find me. They wouldn't manage it, anyhow – remember I am a master of make-up. If I read in the papers that they are after me, I won't be answerable for the consequences. YOU HAVE BEEN WARNED. I might even slip out of the country with a troupe of dancers and you know what that could mean. But if you leave me alone I will take the greatest care of myself and come home unblemished – in six months.

Goodbye, good luck, and lots of love to you all from your prodigal sister
Merry.

P.S. I have quite a lot of money and am taking my diamond brooch. If pawned, it would get me home even from Land's End or John O'Groats – neither of which places I intend to visit. Trust me – and LEAVE ME ALONE.

She read through the letter and carefully blocked out 'Remember I am a master of make-up.' Why give such a possibly valuable clue? Besides, it was conceited.

Now she was ready to start but it was still too early. The most tricky part of her escape was choosing the exact moment to leave. She must go before it was light but if she tried to cross the fields at the back of the house while it was dark she might sprain an ankle or fall into a ditch. Her objective was a road travelled by an early-morning bus to London. She had worked it all out: the time the sun would rise, the time the cross-country walk – around four miles – would take, the time the bus would pass. She ought to wait a while. But she was getting nervous. Better too early than too late and she wasn't sure what time Cook and Edith got up.

She put on the black coat, with its dangling pink rose, picked up her suitcase and her handbag, and then gave a last look around the room. Conscious of a slight catch in her throat she told herself not to work things up – 'You're not going to execution.' The voice of Mavis said cheerfully, 'Bye bye room.'

Lights off, torch on, door opened and quietly closed. Now along the gallery – and don't bang the suitcase into the banisters. She reached the top of the stairs. No sailing down in the middle now; she put the torch in her coat pocket, grasped the handrail, and felt her way step by step. Placing her letter, addressed to Richard, on the hall table she imagined the moment when he would open it and read it aloud. Poor darlings, would they all be terribly worried? She gave a loving look up towards the bedroom doors. But she must not think about that now – already the dome above her was paler than the darkness around her. Perhaps it was already dawn.

But when she let herself out of the back door it was still so dark that she had to use her torch until she reached the lawn. Then there was nothing to bump into but a herbaceous border – which she did once and felt some tall flower brush her cheek. How terribly exciting this escape was! This thrill of fear that she might be caught, she must store it up to be acted later... The dark mass on her right now was the barn – and ahead, a glimmer of white, was the gate. She opened it quietly, then looked back at the house. No lighted windows, no pursuers... She was out in the lane, free.

She was also cautious. It was still too dark to venture into the fields. She sat down on her suitcase and waited. Soon she heard a cock crow – and almost as if on cue, the darkness began to pale. She could start now, if she went carefully.

It proved to be a gruelling walk, for the suitcase, though not particularly heavy, soon seemed so. But she spurred herself on by reciting speeches from *Henry V*, and the village church clock, chiming the quarters, repeatedly assured her she had enough time for frequent rests. She heard it again as she reached the road, a faint, farewell chime which now told her she would have a twenty-minute wait for the bus.

It had begun to rain and she had forgotten to bring her raincoat. But there was a barn close to the road and no nearby farmhouse whose occupiers were likely to see her. She went in, set her suitcase close to a bale of hay which would provide her with a backing, and sat down thankfully.

Soon she would be on the bus. She saw herself hail it, jump on, then off it would go at full speed. She'd be miles and miles away before anyone missed her. And soon, soon – in not much more than two hours – she would be in London.

2

The Anonymous Town

Her head jerked forward. She was instantly, guiltily aware she had been asleep. Only for a moment, of course.

She looked at her watch and panic struck. The time shown was two-thirty. Two-thirty? Already she would have been missed for hours and hours! And suppose Richard had ignored her warnings? Already the police might be after her. And was there an afternoon bus? She doubted it.

Grabbing her suitcase, she hurried out of the barn – and saw, not a hundred yards away, a bus approaching. It was travelling in the wrong direction for London but she instantly hailed it; at least it would take her away from where she was. It stopped. She sprang on and found she was the only passenger. Quickly she made her way to a front seat, behind the driver. Anyone who got on now would see only the back of her head.

The conductress approached and said: 'Where to?' Where to, indeed – Merry had no idea where the bus was going and was determined not to draw attention to herself by inquiring. Handing a pound note, she said in the voice of Mavis: 'All the way, thanks, dear.' She got back only fourteen shillings change, so all the way was obviously going to be some distance. But she would get off as soon as she reached a town with a railway station. Meanwhile she was at least getting further from home and was also in out of the rain.

Soon the bus pulled up in a village she recognized. She knew no one who lived there; still, she partly covered her face with her handkerchief, ostensibly blowing her nose. The bus acquired two more passengers – to be heard but never seen by her – before it went on through the village, which seemed unusually quiet, with none of its shops open; presumably it was early closing day.

As they came to the church, a bus travelling in the opposite direction passed them. One of the passengers said: 'London bus.' At the same instant, Merry caught sight of the church clock. It stood at 7.52. Frantically she looked at her watch. It still said 2.30. Then it had stopped – in the middle of the night! She had forgotten to wind it, depending on her bedroom clock and then on the church clock's chimes. That was *her* London bus which had just thundered past. Soon it would be passing the barn where she would have hailed it – but for that disastrous nap which could not have lasted five minutes. Oh, maddening watch! No: maddening, careless Merry. And maddening, most reprehensible panic.

But all was not lost, all was very much not lost. A whole half day had been given back to her – and she was now speeding in the opposite direction from which her family would expect her to speed; nobody looking for a job on the stage would plunge into the depths of Suffolk. This was a most subtle method of escape, as subtle as disguising herself as Mavis. And she would get a train that stopped at some London suburb. The police might be waiting for her in London, at both the station and the bus terminus. Clever Merry! Resourceful Merry! She leaned back and relaxed.

Soon she was travelling through villages that were unfamiliar, all too small to possess a railway station. People got on and off the bus, always remaining voices, never faces, to her; for she kept her own face averted. It was fun, listening without seeing; she made a game of it, trying to pick up where she was and where she was going. It was a game she never won, not even when the bus reached its terminus soon after nine o'clock, for the conductress announced the name of the place in a blurred roar which conveyed no information whatever. But at least Merry could see this was a small market town, not a village, and it was likely to have a station.

Tidying up in the Ladies' Room she was shocked at her appearance. That awful hair! The sooner she got to a London hairdresser, the better. She must ask her way to the station but not here – the bus was a link with her own locality, someone might remember her later. She would walk a little way into the town.

The rain had stopped now and the day, though not sunny, was whitely bright. Her spirits rose. This not knowing where she was gave her a sense of adventure and freedom – and also security; for surely a person who didn't know where she was would be particularly difficult to find? This idea was pleasant but also confusing. She even felt a little dizzy, but most cheerfully dizzy, with a tendency to giggle.

Now she was in the little town's High Street. A glance at the roof line and the upper storeys showed her that the houses were very old, but they had all been turned into shops and most of the shops, refronted, were very modern indeed. Their contents struck her as being unusually highly coloured – such yellow loaves, such emerald vegetables, such scarlet meat! As for the clothes' shops, they were displaying the most dazzling shades, with a preponderance of turquoise, flame and canary. Nothing looked quite real; it was like walking through a dream. No, not a dream, for her dreams were always dimly coloured. This was like walking through illustrations of nursery rhymes.

She pulled herself up. These were the thoughts of Merry. Mavis had not been heard from since she'd said, 'All the way, thanks, dear,' on the bus. And it was Mavis who must ask where the station was. She came back on duty by saying: 'Stop dreaming, ducky. Shouldn't wonder if you're a bit light-headed. How about some breakfast?'

Not that Merry was really feeling hungry. And the only café she passed was not yet open. Better get to the station at once or she might miss some good train. She would ask her way now. There were few people about but two fat women were approaching. Mavis rehearsed her question to them. Then Merry decided they were looking at her curiously. She would speak to no one who looked at her curiously. Mavis said: 'Oh, don't be daft, dear. Ask the next person you see.' Merry looked for the next person – and saw her, not in

94

the street but in a shop window, picking up a fallen showcard. She was young and pretty, with hair just the colour Merry had hoped to achieve; and the showcard, now righted, said:

DAURENE
Hair stylist
Tinting a speciality

Without consciously making any decision, Merry found herself in the shop.

The red-haired young woman emerged backwards from the window. Mavis said: 'Could I consult Madame Daurene, please?

'I'm her,' said the young woman. 'Just Daurene – everyone calls me that. What can I do for you, dear?'

The voice was the *perfect* voice for Mavis. Merry, subtly adjusting her tone, said: 'Do you do *de*-tinting?'

'Pardon, dear?'

'Well, *un*-tinting.' Merry pointed to her hair.

Daurene got it. 'Went a bit far, didn't you? Well, let's have a look.'

She ushered Merry through pink plastic curtains into one of four cubicles gleaming with chromium, looking-glass and glossy pink paint. Everything looked new.

'Only opened last week,' said Daurene. 'Oh, I've been in the trade since I was sixteen but this is my first venture on my own. Sit down, dear. Whatever did you use?'

Merry told her, adding, 'I wanted it to look just like yours.'

95

'Well, thanks, dear.' Daurene flicked the hair about with a comb and then passed judgement. 'You won't get rid of this muck for at least six washes. And you'll never get a shade like mine out of a packet. Let me give you a proper bleach and tint.'

'That'd be permanent, wouldn't it?'

'Oh, definitely – except for touching up the new hair as it grows.'

'Suppose I wanted my own colour again?'

'You could be tinted to it, while the new hair grew – but you won't want to be. Girls usually want to go redder and redder, or if I give them a blonde tint, they want to go blonder. None of them want to go back.'

Should she risk it, and arrive in London ready for the fray? But before deciding, she asked the times of the trains.

'Only two good ones a day and you've missed the nine-twenty. The other's not till two-thirty so you've lots of time. Oh, come on, dear – I'm in the mood to do you a lovely job. And I'll style it for you, too. A windswept might suit you or an urchin. I'd rather not decide until I've got the colour right. Okay if I go ahead?'

'Okay.' Merry, looking at her reflection disgustedly, had decided almost anything would be an improvement.

'Then that's the last you're going to see of yourself until I'm through,' said Daurene, swinging Merry's chair round so that it faced away from the looking-glass. 'You'd be surprised how many girls lose their nerve the first time and want me to stop. They say children and fools should never see a job till it's finished – not that I mean you're either, dear, still... Take your coat off and put this on.' She produced a surplice-like overall. 'We'll start by getting the soap out.'

A shallow metal bowl was fixed to the chair. Merry was tilted backwards so that her head rested on it. Full-length, with her feet supported by a stool, she felt as if about to be guillotined – face upwards.

She was never able to recall clearly all the stages and details of her metamorphosis: the washings and dryings, the dampings and dabbings, the strange smells... Twice, a dryer was lowered over her head and she was handed what Daurene called 'books', actually the floppiest of women's magazines. At first Daurene talked willingly, prodded by questions. Merry was anxious to avoid being questioned herself as she had not yet invented reasons for arriving wherever she had arrived. She learned how Daurene had got backing for her business, 'And I'm doing ever so well, dear – booked solid from twelve o'clock, couldn't have taken you if I hadn't had a cancellation. It's quite a job, running the place single-handed. Excuse me a minute, dear.' She dived into the shop to serve a customer, giving Merry time to decide on being a typist about to look for work in London.

Daurene, on returning and hearing this, merely said:

'Fancy! Well, good luck, dear – and now don't talk for a bit. I've got to concentrate.' From then on, she spoke mostly to herself, giving advice and encouragement. 'A bit more – no, don't overdo it... That's got it. Now we're getting somewhere.'

At last the tinting was finished but Merry was still not allowed to see herself. 'Not till I've styled you, dear,' said Daurene, brandishing the scissors. 'They say it takes a man to cut hair but don't you believe it.'

The next quarter of an hour was alarming. Daurene cut, combed, flashed and clashed her scissors, to the accompaniment of remarks such as, 'My word, you've got a lot to get rid of – what a mop!' Hair flew into the air, the floor was thick with it – or rather, Merry guessed it was; she did not dare to look down, fearing that unless she kept quite still she might lose an ear. Once she ventured: 'Surely that's enough?' Daurene went on cutting.

But at last she put the scissors down, combed the hair carefully and said: 'Well, there we are – and if you don't like it I'll break my heart.' She then swung the chair round to face the mirror.

Merry's first sensation was one of utter astonishment – not at the colour, which she adored, or at the styling; she knew instantly that this ordered disorder was both fashionable and becoming. What astounded her was that she simply did not recognize herself. The face in the glass might have been that of a stranger. But how splendid – especially as the stranger was far prettier than she had ever hoped to be. And she looked *years* older, *quite* grown up. Her delight was so great that she forgot all about Mavis, and it was the voice of Merry at her youngest which exclaimed: 'Oh, thank you, thank you! It's marvellous – like a lovely copper cap! Oh, darling

Daurene, you're a great artist.'

She then sprang up and hugged Daurene who looked extremely astonished. Fortunately she then heard a customer in the shop, so Merry was left alone long enough to calm down and grow older.

After gazing at herself again, most blissfully, she opened her suitcase. Now she would change into the white sweater. Daurene, returning after showing the customer into the next cubicle, said: 'My word, that suits you! Well, here's your little bill.'

It was a large little bill but Merry grudged not one penny of it. She even added a handsome tip – then wondered if she ought to have tipped a proprietress. Daurene obviously did not share that doubt. She just said, 'Thanks ever so and ever so glad you're pleased. Well, bye bye,' and then went off to the next cubicle. The customer had brought a hairstyle cut out of a 'book'. 'Might do a lot for you,' Daurene pronounced earnestly. Merry knew she was already forgotten. Her magical transformation had, for the magician, been just a run-of-the-mill morning's work.

Now Mavis must be left behind in the hair-strewn cubicle. Merry unpinned the wilted pink rose and dropped it into the wastepaper basket. 'But who am I now?' she wondered, stepping out into the bright little High Street.

She had, when planning her escape, chosen the name she would use: Mary Young – Mary because it would sound to her like Merry, and Young because it seemed to her funnily suitable. But she now thought the name insufficiently dashing for her new appearance. She would be ... Mary le Jeune. A charming name – but not right yet; 'Mary' was too meek. She could risk sticking to 'Merry' now that she looked so different. Yes, Merry le Jeune. And now she must invent a voice.

But could she really sustain any voice but her own? How carelessly she had forgotten to be Mavis! Safer to use her own voice and concentrate on speaking more slowly – and thinking before she spoke. Extreme calmness must be her keynote: confident calmness. And she felt calmly confident now, strolling along with her copper-capped head held high. She also felt hungry – and here was a café open. She went in.

It was a bleak little place, most unlike the glorious and dimly lit Espresso coffee bars she had visited in London. But there was a massive juke-box (to her shame, she did not know how to work it) and the girl behind the counter was obviously a teenager. One might add to one's sparse teenage vocabulary. Merry made her way through the almost empty café, perched herself on a high stool, and remarked: 'I guess I'm early. Not many cats around the joint yet.'

'Haven't got no cats – nor no joint either,' said the teenager. 'Only do ham sandwiches.'

Deflated, Merry ordered a couple.

While waiting for them, she sustained a shock. Staring at her from the looking-glass behind the counter was a very different girl from the one seen in Daurene's discreetly lit cubicle. By the crude light of day the copper cap was ... well, very highly burnished copper. However, it still pleased her; what did not was her face. Mavis still lingered blue of eyelid, plastered with powder and flaunting a lipstick which gave the impression that her mouth had been dyed with her hair. Abandoning teenage conversation as a dead loss, Merry hurried to the Ladies' Room and did what she could to improve matters, which wasn't much; a complete cleansing was needed and a new, very tactful make-up. Copper cap undoubtedly called for discretion.

The sandwiches proved to be stodgy but she wolfed them down, drank a glass of milk, paid her bill and asked the way to the station. Only ten minutes walk, she was thankful to hear – though what she was going to do for two hours she couldn't imagine, burdened as she was with her suitcase.

The High Street was now crowded with shoppers. Wandering along, she remembered her first impression of it. How changed everything was now! The shops still looked bright but their brightness was normal; gone was that early-morning clarity of vision. For a few moments she regretted it, tried to hold it in the mind's eye. Then she began window-shopping. There were so many things she needed as a grown-up but she didn't dare spend any money – not after Daurene's little bill.

It was only one o'clock when she reached the end of the High Street and came to a small, cobbled square; a market square undoubtedly, but there was no market today. She was attracted by a porticoed, eighteenth-century building, on the upper storey of which were incised the words 'Assembly Rooms'. Inspection showed that the place was now used as Auction Rooms. A poster announcing a sale had a strip pasted over it saying 'On View Today'. The doors stood open revealing a large collection of second-hand furniture. Well, to go in would pass the time – and one could find something to sit on.

Never could she have believed that so many hideous things could be gathered together under one roof. As well as deplorable furniture there were pictures and pottery, bundles of bedding, carpets, draperies, old gas-stoves and oil-stoves. She began to play a game; she would win it if she could find one thing she would have accepted as a gift. Absurdly – and though she knew it was absurd she felt it quite strongly – failing to win would be unlucky.

There must be something! Looking up at the gallery which ran round the room she saw a table loaded with books. Surely among so many... But it was still no good. She read title after title. Sermons, books about chemistry, mathematics, agriculture... Well, she would walk right round the gallery.

And in a corner she found it: a rosewood sofa, upholstered in faded moss-green brocade. She wouldn't have paid for it but as a gift – yes, she could consider the game won. Gratefully, she sat down.

Still nearly an hour to waste, even if she got to the station early. She leaned back and put her feet up. This was the kind of one-ended sofa that invalids in old novels spent so much time on. How quiet this place was! She had seen only one person, a man working in an office.

Strange to think of people dancing here – poor Assembly Rooms, now filled with junk. Antique furniture was romantic; junk just depressing. But would junk turn into antiques in, say, a hundred years? No, not most of the junk here – for one thing, it wouldn't last long enough; as well as being hideous it was badly made. But this was a pleasant little sofa. She wondered if it had belonged to people who came to dances here, girls in Jane Austen dresses, or crinolines. What would they think of her thick white sweater, her short, boldly checked skirt? Then and now ... fascinating to think about.

Sliding lower on the sofa she stretched her long legs and lay looking up at the delicate mouldings of the ceiling. 'Don't go to sleep,' she warned herself. No fear of that now; she had never felt more wide awake. Surprising, that, when she remembered she had only had that tiny cat-nap in the barn in – how long? She had awakened at eight o'clock yesterday morning, nearly thirty hours ago. She had got out of bed then a mousy-haired schoolgirl and now... It was kind of fate to bring her to Daurene; the morning had been more than well spent. And soon, soon – in not much more than three hours – she would be in London.

3

Night Thoughts

How dark it was ... she must have forgotten to draw back the curtains before getting into bed. She reached for the switch of her bedside light, failed to find it, failed to find the bedside table, almost overbalanced–

Then it began, the rushing return of memory in a turmoil of bewilderment and fear. She sat bolt upright and swung her legs over the side of the sofa; then restrained herself, grabbing the edge of the sofa as if on a raft from which the waves of surrounding darkness might dislodge her. She must keep still, control herself, think.

Now that she was sitting up, the darkness wasn't so absolute. She could see the pale shapes of round-topped windows, along the gallery; and at the far end, two slightly brighter windows which must look onto the lights of the market square. People would be there. She would attract their attention, break a window if necessary. She felt in her coat pocket for her torch. As her hand closed on it, a church clock began to strike.

She counted the strokes carefully – and astoundedly, as the count increased. Ten, eleven, twelve! She had slept over ten hours. She raged at herself. But there was no time for that now. Snapping the torch on, she made her way along the crowded gallery to the front windows.

The little cobbled square was entirely deserted, the shops shuttered, the windows above them dark. By the light of one of the small, old street-lamps she read a signboard on which was painted: J. Birdswell, Seedsman, Established 1760. It seemed to her that the square must have looked much the same when J. Birdswell first set up in business except that the lights inside the old lamps were now electric – and as she noticed this, they all went out.

But surely if she screamed loud enough some-one would hear? Perhaps a policeman would patrol the square. She pulled herself up. A police-man was the last person she wanted to meet. And why take it for granted she was irrevocably locked in? Surely she would be able to open some door or some window?

Should she go back to the sofa for her suitcase and handbag? No, they would hamper her. She would get them when she had found some way of escape.

Carefully, she lit herself down the staircase, the foot of which was near to the large front doors. Well, of course they were locked on the outside – she had expected this – and the tall windows that flanked them were unopenable and also barred. She threaded her way along one side of the huge room. All the windows were barred. At last she came to a door which opened. But it only admit-ted her to a dilapidated cloakroom. Her torch, after shining along a row of pegs, was reflected in the gilt-framed pier-glass above the fire-place. She turned the light on herself and saw her face floating in the darkness ... frightening; no more of that.

Exploring further, she saw a marble-topped wash basin; also, through an open door, a mahogany-surrounded lavatory of most antiquated design – but it still worked, she was glad to find. And the cold tap of the basin obliged with a stream of water which issued from the mouth of a china lion's head. She wondered if the water would be fit to drink and risked a little, from the palm of her hand.

Now she would go on looking for some way out, though where she would go when she got out, she couldn't imagine. There would be some hotel but it would be closed by now. She could bang on the door but they might refuse to take her in. Why not stay just where she was?

Could she bear it, all the long hours of the night? 'You will bear what you have to bear,' she told herself sternly. 'And serve you damn well right for falling asleep.' Yes, of course she would stay here. She would go back to her suitcase and have a meal of biscuits and chocolate. And she would take an alarm clock with her; she had noticed several amidst a welter of old saucepans.

Returning to the rosewood sofa had a feeling of homecoming. She sat down and experimented with the alarm clock, hastily snapping it off as soon as she had proved it worked. Only a few minutes before, she had longed to draw attention to her plight; now she was determined not to. She used her torch very guardedly and, after finding her biscuits and chocolate, snapped it off. The windows along the gallery seemed lighter now; she guessed that a moon had risen, though no moonlight shone in on her.

She could dimly see the gallery railing. It reminded her of the gallery at Dome House. Not much more than twenty-four hours ago, she had stood there taking a last look down. She felt years and years older now, but that was an illusion and a dangerous one. In her letter to Richard she had said: 'I am older, in myself, than any of you know.' Was she not, rather, younger than she herself knew? Twice she had fallen asleep on duty and panicked on waking up. She had checked the second panic, but–

An inner voice, her own but weightier, kind but extremely firm, addressed her: 'It is normal that anyone of your age should need plenty of sleep. You should have known that and been on guard. And there will be other things to be on guard about because you are still so young. Remember, however mentally grown-up you may feel, physically you are only fourteen and a half. You must learn to think of yourself as an adult in charge of a child.'

The voice ceased – because she was so impressed with its last words. Brilliant! Undoubtedly, she was unusually intelligent – and was she not, at the moment, behaving most shrewdly, turning disaster to advantage, saving the expense of a night at a hotel? And what admirable forethought, to have found an alarm clock and set it for seven a.m.

She also praised herself for not being afraid, in this place of dim shapes and musty smells. She would rather like to see a ghost – or would she? A tremor in her solar plexus warned her to think of something else. And an attractive topic had suggested itself through comparing her mental and physical ages. She would explore it after settling down to sleep – if sleep she could, after all those hours of it.

She made a pillow of some sweaters and covered herself with her dressing gown. A clock struck one.

This question of her age: in one respect she was in advance of it physically as well as mentally – very much in advance, compared with Betty. True, Betty had been attracted by a locum tenens who had replaced the Vicar for a month, but she had refused to imagine being kissed by him. Even Clare, turned twenty-one, had only admitted (under cross-examination) to having imagined being kissed by Charles II – or rather, she'd tried to and failed; Clare could read imaginatively but couldn't imagine anything all on her own. Merry was apt to imagine being kissed by every attractive man she met, saw on the stage or on television – and by some quite revolting men, too. (The revulsion was part of the exercise in imagination.) At no time had anyone kissed her amorously; but imagination, thank goodness, didn't have to wait on experience.

She had been falling in love since the age of nine and had recently been in love with three men at once: two famous actors and a waiter at a hotel in Ipswich. And nowadays her imagination went beyond merely kissing men; she considered the implications of going to bed with them, though hampered by being none too sure what the implications were, having found Weary Willy's biology lecture so dull that she had (a) not listened carefully and (b) discounted much of what she heard. No doubt the rough outline was correct but as to the details ... well, Weary Willy's knowledge was likely to be purely academic.

And sex couldn't really be dull or it wouldn't be so popular. Anyway, Merry *felt* it wasn't dull – and the still remaining veil of mystery made it all the more exciting. And one could hardly be a great actress unless one had a passionate temperament. She was sure she could count on one; the question was, just how soon should one make use of it, in practice as well as in imagination? Not before she was seventeen, she had decided – but that was when she hadn't expected to be let loose in the world until she was seventeen. Now that she intended to live as an adult...

But she had promised Richard she would return unblemished (provided she wasn't hounded) so she must indeed consider herself as an adult in charge of a child, particularly when she sought interviews with the two famous actors she was in love with. (She waved a mental goodbye to the Ipswich waiter; he'd never been more than a poor third.)

A clock struck two. The sofa now seemed very hard. She was restless and thirsty and her teeth felt guilty of biscuits. The alarm clock, close to her ear, ticked noisily. Obviously she wasn't going to sleep another wink...

She woke soon after eight, without benefit of the alarm clock, which had not fulfilled its promise. Looking over the gallery rail, she saw that the front doors of the building were still closed. They would be open at nine, she guessed, and she must be ready to rush out and catch the nine-twenty train mentioned by Daurene. Swiftly she re-packed her suitcase and carried it down to the cloakroom – which, by the light of day, was even more dilapidated than she'd realized, but reasonably clean. Having brushed her teeth and washed, drying herself on handkerchiefs, she studied her face.

How much younger she looked without make-up! She put on a tactful amount, carefully considering it in juxtaposition to her hair, which still delighted her. She spent a long time combing it and admiring it in the misty old pier-glass. Suddenly she heard sounds in the auction room. Opening the door a crack, she saw that a man was now sitting in the office. The front doors stood open but how was she to reach them unseen?

Her best plan would be to crawl. She stuffed her sponge-bag and damp handkerchiefs into her suitcase, closed it and laid it down flat; then, on her knees, she opened the door wider. If only the man would not look round! For three or four yards she had no cover whatever. Crawling, she pushed the suitcase in front of her as fast as she could ... thank heaven, she was now behind a row of wardrobes ... now sideboards ... now a dangerously low settee ... now three blessedly high-backed chairs ... nearly at the doors now but no cover worthy of the name... She sprang up, bruised of knee, grabbed the suitcase and ran without looking back – and as she dashed between the pillars of the portico she heard the alarm clock, left beside the rosewood sofa, going off at last at the top of its very loud voice.

Treacherous of it – still, it might have done worse by her; perhaps it had been bottling itself up until she was free, as she certainly was now. But a clock was striking nine – and she had forgotten which way the station was. Frantically she looked round for someone to ask.

It was then that she saw, across the square, in front of J. Birdswell, Seedsman, a large glittering bus which, unlike the bus she had boarded yesterday, stated where it was going. A splendidly clear sign on the front said LONDON.

A bus would take longer than a train, but the bus was there and she was sure of catching it – or was she? It was already almost full and the driver was at the wheel. She started to run – oh, heavens, it was moving! Then the driver saw her, slowed down and waved reassuringly. Another minute and she was on.

Unlike local buses, this one had no conductor. Merry paid her fare to the driver, then sank into a seat. She had just time for one look back at the Assembly Rooms. She would always remember them and this town. She was glad she still didn't know the town's name; she wished it to remain a mystery town, anyway for the present. It would be fun to come here again quite by accident, when driving through Suffolk; perhaps she'd find out the name then. And perhaps she'd die so famous that Posterity, reading about last night in her journal, would put a plaque on the Assembly Rooms saying 'Merry le Jeune slept here'.

Sad they never put plaques up while one was living.

Now the bus was out of the town and gathering speed. She was going to get very hungry and she'd finished her biscuits and chocolate. Perhaps she could pick up some more on the way, and she'd have a real meal at the end of the journey, before finding a cheap hotel or bed-sitting-room. Anyway, hunger didn't matter – nothing mattered now, because now nothing could stop her getting to London.

4

Green Lane to Crestover

The bus broke down soon after ten o'clock, in deep country two miles from the nearest village. Never, according to the driver, had it done such a thing before and he could not find out what was the matter with it. Merry could have told him: she was aboard. Obviously she had no more chance of getting to London than the three sisters in Chekhov's play had of getting to Moscow.

By then many passengers had got off the bus. Of those who remained, four were bound for the next village; they decided to walk on. The driver decided to walk back for a mile, to an inn from which he could telephone for a relief bus. Only Merry and a fat, elderly woman were bound for London. They would just have to wait.

The fat woman sat in the bus, reading a paper. Merry, attracted by the sunny morning, strolled along the lane for a little way. As she sauntered back towards the bus, the fat woman lowered her paper and stared; then ducked behind the paper. Merry walked past the bus for a few yards, then turned her head quickly. The fat woman had turned hers too, and was again staring. Instantly she turned back to her paper. Merry was close enough to see it was a Suffolk paper and there was a photograph reproduced on its front page.

She went on walking away from the bus.

'Keep absolutely calm,' she told herself. 'Remember how your hair has changed you.' But might not red hair look the same as brown, in a photograph? What photograph was it? She tried to recapture her glimpse of it. A girl in a white dress – that last snapshot, taken in the summer. Oh, she'd never forgive Richard!

She must escape – but not without her suitcase, and let that fat woman try to stop her taking it! She turned and marched towards the bus. Just before she reached it she noticed a weather-beaten signpost saying: 'Green Lane to Crestover'. If she could get between the high hedges of the green lane without being seen getting there, she would have vanished as if by a conjuring trick. The woman was at the front of the bus, the suitcase was at the back. Merry tiptoed forward, seized the case, and sprinted for the green lane. Before dashing into it, she gave one look back. The woman had not turned back

Marvellous! And such a beautiful green lane. Merry had always loved them and there were so few left now, when farm workers cycled to work instead of walking. Soon 'Green Lane' would be as obsolete as 'Bridle Path'. And the hedges would either be cut down or just grow together and form a thicket. But this lane was obviously still used. The hedges, though tall, scarcely encroached on the grass, which was as lush as summer grass. And the mild, windless day might have been a summer day. Only the hedges, tangled with bryony and old man's beard, were autumnal.

She swung along quickly, barely troubled by her

suitcase – at first; within five minutes it had become, as it always did, an exhausting burden. How far was Crestover? The signpost had given no clue; and as the lane kept twisting and the hedges were too high to see over, there was no chance to get the lie of the land. She might have to go on for hours, and she was hungry and very thirsty – with every right to be. The voice of the adult in charge of a child told her: 'Since dinner at home nearly forty hours ago you have only eaten two sandwiches, some chocolate and biscuits, and only drunk a glass of milk, and some water from the palm of your hand. It is not enough!'

Suddenly weak, she sat down on the grass. It was thirst that troubled her most. If only she could find a stream! She must struggle on while she still had a little strength left.

Round the next bend – and still the lane continued. But now one of the hedges was broken by a gate. It only led to a ploughed field but across the field and a stretch of parkland she could see a large house, which must surely be near some road where she might get a bus – or a lift from a passing car (strictly forbidden but no holds were barred now Richard had betrayed her). And she would go to the house and ask for water; no one could grudge her that. Climbing the gate, she quoted from *The Taming of the Shrew:* 'Beggars that come unto my father's door, upon entreaty have a present alms'; then choked with self-pity.

Walking across the ploughed field was hell and she had to scramble through a deep ditch to get into the park surrounding the house, which she could now see was a really vast house. On the side nearest her, tall sashed windows looked onto a terrace. No doubt anyone needing alms ought to go to the back door, but she couldn't see a back door and she could see the double flight of steps which must lead to the front door, so she went straight to them. She found they were of white marble and the door at the top of them stood open onto a white marble hall. The grandeur was intimidating. Still, she rang the bell – or rather, hoped she had rung it; she heard no sound but, with a house of this scale, it probably rang a quarter of a mile away.

She waited several minutes. Nobody came. It then occurred to her that the open door might indicate that the house was on view to the public and the custodian might be showing people around. She stepped across the threshold. On her left were tall closed doors and a white marble staircase.

On her right, tall doors stood open onto a room she could not see. A vast mirror above a console table reflected a white expanse of marble walls and floor.

'It's like a tomb,' she thought. 'Perhaps I shall lie down and die in it.'

But before dying, she must get a drink of water. She approached the open door on her right, then stopped short, staring in amazement.

At the far end of a long room, on a raised platform framed by a proscenium arch, was a group of people in eighteenth-century clothes. Her first thought was, 'Amateur theatricals!' But the group was completely silent and strangely still, and she saw that the clothes were genuinely old, such as she had seen in a museum, worn and faded compared with modern reproductions of such clothes.

In a flash, she remembered the two Oxford ladies who claimed to have seen ghosts at Versailles. Could she now be seeing...? Her legs went weak. Was she going to faint? A dreadful but interesting feeling; she had never fainted before. Blackness, like a curtain, descended in front of her eyes. She dropped the suitcase, dimly hearing the thud. Blackness became less intense and she saw that the frozen group had turned towards her in astonishment – at which her own astonishment completely vanquished the blackness. She was *not* going to faint. Oh, yes she was! But the blackness in front of her eyes now was an imagined blackness and her collapse onto the marble floor was a graceful stage fall.

Footsteps came running the long length of the room. She also heard footsteps in the hall. A woman's voice called: 'Binner, get some water, quickly – and brandy.'

'Very good, my lady.' Binner, presumably, was the butler, who had at last deigned to answer the doorbell.

A man's voice said quietly, 'What a lovely girl.'

Her dead faint became deader as she thought of the picture she must be making, with her red hair and black and white clothes against white marble. Still, she must come round before she was doused with water and dosed with brandy. She opened her eyes, looked piteously around her, and murmured, 'Where am I?'

It was, she feared, a conventional speech with

which to regain consciousness and it received a conventional answer. A man's voice – not the one which had called her lovely – said, 'Oh, among friends – of course.'

She thought the tone satirical but saw that the speaker was smiling down on her quite kindly. He was a slim, elderly man wearing his plum-coloured satin suit with great elegance.

'Just relax!' This was the voice which had sent for water and brandy, and it came from a beautiful but no longer young woman who had knelt down by Merry's side. Just beyond stood two plain girls, and a pleasant-looking boy who was wearing ordinary modern clothes.

'I'm so terribly sorry,' said Merry, weakly.

'No one can help fainting.'

That was the voice that had called her lovely. She turned her head and saw a tall, extremely fair man in blue brocade. She thought him handsome though almost middle-aged.

'Seeing you all in those clothes...' She let the words trail.

'Heavens, did you think we were ghosts?' said the woman kneeling beside her.

'Well, just for a moment.'

'You didn't notice our twentieth-century hair?' Again the elderly man sounded satirical.

'How stupid of me not to. But I was feeling faint when I got here. I came in to ask for water.'

'Tom, go and meet Binner,' said the tall, handsome man. 'He allows himself ten minutes to walk from his pantry.'

The boy said, 'Right, Father,' and hurried away.

'And could I please have something to eat? Just

a little bread...'

Instructions were hurled after Tom. The kneeling woman said, 'Hot soup!' The tall man said, 'Sandwiches!' The two plain girls said, 'Biscuits!' at the same moment and in identical voices. Only the elderly man remained silent.

'I got up early and didn't have any breakfast,' Merry explained. 'And then the bus broke down and my suitcase was so heavy and the green lane went on for ever.' She closed her eyes exhaustedly.

The woman beside her slid an arm under her shoulders, saying, 'Claude, help me to get her to a sofa.'

'I can walk,' said Merry, bravely.

But the tall man picked her up and carried her.

'You must be strong,' she said admiringly, as he set her down. 'I weigh a ton.'

They were now in the long room, a library; the walls were lined with old leather-bound books behind gilt grills. Looking at the stage at the far end, she asked if they had been rehearsing a play.

'Tableaux,' said the elderly woman. She had magnificent dark eyes and black hair with a streak of white. 'For an entertainment we give every year. The village amateurs do most of it but we're expected to put on some kind of an act.'

'Those are genuine eighteenth-century clothes, aren't they?' said Merry. 'Exquisite.'

'We thought they were rather dowdy,' said the tall man.

'That's because they're genuine,' she told him. 'Clothes from a theatrical costumier would be cruder but more effective.'

The elderly woman looked pleased. 'That's exactly what I said. Are you, by any chance, a professional?'

'Well, I haven't done much yet,' said Merry, modestly. 'Just ... er, repertory. I'm on my way to London, to find work.'

'How delightful! I was on the stage, many years ago. We must introduce ourselves. I'm Lady Crestover. Lord Crestover—' she indicated the tall man. 'My daughters, Georgina and Caroline; they're twins and it doesn't matter which is which. My brother, Desmond Deane. He was on the stage, too.'

Merry looked at the elderly man, then back at Lady Crestover. 'But how terribly exciting! You must have been Donna Deane.'

Lady Crestover smiled quite dazzlingly. 'How amazing of you to know!'

'I read about you, in an article on actresses who married peers.' Merry turned towards Lord Crestover.

'Oh, my husband's been dead many years. That's my son. And this is his son, Tom.'

The boy had come back with the water and brandy.

'Just water, please,' said Merry. She drank a tumblerful and held out her glass for more.

'If you *could* lay off,' said Tom, 'I've ordered some champagne.'

'Tom, how bright of you,' said Lady Crestover. 'It's just the morning for it.' Again she smiled at Merry. 'May we know your name?'

For the first time, she said it aloud, and felt that her new self was now truly alive. 'I'm Merry le Jeune.'

'What an enchanting name for a young actress,' said Lady Crestover. 'Is it real or did you invent it?'

'A bit of both,' said Merry.

'What repertory company were you with last, Miss le Jeune?' said Mr Desmond Deane.

She felt herself flushing. She hadn't had time to invent a history for herself. Then inspiration came. 'Do you mind if I don't talk about it? You see, I had ... rather a difficult time and had to dash away.'

'Some brute of a man, no doubt,' said Lady Crestover.

'Don't worry her with questions, Desmond. Ah, here's some food.'

Binner, who was portly as well as stately, arrived with chicken sandwiches.

'And bring some more, with the champagne,' said Lady Crestover. 'I can never see food without wanting some. But these are all for you, my dear.' She handed the plate to Merry.

'How kind you are! I really am terribly hungry. Will anyone mind if I eat rather fast?' She barely waited for the voices that reassured her.

'Sit down, everyone,' said Lady Crestover. 'We're standing watching her as if she were a wild animal.'

'Well, I'm eating like one,' said Merry, and went on eating. By the time more sandwiches arrived with the champagne, the edge was off her appetite and she was talking with her usual ease, though with an assumption of maturity. (Lady Crestover's aristocratic tones were beautifully catching;

Merry gave herself a dispensation as regards the slurred vowels.) Genuinely interested, she reverted to the projected entertainment.

'We did tableaux at school, once–' She added hastily, 'Years ago, of course, when I was a child. They bored people quite a bit. Couldn't you do a play, or scenes from one? Perhaps Sheridan, if you want to wear those clothes. Let's see what you have a cast for.' She assessed the group with a highly professional eye.

'You should stay and advise us,' said Lord Crestover.

'I'd love to – but I have to find a job.'

'Naturally, I meant on a professional basis.'

She saw Lady Crestover look at him with astonishment which changed instantaneously to warm enthusiasm.

'What a splendid idea, Claude! Seriously, Miss le Jeune, would you consider it? And you could act with us. A month would see us through our entertainment.'

'May I suggest a fee of one hundred guineas?' said Lord Crestover.

'Oh, goodness!' How childish that sounded. She added in a more grown-up voice, 'I don't earn twenty-five pounds a week yet.'

'I'm sure you ought to,' said Lord Crestover.

Could this staggering offer be a trap? The room was littered with London newspapers. If her photograph had been in a local paper, might it not be in these, too? Had she been recognized?

Mr Desmond Deane was saying: 'You mustn't rush her. She's had a difficult morning. Starts off without breakfast, exhausts herself by a long walk,

122

sees ghosts, faints – and now, I suspect, is being given champagne when she still wants water.'

Merry shot him a grateful if puzzled glance; though his words were kind he still sounded satirical. She said: 'I *would* like some more water. And then, please, could I be left alone for a few minutes, to think over your very kind offer?'

'But of course,' said Lady Crestover. 'Or would you like a bedroom to rest in?'

'Oh, here will do nicely,' said Merry. She wanted to be left alone with the newspapers.

'There's no hurry to decide,' said Lord Crestover. 'Why not stay for a few days, anyway, and see how you like us?'

'Thank you, but I must decide quickly – because of appointments in London.' This sounded most authentically professional.

'Then we'll leave you to think. We shall be in the drawing-room – just across the hall.'

Could he smile like that if he meant to trap her? She smiled in return and said: 'You do really want me to stay?'

Both he and his mother assured her they did. And the twins too said they would like it – speaking together, in girlish voices; though Merry had now realized they were very elderly girls.

'Well, I'm terribly tempted.' Pleased with her sophisticated tone, she lay back and watched them file out of the room. The doors closed behind them. She waited a few moments, then dived for the papers.

There was no mention of her on any of the front pages. It would take ages to go through so many papers carefully but she could quickly spot a photograph – and only a photograph would endanger her. She was about to hunt for one when she saw the local paper the woman on the bus had been reading – and there was the photograph.

But it was not a photograph of her. It was of a local bride and bore no resemblance to the snapshot she had mistaken it for.

'You just panicked again,' she told herself furiously. But panic had brought her here – and to an offer of one hundred guineas. How splendid to have so much in hand when she besieged London! Not that she would keep it all. Some should go to Richard from 'A friend and well-wisher'. Dear Richard – she finished glancing through the London papers – he had not betrayed her.

But she was still wary. It was true she was capable of helping these people with their theatricals but could they have guessed that so quickly? It was Lord Crestover who had suggested it, Lord Crestover who had admired her as she lay on the floor. Could he have fallen in love with her on sight?

The adult in charge of a child began to formulate a warning but was cut short. She could cope. She found her unfinished glass of champagne, raised her glass and gave it a smouldering glance between half-closed eyes, then drank to herself coping.

Now she must do some quiet thinking, before telling her new friends she would be delighted to stay with them. Slowly pacing up and down the library, she began the comprehensive invention of a suitable past life.

5

Marble Halls

She was ageing fast – and she knew why. At home, though loved and admired, she was frequently quelled. There was a tendency to think her conceited and too talkative; someone was always saying, 'That's enough, Merry' or otherwise attempting to deflate her. And she was never treated as a grown-up. Here, she was so frequently inflated and her good sense discounted some of the compliments. And she was not only treated as a grown-up but also as a grown-up of unusual intelligence, talent and charm – and this by every member of the family. She had at first thought Mr Desmond Deane was a trifle antagonistic but he had soon become particularly kind. And if he still, at times, looked at her quizzically, no doubt that was just his dryly humorous way.

Never had she run into any difficulties. She had told them she was an orphan, brought up by an aunt now dead, in the Lake District. (Having spent a holiday there, she could come out strongly as to local colour.) She'd admitted that much of her acting had been with amateurs, when she'd had the chance to play important parts. No one had questioned her further about her 'difficult time' in repertory. Her reason for travelling through Suffolk on a bus was that she'd been staying with a married schoolfriend in a remote village with – as she laughingly said – the unlikely name of Long Wimple. Occasionally she wrote letters to this friend, leaving them on the hall table to be posted. She also left letters addressed to London theatrical managers – ostensibly, to postpone appointments. All envelopes contained blank sheets of paper.

She had chosen to be twenty-one, because it gave her a feeling of independence. No one had accused her of looking younger. The only comment made when she mentioned her age had been Lord Crestover's: 'What a delightful age to be!'

Even the problem of her lack of clothes had been speedily solved. She had said frankly that she owned little more than she stood up in, owing to a fire in some theatrical lodgings. (No loss of life, fortunately.) It had then been discovered that she was the same height, and much the same build (if she flattened her bra a bit) as Lady Crestover and the twins, and she'd been invited to use their wardrobes like a circulating library. Every night, a dinner dress (usually dull, but undoubtedly expensive) was laid out on her bed, and many things had been given to her outright – sportswear, underwear, shoes... Such kindness! As she frequently remarked.

Everyone liked her, everyone thought her brilliant – and compared with some of them, she certainly was. There were times when she wondered if Lady Georgina and Lady Caroline were quite normal, so little did they say and so blank were their long, gentle faces. They were thirty and looked it, yet they also managed to look completely immature. And Tom, who had now gone back to school, was hardly brainy even for a boy of sixteen.

She did not consider Lord Crestover stupid; merely quiet. He was thirty-nine, she had discovered (not really middle-aged), and had been a widower for five years. When first she had seen him in an ordinary suit she'd been a little disappointed; blue brocade and lace ruffles had done quite a lot for him. And she did not, as a rule, admire aquiline noses. But she had got used to his; like everything else about him it was so truly aristocratic. Still, she hadn't fallen in love with him, and though he treated her with the most flattering attentiveness, she had stopped thinking he might have fallen in love with her; certainly, she'd never had to do any coping. He just *liked* her, as did all these kind people.

Lady Crestover, in spite of her black hair, must be getting on for seventy, judging by an old theatre magazine Merry had found in the library, which showed Donna and Desmond Deane in a musical comedy of 1913. It had been puzzling to see that though Donna looked very young, Desmond looked much as he did now; but the letter-press revealed that he had always specialized in elderly, eccentric parts. Sometimes Merry pretended to herself that he was still a young man disguised as an old one. She liked him extremely, even more than she liked Lady Crestover whose kindness was a little gushing; not insincere, exactly, but a little overdone, like her tendency to smile too often, and too widely. She and her brother were certainly not stupid, though they didn't seem to read any books. Merry often got them to talk about their life in the theatre. Lady Crestover had retired on her marriage, Mr Deane when he was sixty; he was now seventy-two.

'There was no fun in playing old men when I became one,' he told Merry. 'And I got too stiff for eccentric dancing.'

But he was still a marvellous ballroom dancer. He felt like a bundle of twigs but held one with the most delicate strength. She could follow even his most intricate steps. They often danced after dinner. Lord Crestover was far more difficult to follow. He seemed nervous when dancing and that made her nervous too.

Plans for the entertainment were now progressing well, after an unpromising start. Urged by Merry, Lady Crestover had telephoned to London for enough copies of Sheridan's plays and Merry had organized a reading of *The Rivals*. She had cast herself as Lucy, the twins as Lydia and Julia, Lady Crestover as Mrs Malaprop and Mr Deane as Sir Anthony Absolute. Lord Crestover had doubled the parts of Captain Absolute and Sir Lucius O'Trigger, it being Merry's idea to try out her cast and see which scenes suited them best. Mr Deane had been excellent, Lady Crestover efficient (though Merry doubted if Mrs Malaprop had ever before been interpreted with enormous charm and a crescent-moon smile). Unfortunately the twins seemed barely capable of reading, let alone acting. And though Lord Crestover read without difficulty, he also read without expression.

'Now you'll see why we thought of tableaux,' said Mr Deane, when they paused for a discussion.

'They just can't act,' said Lady Crestover. It was obviously no secret.

'What did you do last year?' Merry inquired.

The twins, it transpired, usually played a piano duet, but had run out of piano duets. Lady Crestover and her brother usually did a duologue but had run out of duologues. Lord Crestover merely made speeches to open and close the show. 'You know the kind of thing,' said Lady Crestover. 'Hoping people will enjoy themselves – and then hoping they *have*.'

'Why don't you and Mr Deane revive some of your musical comedy songs?' suggested Merry.

It was said to be out of the question – they hadn't sung for years, they'd be undignified, old-fashioned... But Merry got them to try and was enchanted.

'You'll be an enormous success,' she insisted, and eventually she prevailed. The twins would share the accompanying, Lord Crestover would make his usual speeches, and – as they all so much wanted her to appear – she and Mr Deane would play the Teazles in the quarrel scenes from *The School for Scandal*.

'We must warn the village amateurs we're going to hog half the show,' said Lady Crestover. 'They won't mind. What they really come for is the supper.'

Since then there had been plenty to plan and rehearse and time was passing incredibly fast – in spite of which, Merry felt years had elapsed since she had run away from Dome House. She seldom, now, thought of herself as a child pretending to be grown-up. Almost always she *felt* grown up, and her grown-up behaviour was becoming more and more automatic instead of considered.

The pattern of the swiftly flying days varied very little. Breakfast in bed came at nine. She had been given a beautiful room overlooking the marble steps leading to the front door. The bulbous, elaborately inlaid furniture must, she thought, be valuable; the bed, she knew, was uncomfortable – but how romantic, with its brocade draperies held up by a gilded cupid! Sitting up drinking chocolate (never before had she been given the chance of chocolate for breakfast) she felt like an eighteenth-century *marquise* – except for the eiderdown she wrapped round herself as soon as the maid who brought the breakfast tray was gone. The room was so cold and so large and the small electric fire in the vast marble hearth made little impression on it. All Crestover House was cold, the radiators few and far between and never more than lukewarm, and the prevalence of white marble added to the coldness.

After breakfast she had her bath in her own private bathroom which was even colder than the bedroom. For her first few days the water was nowhere near hot. Rising rather earlier one morning, she got a comfortable bath – since when, she had made a point of running her bath water before nine-thirty. While lying in it, she often wondered whose hot bath she was stealing.

She always spent a long time dressing, making-

130

up carefully and taking trouble with her hair (after a week she had, with great trepidation, washed it; all had gone well). There was no point in getting down before eleven as no member of the family put in an appearance before that time, when coffee was served in the library; after which there was usually a rehearsal – much interrupted by conversation, in spite of Merry's attempts to be professional. Lord Crestover had nothing to rehearse but he made an enthusiastic audience and he, plus all the others, frequently incited her to entertain them with speeches from her repertoire. She treated them to Shakespeare, Shaw and Chekhov and they praised everything, except that the twins did not greatly like 'that one where you keep saying you're a seagull'.

Luncheon was at one-thirty, quite an elaborate meal though not well-cooked. After that, Lady Crestover and her daughters rested until tea-time while Lord Crestover and Mr Deane entertained Merry. Sometimes they walked in the park; sometimes they drove round the countryside in a large Daimler. The drives made Merry anxious as she had soon realized she was only about thirty miles from Dome House; but they never went anywhere near it. On wet days they sat over the library fire. Occasionally Lord Crestover was absent on some business connected with the estate, thus leaving her alone with Mr Deane. But never was Mr Deane absent, leaving her alone with Lord Crestover.

After tea it was soon time to dress for dinner, which was more elaborate than lunch and no better cooked. Here Merry ran into a problem: a number of wines were served. She was nervous of drink, thinking it might be bad for her and also loosen her tongue dangerously. So at her first dinner she said she was teetotal except for champagne on 'occasions'. Lady Crestover then said she was always glad of an excuse to drink champagne, and had it served to herself and Merry every night. Merry limited herself to one glass. It had no effect on her except for a pleasurable sense of guilt at becoming such a hardened drinker.

After dinner they talked, danced, and only very occasionally watched television. Lady Crestover complained that it tired her eyes and she disliked hearing so many ugly voices. Merry found it made her homesick: would they, at Dome House, be watching what she was watching? She was always glad when it was turned off.

Tea was brought in at eleven, after which they all trailed up the white marble staircase to bed, and another day was gone.

No visits were paid; no visitors called. Lady Crestover once spoke of being understaffed and of the impossibility of entertaining, but added that there were no neighbours worth knowing and all her friends were in London. The family appeared to live isolated, using only a small portion of their huge 'house, which was said to contain a hundred rooms. The thought of all those closed rooms weighed on Merry strangely, almost frightening her, yet she longed to see them and had asked if someone would show her over the house. No one had jumped at the job; she'd been told it would be a long walk and very dull.

But on her sixteenth day, after tea, she asked again and had better luck.

'Why don't *you* take her, Claude?' said Lady Crestover.

Lord Crestover said he would be delighted to. Merry had already seen the ground-floor rooms (only the library and dining-room were in general use but there were also two drawing-rooms, several indeterminate sitting-rooms and a billiard-room) so they began by walking to the first floor. Here Lord Crestover opened the door of the Long Gallery, which ran the full depth of the house.

She had been in here before, to go through the chests full of ancient clothes and choose a dress for Lady Teazle. No clothes had been saved since the Victorian era. She had suggested that the collection should now be added to but Lady Crestover had said that modern clothes weren't worth saving.

'But they will be, to posterity,' said Merry. 'You could put in some cashmere sweaters. They're so very twentieth century.'

'What, waste good cashmere sweaters?' said Lady Crestover. She had, most generously, made Merry a present of several but saw no point in making presents to posterity.

Lord Crestover now opened one of the chests, took out a Paisley shawl and wrapped it round Merry, saying that the radiators weren't in use on the upper floors. They weren't doing much for this floor, Merry decided. She was glad of the shawl already.

The Long Gallery led into the Picture Gallery,

which ran across the back of the house. The paintings were either mediocre portraits or vague, dark landscapes and they all needed cleaning. No attempt had been made to fill the gaps caused by the sale of more valuable paintings which had helped to pay death duties on the death of Lord Crestover's father.

She was mildly attracted by one portrait, of a very young girl holding a cherub-like little boy.

'My great, great – oh, lots of greats – grandmother,' said Lord Crestover. 'She married the sixth earl when she was fifteen.'

Merry's interest increased and she peered more closely; not much daylight came in now as the windows looked onto the courtyard round which the house was built. Lord Crestover switched on the lights but only one dangling bulb functioned.

'Oh, put it off,' said Merry. 'It makes things gloomier than ever.' She added hastily, 'I mean, dark old pictures always are a bit depressing, aren't they?'

'It's the gaps I find depressing,' said Lord Crestover. 'There's so little left for Tom to sell when I go.'

They went on into the ballroom. This, Merry felt, was melancholy rather than depressing, and sadly beautiful. Rose-brocaded sofas, along the walls, were surmounted by ceiling-high mirrors. Four shrouded chandeliers hung from the elaborate plaster ceiling. The great stretch of parquet floor was lustreless.

'How long is it since there was a dance here?' asked Merry.

'Not since before the war. I fell in love with my

wife at it – though we didn't, of course, marry until some years later, when we were both twenty-one.' He looked up at the ceiling and shook his head, pointing out new cracks in the plaster.

The door at the far end of the ballroom brought them back to the front landing, onto which Merry's room and all the bedrooms occupied by the family opened. From here, the staircase led up to a floor of closed bedrooms.

'Mother had these rooms done up soon after she married,' said Lord Crestover. 'She's never cared for bright colours herself but she let some interior decorator fellow get round her.' He opened a door to reveal a large, square room with a wallpaper splodged in orange, magenta, emerald and gold. 'Influenced by the Russian Ballet, I believe. The colours have faded a little.'

Lovely colours for a ballet, Merry decided, but hideous for wallpaper. Lifting dustsheets, she found satin upholstery, worn and grubby but as violent in colour as the walls. Numerous tarnished gilt tassels increased the general impression of tired gaudiness. Room after room after room was shown to her, each a large, square box with two sashed windows, and though the violent colours of the furnishings and decorations varied, the total effect was always the same.

'The next floor's utterly dreary,' said Lord Crestover, as they went up to it. 'Just bedrooms for servants – our own, and the maids and valets visitors brought with them.'

They began with the west-facing rooms, now flooded with sunset. Squat, drably distempered, furnished with oddments ... after half a dozen of them, Merry admitted she'd seen enough.

'Then that only leaves the attics,' said Lord Crestover. 'It's about time I went round them to see if the roof's leaking anywhere.'

She asked if he and his sisters hadn't had a nursery.

'Oh, yes – the nurseries were over the kitchen. They got turned into rooms for the few servants we still have.' He was now leading the way up a narrow back staircase. 'It's pretty awful up here. I doubt if anyone's slept here since my grand-parents' days, when there must have been as many lower servants to wait on the upper servants as there were upper servants to wait on the family.'

She found 'pretty awful' too mild a description of the attics. They were truly horrifying. Their small windows, only a few inches from the floor, looked onto the parapet surrounding the house, and let in hardly any light. The outer walls sloped so much that there was little space in which one could stand upright. Thin, stained mattresses lay on iron bedsteads. The sparse furniture was almost all damaged; she did not see one chest of drawers with its full complement of handles. Hooks on the walls did duty as wardrobes. The floors were bare except for occasional strips of worn linoleum. Each attic contained a battered enamel jug and basin on a metal stand.

Ironically, the wallpapers, though faded, dam-aged, and discoloured by damp, were charming: delicate floral patterns tiny enough for a dolls' house, relics of Victorian taste now back in fashion. Perhaps the nightmare papers below would one day seem as charming.

'This used to be a hidy-hole of mine,' said Lord Crestover opening a door. 'I suppose the window attracted me.'

It was a circular window, high in the wall and unbaulked by the parapet. She recalled seeing, from the outside, one such window in the middle of each side of the attic storey.

He went on, 'I thought it was like a port-hole. Of course I had to stand on a chair then, to look out. I used to come up here with my cat.'

She joined him at the window, now a circle of sunset, framing both their heads. 'No dog, ever?' She had been surprised to find a country house without a dog.

'Never a dog. They're supposed to give my mother hay-fever; anyway, she doesn't like them, or cats, much, for that matter. I used to smuggle this cat in from the stables.'

He began to tell her about the cat's unusual intelligence. She listened with sympathy, thinking how much she liked him and noticing how white his teeth were and how particularly clean his face looked; it was extremely close to hers. Perhaps she *was* a little in love with him. And surely he was gazing at her very intensely – was she at last going to have to do a bit of coping? But perhaps he was just thinking about his cat. He spoke of his misery when it died, caught in a trap – oh, poor little boy, and poor, poor cat, which had obviously done its level best to substitute for a dog. Her eyes filled with tears. He saw them, bent his head, and kissed her.

In a split second she reminded herself of two

things: that this was her first kiss, and that she'd read somewhere that a girl should not respond too eagerly when a man first kissed her or he might think she was over-eager. In any case, she was too busy noticing this kiss to respond to it. She expected to be thrilled, shaken by emotion; nothing of the sort happened. She merely felt a warm, meaningless pressure on her mouth. Then Lord Crestover moved away and said:

'I'm sorry. Forgive me.'

She saw his disappointment and embarrassment. To hell with avoiding eagerness – she had hurt him! Instantly, she moved towards him, raising her face. This time, she would be Juliet, kissing Romeo. That should work.

It did indeed. She had not known that emotion could be experienced by one's whole body as well as one's mind. She swayed and had to clutch him for support. He looked as astonished as she felt, and then delighted. Clinging together, they kissed again and again until he paused long enough to say: 'My darling, will you marry me?'

She was so astounded that she not only backed but also pushed him away.

'Oh, no, no! Oh, my goodness! I can't, I can't!'

'My dearest child, what is it?'

'Oh, what a thing to happen!' Never had she dreamt of coping with *this*. In the very beginning she had visualized some kind of dangerous romance, he pursuing, she running away perhaps not very fast, the outcome uncertain. But marriage–!

'Don't you care for me?'

'Of course I do!' She had no doubt of that now.

138

'It's just that ... I'm too young.'

He looked stricken. 'Oh, I know I'm too old for you–'

'You're not, you're not,' she interrupted. 'But–' For a second she was on the point of telling him the truth. Then she thought of a way out. 'You see, there's my career. I've barely made a start.'

He laughed with relief. 'But marriage won't interfere with that – I promise. My mother will help you; she still has theatrical friends.'

'But surely she won't want you to marry me?'

'Why, it was her idea! I mean, she mentioned it to me before I mentioned it to her – of course I thought of it for myself. I think I fell in love with you when you were lying on the floor, that first day.'

'And I with you, as soon as I opened my eyes and saw you standing there in blue brocade.' She began the sentence simply wanting to please him; she finished it believing every word to be true.

'Then it's all right?' Again he drew her to him. She must think. And it was difficult, while he was kissing her. At what age could one legally marry? Presumably not till school-leaving age. Fifteen? Yes, that would be it; the girl in the painting had married at fifteen. Looking up between kisses, she said: 'Could we have a six months' engagement?'

'But why, my darling?'

'If I could do even one job on the London stage, before I'm a countess...'

'You absurd child!' He kissed her again.

From far below came the faintly heard boom of the dressing gong. He sighed and said he must take her downstairs. The sunset had faded now, the little room was growing dim. With his arm around her, he steered her along the dark passages and down the darker back stairs, then past the closed bedrooms to the wide front staircase. When they reached her door there were lights under the other bedroom doors, where the family were now dressing for dinner.

He said he must go and tell his mother. 'She'll be so happy.'

'Please make her understand we're going to have a six months' engagement,' Merry begged. 'We are, aren't we?'

'We'll see,' he said tolerantly.

Too well she remembered, from early childhood, that 'We'll see' was often a kindly postponement of 'No'.

6

Forty-eight Hours

She dressed as fast as she could, hoping to have a little time left in which to think. But she had barely begun when Lady Crestover and her daughters arrived to express their delight about the engagement. The twins, for once, were positively vivacious, and Lady Crestover combined her most dazzling smile with tears of emotion – not that Merry actually saw the tears, but a lace-edged handkerchief was very prettily used.

The three of them bore her triumphantly downstairs, where Mr Deane kissed her and expressed warm wishes for her happiness. Then there was a great deal of laughter when she had to be told to call Lord Crestover 'Claude'.

At dinner she drank two glasses of champagne instead of her usual one, and tried some valuable, historic and revolting brandy which was ostentatiously brought in by Binner to mark the occasion. And she listened blissfully, if a trifle hazily, to Lady Crestover's plans for shopping, and a winter in London after the wedding. Only Mr Deane appeared willing to consider her request for a six months' engagement during which she could make a start on the West End stage.

'Anyway, it won't take you six months to make a start,' said Lady Crestover. 'Remember, your engagement will give you some very useful publicity.'

No doubt that would have been the case in Donna Deane's day, but would it now? And did one, as a serious actress, want to be helped by any such publicity? Well, at least Merry could feel thankful that the engagement wasn't to be announced until the night of the theatrical entertainment. Long before then she would somehow straighten things out.

The straightening-out process was due to begin as soon as she got into bed. But as she lay down, she decided she would first allow herself to re-live the moments after Claude had proposed. (She would have welcomed some more love-making during the evening but had never been left alone with him for an instant; and his good-night kiss outside her bedroom door had been witnessed by the entire family, every member of which had also kissed her good night.) She set the scene by remembering the attic he'd called his hidy-hole, saw most vividly the porthole window flooded by sunset. And the next thing she saw was the maid arriving with her breakfast tray.

Well, perhaps it was a good thing she hadn't racked her brains last night, for – having tottered to the bathroom and banished sleepiness by splashing her face with cold water – she was now back in bed drinking chocolate and feeling most splendidly clear-headed. The situation was really quite simple: it was just a matter of *insisting* on a six months' engagement. Not that, even at fifteen, she could just rush off and get married; she knew that until you were twenty-one, you needed the consent of your parents or guardian. But if her father turned up within six months, she felt sure he would oblige (he'd probably be in jail; she hoped the Crestovers wouldn't mind). And if he remained absent, as she hoped he would, then Richard, ranking as her guardian, would give his approval. How could anyone not approve of her marrying a kind, handsome earl? (She was thrilled at the thought of being a countess but sure her feelings about this were romantic, not snobbish.) Of course she must (fairly soon – but not yet) tell Claude her real age, but why should he mind her being a few years younger than he expected? Anyway, she would remind him of his ancestress who had married at fifteen; and already, after treating the family to Juliet's major speeches, she had told him Juliet was only fourteen when she married Romeo.

Yes, it would all work out. She had just reached this pleasing conclusion over her second cup of chocolate when the maid returned, bringing a message from Lady Crestover.

'Her ladyship wants to take you to London for shopping and the car will be waiting at ten o'clock, if you can be ready then. And please, miss, we're all ever so glad about the engagement.'

'Oh; bless you!' said Merry, feeling the whole world was on her side. 'Please say I'll be ready.'

She put on the black-and-white outfit in which she had arrived at Crestover; none of the clothes

143

which had been given or lent to her seemed suitable for London. Ready a little before ten, she went along to Lady Crestover, whose room, unlike the bedrooms upstairs, still represented her own unchanging taste. Merry, judging by the old theatre magazines, thought it must be very like the sets of old musical comedies. The panelling and the furniture were white and gold, the pink satin curtains elaborately draped; taffeta and lace abounded, also a great many photographs and theatrical souvenirs. Even two long-legged dolls, known as Donna and Desmond, had survived and, though faded and dilapidated, were still limply elegant.

'Oh, you're wearing *those* clothes,' said Lady Crestover. 'Well, I must say they suit you, if they are a bit...' She let the words trail, as she saw through the window that the car was waiting.

They went downstairs, to be seen off by the assembled family. Everyone kissed Merry. She was helped into the car and the chauffeur solicitously spread a rug. Lord Crestover said he wished he were coming too. 'Oh, men are a nuisance when one's shopping,' said Lady Crestover. They drove off through the misty autumn morning.

The journey to London took nearly three hours, during which they conversed pleasantly – 'conversed' was the right word, Merry decided. She was discovering that Lady Crestover had a talent for talking almost continuously without saying anything one could remember, unless one could get her onto the subject of her youth in the theatre, and this wasn't always possible; Merry tried this morning but had no luck. During the entire drive, only one remark interested her – to the effect that she would be 'so splendid for Claude'.

'In what way?' she instantly asked.

'We must discuss that later,' said Lady Crestover. 'Yes, indeed, we must have some very serious discussions.'

Then the small talk flowed on.

They lunched at a quiet hotel of which Merry had never heard. Lady Crestover asked for a secluded table. 'I want to keep you under wraps until the engagement's announced,' she whispered to Merry, flashing her swift, wide smile.

After lunch they drove, not to a shop as Merry had expected, but to a tall house without even the hint of a shop window.

'They've made for me since I was a girl,' said Lady Crestover. 'Of course the old lady's dead now, but they still do beautiful work.'

She rang the bell and they were ushered upstairs into a grey-carpeted double drawing-room where Lady Crestover's own saleswoman, white-haired, grey-robed, came to them. The whole Collection, they were told, would be shown at three-thirty.

'Oh, we won't wait for that,' said Lady Crestover. 'Just show us some simple evening dresses for this young lady, and a day dress or two and a good warm coat. You know the kind of thing I like.'

Merry's hopeful excitement lasted until she had seen half a dozen dresses, all displayed by girls so slim they looked breakable. After that, she be-

145

came dispirited. The clothes were certainly well made but the evening dresses seemed to her insipid, the day clothes extremely ordinary. And she had not the courage to say so. She allowed Lady Crestover to choose two 'sweetly pretty' evening dresses, and a woollen dress and coat which, though of admirable black cloth, were deadly uninteresting in shape. Even the prices depressed as well as impressed her. Let loose in a shop, she could have bought herself a complete and far more exciting outfit for less than the cost of just one of the evening dresses.

Her measurements were taken, a fitting arranged for the next week. Then they left, just as people began to arrive to see the Collection. Merry wondered if it contained clothes she would have liked better. Perhaps the saleswoman knew only too well the kind of thing Lady Crestover liked.

They drove next to a house agent, to make inquiries about a London flat. Merry, left waiting in the car, looked out on the sunless London afternoon. What had been mist in the country seemed like fog here. Why had she been so spiritless about the clothes? Somehow, she felt ... undermined. By Lady Crestover's kindness? And by her own guilt, she decided gloomily. It was dreadful to deceive anyone so generous, so unsuspecting. She was almost annoyed by the lack of suspicion. Surely it was ... a bit stupid, not wanting to know more about a son's future wife? Suppose one was a criminal? Perhaps one was. Certainly one was a liar. No use pretending all the lies told at Crestover came into the category

146

of 'playing a part'. One couldn't play the part without lying.

Oh, she must tell Claude the truth – soon, soon now! But not *just* yet.

The clothes, guilt and the dreary afternoon all combined to sadden her. But she cheered herself up by remembering the previous afternoon. Not much later than this, she and Claude had begun to explore the house...

Lady Crestover returned in good spirits; she had heard of several possible flats – 'Ruinous, of course, but ... I shall see them when we come up for your fitting. Oh, you poor, patient child, waiting for your tea!'

They went back to the quiet hotel.

After tea, the return journey began. As they drove along Shaftesbury Avenue Merry leaned forward eagerly, trying to see photographs outside theatres.

'All the shows sound so dreary nowadays,' said Lady Crestover. 'There's nothing one wants to see.'

There was nothing Merry did not want to see.

She found herself remembering a day trip to London with Betty, when they had rushed around shops in the late morning, lunched and dined at Espresso bars, done a matinee and evening performance, and dashingly gone home on the last train, to be met by Richard. Perhaps Betty could come and stay ... eventually, when everything was straightened out.

'How ghastly these interminable suburbs are,' said Lady Crestover, as the journey proceeded.

Merry had been finding them interesting – or

rather, their shopping districts, where the crammed, colourful windows of dress shops were now garishly lit. Most of the clothes were gaudy but some of them were fun. But she reminded herself she was seeing them with the eyes of a teenager. Obviously the future Countess of Crestover couldn't wear such clothes.

They were half-way home when Lady Crestover, who had been unusually silent for some time, leaned forward to make sure that the glass division between them and the chauffeur was completely closed. She then said: 'Merry, dear, I think we mustn't tell Claude yet that I'm considering *un*furnished flats. Of course you must have a permanent home in London, not just a flat for a few months. But he'll be alarmed at the expense – until we can, well, swing his thoughts away from Crestover. You'll help me, won't you?

'How do you mean?' said Merry, puzzled.

'Well, by getting him more and more interested in your career, to start with. You see, dear, he must let Crestover go. He should have done so years ago but ... he was influenced against it. Our life there is finished. Even with a skeleton staff, the house eats money. And we're all so bored. Thank goodness you came along to cheer us up, dear child.' She patted Merry's hand affectionately.

'But if Claude's fond of Crestover–'

'He isn't. And there's nothing for him to *do* now the estate's let to a syndicate – quite advantageously, I'm glad to say. Oh, Claude's consulted occasionally but that's purely a courtesy. The trouble is that ... well, he may *think* he's a little fond of the house and he feels Tom should have the chance to inherit it. As if Tom cared one straw about it! No, my dear. We've just got to make Claude see there's a new life ahead of him – and of all of us – once he lets Crestover go.'

'Could you sell it to ... isn't it the National Trust that takes care of old houses and opens them to the public?'

'We couldn't even *give* it, I fear – even with an endowment, which we couldn't afford. It's so dull, and the architecture's said to be bad. And the public won't pay to see houses unless there are interesting things inside them; we've practically nothing left. But we might sell it for a school or something, once Claude's willing. Luckily it isn't entailed. Anyway, we could close it, in which case we should have enough income to live in London, provided we pooled our resources and all kept together. You wouldn't mind that?'

'Me?' said Merry, astonished. It then dawned on her that most married women expected to have their husbands to themselves, but it was too late to disguise her astonishment.

'I knew you wouldn't,' said Lady Crestover happily. 'And of course you'll need someone to run things for you while you're busy with your career. Oh, it'll all work out. Already Claude's a different man. There's just one thing more, my dear. Please don't insist on this six months' postponement of the wedding. It will distress us all greatly if you do. And really, Merry, it could prove a most serious mistake.'

'How?' said Merry, abruptly.

Lady Crestover was silent for a moment. Then she said:

'Yes, I'd better tell you. I'm sure you're sensible enough to understand. Dear Claude cared very deeply for his wife; indeed, I never expected him to fall in love again – as he undoubtedly has, with you. But during his years of loneliness he ... formed a close friendship with a near neighbour of ours, a married woman with an invalid husband. None of us like her and she's had a very bad influence, perpetually enthusing over Crestover House. She's a countrywoman, born and bred, always hunting or shooting or fishing – or ratting, heaven help us, with a pack of yelping dogs. If she married Claude–'

Merry interrupted. 'But didn't you say she was married?'

'Her husband died some months ago and she went on a long visit to her family in Ireland. Merry, dear, you're not to imagine there's any question of ... an entanglement but all the same I'd like to see Claude happily married before she returns. She has no claims whatever on him, but ... well, there it is, my dear.'

'I see,' said Merry. 'Worrying, isn't it?'

'Not if you'll be a dear, sensible girl – as I know you will,' said Lady Crestover. 'Now let's talk of something else.'

'Something else' proved to be the history of her intense dislike for Crestover House, ever since she had married its owner. The 'twenties hadn't been so bad, one could stand the place just for weekends, with large house parties. But in the 'thirties, they'd had to sell the town house and

150

there'd been less and less money for entertaining. The war had at least been a change, with Crest-over closed. 'We offered it for a hospital but they wouldn't take it. *Nobody* wanted the damn place. I begged my husband not to open it again...' The chronicle went on and on. 'For over forty years that house has bored... Such long years and yet they've somehow gone so fast.' For once, her bright, confident voice sounded sad and be-wildered; then she fell silent, gazing out into the dusk.

The car slowed down so that the chauffeur could study a signpost. Looking at it, Merry felt her heart beating wildly as it dawned on her that they were only a few miles from Dome House. She had realized they were returning by a different route from that taken in the morning but hadn't anticipated– The car drove on. Would they actually pass the house?

She found she longed to, even more than she dreaded to. Eagerly she watched for landmarks. Soon they were on the hill outside the village. Looking downwards, she could see the dome, dimly lit. As they drove down the hill she remem-bered with a pang that the house would be hidden by trees; the leaves were tinged by autumn now but still thick. Then she was past the gate and driving through the village, past Betty's house, past the Swan. Not one person did she see in the street. Soon they had left behind the last lighted window.

She leaned back in her corner shaken by home-sickness. If only she could talk to them all, ask their advice! If only she could be *told* what to do!

Things were even more difficult now, after what she had learned.

But she cheered up once she reached Crestover. Everyone was so pleased to see her and Claude kissed her so lovingly. She would *not* let that hard-ratting woman have him. And again she promised herself she would think it all out in bed. But again she was vanquished by her old enemy, sleep.

The next morning rehearsals were resumed with unprecedented energy, 'I'm hoping this will be the last entertainment we give,' Lady Crestover whispered to Merry, 'so let's make it a good one.' Merry enjoyed herself, in spite of the undercurrent of worry, and planned to take a long, thoughtful walk in the afternoon when, for once, Lady Crestover, her son and her brother were all going out, having promised to attend a committee meeting of some local charity. But the twins remained at home and insisted on sacrificing their afternoon naps in order to accompany Merry. Now that they were at ease with her she found they could talk almost as much as their mother. They chattered – 'twittered' described it better – throughout her walk and throughout tea, after which, hoping to silence them, she picked up the local paper.

Almost instantly a headline caught her attention. Below it was the report of a case dealing with a labourer and a girl of fifteen who, though obviously a most co-operative consenter, was said not to have reached the age of consent – which was, Merry gathered, sixteen. If one could not legally consent to be seduced before that age, could one legally consent to be married? One

152

could in the eighteenth century – there was that portrait in the Picture Gallery – but the law might have been changed. If so, her case was hopeless. It was proving hard enough to stave the wedding off for six months; eighteen months would be out of the question.

She must find out what the law was now. Surely there must be some reference book in the library? Yes, she remembered seeing a many-volumed encyclopaedia. If only she could get rid of the twins!

After a couple of well-simulated yawns, she suggested they should all have a rest before dinner, saw them safely into their rooms, and then hurried downstairs again. The encyclopaedia was housed on shelves which were now, so to speak, in the wings of the little stage erected in the library. She got out the index, rested the heavy volume on the floor of the stage, and squatted in front of it. She would look up 'Marriage Laws'. A moment later, she heard Binner enter the library to remove the tea tray. She was glad that, though the proscenium curtains were drawn back, one of them hid her from him. She had located Marriage Laws and was reading absorbedly when she heard other sounds in the library. From where she was squatting the drinks table by the fireplace was partially visible. As she looked up, she saw Mr Desmond Deane standing there with his back towards her. Then she heard Lady Crestover say: 'I wish I'd time for a rest before dinner. Really, I'm quite exhausted. I suppose Merry's gone up already.'

Was Claude there too? Whether he was or not, Merry decided she must disclose herself, but first she must think of a reason for being where she was. She had it: Sheridan. She'd say she'd been about to look up the first performance of *The School for Scandal*. Her hesitation lasted only an instant, but in that instant Mr Deane began to speak, in his dry, penetrating voice.

'My dear Donna, may I make one last appeal to you? Are you really determined to marry Claude to this girl?'

Merry froze. Then – while Mr Deane, pouring drinks, still had his back to her – she silently moved forwards on her knees until she was so close to a proscenium curtain that she could not be seen from any point beyond it. Meanwhile, Lady Crestover was answering her brother defensively.

'I couldn't break the match now even if I wanted to. Claude's in love. Why can't you stop fussing, Desmond? She's well bred, well educated and extremely talented – and a godsend in our circumstances. Do you want us to spend the rest of our lives shut up in that mouldering dower house? What's wrong with the girl, anyway?'

'I don't know what's wrong with her, that's what's so alarming. But she's been lying to us ever since she opened her eyes after that bogus faint on the hall floor.'

'Who says it was bogus?'

'Don't you know a stage fall when you see one – with the feet gracefully crossed? Did you plan it all from the beginning, Donna – when you asked her to stay?'

'It was Claude who suggested it, and I was delighted to see him so attracted. I tell you she's

154

a charming girl. Who cares if she lies occasion-ally?'

'She never stops lying. I wonder Claude doesn't realize it. Of course he's not very bright. But he's a good man, Donna. Do you really want him tied to an adventuress?'

Merry, sick with rage and misery, struggled to her feet. She must go out to them, stop them...

'You grow narrow-minded in your old age, Desmond,' said Lady Crestover. 'I'd say she's quite as respectable as I was, when I married his father. Anyway, what does it matter? He's got Tom. She won't have to be the mother of a future earl, though that wouldn't worry me. What does, is this insistence on waiting six months. Do you think she has a divorce pending?'

Merry leaned back against the bookshelves, closing her eyes. It was too late to go to them. Besides, she felt so sick.

'I should doubt it,' said Mr Deane. 'I have the strongest impression that she's a virgin – and almost childishly innocent. It's sometimes hard to believe she's twenty-one.'

'Women don't usually say they're older than they really are,' said Lady Crestover, dryly.

'What beats me is why she's *willing* to marry Claude – with her looks and talents.'

'Don't be idotic, Desmond. She's penniless and ambitious, and she may even be in love with him.'

'Or with his title,' said Mr Deane. 'I've often thought titles have a sexual attraction for women. But only *before* marriage, I gather.'

'That's extremely astute of you, my dear. But

it's of no importance.'

'Perhaps not when one's seventy, Donna, merely looking back.'

'Anyway, that side of it's her look out. Do leave well alone. She's happy, Claude's happy. We shall get him away from Crestover at last and out of that woman's clutches. I've given Merry a hint about that and I'm sure she'll co-operate. She's a dear, whatever she's hiding from us. I thought you liked her.'

'I don't think I've ever liked a girl so much,' said Mr Deane, raising his voice slightly. 'That's why I dislike seeing her victimized.'

Lady Crestover laughed shortly. 'If there's any victimization it's on her side. Only a couple of minutes ago you called her an adventuress.'

'Nevertheless, I wish her well. And I hope she knows it.'

'The whole house will know it, if you shout like that. Now we must go up and change.'

Merry, while waiting until the door closed behind them, knew why he had raised his voice. It had come to her that, as she had been able to see him at the drinks table, he must – before he turned his back – have been able to see her. She felt quite sure that he had intended her to hear the entire conversation and that his last words were a direct message, though when they met again, she could pretend she had not heard them. He had left her that freedom.

She no longer felt sick or even very much distressed; quite suddenly, she had become calm and particularly clear-headed. Deliberately she went on reading the entry in the encyclopaedia until she found what she sought: in England, sixteen was the earliest age at which a girl could marry. Well, that settled it. But it was settled without that.

She replaced the volume and hurried out of the library, then went cautiously upstairs. All the bedroom doors were safely closed. As she entered the room the hall clock struck. She reckoned she had three-quarters of an hour before dinner.

She worked fast but without panic. Crestover clothes went on the bed, even those that had been given, not lent; her own were tossed into her suitcase – so carelessly packed that it was hard to get everything in, but she managed. She had put on her checked skirt and was about to struggle into the polo-necked sweater when she changed her mind and extracted an old grey sweater from her suitcase. She had other plans for the white sweater.

She was ready, packed and dressed, soon after the dressing-gong boomed. Now for her letter. She sat down at the writing-table and took a sheet of paper, sparing a moment to look with regret at the coronet on it. How right Mr Deane was about the attractiveness of titles!

The hall clock struck as she finished writing. She was still all right for time. Only five minutes' walk across the park would bring her to the road where, on many nights as she walked past the hall windows on her way in to dinner, she had seen a lighted bus go by. She only had to get out of the house unseen. And there was her plan for the white sweater; an unnecessary risk but she was going to take it.

She scribbled the date on a piece of paper and pinned it to the sweater, then opened the door and made a dash for the Long Gallery. There, she lifted the lid of one of the chests containing clothes, delved down and put the sweater at the very bottom, hoping it would remain undisturbed for many years – for generations, perhaps, if Claude married the lady who loved poor unloved Crestover and they kept the house for Tom to inherit.

'That's from me to posterity,' she thought, closing the chest.

Back to her room for her suitcase ... down the marble staircase ... across the cold white hall, pausing only to leave her letter on the table. She was through the front door, down the steps and running across the park. 'Stop running, you fool,' she told herself. 'They can't send bloodhounds after you. They haven't so much as a Pekinese.'

She reached the road. The bus, she reckoned, would be along in less than five minutes. She sat down on her suitcase and looked back at the house.

All the bedrooms occupied by the family were still lit. Then she saw Claude's lights go out. Now he would be coming downstairs. She imagined him finding her letter, opening it, reading it. She remembered every word:

My dearest Claude,
This is to say goodbye. I thought I could work things out. I thought I could marry you but the law won't let me. I am terribly sorry that I have victimized you and the fact that I truly love you

does not excuse me.

I thank you all for everything. Lady Crestover and your sisters have been so generous. I have left their clothes on my bed. I send special thanks to Mr Deane who has taught me many things. I thank you for loving me but hope you will soon stop – it may help you to when I tell you everything about me is false, even my figure. My hair is dyed. I have told you any amount of lies. My father is not dead but a fugitive from justice.

I'm afraid the clothes Lady Crestover ordered for me yesterday will have been started and cannot be cancelled. So I am leaving a diamond brooch (honestly mine, once my mother's) to help pay for them.

Please forget me but I will never forget you.

Yours lovingly,

Merry.

P.S. I almost forgot to mention that I am only fourteen years and nearly seven months old.

At least, she thought, it was a humble letter and did not give away that she felt resentful as well as guilty. And the resentment, directed only towards Lady Crestover's scheming, was already abating. What right had she to resent anything? And Lady Crestover had genuinely liked her.

She sat there, staring across the park and thinking of them all. Perhaps no one would notice her letter tonight–

The front door was flung open and a man's figure was silhouetted against the lighted hall. It must be Claude, looking for her – perhaps calling her name! Suddenly she knew she had done wrong, leaving him like this. She should have told him the truth, not written it. How cowardly just to run away! She was flooded with love, pity and the blackest guilt. But it was too late to turn back.

Now the large, lighted bus was approaching. She stood up and signalled. It stopped and she jumped on.

Interlude Under the Dome

Jane

In the battle which raged after Merry's flight from Dome House was discovered, Jane found herself sympathetic with both the warring factions and quite undecided which to back. Richard and Drew were determined that no pursuit should be instituted. Cook and Edith, with no less firmness and much more noise, demanded that the police should be notified. Clare, after wavering, sided with her brothers, though not very firmly. Her main reaction seemed to be envy of Merry's courage.

For the third time Richard read the farewell letter aloud, stressing the passage which referred to the police: 'If I read in the papers that they are after me, I won't be answerable for the consequences. YOU HAVE BEEN WARNED. I might even slip out of the country with a troupe of dancers and you know what that could mean. But if you leave me alone I will take the greatest care of myself–'

Cook broke in, loudly emotional. 'How can she take care of herself? She's just a little, little girl.'

'She's five foot seven,' said Richard. 'And probably has the best brains in the family.'

'I doubt if she could get out of England,' said Jane.

161

'There's plenty of trouble she can land in without that,' said Edith. 'She ought to be found this very day, before the sun sets – before she faces night in the London streets.'

Drew said: 'All she'll face tonight is a London theatre and a London hotel. Truly, it's *safer* to let her have her head.'

Argument continued, Cook and Edith becoming more and more excited. Richard's firmness turning to anger, Drew's support of his brother remaining quiet and therefore mainly inaudible. A climax was reached when Cook announced that, if Richard would not telephone the police, she would do it herself and at once. He then seized her by the shoulders, thrust her into a chair, and said: 'If the police or anyone else in the village learn the true facts of Merry's disappearance from you or Edith, you will both leave this house for good. I'm deeply fond of you, deeply grateful to you. But while you live here, you will do as you are told.'

There was a moment of utter silence. Then Cook said:

'Edith, we pack,' and led the way out of the hall. Edith, before following her, gave Richard a look of bitter outrage.

'Well, that's that,' said Richard.

'I doubt if you've realized what "that" amounts to,' said Drew. 'The minute they're out of this house they'll feel free to notify the police – not to mention everyone else in the village. Our only hope was to convince them we're right. I shall give them a few minutes and then try again. May I say you're sorry?'

'Certainly not. Oh, God, perhaps you'd better. If Merry finds out the police are after her...'

'But surely it could be kept out of the papers?' said Jane. 'Then she wouldn't know.'

'She'd know if they found her, and she'd never forgive me. What's more, she's capable of doing something desperate, just as a reprisal. Say anything you like, Drew, if you feel you can muzzle Cook and Edith. But I don't believe you'll manage it.'

Neither did Jane believe it; but in twenty minutes Drew returned to say all was well. He even bore an apology for Richard. 'That is, they said they hoped you'd understand it was all due to their fears for Merry. I found the poor loves sitting on their beds crying, and wondering how they were going to pack the accumulations of fifteen years into the two suitcases they brought with them originally. And they were afraid you wouldn't let them take Burly – or that, if you would, their sister wouldn't give him a permanent home. And they couldn't work at the Swan if they didn't live here – and so on. Still, they kept on saying nothing mattered except that Merry must be found by the police so they did need quite a bit of convincing she shouldn't be.'

'How did you manage it?' asked Jane.

'Oh, I just explained, very gently. And they finally had the nerve to say they'd have understood if we'd explained before. As if we didn't! Anyway, they're now loyally prepared to back our story that Merry's staying with an aunt. Let's have breakfast. Cook's making fresh tea.'

Later in the morning, Drew went to get the

support of Merry's friend, Betty.

'Just explain, very gently,' said Richard, smiling at his brother.

Drew brought back the news that Betty's conscience had given only a feeble flutter and been satisfied by a simple formula. She would say to people: 'Drew tells me Merry has gone to stay with an aunt,' thus leaving the lie on Drew's conscience, not on hers. Asked by him if she knew how Merry would set about getting a job, she'd replied: 'I suppose she'll go to theatres and ask for one.'

'I shouldn't think that would work,' said Jane. 'Though there is something invincible about Merry.'

'And she knows what she wants,' said Clare. 'That's half the battle. How I wish I could run away and get a job!'

'No need to run away, dear,' said Drew. 'We'll give you our blessing.'

'I shall start hunting this afternoon – in grim earnest.'

Jane offered to drive her to the nearest Labour Exchange but it turned out that Clare's hunting was merely to be through newspapers. After lunch, she spread various Situations Vacant pages on the hall floor and proceeded to crawl over them on her hands and knees. Jane was invited to sit near by and give advice. Drew shortly joined the crawl. Richard, for the first time since his father's flight, went to his music room.

'Really, it's humiliating,' said Drew. 'Hundreds of firms simply shouting their need of employees in large, expensive advertisements; offering huge salaries, brilliant prospects, positively coaxing one to work for them – and not one job one could conceivably do. Metallurgists, mathematical physicists, organic chemists, estimators – well, I could estimate some things; ah, no, not boilers. Intermediate engineers – what could that mean? Jig and tool draughtsmen. Oh, if only one had been trained to jig and tool!'

'And thousands of shorthand typists needed,' said Clare. 'Jane, how long does it take to train as a shorthand typist?'

'It took me a year.'

'Then I'd have to allow at least three. And the training would cost so much.'

'Can't you think of some job you'd actually enjoy? Do try, both of you.'

Clare sat back on her heels and considered. At last, looking pleased at her sudden initiative, she said: 'I wouldn't mind travelling abroad with someone – provided I was well looked after.'

'You'd have to do the looking after,' said Jane. 'That's what you'd be paid for.'

Drew said he could fancy running the Correspondence Corner of a woman's magazine. 'You know – advice to the lovelorn. I wrote for advice myself once – Merry dared me to – and got my letter published. I began, "May a puzzled lad crave the courtesy of your column?" and signed the letter "Tuffy Roughwell". I said I was six foot three and terribly strong but gentle as a lamb, and why were nice girls so scared of me? Six letters were forwarded from nice girls who weren't one bit scared. I had to write and tell them I was emigrating. Well, failing a Cupid's

Corner with me as Uncle Andrew, I can't think what I'd like – all I really want is to work at my novel. Of course I get on very well at tea parties with village old ladies. Do you think I'd enjoy being an old lady's companion?'

Jane laughed. 'Not for long, you wouldn't.'

'Well, perhaps not for very long. But I might be willing to put in a few well-paid weeks with some kind, rich old girl who was young in the early nineteen hundreds – provided she had a good, nostalgic memory; my village old ladies are so much more interested in their presents than their pasts.' He sighed. 'I'm beginning to despair of ever getting the *feel* of the period for my novel. Research isn't the same as meeting people who remember.'

'This sounds the right job for you,' said Clare. '"Elderly lady needs secretary-companion. Two maids kept. Good salary... Apply Miss Blanche Whitecliff, White Turrets, Whitesea." What a name and address!'

'Fascinating,' said Drew. 'I pine to see those turrets.'

'I have seen them,' said Jane. 'That's a job I investigated five or six weeks ago. Seriously, I wonder if Clare–'

Clare interrupted. 'It says *secretary*-companion.'

'She didn't need shorthand, and you might even manage without typing. She talks about writing a memoir of her parents, but I doubt if it'll get any further than talking about it. Her father was a composer named Albion Whitecliff who set her mother's verses to music. I had to confess I'd never heard of either of them. She was

166

so nice, Clare, and rather beautiful. And the house was just right for your novel, Drew – lots of fancy white-painted balconies, and I've never seen such a perfectly preserved Edwardian interior; silver vases and a satin-striped wallpaper with a frieze of roses and blue ribbons.'

'Sheer bliss,' said Drew. 'Why didn't you take the job?'

'Well, the word "companion" always alarms me, and the maid who opened the door looked a bit of a menace – very old and rather like a little black fly, but a lovely lace cap and apron. However, I did say I'd think it over, because I liked Miss Whitecliff so, and I could see she was lonely. But then I went to see your father.'

'Do try for it, Clare,' said Drew. 'I could come and see you and get all the atmosphere I want. None of my old ladies have preserved the surroundings of their youth; they're all for Georgian antiques and modern American kitchens. Besides, a seaside town would make a splendid setting for my novel.'

'And Whitesea's almost as Edwardian as Miss Whitecliff,' said Jane.

But Clare said she couldn't be shut up with an old lady.

'I might dress up as a female and try for the job myself,' said Drew. 'But my gruff voice would give me away.'

'Not only that,' said Jane, smiling. She found Drew, in spite of his gentleness, cosiness and occasional pretence of feminine interests, essentially masculine, but not yet maturely masculine. He was still only a boy, even when his manner was dryly sophisticated. As for his voice, 'gruff' certainly didn't describe it well; 'veiled' was the most suitable word she could think of.

Soon he gave up job-hunting and went to his room. Clare, looking after him, said: 'If only he'd known this catastrophe was coming, he could have equipped himself for it. Grand always said he had an all-round intelligence – not dead-set on just one thing. Now, poor love, he'll never get his year abroad, the way Richard did.'

'Richard went abroad?'

'When he was twenty-one, to study music. He said a year wasn't nearly long enough, but he was glad to get back. And we were glad to have him. It's the only time the four of us have ever been separated.'

Jane asked if the boys had not been away to school and was surprised to hear they had attended a day school in a nearby town. Excellent, according to Clare, but one would have expected Rupert Carrington's sons to go to a public school. Well, one was probably a snob, but quite unrepentant. As if answering her thoughts, Clare said: 'Grand didn't approve of public schools. And anyway she wanted us all at home. When I think of ... well, what sheltered lives we've led I'm even more amazed at Merry's bravery. I wonder where she is.'

'And where your father is.'

'Oh, dear, it's raining again. I do feel depressed.'

So did Jane; and when Richard shortly returned from his music room he was equally gloomy. Asked by her if he had been working he said: 'Merely shutting up shop. At the moment, I can't imagine ever working again. But one must, at least, down tools in an orderly manner.'

'Surely you need your work more than ever now – to keep your mind off things?'

He said he must keep his mind on things, much as he'd prefer not to. 'And when I work, I forget everything else.'

Jane suddenly decided that she, anyway, must work. She would accept Miss Willy's offer of a job. Apart from the fact that she could then help the family financially, she would need distraction from the changed atmosphere at Dome House. Richard had already given his grateful approval, if she really felt she could stand working for Miss Willy. Well, stand it she must; perhaps she'd look on it as a penance for having failed to get a scholarship for Merry.

She went upstairs and wrote her acceptance. Coming out onto the gallery with her letter, she met Drew, also coming from his room with a letter. He said he would take hers with his, to catch the afternoon post.

BOOK THREE

Drew

1

A Town Embalmed

The answer to his letter came by return of post. Guessing it might, he was careful to be in the hall when it arrived. The name on the envelope, if seen by anyone else, would have given rise to comment.

Miss Blanche Whitecliff wrote to say she would be at home on the following afternoon at three o'clock– 'If you are sure you wish to come all this way to see me. From what you tell me, there is a great possibility you might prove suitable, and I very much admire your handwriting. Forgive the seeming illiteracy of my own owing to arthritis.'

He had written in his best italic script. He had mentioned having been temporary companion to several ladies who would, if required, supply references. (Surely his friendship with local old ladies amounted to temporary companionship?) He had touched on the fact that he had recently met Miss Jane Minton 'who felt that the position might be right for me'. (Well, she'd almost said that.) He concluded by saying that he felt qualified to help with Miss Whitecliff's family memoir

170

as he had already done research on the Edwardian period, and he signed the letter 'Evelyn A. Carrington', a name he had every right to, having been christened Evelyn Andrew.

Naturally, Miss Whitecliff addressed him as 'Miss'. Reading her gracious reply he was smitten by qualms of conscience. He had acted on an impulse born of his intense desire to see her house and talk to the woman who had preserved such a setting; so soon now it would be too late to catch an authentic glimpse of the golden era that fascinated him. But his letter, implying that he was a female, was rather like his letter to Cupid's Corner – just 'one of Drew's jokes', famous in the family; and he now saw it as an offensive joke. But surely he could prevent its being offensive? And in the unlikely event that she would accept him he would stay with her ... yes, a whole month and be very, very kind to her. Anyway, conscience or no conscience, he just must see that Edwardian interior.

After breakfast he speedily packed a suitcase and, being determined not to tell anyone what he was up to, wrote a brief note to Richard saying: 'Another bird has flown the nest in search of a job, but is liable to be back, jobless, within a couple of days. If not, I'll write.' Then, remembering Merry's farewell letter, he added: 'I promise not to go abroad with a troupe of dancers.'

He also wrote to Miss Whitecliff, confirming the appointment.

Getting out of the house unseen proved easy. Cook and Edith had gone for their first day at the Swan, Jane for her first day with Miss Willy.

Choosing a moment when Clare was in the kitchen and Richard in his father's study, he hurried down the drive and stood looking appealingly at approaching cars. Almost at once he got a lift to the station in time for an excellent train to London. There he changed stations, gazing at the crowded streets from the top of his bus on the off chance of seeing Merry, and ate an early lunch. He reached Whitesea, after a complicated journey, well on in the afternoon.

He was glad to find it was quite a small place. Indeed, 'miniature' was the word that occurred to him as he looked out of the window of the taxi he had taken at the station. He felt himself to be in a miniature resort, complete with narrow shopping arcades, an ornate little theatre (now, alas, a cinema) and on the promenade a white bandstand which somehow suggested a toy merry-go-round. Everything was spick and span but old – no, old was the wrong word; this little town was ... embalmed, preserved unchanged since its heyday, as if in order to present him with the perfect setting for his novel. And how fortunate he should have come here in the autumn, with the holiday season over! Even the shopping district was almost deserted and he saw not one soul on the promenade. The setting awaited the characters, with which he would people it.

The sea was so calm that it scarcely seemed to move and so pale, under a high mist, that he wondered if the town had first been given its name on such an afternoon as this. There were no sands; only a stretch of shingle as pale as the sea.

He wished to stay in a hotel on the promenade;

there were only three and the taxi-driver advised against two of them:

'They're not what you might call properly open out of the season. The Royal's all right. They have all-the-year-round regulars there.'

The Royal was the largest but, even so, not very large. It was built of red and yellow bricks and Drew was about to consider it hideous when he noticed, picked out in yellow bricks, the date 1905. This placed it in 'his' period, so he decided to like it. The bedroom to which he was shown disappointed him by having no personality whatever, but he had glimpsed a be-palmed and be-wickered lounge which attracted him and he hurried down in time to be served with tea.

Here, obviously, were some of the 'all-the-year-round regulars': three very old ladies and one slightly less old. He soon decided that the less-old lady was a paid companion. She was sent upstairs for a forgotten book, asked to find out if the evening paper had come, told to go and see why the waiter hadn't answered a bell rung for more hot water. This thought Drew, is the kind of job you are applying for and you're mad to think you could stick it a week, let alone a month. He had no desire to be kind to any of these old ladies, except the harassed companion, and even to her kindness would be more of a duty than a pleasure.

All these women had drab clothes, drab faces, drab hair, and peculiarly unattractive feet. When he went to tea with his village old ladies they usually wore mauve or powder blue, their skins were pink and their hair fluffily white; and their feet, though in one case plump, were neatly shod. Besides, all his village old ladies were spry. The women here looked infirm as well as ugly. Jane had described Miss Whitecliff as beautiful but the lady herself had mentioned her arthritis. Not without shame, he realized that, even for the sake of his book, he was only prepared to serve old age which was both decorative and healthy.

He finished his tea and went out for a walk, far from sure he would not go to London in the morning and then send a telegram calling his appointment off. He would anyway have this ideal background for his novel. The crones under the dusty palms had not destroyed his pleasure in the town; indeed, he now liked it even more than when seen from the taxi. Leaving the sea front he wandered past the shops, already closing, towards the residential district on the higher land at the back of the town.

Somewhere there, he guessed, was Miss Whitecliff's house. He decided he would at least walk past it. He knew from her letter heading that 'White Turrets' was in Chestnut Avenue. (He trusted the chestnuts were white.) A boy locking up a shop directed him.

It was the last of several avenues, reached after nearly a mile walking uphill. The houses on it were large, mainly imitation Tudor (his word for it was 'Pseudor') and not attractive. Most of them had been turned into boarding houses and looked as if already closed for the winter. He passed more than half a dozen of them, with their extensive gardens, without finding White Turrets. Then he unmistakably spotted it, the last house in the avenue, separated from its nearest neighbour by a long stretch of downland. He quickened his pace.

It was built of rich red brick but with so much painted woodwork that the predominating note was white. He counted six white balconies, of different sizes and shapes. There were white wooden frames to bow windows and bay windows and to corner windows that formed three-quarters of a circle; white framed dormer windows in the roof and – joy of joys – four white turrets suggestive of dovecots. Higher even than these, in the middle of the roof, was what looked like a white-painted play-pen.

Nowhere was there a flat, undisturbed stretch of brick wall; always some jutting window or balcony broke the line. Here, as he delightedly told himself, was a supreme, perfectly preserved example of Edwardian Protuberant.

Already the curtains of the downstairs rooms were drawn; but as he gazed, entranced, a bedroom was brightly lit by electric bulbs scarcely dimmed by frosted glass shades. He saw a pale grey wall down which trailed sprays of wistaria. Then a maid in muslin cap (a mob cap – actually!) drew the curtains. He caught one gleam of dark pink satin ('crushed strawberry' he believed) reflecting the bright electric light, before he was faced with the blank drabness of the linings.

Now the house was closed against the night and him. But he would return tomorrow and get inside, even if Miss Whitecliff and her maids finally ejected him by main force. The maid he'd seen wouldn't have much force to contribute; she appeared to be little more than four feet high. He remembered with pleasure that there had been a muslin cuff on her tight black sleeve.

The daylight was fading now. He gave one last loving look at White Turrets, then strode cheerfully along Chestnut Avenue and down the hill to the town.

After dinner (the crones returned his smiling 'good evening'; the poor old things weren't so bad) he went to the pictures, mainly to see the inside of the theatre. It was nearly empty and he learned that the gallery, upper circle and boxes were never used now. He enjoyed most the musical interlude – a piano selection from *Véronique* – though he could have played it better himself. He collected the scores of old musical comedies.

The next morning he explored the town further and had morning coffee at a café established in 1903. Gossiping with the elderly waitress he asked if the town was very different in the summer. She said it got pretty full in August, 'but never what you could call rowdy. Well, it's awkward to get to, isn't it? And there are no sands for the children. We mostly get old people.'

He ate several cakes and decided to skip lunch. Treated as merely an outing to gain local colour, his trip to Whitesea was a colossal extravagance. And he felt more and more that nothing now lay ahead beyond an embarrassing interview – and, of course, a glimpse inside White Turrets.

At one minute to three he opened the wrought-iron gate. The garden was neat but contained little but grass, a few bushes and some stunted trees; it was extremely exposed. Feeling quite sick with nervousness, he rang the bell.

The door was opened by the maid he had seen drawing the curtains the previous evening. Though nearer to five feet than four she was still very small, and he saw why she had reminded Jane of a little black fly. The lines on her face were so deeply incised that they might have been made with a black lead pencil; her eyes were almost as dark as the small amount of hair (a wig, almost certainly) revealed by the mob cap. He thought her black alpaca dress ugly but was enchanted by her spotted-muslin lace-trimmed apron.

Blushing, he asked if he might see Miss White-cliff. 'She's expecting me. Mr Carrington.'

'She's expecting a *Miss* Carrington.' The voice was childishly high but cracked with age.

'I know. I've come to explain.' Would that get him in?

It did. She said, 'Very good, sir,' with no hint of comment in her tone. But when she opened a door and announced him, she allowed herself a faintly satiric stress on 'Mr'.

A tall, painfully thin woman rose from the fire-side. He was astonished that Jane had considered her beautiful but he liked her floor-length, cling-ing grey dress; could it delightfully be a tea-gown? She looked at him in bewilderment, saying, 'Oh, dear! Was Miss Evelyn Carrington unable to come?'

He said: 'I'm Evelyn Carrington. I'm most ter-ribly sorry I misled you.'

She gave a gasp of dismay and then, to his intense relief, began to laugh – a light, musical laugh, no doubt the rippling laughter performed by the heroines of so many old novels.

'Good gracious, what an absurd mistake! And I've let you come all this way. But – do sit down, please – you see, I took it for granted that– Well, companions always are female, surely?'

'But not secretaries, and I would so like to help you with your memoir. And I play the piano – and even sing a little. I was looking forward to trying your parents' songs. And *I* think I could make you a really good companion.' He found himself speaking with the utmost earnestness and gazing at her appealingly.

'Do you mean you really want to work for me?'

He assured her he did and meant it. He had now realized that she was, indeed, beautiful. Her features, once one got used to thinness amounting to emaciation, were exquisite, the expression of her grey eyes flowerlike. She was certainly no pink-cheeked, white-thatched old lady; her skin was ashen and her hair, worn parted down the middle and looped over a black velvet ribbon, was a faded brown. But she was far more appealing than any of his conventionally pretty old ladies and he knew, he absolutely knew, that she was as Edwardian as her room – not that he'd dared take time to look at it fully yet.

'I can't understand it,' she said. 'Why should a charming young man want such a dreary job? Being a companion is considered dreary – very few people have answered my advertisements, and no one at all nice has come to see me except

Miss Jane Minton. How surprising she should think the work might suit you!'

It was then he decided to tell her the truth about himself. He described his background and the family's present difficulties, even spoke frankly about his father's troubles, for he felt that, if he did persuade her to let him work for her, he would have to be on an honest footing. She listened with great interest, frequently expressing sympathy. His father must, she insisted, simply have been unfortunate; no doubt his name would eventually be cleared.

'And how I wish I could offer you work,' she added. 'But I do assure you, ladies don't have gentlemen companions.'

'Do you feel it wouldn't be respectable?'

Again she laughed ripplingly. 'My dear Mr Carrington, I'm seventy. It's just that ... well, it wouldn't do.'

He said with resignation, 'I understand. You couldn't be at ease with me – as you would be with a woman.'

She considered this for a moment, then said in a faintly surprised tone, 'I'm more at ease with you – already – than with my great-niece when she comes to see me. And I think I'm more at ease than I was with Miss Jane Minton – I was a bit in awe of her. Let me ... try to get used to the idea of your coming here – while we talk of something else.'

He assented eagerly, his hopes springing up. She rose and rang the bell, twice; then turned to him smiling. 'Once would mean Annie was to show you out; twice means "Bring tea".'

He had risen when she rose, and had time for a swift glance around. He noted gilt-framed, gilt-mounted watercolours, anaemically pretty. Then his eyes rested on a white-painted cosy corner. Its carved roof was supported by delicate pillars and there were oval portraits let into the blue silk upholstered back. He said: 'What a lovely room this is!'

'You like it? I haven't *quite* got used to it. Our local decorator has always been able to repeat the satin-striped paper but last year he had to make a change in the frieze under the picture rail – the roses are larger and the blue ribbon wider. My mother was distressed; she considered our regular re-decorations were a memorial to my father's superb taste and liked everything to be just as it was in his day.'

'When did your parents die?' asked Drew, puzzled. Surely she couldn't have meant her mother was alive as recently as last year?

'Oh, my father died many, many years ago. My mother lived until last March – just after her ninety-fifth birthday. She was a wonderful woman, fully alert until a few days before her death. And my father was a wonderful man. Such admirable characters – and they were both so gifted!'

She went to the glossy grand piano near the semi-circular window and opened the long piano stool. 'I used to play their songs almost daily until my right hand became arthritic. Such a nuisance – and so unsightly.'

'I hadn't noticed it,' said Drew, truthfully. 'Though I had noticed the beauty of your left hand.'

She smiled. 'That's the hand I *let* people notice – not that I see many people nowadays.'

He joined her in looking through the songs she had taken from the piano stool. Most of the titles suggested love combined with patriotism. *Stay not if duty calls, love, Beloved, when the trumpet sounds, Love's Banners Blow* ... elaborate penmanship curled itself round 'Words by Melicent Whitecliffe. Music by Albion Whitecliff'.

'An unusual name, your father's,' Drew commented.

'It was originally Albert Whitely. He adopted Whitecliff by deed poll and – well, just assumed Albion. My mother felt the whole name so suitable for a composer of such typically English songs. We often laughed about the many "Whites" in our name and address. Ah, here is tea.'

The black fly had entered with a silver tea-tray obviously too heavy for her. Should he offer to help? He was about to when she got the tray down safely, to his relief and her own; her grimly set lips parted to emit a gasp, and her firm tread as she left the room was suggestive of triumph.

'You must have impressed her,' said Miss Whitecliff. 'We never use the silver tea service nowadays and I'm far from sure I can lift the teapot.'

'Then let me pour out for you,' said Drew. 'I'll always do that if you let me be your companion. And I could carve for you, too. I'm quite good at it.'

'Really? No joint has been properly carved in this house for many years. Yes, do pour out, please. I hope you don't dislike Indian tea. I do, but Annie and Lizzie prefer it.'

'But surely you've only got to tell them—'

She interrupted him. 'One doesn't wish to. It would be difficult. You see—' She looked vaguely distressed and left the sentence unfinished; then, as if pushing the subject away from her, she added brightly: 'Annie and Lizzie are sisters.'

It seemed to him no valid reason for putting up with tea she didn't like. But he only said: 'Oh, our maids are sisters too. They've been with us fifteen years and they're absolute angels.'

'Mine,' said Miss Whitecliff, 'have been here over fifty years. And they're absolute fiends.'

2

Miss Whitecliff

He took it for granted that she was joking and responded only with a smile, being much occupied in pouring out tea. Undoubtedly a companion ought to be an adept tea-pourer and he was finding the heavy silver teapot more awkward to handle than he had expected. However, he managed without disaster.

Having skipped lunch he was glad to see a plate of solid bread and butter. He handed it to Miss Whitecliff, then helped himself. He found the bread stale and the butter so rancid that it took him all his time to finish his slice. The cakes, in splayed-out paper cases, proved staler than the bread. But what worried him far more than the food was that the conversation had ceased to flow easily. And his hostess, somehow looking thinner than ever, kept avoiding his eye, until, with sudden directness, she not only faced him but spoke in a tone of defiance.

'It's no use, Mr Carrington. You mustn't go on hoping – if you really do want to come here and aren't just being kind. It's out of the question, anyway. A cheque will be sent to you, to cover the expense you've incurred.'

He looked at her in bewilderment. 'Dear Miss Whitecliff, what is it? Have I offended you?'

'No, no, you couldn't have been more charming. I'd like to have you here – I'm sure of that now. But it wouldn't work. No man could live here. Apart from everything else, you'd starve. Hasn't this tea convinced you?'

He decided to be blunt. 'It's convinced me you need looking after. Your maids shouldn't give you such a tea.'

'It's partly my fault – or misfortune.' Again she avoided his eyes. 'And one has to economize.'

'One can be economical without having stale bread and rancid butter, surely?'

'Oh, that's just Lizzie's fiendishness. She decides about the food and does the cooking. She's much worse than Annie.'

'Do you really mean they're fiends?'

'It's only since my mother died. And they may not be completely to blame, about the staleness. One can't any longer do the shopping. One can't face the pull up the hill.'

'Don't the tradesmen call?

'Well, sometimes – or one would starve completely. But ... oh, it's all so complicated. And one doesn't like talking about it.'

'Then don't, please,' said Drew. 'Let me come to you for a trial month and I'll find out the difficulties for myself.' He felt a pang of guilt. The word 'trial' implied that he would be willing to stay longer than a month. Well, perhaps he could manage a little longer, especially now he felt she was in real need of help. He added firmly: 'You leave it all to me.'

'Do you mean you're *determined* to come?'

Was he persecuting her? He looked at her

184

anxiously. She now returned his glance, and surely her eyes looked hopefully expectant? She *wanted* him to insist.

He said: 'Absolutely determined.'

'Oh, well, then. That's decided.' She sounded relieved, if not actually pleased. 'We must fix your salary.'

She then named a figure which surprised him by its lowness; he could not believe Jane would even have considered it. But he hadn't Jane's qualifications as a secretary. And Miss Whitecliff had spoken of having to economize. He accepted eagerly – on which, she appeared to become conscience-stricken: 'Oh, no, it isn't enough. Not as much as– And a man expects to get more than a woman.'

'This man doesn't,' said Drew. 'We'll consider it settled. I shall be your secretary, your companion – and perhaps I can even help a little with the housekeeping.'

'Oh, that would be wonderful. But one couldn't expect it of a man.'

'You wait and see. Anyway, tomorrow you shall have China tea and anything else you fancy. Remember I can walk up and down the hill and get what you need. Now may I go for my suitcase?'

'You'll come at once?'

'If that's all right?'

'Well, yes. It's all *decided,* isn't it?'

There was something odd about the way she stressed the word and she was again avoiding his eyes. 'Yes, yes,' he said firmly. 'And this evening we'll have some music.'

She relaxed. 'Oh, that will be delightful.'

He rose to go and stopped her as she moved towards the bell. 'No need to have me shown out. I'm one of the family now.'

She then came to the front door with him and when he looked back, after closing the gate, she was still there smiling.

He strode along Chestnut Avenue feeling triumphant. He had the right to return to that marvellous house, the perfect house in the perfect town for his novel. And for the first time in his life he would be earning – if not, admittedly, much. Of course it was a ludicrous job to have got himself, but really quite a good joke. All that troubled him was a definite uneasiness about Miss Whitecliff.

Her mention of having to economize had worried him. But surely she couldn't be really poor if she lived in such a large, well-kept house with two maids. What troubled him far more was that he wasn't certain she was ... well, one hundred per cent right in the head. Would a completely sane woman allow maids of even fifty years' standing to give her Indian tea when she preferred China? Besides, just occasionally... He pulled himself up. It had only been occasionally that she'd seemed strange. Most of the time – all the time before tea had been served – she'd been both normal and delightful. Really, he quite adored her already, and longed to see that she got a great deal of good food. It positively hurt him to remember how thin she was.

Somehow those fiendish maids would have to be coped with. Actually, he'd quite liked the look of Annie. Perhaps Lizzie, described as 'worse', was fiend-in-chief.

He stopped at the post office and wrote a postcard to Richard, giving his address and saying: 'Got the job. Jane will describe my surroundings which are eminently suitable for me. Will write fully in a few days.' He then bought a packet of chocolate and ate it exuberantly, walking along the sea front. Judging by tea, it would be as well to spoil his appetite for dinner.

He had already given up his room at the hotel, having intended to leave Whitesea at once if he didn't get the job. All he had to do was pay his bill, collect his suitcase, and ask the desk clerk to telephone for a taxi. He sat waiting for it in the lounge, where all the crones now beamed on him. He no longer disliked them but still thought their feet should be better shod. Miss Whitecliff had worn thick grey silk stockings and kid shoes trimmed with cut steel buckles. The fact that her feet looked about half a yard long merely added to their elegance.

It was dusk by the time he was again ringing the bell at White Turrets. He now felt more pleasurably excited than nervous. He also felt amused – at himself. Was he not the young governess of some old novel, arriving at a mysterious house?

'Here I am again,' he said ingratiatingly, when Annie opened the door.

She didn't get as far as returning his smile but her tone was respectfully pleasant. 'Yes, sir. Your room is ready. Let me take your case.' When he said he would carry it himself she merely said: 'As you wish, sir,' and led him across the hall.

187

The banisters of the staircase were giant carved wooden tulips. On reaching the first floor, she showed him into a front room and snapped the lights on. Dinner, she informed him, would be ready in half an hour.

Left alone, he looked around delightedly. Here the wallpaper was entirely covered with roses, life-size, in clusters of three. All the draperies were shell pink, the furniture white; everything seemed shiningly new. He had been a little disappointed to learn from Miss Whitecliff that the house had been frequently re-decorated, but it now occurred to him that any genuine Edwardian interior would be over fifty years old and therefore faded and shabby. He was far nearer to the true atmosphere of the period in this house, which was really an apostolic succession of houses.

The pink silk eiderdown was raised into a strange hill, caused, he found, by a stone hot-water bottle. He could well believe the bed needed airing, for the room felt both cold and damp. The grate did not look as if it could remember a fire and there was no other form of heating available. Life at White Turrets was going to be spartan as regards climate as well as food.

There was a knock on his door. He called 'Come in' but no one came, so he opened the door. A large copper can of hot water had arrived. He carried it to the white washstand and surveyed the equipment of rose-sprigged pottery: jug of cold water, basin, sponge bowl, soap dish, and a curious vase – intended for toothbrushes? Below, a mammoth slop pail was flanked by two chamber pots. It was all just a little alarming.

He lifted out the jug of cold water and poured the hot water into the basin, added too much cold water, crashed the jug into the soap dish (thank God, it didn't break), kicked over the copper can (thank God, it was empty), failed to find any soap (thank God, he'd brought some). Having at last washed his hands, he wondered what he was supposed to do with the water in the basin. Did one leave it where it was or pour it into the slop pail? After considering the heavy pottery in relation to the lightweight Annie, he decided to pour – with disastrous results. He sopped up the flood as well as he could and wrung out his towel. All this to wash only his hands. Pray heaven he could in future use the bathroom.

After his bout with the washstand he unpacked hastily, and had barely finished when a gong sounded. As he went out on to the landing, Miss Whitecliff came from her room, which was next door to his. She now wore mauve, and her velvet head-band was purple. The dress – long, loose, girdled, and heavily embroidered with grapes – suggested no period known to him. Would it be the artistic, as opposed to the fashionable, style of her girlhood? It had, he thought, as he followed her downstairs, an affinity with the giant tulip banisters.

'The fiends seem quite pleased about your-arrival,' she whispered, before they entered the dining-room. 'I asked them to make a special effort tonight.'

Judging by the table, they had done so; it gleamed with silver and cut-glass set out on a damask cloth. In the centre was a nine-vased épergne, highly decorative in its own right – which was just as well as it contained no flowers. Above it hung a beaten-brass electrical fitting from which descended a foot-deep red silk frill. In the outer darkness, Annie hovered.

Soup arrived; it looked like weak tea and tasted like weak Bovril. Next came two unusually small frilled cutlets leaning against a little hill of mashed potatoes. The entrée dish in which they were served would have accommodated ten times as much. He made his cutlet last as long as he could and accepted a second helping of mashed potatoes. Choosing a moment when Annie was absent Miss Whitecliff said:

'Lizzie couldn't manage a pudding at such short notice but one understands there's to be a savoury.' Two sardines on toast were shortly placed in front of him.

'One doesn't often use tinned food,' said Miss Whitecliff. 'My mother greatly disapproved of it. But even she made an exception for sardines.'

None had been served to Miss Whitecliff. Drew asked if she wasn't having any.

She looked surprised. 'Oh, I never take savouries. My mother considered them unsuitable for women.'

The meal concluded. Drew, his appetite stimulated by the tastiness of the sardines, felt hungrier than when he had begun, but Miss Whitecliff obviously thought he had done quite well.

As she led the way from the dining-room she murmured smilingly: 'That was a better dinner than I expected.'

'And so beautifully served,' said Drew, hoping Annie might hear him. He had been fascinated by the little black and white figure moving around swiftly and silently.

The dining-room, heated by a gas stove, had been reasonably warm. The drawing-room was cold by comparison. For a while he stood by the small fire, vainly hoping for coffee. At last he walked manfully to the piano. Now for Melicent and Albion Whitecliff.

At first he wondered which he disliked most. But after doing his best with half a dozen songs, enthusiastically encouraged by Miss Whitecliff, he decided that Melicent was his least favourite. The music, consisting mainly of chords and arpeggios repeated in various parts of the piano, was merely feeble; the verses were both feeble and objectionable. Melicent constantly incited her 'lover' to go and get killed in battle, making it plain she would prefer him gloriously dead to ignobly alive. And she seemed unprepared to allow him even a chance of survival, for when she did refer to a possible return it was always a return on a 'bier'.

Drew learned, in a snatch of conversation between songs, that Albion himself had not been sent off to any war. But Miss Whitecliff's three brothers had all been killed in 1914. Had Melicent taken that as well as her lyrics indicated she would?

At last, after responding to encores for nearly two hours, he closed the piano. His hands were tired and his pleasant but quite untrained voice was becoming hoarse.

'I can't thank you enough,' said Miss Whitecliff.

She was sitting in the cosy-corner. He joined her there and looked at the portraits let into the back of it.

'I call this my memory corner,' she told him. 'Here we all are: Father, Mother, my three brothers and myself. They are paintings on opaline – from photographs taken in 1906, the year this house was built.'

She could then have been only in her early 'teens, yet she still looked surprisingly like the portrait, and the fact that in it, as now, she wore her hair looped over a ribbon, stressed the resemblance. But there was a cruel difference between the thinness of youth and the thinness of age. And her expression in the portrait was untroubled; now, unless she was smiling, it was faintly agonized – or was that putting it too strongly?

Perhaps lost, bewildered expressed it better. He had never seen anyone look ... so undecided.

He asked her questions about the family and was glad to hear that her elder brother had achieved marriage before his early death; the great-niece mentioned in the afternoon was his grandchild. 'A beautiful girl – but one is a little nervous of her.' The younger brothers, children in the portraits, had been killed while still under twenty.

'You're like your father,' he told her, studying Albion's delicate features.

'I'm very proud to be. Dear Father ... he could have been successful in so many professions had his health permitted him to adopt one. There was a time when he hoped to be an architect – indeed, he was his own architect for this house.

'But he was never strong – a constant anxiety to us. We were fortunate to keep him as long as we did.'

He had, Drew learned, managed to reach the age of sixty-nine, owing to his wife's unremitting care. Her portrait showed her to have been a dark, heavily handsome woman whose jaw would have made two of her husband's.

'Never did I think she would survive his loss,' said Miss Whitecliff. 'But she did – for thirty years, though she said she only lived from day to day, waiting to join him. Dear, brave Mother.'

He led the conversation back to times when the whole family had been alive, and was told of picnics and parties, a concert of the Whitecliff songs – 'Madame Ada Warburton came down to sing them – such a rich contralto.' It was a pleasure to see his employer so happily animated but it was getting late and he was thankful when the chime of the gilt clock brought this to her notice.

'Eleven! The evening has flown! We must go to bed.'

'Let me make you some tea,' said Drew, now painfully hungry. If he could get to the kitchen he would look for something to eat.

'Oh, no thank you. I never have anything at night.'

He then asked if he might make some tea for himself and perhaps find a biscuit.

Her eyes became tragic. 'I'm afraid we never have biscuits. My mother thought them bad for the teeth. I can't think of anything we could find.'

'Let's look, anyway,' said Drew. 'I might even manage one of those cakes we left at tea.'

She brightened. 'Yes, you could have one of those – I shouldn't think Lizzie would need them. We mustn't take anything she's counting on.'

'If we do, I'll go shopping tomorrow.' In any case, he'd go shopping. Unstale bread and un-rancid butter at least were coming into this house.

She led him through a dim, cold passage and switched on the solitary light which dangled from the kitchen ceiling. The old range was a little like the one at Dome House, but it was fireless and there were no armchairs in front of it; only two deal chairs by the bare scrubbed table.

'Don't they ever have a fire?' he asked.

'Yes, once a week – to heat the bath water. Oh, dear!'

She had noticed his dismayed expression. 'Are you like my great-niece, who expects a daily bath? My mother considered that quite dangerous. So weakening!'

He said he might manage with fewer baths. 'But don't Annie and Lizzie need a fire?' The kitchen felt cold as a cellar.

'Oh, no, they cook by gas.'

He eyed the ancient cooker with respect, sur-prised that such an antique was still in active service. 'But don't they feel cold?'

'One doesn't think so. They're always so busy. Now, where would those cakes be?'

He followed her into a stone-slabbed larder which appeared to be empty except for two bottles of milk. Delighted to see them he said:

'Never mind the cakes. We'll have bread and milk.'

Miss Whitecliff looked doubtful. 'Lizzie planned a rice pudding for tomorrow.'

'Well, the milkman will call, won't he? If not, *I'll* get the milk.' He had now found the earthenware bread-jar and taken out half a loaf. Its staleness would not matter for bread and milk. He went back to the kitchen, got a saucepan and two bowls, and measured out the milk.

'Oh, my dear boy, none for me! Well, perhaps just a very little. It's years since I had bread and milk.'

He found the bread knife, spoons, sugar, matches. She made only the vaguest attempt to help and obviously had no idea where anything was kept. But while he watched over the heating milk she managed to discover a large tray.

'Do we need that?' he asked.

'Why, yes – to carry the bowls to the dining-room.'

'Can't we have it here?'

'Here?' She looked astounded, but raised no objection when he set the bowls out on the scrubbed table and drew up the deal chairs. Once they began to eat she seemed little less ravenous than Drew felt.

'One was hungrier than one knew,' she said, tilting her bowl to get the last of the milk. 'Well, this has been an adventure. I only hope Lizzie won't be angry.'

'We've left her plenty of milk for breakfast,' said Drew, carrying the surplus milk back to the larder. 'By the way, have you never thought of having a refrigerator?'

She looked faintly shocked. 'Oh, no – my mother very greatly disapproved of them. She thought all food should be *fresh.*'

'But–' No, it was too late at night to start a campaign against her mother's prejudices. He located the scullery, put the bowls in the stone sink and filled the saucepan with water; then steered Miss Whitecliff upstairs. When they reached the landing she said: 'Annie will call you at eight o'clock, with your hot water.'

'Please may I take it to the bathroom – and which is the bathroom?'

'*That* door – and *that* door.'

He guessed from her air of embarrassment that she did not mean there were two bathrooms.

She opened her bedroom door and put the light on. He saw an empty fireplace and said: 'Dear Miss Whitecliff, oughtn't you to have some heat in your bedroom? Why not a gas fire?'

'In a bedroom? My mother considered that highly dangerous. I confess one does sometimes miss the pleasant coal fire we had in here when she was alive, but one can't pamper oneself to that extent unless one's ill. I do hope you've everything you need in your room. It was my room until my father died and I moved into Mother's. She didn't like to be alone. Goodnight, Mr Carrington. I have so enjoyed our evening.'

'So have I,' said Drew and meant it. Yet he wondered, while undressing in his cold, rosy room, just how long he could stand life at White Turrets. He was not particularly worried about the living conditions; he could improve them or

196

weather them. What really disturbed him was that, while he was more and more charmed by his employer, he was less and less sure she was mentally normal. In fact, he was quite sure she wasn't; not all the time, anyway. But he wasn't going to think about that tonight.

Determined to have no more truck with the washstand, he paid quick visits to 'that door and that door'. Then he got into bed and stubbed his toe on the stone-cold stone hot-water bottle.

3

The Fiends

He slept badly, troubled by an elusive eiderdown and weighty blankets; all night he was either too cold or too warm. Annie's knock wakened him to a grey morning with a high wind shaking the windows. Looking out at the stunted trees in the front garden he saw how advanced the autumn was here, and the sea far below looked wintry.

The bathroom proved little less awkward than the washstand. He accidentally pulled the plug out of the basin and lost most of his can of hot water. However, when finally shaved and washed, he felt slightly warmed by a sense of virtue. There was a glow of merit about cleanliness which entailed so much discomfort.

Miss Whitecliff awaited him at the breakfast table. She now wore a curious long housecoat which she referred to as her morning gown, when apologizing for its informality. He was touched to see the radiant smile with which she welcomed him, and even more touched when she said: 'Oh, I had such a wonderful sleep after our stolen feast.'

Having seen the vast open spaces of the larder he expected little for breakfast, but there was enough marmalade to disguise the taste of the butter.

'Tomorrow Lizzie will achieve an egg,' said Miss Whitecliff.

'That reminds me, I'm going shopping for you today and I think I should consult Lizzie first. All right if I see her after breakfast?'

Miss Whitecliff looked dubious. 'They'll be so busy then. But perhaps ... one believes they have a cup of their nasty tea at eleven – my mother permitted that. It might be a good moment.'

When they finished breakfast Drew asked what she would like him to do. 'Shall I read the morning paper to you?'

'I'm afraid we don't take one. During my mother's last years she wouldn't allow the news to come into the house – and one has gone on doing without it. It's seldom *good* news, is it?'

He looked at his watch. 'Perhaps I could just listen to the news summary on the radio.' But even as he spoke he guessed that there would be no radio; in fact, not until he substituted the word 'wireless' did she understand what he meant. She then said: 'Ah, yes, what a wonderful invention! So helpful in shipwrecks. And I found it quite fascinating, when an instrument was lent to us once. But my mother considered the distortion of music and voices most painful.'

They moved to the drawing-room.

'Well, let's talk about your memoir of your parents,' said Drew brightly. 'Do you plan to dictate it?'

She looked blank, then harassed. 'One doesn't quite know. One hasn't thought...'

'Suppose you just talk and I make notes?'

He got out the notebook he always carried and

gently prodded her with questions but soon found that his note-taking was inhibiting her. So he gave it up, feeling almost sure the memoir would never be written – and quite sure it oughtn't to be. Melicent and Albion Whitecliff had obviously been without any genuine talent and it would do no one any good to read about them. But it might do their daughter a lot of good to talk about them, or about anything else she fancied talking about. And he never found her boring, though he did find her vagueness and her transitions of mood – swift unaccountable distress followed by equally swift unaccountable recovery – very confusing. Sometimes he felt as if buffeted by a storm of feathers.

Just before eleven he said he would go and see Lizzie. Miss Whitecliff offered to introduce him, then added: 'Or will that make it worse?' She looked so apprehensive that he thought it undoubtedly might. He said he would go alone.

'I shall be thinking of you all the time,' she assured him, earnestly.

Well, now for the fiends. He paused in the hall and told himself he might need to be stern, especially with Lizzie. And he must guard against his instinct to like Annie. There was no doubt whatever that Miss Whitecliff wasn't being properly looked after. He strode firmly along the passage – and resisted a sudden temptation to knock on the kitchen door.

Two little figures rose from the table as he entered. Lizzie was even smaller than Annie and more wizened. Her eyes were pale and her sparse hair was a dusty white. If Annie was a black fly,

Lizzie was a colourless one – a midge, possibly.

He told them to sit down, and as there was no third chair he perched himself on the edge of the table. He then asked if he too might have a cup of tea. Annie provided him with a china cup and silver spoon. Lizzie enquired what his wishes were as regards milk and sugar. Both maids treated him with perfect civility but neither of them returned his smile – not, he decided, that they looked inimical; they merely looked wary.

He drank some of his stewed, strong tea and then said cheerfully: 'Well, we'd better have a talk about meals. Don't you think so, Lizzie?'

'As you wish, sir,' said Lizzie.

'I thought I'd go shopping for us all and buy some nice, fresh food.' He paused for encouragement.

'Very good, sir,' said Lizzie.

'Then will you let me have a list of what you need?'

He expected another formal 'Very good, sir'. Instead, she said distantly: 'That's for Miss Blanche, sir.'

'Well, I know one or two things she needs but I'm sure she'd prefer you to make the main list, as you plan the meals. Now, let's see–'

To his surprise, she interrupted him, in a voice shaking with angry distress. 'I don't plan the meals. I won't – I keep telling her. And it'll be worse than ever now, with you here – a gentleman must have proper food. I can't do it, sir. It's making me ill, and Annie too – all that's being pushed on to us. The mistress never expected it of us, not in fifty years.'

'It's worse for Lizzie than for me,' said Annie. 'I know the order of my work and it doesn't change – except during spring cleaning; that was awful, with Miss Blanche refusing to give instructions.'

'It's every blessed day with me,' said Lizzie. 'What shall we have, miss?" "Oh, anything will do, Lizzie." "But we haven't got anything, miss. Nobody's ordered anything." "Oh, haven't they, Lizzie? How difficult." And away she goes.'

Drew asked how the ordering was done.

'We have to tell the tradesmen when they call, but that only works with the milkman. It's not like the old days when the butcher called for orders and brought what you asked for. You have to write it down now, and if there's nothing on order he doesn't come at all. And the grocer only delivers up here twice a week and he wants a list – and she won't make a list.'

'But couldn't you, Lizzie?'

'No, sir. It's for her to make lists and plan meals – and give me my orders as the mistress always did.'

He said gently, 'I think perhaps Miss Whitecliff doesn't feel capable of it.'

'But she could try, sir,' said Annie. 'Lizzie's tried and I've tried to help her but we're not clever enough. And it makes Lizzie ill. All the blood rushes to her head.'

He was smitten by guilt. 'I oughtn't to have persuaded her to engage me. She needed a lady companion who could take over the housekeeping completely.'

'No!' Lizzie's tone was violent. 'Miss Blanche should do it herself. We wouldn't want a strange woman giving orders. But we don't mind you being here, sir. You can play to Miss Blanche – we heard you – and help her with the book the mistress wanted her to write. And Annie liked you the minute she set eyes on you.'

Enormously cheered he said: 'And I like you both, very much indeed. We'll work together, won't we? I'll help all I can.'

'Please make Miss Blanche *try*,' said Annie.

He said he would do his best. 'But by degrees, Annie – I don't want to upset her. And until she's, well, ready to try, we must manage on our own. Now please help me with a shopping list. Have you a pad of paper? I've got a pencil.'

'The pad's finished,' said Annie. 'And Miss Blanche won't get us another.'

He tore the middle sheets from his notebook. 'First of all, tell me the shops you usually deal with.'

'That's for Miss Blanche to tell you,' said Lizzie, her expression becoming wooden.

Annie clicked her tongue disapprovingly at her sister. 'Someone's got to help him.' She then gave him the names of several shops.

'And now, please tell me what you need,' he said coaxingly. Annie looked at Lizzie who merely rose and said she must start getting lunch. 'Not that it'll be anything but scraps.'

'Well, I'll have mine out – that'll make it easier, won't it? And we'll concentrate on a good dinner tonight. How about chicken, Lizzie?'

'Not for me to decide,' said Lizzie, with cold disinterest. He looked beseechingly at Annie. She sighed heavily, then said she'd do her best. 'But I don't know where to start, sir. There's nothing we don't need, really.' He made suggestions, dragged item after item out of her. Again and again she broke off, saying she just couldn't think any more, her dark little face quite agonized by the effort she was making. But eventually they achieved an enormously long list, not limited to food: cleaning materials were needed, tea towels, dusters, a new kettle... He began to feel daunted by the shopping ahead of him, and Annie suddenly alarmed him by saying, 'I suppose it's all right, such a terrible lot of things, when the money's all been taken. The mistress's money, sir – when she died, the Government took it.'

After a blank moment he guessed she was referring to death duties. 'Not all of it, surely, Annie?'

'Well, a lot of it, sir – according to Miss Blanche. And she has to go to her solicitor for every penny. You'll ask her if it's all right, this list? Tell her I've no more rags I can use for dusters and the tea towels are nothing but holes and the kettle's leaking.'

'Don't worry, Annie,' he said soothingly.

Lizzie came back into circulation. 'That's what I tell her. It's not our business to wonder where the money's coming from. The house has to be kept clean and we all have to eat.'

'And more than you have been eating or you two girls will blow away.' It was his habit to call Cook and Edith 'you girls' and he used the phrase without thinking. To his delight, both Annie and Lithe gave wintry little giggles. Following up his advantage, he said, 'Let's have a nice heavy pudding tonight. What do you suggest, Lizzie?'

'I'll make what I'm told to,' said Lizzie, and again retired from the conversation.

'Jam roly-poly,' he said decidedly. 'That needs suet, I believe.' He added it to his list. 'And now I'm off.'

He wished he could go without seeing Miss Whitecliff. What was he to say to her? Just as little as possible, he decided.

When he entered the drawing-room she gave him one apprehensive look and then avoided his eyes.

'Well, that was all right,' he said cheerfully. 'They weren't at all fiendish.'

'Not even Lizzie?'

'Not really – though she wasn't as helpful as Annie.' He was careful to speak casually. 'I fancy Lizzie feels the need of definite instructions.'

Still she averted her gaze. 'That's silly of her, isn't it? Oh, Lizzie's terrible.' Suddenly she looked at him directly, her eyes blandly innocent. 'Well, play me something.'

He said he must go shopping first and offered the list for her approval. She waved it away, saying she would leave it to him. He then asked if he could have some money in case he went to shops where she had no account.

She opened a drawer and took out a money box shaped like a safe. 'Oh, dear! There's none left. I must write for some more.'

'Could I get it for you? I could take a cheque to your bank.'

'Oh, I've no bank account. My mother had, of

205

course, but I never needed one. And now Mr Severn keeps my money for me – my solicitor. He'll send a clerk here with some – if one can only remember to write.'

'I'll do it for you when I come back,' said Drew. 'And for now, I'll use my own money.'

'How kind of you.'

When he said he would be out to lunch she looked distressed and suggested he should have it before he went. But he was determined to get out of the house as soon as he could. She was a sweet, touching creature but far dottier than he had thought, and the poor misnamed fiends were a bit peculiar, too. He needed a respite from them all.

What the hell was the real trouble? He tried to puzzle it out as he started his walk to the town. Miss Whitecliff obviously suffered from mental inertia which was, no doubt, very trying to her maids. But couldn't they, after fifty years' experience, help her out? Perhaps Lizzie's obstinacy did deserve to be called fiendish. Anyway, it was preferable to think so rather than to suspect Miss Whitecliff of persecution mania.

Though he couldn't help sympathizing with Lizzie, knowing that Cook, younger and more intelligent, expected Clare to plan all meals. And did Clare make heavy weather of it! Could it be so difficult? Surely if one used one's wits...

By the time he was striding down the hill his spirits had risen. The sun had come out, the wind was less strong; he was hungry and intended to treat himself to a square meal – and at once. The shopping could wait until afterwards.

Reading a newspaper at the café he had the sensation of returning to the present-day world after a long, long absence.

Now for the shopping. He went first to the grocers – established, he noticed, in 1896. As soon as he said he was Miss Whitecliff's secretary, the manager was sent for. Was her credit no longer good? But it turned out that extra courtesy was intended. The manager was overjoyed to have an order.

'Believe me, sir, not enough food has been going into that house to feed one woman, let alone three – and you'll hear the same from other shops. The boy on the van asks for instructions every time he calls but more often than not they won't give him any. We'll make a special delivery this afternoon – it'll be a pleasure. I tell you, we've been worried, after serving the family for over sixty years...' If he felt any surprise that Miss Whitecliff had acquired a male secretary, he did not show it and again and again said he would do anything to oblige.

At every shop Drew went to he was received with the same eager courtesy and there was always an undercurrent of anxiety about Miss Whitecliff. But no one asked direct questions about her. He found this alarming. Was everyone tacitly admitting she wasn't normal? He longed to ask questions himself but felt he couldn't for various reasons, one of them being that he dreaded the answers he might get.

And smoothly though the shopping went he was bewildered when it came to buying perishable food. How long would it keep without refrigeration – and what quantities did one need? The butcher and the fishmonger helped with advice and he managed to order enough for several days and arrange for deliveries. But his sympathy with Lizzie was increasing. He now understood why planning meals made the blood rush to her head.

Still, he was pretty cheerful when he started his journey back to White Turrets, laden with everything for that evening's dinner, plus a cookery book to help with meal planning, and flowers which were to be a present to Miss Whitecliffe. And at the last moment he bought another present: some womens magazines, intended for the fiends as well as their mistress; somehow he must get news of the present into that shrine of the past which now housed him.

He went indoors the back way, to leave the food and half the magazines in the kitchen. There was now a fire in the range so presumably he'd get a bath. Lizzie made no objection to going through his purchases with him and looked approvingly at the China tea. 'Miss Blanche'll be glad to have that. We've been out of it for weeks.'

'And she'll be pleased with those flowers,' said Annie.

'Who arranges flowers? I'm sure you do it beautifully.' He looked hopefully at Annie.

'Oh, no, sir. Miss Blanche will want to do those.'

Would she? Surely arranging flowers was far more trouble than ordering the tea one wanted? But Annie was right. Miss Whitecliff, after thanking him ecstatically for his not very expensive pink chrysanthemums, hurried off to the pantry with them. He had a flash of understanding; this was a job she'd *always* done.

While she was gone, he made a list of his out-of-pocket expenses and asked, on her return, if he might write to her solicitor for her.

'Oh, I've written already,' she said proudly. 'I've asked him for *lots* of money – and told him all about you.'

He thought she looked both happy and normal, standing there with the flowers, which she had arranged most efficiently. He asked if he could post her letter for her.

She said she'd posted it already. 'That is, the postman took it; he's very kind about taking letters. Oh, dear...' Her happiness had clouded. 'He brought me a letter from my great-niece. Do you think I need answer it?'

'Does it call for an answer? If so, I could write – at your dictation.'

She shook her head. 'I'm not sure I shall let her know you're here. She's ... a very interfering sort of girl. I must think about it.' Then, casting all doubts aside, she said, 'No, I won't. I *will* write – at once. I want everyone to know how clever I've been to find you.'

4

Mr Cyril Severn

A week later, seated at his washstand now become his desk (Annie had obligingly removed the crockery), Drew took stock of his achievements. The household was now well fed. The bath water was always hot. Lizzie and Annie were cheerful, and Miss Whitecliff appeared to be blissful – except immediately after lunch when she looked slightly woebegone, it then being his custom to leave her for a couple of hours. He found this essential, as the planning of meals, without telephone or refrigerator, was most complicated. He had to think ahead, arrange that food came exactly when needed, either post his orders or have them ready for visiting tradesmen. And he could still get no help from Lizzie. She would take any amount of trouble over her admirable cooking, she welcomed every order he gave her, both she and Annie treated him with friendliness and gratitude; but he had come to realize that, though they would labour physically from morning till night, they were virtually incapable of the labour of thought.

He was distressed at the extent of the physical labour. Every room in the house was kept not only clean but highly polished. Bedrooms not slept in for over forty years were religiously 'done'

210

every day. 'Religiously, was, he thought, the operative word; White Turrets had been the late Mrs Whitecliff's cathedral, and the care of it, including frequent re-decorations, had become a cult. He hoped to get two-thirds of the rooms dustsheeted and closed eventually but felt he must not suggest this yet. For the moment, he satisfied himself by making sure the maids were well fed (he carved for them himself) and always had a fire. And he had found two wicker chairs in disused bedrooms and carried them down to the kitchen.

Miss Whitecliff now called him 'Drew' and seemed completely at ease with him. And for most of the many hours they spent together her behaviour was perfectly normal; indeed he was often impressed by her almost sophisticated poise, which reminded him of the unembarrassed grace with which she had first received him. Only if asked for some definite decision did she become distressed, evasive and curiously childish. It was therefore easier to make all decisions himself. But he could not feel it was right to do so. Surely he ought to awaken her will-power, not acquiesce in its paralysis? So he would often ask her to decide some small matter, and every now and then she would give him a swift, clean-cut answer. But, if she stopped to think, her eyes became troubled and she either took refuge in silence or changed the subject.

In the mornings he often took her for a walk. In the afternoons, after going back on duty, he read to her or talked. In the evenings he played and sang to her. He had discovered, in the piano stool, a great many songs that mercifully were not the work of Melicent and Albion Whitecliff: *Because, An old Garden, Love's Coronation, Beloved, It Is Morn, Down the Vale,* and others, all tuneful, all accomplished, inoffensively sentimental and blessedly unmartial. Each of them drew some reminiscence from Miss Whitecliff, and these musical evenings had for him a charm which emanated from Miss Whitecliff, the songs and his own imagination. Gradually he came to feel he was being given access to the days when the old songs were new.

He had noticed that *Down the Vale* was inscribed: 'To Blanche, from Cyril'.

'Cyril Severn, my solicitor,' Miss Whitecliff explained. 'I mean, he is now. Then he was just a young man in his father's office – until the war broke out. He joined up with my brothers. We were engaged for five years, and even when I broke it off he waited. But of course I couldn't leave my parents after all my brothers were killed.'

There had been no sadness in her tone and she had gone on to talk about the young Cyril Severn in quite a matter-of-fact way. But she did remark that he had been considered handsome. Drew saw him as a tall, fair youth, a suitable partner for the young Blanche Whitecliff. Now he would be an ascetic old man. Drew wanted to meet him and not merely out of curiosity.

He felt he must get Mr Severn's approval before launching out on expenditure which, if mentioned to Miss Whitecliff, might worry her. Indeed Drew was worried about it himself, but he feared that without it he could not stay for even a couple of months. Running the house would soon cease to be an amusing challenge; and fond as he was of Miss Whitecliffe and of the maids too, life would not be bearable unless he could work on his novel every afternoon. He could only make time for this if the housekeeping could be simplified. Also his room must be warmer. One way and another, the expense would be considerable.

He was thinking about this, sitting at his washstand desk, after patting himself on the back for what he had accomplished in a week. Before making any demands he must decide what was essential. Under a heading 'Minimum Basic Needs' he began a list.

He had made little headway when the front-door bell rang. The postman? No, he always knocked. Drew went to the window. A car – it looked up-to-date and expensive – was parked outside the house. A visitor? Miss Whitecliff had told him she had few friends left– 'They were my mother's friends, really, and so many died before she did.' He heard the front door close. No one came down the steps. The caller must have been admitted.

Drew wondered if he ought to go down, then decided against it. She was capable of receiving someone on her own. He went back to Minimum Basic Needs.

Some ten minutes later, as he was finishing his list, there was a knock on his door and Miss Whitecliff quaveringly called his name. He hurried to open the door and saw at once that she was distressed.

'It's Cyril,' she said. 'Mr Severn. He's here and he wants to see you.'

'Oh, good,' said Drew. 'I was hoping to meet him.'

She looked even more distressed. 'You didn't say so. And when he asked to see you, in the letter he sent with the money, I forgot. Well, I didn't *exactly* forget but... Oh dear, he was so cross – but I've told him it wasn't your fault. Please go down at once.' She hurried into her bedroom and closed the door.

Drew, worried to see her so upset, grabbed Minimum Basic Needs and went to the drawing-room feeling belligerent.

Mr Severn was looking through the songs which lay on the top of the piano. He turned – and Drew had seldom been so astonished. Instead of the thin, ascetic old gentleman he expected to see, now probably much annoyed, he found himself facing a robust, handsome man who looked years younger than Miss Whitecliff. And the solicitor showed no signs of annoyance. He gave Drew one swift glance, pleasant if also appraising, and then greeted him heartily.

'Ah, there you are! Let's sit down and have a look at each other. Do you smoke? Wise man – wish I didn't. Well, well, this is a very pleasant surprise. If you knew what I've been expecting!'

'The worst, I'm sure,' said Drew, relaxing.

'Frankly, yes – when I got Blanche's letter. And I really was very much annoyed with her. Well, imagine: I'd taken the greatest trouble to find her a suitable companion – it was my idea that she should have one. I'd dealt with a highly respectable London agency, vetted all the applications, only put advertisements in papers because we couldn't find the right woman. Of course I told Blanche to send me all the answers she received. But does she? No, indeed. She merely informs me she's engaged a *man!* Naturally I wrote saying she must send you to me at once; and believe me, I was prepared for anything – a crook or, at best, a willowy type. Not that I mind the willowy lads; got one in my office, excellent worker, and they are often very good to old women. But actually, you're not, are you? I mean willowy.'

'If so, I haven't noticed it yet,' said Drew, slightly dazed.

'Doubt if you will now. No, no, you can take it from me. And you're not a crook – I knew that even before I saw you. Blanche has just told me about your father. You'd never have mentioned him if you'd had any underhand plans. No news of him, I suppose? Let's hope he's out of harm's way. These things happen in my own profession. I could swindle Blanche with the greatest ease. Well, now, are you really going to stay with her?'

'That's just what I was asking myself when you arrived,' said Drew. Though still a bit dazed by Mr Severn he felt that such a direct approach called for a direct response. 'Do these demands seem to you reasonable?' He held out Minimum Basic Needs.

The solicitor put on his spectacles and studied the list. 'Telephone? Of course. We *must* make her have one. Her mother never would. Refrigerator – Good God, isn't there one? Electric fires? Yes, indeed, though you'll never make this ghastly house really warm. Don't you want television?'

'Not yet, anyway. I'd rather start with a radio – and perhaps a gramophone; though I don't want to interfere with our musical evenings.'

'Ah, yes, Blanche told me about those. What are you up to, exactly? She tells me you write. Going to put her in a book?'

'Not *her*, but...' He gave a brief explanation of why he had tried for the job, concluding apologetically, 'Of course I ought never to have written to her. I see it now as a joke in very poor taste. But I was so madly keen to get atmosphere for my novel.'

'Very enterprising of you. And we must make sure you have time to work on it. Now I'm going to be frank with you–' Mr Severn interrupted himself. 'Dreadful remark that – so apt to precede something unpleasant or else an outright lie.'

'Not this time, I'm sure,' said Drew smilingly. 'Anyway – not a lie.'

'Thank you. It's not unpleasant, either – for you. It could be damned unpleasant for me, if I've estimated your character wrongly, but I'm sure I haven't. The truth is, my dear boy, that as far as I'm concerned you've dropped from heaven and there's practically nothing I won't do to keep you here. Of course you can have what's on this list. Don't trouble Blanche with it; I settle all her bills. And the salary she offered you is ridiculous. I'll see you get double.'

'But she spoke of having to economize.'

'Rubbish. She's extremely wealthy. The trouble is that her ideas of expenditure are conditioned by her miserly old mother's – on top of which, she feels persecuted by death duties. Naturally they're heavy, on a fortune the size of her mother's, but when I get the estate cleared up Blanche will still have enough to live extravagantly, let alone comfortably. Why not buy a car? Take her some pleasant drives – or even abroad, if you fancy the idea. You're looking puzzled. Why?'

'I'm wondering what the catch is,' said Drew.

Mr Severn laughed. 'Don't blame you – but there *is* none. It's just that I want you here, for my sake as well as hers, I think, perhaps...' He was silent for a moment and when he went on his eyes and his voice were grave. 'Yes, I'd better explain my own position, otherwise you'll think it strange that I should wish to hand over so much responsibility. You see, Blanche is greatly on my conscience. I once hoped to marry her and was prevented by her parents. For twenty years I miserably watched a delightful girl on the way to becoming what she is now. And then ... well, I stopped minding and married a woman half my age. I've been, I am, exceedingly happy. And I want to go on being happy – as long as I can. I'm seventy-two, you know.'

'You certainly don't look it,' said Drew.

'Well, I try not to, on my wife's account even more than on my own. I make a practice of youthfulness and it's hard work at times. Now, the point of this embarrassing confession is that I simply cannot bear being with Blanche. I see my true age reflected in hers. And she fills me with guilt because – let's face it – I no longer have any real affection for her; God forgive me, she makes me impatient. Now you'll understand why I'll do practically anything to ensure her happiness without, to put it bluntly, interfering with my own. Are you thinking me callous?'

'No, no—' Drew was actually engaged in thinking how much older the old man was looking. It was as if a mask had fallen. 'No, really. But it's rather awful for me, isn't it? Makes me feel I've *got* to stay with her.'

'I'm afraid it was intended to.' Mr Severn now spoke smilingly; the mask was up again. 'And do consider the advantages. You can order anything you like to make this house tolerably comfortable. Re-decorate your room if you like – but of course Edwardian taste suits your book in every sense of the word. Well, get the book written. Invite friends to stay, or your family. And you must make friends here; I'll talk to my wife about that and we must see you take time off to meet people. Send for any books you want, gramophone records... In short, do any damn thing you please as long as you keep dear demented Blanche as happy as she seems to be with you.'

'Just how demented is she?' asked Drew, looking at Mr Severn searchingly.

'I used that word ill-advisedly.' Mr Severn's glance had become oblique. He then thought better of evasion and met Drew's eyes squarely. 'As far as I know there's nothing wrong with her except that she hates making decisions. No doubt it's the result of never having been allowed to make any while her mother was alive. The tricky thing for me is that she both counts on me to run her life *and* resents my authority. And every now

218

and then she's unpredictably self-willed – as when she decided to engage you; thankful though I am that she did.

'Actually, I decided for her,' said Drew, remembering.

'Ah! Well, go on deciding for her. I doubt if she'll ever resent it, from you. I'm not tactful enough – I try to be but my irritation shows. You may be glad to know that she said she wouldn't let you go whatever I felt about it. That could mean a real awakening of will-power but it's more likely that she just prefers your authority to mine. Now, will you help me? Give me your promise to stay with her at least a year.'

Drew, after a moment, said: 'I can only promise I'll try to.'

Mr Severn nodded acceptance. 'I've no right to ask for more. But I'll just add that if you do leave I may have to, well, coerce Blanche into some kind of ... well, nursing home. Beastly of me to hold that over you but it's true. And I might mention that if she wants to put you in her will she'll get every encouragement from me. Oh, dear, dear – you're looking outraged. That's conventional of you.'

Drew smiled. 'Quite true. One just has a horror of appearing mercenary.'

'I'd advise you to *be* a bit mercenary, if you can. It'll help you to stick this job. Seriously, Blanche has nobody to leave her money to but one very well-off niece whom I happen to dislike, and those midgets in the kitchen. Thank God, she let me talk her into making provision for them. Her mother wouldn't; to be fair, she feared they'd leave Blanche if she did, but it was pretty shocking – not one penny after well over fifty years of service. She got them from an orphanage and paid them eighteen pounds a year each, which with princely generosity she eventually raised to twenty-five. Imagine! With domestic service at a premium, they were still getting less than ten shillings a week each when she died.'

'Good Lord! What are they getting now?'

'Oh, the same, from Blanche. I told you, she's half convinced she's ruined. But I'm paying a normal wage into an account for them and I've made them understand they'll always be taken care of. I daren't let them know quite how shockingly they've been treated in case they count it against Blanche. There's something approaching enmity there – on both sides. I've no idea why. It's just one of the mysteries of this frightening household.'

'Frightening indeed,' said Drew. 'And I can't understand how such a fantastic state of affairs could have gone on so long here. This house isn't–'

'Its inmates were, by the iron will of one old woman. But don't harrow yourself about the past. Just concentrate on making the present as comfortable as possible, for yourself, Blanche and those poor victimized midgets – who would, by the way, be utterly lost if ever I had to send her away and close the house. Tomorrow you must start spending money; that's always cheering. And now let's have Blanche down. I'll tell her I've given you my blessing and do my level best to behave nicely.'

Drew went for Miss Whitecliff. She came out of her room still looking distressed and seemed unable to believe that all was now well. Only after considerable effort on Mr Severn's part did she relax. He treated her with a mixture of gallantry and playful brusqueness which, to Drew, was most obviously false; but it undoubtedly pleased her and by the time tea came in she was responding gaily and laughing her pretty laugh. Her whole manner, particularly the delicate flicker of her eyelids, had a faded coquetry Drew found heart-breaking.

'Well, I must get back before my office closes,' said the solicitor at last, and bade Miss Whitecliff an almost lover-like farewell. Drew then accompanied him to his car.

'Didn't do too badly, did I?' said Mr Severn, once they were out of the house. 'But, oh my God, the strain! Now drop into my office whenever you need to and I'll fix a date for you to dine with us; but don't, I implore you, ask me to see Blanche more than is strictly necessary. Oh, I know I'm heartless.'

'A heartless man wouldn't mind seeing her,' said Drew.

'Still, I don't acquit myself – and I've no right to feel such rapturous relief on getting away from the poor dear.' He waved gaily to Miss Whitecliff at the drawing-room window, then turned again to Drew. 'Well, don't dislike me too much. How nice of you to look genuinely astonished at such an idea! I suspect you haven't acquired the knack of disliking people. Good night, my dear boy, and the best of luck.'

221

Drew, watching him drive away, asked himself if he'd ever really disliked anyone and couldn't remember doing so. Perhaps it was a bit milk-and-watery of him. But he took a pride in being able to see other people's points of view and once one did that... He certainly saw Mr Severn's point of view. Darling Miss Whitecliff was harrowing enough even when one hadn't shared her youth.

Turning to go in, he looked up at White Turrets. Such a cheerful house, with all its gleaming paintwork! He shuddered to think of its cheerless past – and reminded himself of the good dinner Lizzie would be cooking. Now Annie was drawing the bedroom curtains, and Miss Whitecliff had come to meet him at the front door. Why should these three harmless old women feel 'something approaching enmity' for each other? Well, he'd go on doing his best for them all.

5

Rosalind

The next morning he took Mr Severn's advice as regards spending money. Miss Whitecliff's name, and instructions to send all bills to Mr Severn, instantly secured him credit wherever he went. After that shopping spree he was never able to recapture his first picture of Whitesea as a town embalmed, for there was no lack of modernity if one wanted to find it rather than avoid it. Indeed, he amused himself by wondering if he had invented that first town to please his mood, and was now inventing a second one to fit his needs. Certainly there were shops overflowing with electrical equipment, all the latest gadgets... He had to resist the temptation to streamline the entire kitchen; for the moment it would be enough if he ordered a refrigerator, new saucepans, and a radio for the midgets. (He had now accepted Mr Severn's name for them; it finally ousted 'the fiends'.) For Miss Whitecliff and himself he bought a radio and gramophone combined and a first selection of records. He also chose four electric fires, one intended for the midgets' bedroom, wherever in the heights of White Turrets they slept; and was promised that an electrician should start work at once on the necessary new wiring. Only when he went to inquire about a telephone was he warned there might be some delay.

Having finished what he thought of as the solid spending he got flowers and chocolates, including some of each for the kitchen, also some books for himself. And on his way home in a taxi he decided Mr Severn had been right: spending money was certainly cheering. One was, in fact, just a little drunk on spending.

And his pleasure was increased by Miss Whitecliff's pleasure – at having him back, at the history of his shopping, and his purchases in hand and to come. Before setting out he had merely told her they needed many things which Mr Severn said she could afford and ought to have, and they were all to be a lovely surprise. This had delighted her and she was even more delighted now. Told that a refrigerator was coming she confessed that, in spite of her mother's views, she had often wished for one because it would make ice-cream. Drew doubted this but if she wanted ice-cream he would, of course, get her some. He gathered that she'd had none since she was a girl, when it had been made 'for garden parties in a funny kind of bucket'. He'd neither seen nor heard of such a bucket; this must be a gap in his knowledge of Edwardiana.

Lizzie and Annie, too, were pleased about the refrigerator. He had already noticed that their outlook had been changed by the women's magazines, which he had several times found them studying through steel-rimmed spectacles. (The advertisements interested them most; he guessed that their imaginations had not had enough practice to let them enjoy fiction.) And the general excitement rose higher in mid-afternoon, when the refrigerator, radiogram and electric fires were delivered. None of them could be used as yet and Drew felt it was just as well their potentialities should be considered before their actual performance. He was beginning to fear his three old ladles were a bit too excited.

Miss Whitecliff's spirits suffered a set-back when the afternoon post came. Having read the only letter it brought, she turned to Drew with dismayed eyes. 'It's from my great-niece. She's coming here – on Saturday. Oh, dear, she always makes me so nervous.'

'Well, we won't let her, this time,' said Drew firmly. 'And think what fun it'll be to show her all your new possessions – including me.'

Miss Whitecliff regained her spirits and laughed her pretty laugh. 'Oh, *yes!* And I shall tell her how much Cyril likes you, and then she won't dare criticize. Rosalind is critical.'

Rosalind! It was a name he particularly liked. He had never been romantically attracted by any living girl but had often been half in love with girls in history and literature. Of these, Shakespeare's Rosalind took pride of place. He instantly pictured Rosalind Whitecliff as tall, boyish yet essentially feminine, striding through the Forest of Arden in spring. He was strongly disposed to fall in love with her – if only for practice. One was confident Mr Severn was right in believing one would not become 'willowy'; but it was high time one became *something.*

'Does she usually have my room?' he asked. 'I

could easily move out.'

'Oh, she's only coming for lunch, on her way somewhere else. She'll drive; she always does. Imagine, a girl of nineteen, driving her own car! Though I remember now, at her age I longed for a bicycle. I suppose a car to her is only what a bicycle would have been to me.'

He was glad to hear her say this; it suggested a dawning acceptance of a changed world. He asked if she'd ever had the bicycle.

'Good gracious, no! Though father was on my side – well, just a little, at first. How well one remembers! I still hanker for that bicycle.'

'I'm afraid you'd find it...' He broke off, interrupted by her charming laughter.

'Oh, I only hanker for it *then,* not *now.* It's strange, but "then" is often quite as real to me as "now", sometimes realer.'

He wondered if that was the cause of her slight derangement, if her will-power was paralyzed because she was imprisoned in her youth, subservient to authority that no longer existed. But surely she was showing signs of independence? Unless, of course, in accepting new ideas, she was now merely subservient to *his* authority.

He was, anyway, certain she was acting independently when, the next morning, she asked him to take a letter to Mr Severn and did not tell him what it was about. He found himself faintly irritated, particularly as an electrician had just arrived and needed instructions.

'Couldn't I just post the letter?' he asked.

'I *particularly* want him to have it this morning.'

Independence, certainly even a touch of bossiness. Well, one ought to be pleased. And a little more shopping might be useful, to ensure a specially good lunch for Rosalind. So he swiftly instructed the electrician and then hurried out.

Having delivered the letter and made sure Mr Severn would soon be in to receive it, he did his shopping. This, on a sudden inspiration, included something he paid for with his own money. He had noticed that Miss Whitecliff sometimes wore a long chain to which small charms were attached. He had the good luck to find a charm in the form of a bicycle.

She received it with ecstasy. And when he had put it on her chain for her she repeatedly looked down on it and fingered it. What with this, and the fact that the radiogram was now working, she passed the rest of the day in a visible daze of bliss. The refrigerator, too, was in action and Drew saw that the midgets were going to be fondly possessive of it. When he suggested Miss White-cliff should be invited to see it working, Lizzie said: 'Not till we've had a little more practice, sir.'

Mr Severn's reply came the following morning. Miss Whitecliff, having read it, looked pleased and important.

'I have to see Cyril at once,' she informed Drew. 'He's sending a car for me.'

Drew felt guilty at having failed to protect Mr Severn. And this was the morning of Rosalind's visit. He asked Miss Whitecliff if she had forgotten that.

'Oh, I shall be back in good time,' she said, airily.

He offered to see Mr Severn for her but she

smilingly refused. 'It's something I have to do myself. And you mustn't ask me what it is. You'll know later.'

She looked so happy that his slight annoyance faded. He said: 'Well, anyway, I'd better come with you, hadn't I?' So far, he'd never known her to set foot out of the house alone.

But she said firmly: 'No, you must stay here in case Rosalind *should* arrive before I get back. Oh, I do hope you'll like her!'

'Let's hope she likes me,' said Drew. He did not usually worry as to whether people would like him, perhaps because they usually did, just as he usually liked them. But he was very, very anxious that Rosalind should like him.

The car came and he saw Miss Whitecliff off. She was wearing a voluminous fur coat – squirrel, she told him; she'd had it for her twenty-first birthday and always taken great care of it. He imagined it must have gone in and out of fashion (well, never quite in) at least half a dozen times. At the moment, it was a foot or so too long.

Left alone, he was conscious of behaving like a houseproud young wife before her first luncheon party. He visited the kitchen, discussed with Annie the laying of the table and approved a lace-edged tablecloth. (The épergne was now filled with clove carnations.) He then turned his attention to the drawing-room, moved various vases of flowers and then moved them back again, placed a screen round the too modern radio-gramophone on which he put, in readiness, a recording of Mendelssohn's *Songs Without Words,* bought because Miss Whitecliff had played them in her girlhood. He would start the record, very softly, when Rosalind's car drew up. She should enter a flower-filled, warm room (an electric fire was now augmenting the coal fire) which had become comfortable without any sacrifice of its own period charm.

He was fully ready by eleven and watching for her. She arrived at twelve-thirty.

Quickly he switched on the record-player, then turned again to the window. Rosalind was just coming through the gate, a tall girl, tall as Miss Whitecliff and of the same slim build though not, as her great-aunt was, painfully thin. Was there a facial resemblance? In the eyes, surely. And Miss Whitecliff's faded hair must once have been the same bright brown as Rosalind's, now stirred by the wind. A scurry of leaves blew down on her and she flicked one from the white lamb collar of her russet leather jacket. His Arden in spring changed to Arden in autumn. And he was suddenly sure he would remember this moment all his life.

The front-door bell rang. Should he go out and welcome her? Better wait here; the hall would be cluttered by Annie. He heard the door opened, a murmur of voices. Then Annie, with strict formality, announced: 'Miss Rosalind Whitecliff', and withdrew.

He said: 'I'm Drew Carrington. I believe Miss Whitecliff wrote to you about me.'

She failed to return his smile. 'Yes, indeed. What's been going on here?' She was now looking around the room.

He thought her tone rude but hoped she was

merely astonished. Still smilingly, he said: 'I think you'll find things a little more comfortable.'

'Comfortable? Those flowers must have cost a fortune. Does Mr Severn know you're here?'

There could now be no doubt about her rudeness but he could still make excuses for her. She had surely a right to be suspicious until she knew more about the situation. He said:

'Oh, yes, I've met Mr Severn. He's been most—'

She interrupted him. 'Where's my aunt?'

Before he could reply the front-door bell rang. Glancing quickly towards the window, he saw Mr Severn's car and said, 'This'll be Miss Whitecliff, now.'

Rosalind was again staring around, now seeking the source of the music. Looking behind the screen she said, 'My poor dear aunt must have gone quite out of her mind at last.'

'She's well and happy,' said Drew, suddenly angry. 'And please don't say anything to distress her.'

Rosalind glared at him. 'I shall say exactly what I like. It's what I've come for.'

'As you please. But I warn you, don't upset her. If you do, I shall put you out of the house.'

The words astonished him as much as they astonished her; but he didn't regret them. She had barely time for one scornful snort before Miss Whitecliff entered laden with carrier bags.

'Oh, you've met!' She kissed her great-niece affectionately, then disentangled the strings of the carrier bags. 'I've been shopping. This is for you, dear Rosalind. And this is for you, dear Drew – Cyril thought it would be right for you.

And this is for me. Cyril made me buy it, though I shan't really need it now the house is so beautifully warm.' She took a lacy shawl from her own bag.

Drew had taken an expensive cardigan from his. As he thanked her for it he caught sight of Rosalind's expression and flushed deeply. She was now smiling but it wasn't a pleasant smile; he felt assessed as a youth who cadged presents from old women. But she had, presumably, heeded his warning for she said nothing to distress Miss Whitecliff, merely thanked her for the silk scarf which was her own present and asked how she was.

At that moment Miss Whitecliff delightedly noticed the music. 'Oh, Mendelssohn's *Spring Songs*. You must see our marvellous machine – or does one call it an instrument? But first come upstairs and take your things off.'

Drew quickly recovered himself. It was only a question of time; Rosalind would soon see she'd made a mistake. But he blushed again, remembering her supercilious smile on seeing the cardigan – which was, incidentally, exactly what he would have chosen for himself; he gave Mr Severn full marks.

Nothing untoward appeared to have been said upstairs, judging by Miss Whitecliff's unchanged cheerfulness when she and Rosalind came down to lunch. The meal was certainly a success as regards the food. But Rosalind never once spoke to him, nor he to her. However, he doubted if Miss Whitecliff noticed; she was too busy talking herself. Never before had he seen her so confident. She was still dominating the conversation when they returned to the drawing-room for coffee.

'Dear Drew always pours it for me,' she said with satisfaction. 'And afterwards I want him to play to you, and sing some of your great-grand-parents' songs.' She proceeded to chat proudly about Drew's talents and his many improvements in the house, appearing not to notice that Rosalind showed no interest whatever. Embarrassed, Drew drank his coffee and tried to make plans for convincing Rosalind he wasn't whatever she thought he was. Suddenly he was astounded to hear Miss Whitecliff say: 'And I haven't told you the most exciting thing of all. We're going to have a motor car.'

He had never seriously considered getting a car, let alone mentioned it. He was about to ask if Mr Severn had, when Rosalind, ignoring the reference to a car, said: 'Aunt Blanche, I have to leave quite early. And before that, I want to see you alone.'

He looked at Miss Whitecliff anxiously. She smiled and nodded. 'Yes, Drew. I knew she would. Please take your time off as usual.'

He rose, but doubtfully. She reassured him. 'It's quite all right – really. I'll call you when dear Rosalind's had her little say.'

She now sounded not only confident but as if rather enjoying herself. All the same, he left her unwillingly, knowing how quickly she could become distressed. Up in his room, he sat with the door open, prepared to go back if he heard Rosalind speaking angrily. But he heard nothing for five minutes or so. Then the drawing-room door opened and the front door slammed. Looking out of his window he saw Rosalind hurrying to her car. He dashed down to Miss Whitecliff.

She was sitting with her head held high, looking triumphant. 'I've sent her to Cyril Severn. He said I could.'

'But it's Saturday. Won't his office be closed?'

'Oh, she's gone to his home; it's no distance. Cyril will settle her. I'm afraid I've let her bully me sometimes and she thought she could go on doing it, though she called it being sensible and wanting to protect me. As if I needed protecting from you!' She gazed at Drew fondly. 'And when I did need protecting, when I was frightened after Mother died and asked her to keep me company, she only stayed three days and she thought I ought to go into some kind of home for the elderly – though that was her mother's idea, really, such a horrid woman, Cyril told her not to come here again. After all, she's not related to me, as Rosalind is, and she did so upset me.'

'Are you upset now?' He had noted that her voice had begun to quaver.

'Well, I wasn't ... but I do feel a little tired. Perhaps the wine at luncheon – though I liked it. We often drank wine when my father was alive.'

'Why not lie down for a while?'

'Yes, I think I will, though my dear mother never approved of afternoon naps.'

He had of late not heard so much about her mother's prejudices and wanted to hear even less. 'Off you go then,' he said, and firmly piloted her up to her room, where he put on the electric fire and took off the bedspread. She removed her shoes and lay down under the quilt, then stopped him as he began to draw the curtains. 'Just leave them, please, so that I can see the sky. I don't suppose I shall sleep. Please play *Songs Without Words* again, and leave my door open. I told Rosalind to come back but now I'd rather not see her again. Just tell her she mustn't forget my warning.'

'I don't think I'd like to do that,' said Drew.

'No, it might make for unpleasantness. And I can write, if necessary. Anyway, she'll feel differently when she's seen Cyril. I think both she and her mother are a little frightened of him. He can be frightening. But he was so kind this morning, doing everything I wanted and taking me shopping. And he seemed so pleased with me. He said I was a different woman. And he's going to ask us both to dinner – it's years since he asked me to visit him. And he thinks he can hurry our telephone.'

'That's splendid,' said Drew. 'And now you just rest a little.' Her happiness seemed to him tinged by hysteria.

He went down and put on the Mendelssohn record; then visited the kitchen to congratulate the maids on lunch. They were only now eating their own, having asked him not to carve for them. ('Not when we have company, sir,' Annie had requested.) He was astonished to hear they had never before tasted pheasant or any kind of game. 'Oh, I've cooked it often enough,' said Lizzie, 'but we weren't allowed the same food as was served in the dining-room. I suppose it *is* all right for us to have it, sir?'

He assured her it was and brought each of them a glass of wine. They confessed that they'd sometimes drunk what was left in glasses– 'In the old days, when the master was alive.' The fact that they told him this made him realize how at ease they had become with him.

Surely if he could win the good will of the midgets, Miss Whitecliff and Mr Severn, all of them so much older than he was, he could ... well, at least lose the ill will of a girl his own age? And he'd start by making himself see her point of view – and before she returned.

Leaving the midgets to enjoy their meal, he went back to the drawing-room and sat seeing Rosalind's point of view with such determination that he was soon wondering if he ought to apologize for threatening to put her out of the house. Really, that was outrageous of him...

The Mendelssohn record came to an end. Should he turn it over? He tiptoed upstairs and listened outside Miss Whitecliff's room, then looked in through the open door. He had never before seen her with her eyes closed. Lacking their liveliness her pale, thin face was so utterly unanimated that for an instant he feared she was dead. Then he saw she was breathing gently, fast asleep.

He went downstairs again and did some more thinking about Rosalind's point of view... *Of course* he'd apologize!

6

Growing Up

She was back sooner than he expected but he was already on the look-out, intending to have the front door open for her. As she came up the steps he said: 'I didn't want you to ring the bell in case it disturbed Miss Whitecliff. She's lying down.'

'Good. I don't want to see her,' said Rosalind. 'I just want a word or two with you.'

Her tone now was casual but neither rude nor threatening. He followed her into the drawing-room, closed the door and turned to make his apology. But before he could speak she said: 'Sit down, do you mind? Over there,' indicating a chair opposite the one she flung herself into. She then favoured him with a long, cool, speculative stare. As a response to such a stare an apology would, he felt, seem like crawling, so he merely stared back, gravely but with a readiness to smile.

At last she said: 'I was told to look at you. Well, I've looked.'

'Yes, I did notice it,' said Drew.

'Mr Severn said no one could blame me for thinking the worst *before* I met you, but I ought to have *seen* at once that I was wrong. He's probably right. Anyway, I do see it now. I suppose I owe you an apology.'

He was surprised she could say this and still

236

remain unsmiling. No doubt she was proud– in which case the apology meant all the more. Smiling himself, he said regretfully: 'Ah, you got in ahead of me. I was going to apologize to *you*.'

'What for? Oh, for threatening to put me out of the house? Damn cheek, still... Do you know what Mr Severn said when I told him that? You haven't half made a hit with old man Severn. He said: "Good. Shows the boy has a temper. I did think he might be a bit too saintly." Are you saintly? I've always imagined saintly youths were dull.' There was the faintest hint of a smile in her eyes now.

'Dull I may be,' said Drew. 'But saintly, no. I assure you.' At last she smiled fully and it was as if a light had been turned on to her fine-boned beauty, illuminating its resemblance to Miss Whitecliff's. For a moment they sat silently, looking into each other's eyes. And while the moment lasted Drew was utterly happy. It had come right, just as he had known it would.

It was she who broke the silence. Still smiling, she said: 'You've got it wrong. Dull you aren't – but you are a bit saintly. Don't worry. It's curable.'

She changed her position, crossing one long leg over the other and drawing her tight skirt upwards. Something about the action surprised him ... yes, of course: Clare and Merry, when crossing their legs, either left their skirts alone or twitched them downwards. He had never before seen a girl deliberately pull her skirt above the knee – and some considerable way above. Perhaps the skirt was too tight to pull down; any-way, it was pleasant to see a little more of such elegant legs and he was in no way shocked. All the same, he quickly raised his eyes from Rosalind's legs to Rosalind's face.

Her expression had changed. She was now looking at him through half-closed eyes and her smile, which he had thought of as particularly frank, had become provocative. But that word was too innocuous. Her expression was tentatively licentious and becoming, every second, less tentative and more confident, expressive of a sexual conceit he found far more shocking than the sexual invitation. But what shocked him most of all was an intuitive certainty that she was not attracted by *him* but by the idea of his supposed saintliness and the prospect of 'curing' it.

He felt no embarrassment, merely a cold revulsion – and one which must have shown plainly in his eyes, for her own eyes grew cold. Then she looked away and he saw that she had flushed deeply. He now became embarrassed, on her account as well as his own. He must ignore what had happened, let her ignore it. Forcing himself to speak with merely casual politeness he said: 'I believe you have to leave early. Would you like tea now?'

She rose, saying, 'No, thanks. Too soon after that excellent lunch. And I ought to start now.'

Her tone was so normal that for an instant he hoped he had made a mistake, misinterpreted her expression or, at worst, been wrong in thinking she had seen his revulsion. But he was quickly undeceived when she continued, 'You can tell my aunt that I quite understand the situation now and I'm sure you'll make her an ideal com-

238

panion.' The last words were spoken with such crude venom that he could not pretend to be unaware they were meant to be insulting. Again their eyes met and this time with unveiled antagonism. Then she walked out of the room and out of the house, slamming the front door behind her.

He found himself thinking she was unbelievable. People just didn't behave like that. It wasn't only her awfulness that amazed him. He was almost as astonished by the instantaneousness of her reactions; her enmity and rudeness on her first arrival had been as sudden as her recent, very opposite behaviour. Was there something admirable in such a complete lack of façade? Did it indicate unusual honesty? Had he still found her attractive he might have thought so but as things were ... no, her directness was just arrogance. And good God, what had she expected? That he'd jump up and grab her? More likely she'd hoped he'd blush and stammer and become shyly adoring. How dare this creature be called Rosalind?

Well, he must pull himself together. No doubt the slammed door would have awakened Miss Whitecliff. He must go up to her.

She smiled at him as he looked in. 'I've been awake some time. I heard Rosalind's voice but I kept quiet because I wanted her to go without seeing me. Did she behave any better?'

Instead of answering directly he gave her Rosalind's message about himself but minus Rosalind's intonation. As he expected, she took it at its face-value and was delighted.

'Did she really say you'd make me an ideal

239

companion? There, now, I knew Cyril would cope with her. And I did quite a bit myself. I told her she wasn't to come again without being invited and if she wrote me worrying letters I might make a new will and cut her out of it. You see, she was so rude about you and I thought she needed frightening. Though I don't think I would cut her out, really, because she *is* my only relation. Anyway, I promised her the will should stay as it is, provided she leaves us in peace – and I was able to promise it quite truthfully. Oh, I've been very, very clever!' She looked like a child proud of a happy secret.

'Splendid,' said Drew, with a heartiness that was slightly histrionic. Obviously it hadn't entered her head that she might put *him* in her will. The money didn't matter but it would have been pleasant to think she wished him to have some little legacy. And why not be honest and admit that the money did matter? That is, it would if one stayed on and on – and it was hard to imagine being cruel enough to leave her...

She was continuing to chatter. 'I was telling Cyril how much you do for me and yet I some-how feel more independent, not less. He says that's because you're making me believe in my own importance. Yes, that was how he put it. I was thinking about it before I fell asleep and I had such a ridiculous idea. I thought: "Not my own importance, exactly. It's more that I'm beginning to feel grown-up." Oh, dear, how silly that sounds – at my age!'

Touched and interested, he had already dismissed thoughts about her will. Returning her smile, he said: 'Perhaps you couldn't feel fully grown-up while your mother was alive. You were such a dutiful daughter.'

'I didn't think of myself as dutiful – it was just the way things were. Naturally one had to do as Mother wished, when she was so near death. That is, she felt she was, for so many years. But she had such wonderful strength of character. Even when she was, well, really near death, she still decided every detail of our life. There was never any trouble with Annie and Lizzie when Mother was alive.'

'But there isn't any trouble with them now,' said Drew. 'May I ask you something? Why did you tell me they were fiends?'

She looked startled, then evasive. 'Did I tell you that? Perhaps it was a joke.'

'Yes, I see.' Better leave it at that.

But she didn't let him. Still avoiding his eyes, she said, 'No. It wasn't a joke. They *were* fiendish – I mean after Mother died. They kept wanting me to decide things, and how could I when there was no one to tell me? And I was frightened of them sometimes. I thought they were punishing me.'

'For what?' Even if it distressed her he must get the truth.

'Well, just for being me – especially when I was young and they were young. I had so much, parties and pretty dresses and Cyril. And they had nothing. They never went anywhere because they had nowhere to go. And Mother warned me never to be familiar with them in case they got out of hand.

'We'd never had *young* maids before. And – well, it stands to reason they must have hated me.'

'It would have been more natural to hate your mother.'

'Oh, they never did that. They admired her. But I came to feel they hated me *and* despised me. And I can see why. I mean I can see it now, this minute, for the first time. I ought to have done more for them, oughtn't I?'

He said gently, 'It's hard to do things for people, or for oneself, when one isn't quite grown-up.'

'How clever of you to understand!' She smiled at him gratefully. 'Especially when I don't fully understand, myself. What puzzles me most of all is the way time slid by. Often when I was going to bed, here in this room with Mother, I'd think "But it's only a minute since last night" – and in another minute, it was the next night, and on and on. Even the years ran into each other – I used to think that, every New Year's Eve. It was confusing...'

He had read somewhere that a monotonous life passed quickly, even in prison. Should he try to explain? But already she was continuing.

'And I felt somehow to blame, though I don't know why. Perhaps being good to Mother wasn't enough. Perhaps it was a sort of excuse for not making more effort, for just letting life slide by. I'm beginning to see so many things, now when it's too late.'

'But it isn't,' said Drew firmly. 'There's still heaps of time. And you mustn't waste any of it in worrying. As for Annie and Lizzie, of course they don't hate you.' If they did, he doubted if they

242

were aware of it. Perhaps they suffered from suppressed resentment, just as she had suffered from suppressed guilt; but even so, he felt sure they'd serve her dutifully if not devotedly as long as she didn't expect them to *think*. 'Now let's forget about it. Shall I bring your tea up here?'

'Oh, no!' She sat up quickly. 'I want to come down and listen to the wireless – and the gramophone, and have you play to me, *and* I want to look at all the nice magazines. So many, many exciting things!'

'I'll go and see to the fire,' said Drew.

He went downstairs briskly enough but, while poking the fire into a blaze, realized that he was heavily depressed. Just why? Surely not because Miss Whitecliff had no intention of mentioning him in her will? No, that wasn't what was weighing on him. Her will could not operate until she died – and the very idea of her dying was unbearable, when she had only just begun to live. Was he dreading the fetters of her affection? Did he fear he might become a captive in this house, even as she had been? If so, he would deserve it for writing to her – such a silly schoolboyish trick it seemed to him now; she wasn't the only one who was growing up. But it was nonsense to think his position here could resemble what hers had been. He would have all the power she had lacked. He could make life interesting for himself as well as for her. Later, they might travel – and for the present, why not ask someone to stay? She had said she would like to meet his family. But Richard couldn't leave Dome House at present and Clare didn't like old ladies. (What *did* poor dear Clare like?) Merry would have been the one, but there was still no news of her...

He put new magazines on a stool by Miss Whitecliff's chair and a new novel by his own – not that he much wanted to read the novel, any more than he now wanted to write one, particularly one steeped in a golden Edwardian glow; he could no longer visualize the glow. But surely the desire to write *something* would return, once he stopped putting all his creative energy into creating a new life for Miss Whitecliff? Really, he should be feeling especially happy at seeing her mental state so much improved. It was something he could be proud of – and he'd done quite a bit for her midgets. (*His* midgets now, he thought, with rueful amusement.) And hadn't he had a victorious day? The detestable Rosalind had been routed.

He went to the window, wondering if he would draw the curtains already against the gloomy late afternoon, and as he looked across the leaf-strewn garden he at last tracked his depression to its true source. He remembered standing at the window that morning, remembered – most poignantly – his first glimpse of Rosalind as she strode through an autumnal Arden.

He had not fallen in love with her on sight; he had simply been willing to fall in love. Instead, he had hated her. No, hate was too much of a compliment; hate involved one's emotions. He merely disliked her, coldly and critically. Never again would he be able to feel he had never really disliked anyone. He wondered why this distressed him so much – and found the answer: he was

244

conscious of a loss of innocence far more absolute than if he could have sensually responded to Rosalind's sensuality. But the distress, he intuitively knew, would not long survive the innocence, for a loss of sensibility follows a loss of innocence, at once a penalty and a compensation.

He drew the curtains. Miss Whitecliff, entering, said:

'Oh, how cosy the room looks!'

Annie brought in the tea.

Interlude Under the Dome

Jane

Jane, returning to Dome House after her first day with Miss Willy, felt cheerful. She suspected the head mistress would be merciless to the inefficient; but as an employer of anyone as efficient as Jane knew herself to be, she seemed-likely to prove reasonably considerate. They had got on well and Jane had found the work interesting. She was looking forward to telling someone about it, preferably Drew.

She found the hall deserted. Then Clare came out of her bedroom on to the gallery and called down lugubriously.

'I've been asleep. Isn't it awful about Drew? He's gone – after a job. He left a note.'

'Why is it awful?'

'Well, it is for me. Drew, Merry, Cook, Edith – and you – getting jobs. Not that we know if Drew and Merry have yet, but I'm sure they will. Everyone will but me. Anyway, I always feel awful if I sleep in the afternoon. Will you light the fire? I'll come down when I've freshened up a bit.'

Jane's cheerfulness ebbed. She would miss Drew as much as she was missing Merry. And Clare's lack of vitality was both depressing and irritating. But later, when they were sitting by the fire together, she felt sorry for the pretty, spiritless girl – who could no more help being spiritless than she could help being talentless.

'I know someone who might help you,' she told her. 'A Miss Gifford, who runs an old-established employment agency. She sometimes has jobs which require no training – like doing people's shopping or seeing schoolgirls across London.'

'But I always get lost in London. And surely it would cost too much to live there unless one had a full-time job?'

'Quite true. But there might be *something*.'

'I can't think what. Why am I so ... so spineless, compared to most people?'

'Has it anything to do with your health?'

'Heavens, I'm as strong as a horse. I think the real trouble is that I'm so conscious of not being good at anything. Years ago I realized I wasn't clever like the others, and I'd have to be an ordinary, domesticated girl. But I never liked it, not even after Aunt Winifred went. She, of course, was utter hell. Running the house was supposed to be her job but I had to dance attendance on her. And nothing I did ever satisfied her.'

'I expect she's to blame for a lot,' said Jane. 'Anyway, you've somehow got an over-developed sense of inferiority. Well, you're bound to marry eventually. Then everything will come right.'

'But I don't *fancy* marrying. The idea bores me just as books about married people bore me. And I never want any children. I can't bear babies.'

'That really is astonishing.' Again Jane felt irritated. A pretty girl who didn't hanker for a career *ought* to fancy being a wife and mother. 'Well, I shall write to Miss Gifford for you, but I do wish I could tell her some job you'd like.'

'Sorry,' said Clare, her expression blank.

'Except, according to Merry, being a king's mistress. But you've probably outgrown that.'

A flash of humour gave a momentary life to Clare's prettiness. 'Oh, no! I'd simply adore it, still. But what a hope!'

'Well, it's not a job you'd get from Miss Gifford,' said Jane, smiling. 'She's an ultra-respectable old lady. I'll write to her now – I want to, anyway, to tell her I'm working for Miss Willy.'

'I've never decided which I dislike most – Miss Willy or Aunt Winifred. I wish they'd fight each other and both win. Well, I'll start getting supper. Cook and Edith will be back soon.'

'Dinner,' Jane noted, had been degraded to 'supper'.

She went to her room and nobly refrained from turning on the electric fire, even though she intended to pay her share towards the heating of the house as well as for her board and lodging. It was, she remembered ruefully as she sat down at her desk, exactly a week since she had first entered this room and found the fire full on and the radiators hot, on a day far warmer than today.

Miss Gifford's reply came by the same post that brought Drew's postcard from Whitesea saying he had got his job. Jane had to tell all she could remember about Miss Whitecliff before even opening her own letter. When at last she had the chance to, she was astonished by one paragraph:

Your little friend who hankers to be a king's mistress strikes me as particularly funny because, believe it or not, I have an ex-king on my books! I supply him with young ladies who read aloud to him. But he'll hardly be in need of a mistress as he must be quite ninety. He was one of my mother's clients, way back in the early nineteen-hundreds when he lost his throne. I can't remember what the name of his country was – or is; I suppose it's under Communist domination now. Seriously, there might be a chance for your girl as you say she's pretty – he insists on that and it's not easy to find pretty girls who read aloud well. Anyway, if your friend thinks she could qualify tell her to see me *soon* as the job's been open for a week. The pay's very good. – Oh, don't on any account mention the old gentleman's ex-royal status as he has always preserved the strictest incognito.

Jane regretted the last sentence. Mention of an ex-king, even one of ninety, might have given the job a touch of glamour. As things were, she could only describe it as 'reading aloud to an old gentleman'.

'How ghastly!' said Clare. 'Though I do read aloud fairly well. I used to read plays with Merry before she got so friendly with Betty – though I never acted them, as Merry does.'

'You're not supposed to act when you're just reading aloud,' said Jane. 'Do try for this, Clare.'

'Oh, dear! Do you think I ought to, Richard?'

'Not unless you want to. Frankly, I'd rather have you here. If you go, I shall have to run the house, now Cook and Edith are out all day. Still, I don't want to stand in your way.'

'I'm afraid I want my way to be stood in, unless it's something more exciting than reading to an old gentleman. I'm sorry, Jane. I know I'm an ungrateful beast.'

'Couldn't you just go and see the old gentleman? You might like him. Anyway, here's Miss Gifford's address, if you change your mind.' Jane tore off the top of the letter and handed it over.

Clare eyed the address with aversion. 'It would cost a lot to go to London.'

Richard asked if she'd run out of money.

'No, I've still a few pounds left but–'

He interrupted her. 'I'll finance this trip if you'll take it.'

'Or will you let me treat you to it?' said Jane. 'I'd particularly like to.'

But Clare would only say she'd think it over.

She won't even do that, thought Jane. 'Well, I must go or I shall be late for Miss Willy.' She put Miss Gifford's letter in her handbag and went out to get her car.

BOOK FOUR

Clare

1

In the Mantle of Merry

She put the torn-off address of Jane's Miss Gifford into the pocket of her frilly apron and told herself she would need some solid aprons or overalls if she was to do as much housework as now seemed likely. How she loathed housework, especially when one did it all on one's own! But she declined Richard's offer to help with the washing-up, saying: 'Let me feel I'm doing something to earn my keep.'

Bed-making without a companion was even worse than dish-washing; so much walking from side to side. But she finished at last and sat on her own bed wondering what to do with the rest of the morning. Her glance rested on her work-table. She would put away all her painting materials. In future any flowers on that table should be enjoyed, not painted. At present the very sight of the table depressed her; for months she had felt guilty when she didn't paint and inadequate when she did.

She went to the box-room for a suitcase and noticed that Richard was below in the hall, reading *The Times.*

'Don't tell me *you're* looking for a job,' she called down.

He said he didn't see how he could take one while everything was still so uncertain. 'I couldn't go away, anyhow – with Jane and Cook and Edith so determined to keep the home fires burning. And Merry might come back.'

'It'd be awful if she found no lamp in the window,' said Clare. 'As for the home fires, we'll die in the real winter if we don't have the radiators on. And we're almost out of coke.'

'I know. And the last bill isn't paid. Why the suitcase?'

She told him and went into her room where she cleared her work-table with satisfaction. Paints, drawing-board, sketch-books, all went into the suitcase with a pile of anaemic paintings – how was it she could see how bad they were yet not do better? She was ready to take the suitcase to the box-room when the front-door bell rang. Stepping onto the gallery, she looked down and listened as Richard went to the door.

A moment later she was back in her room so dismayed that she felt physically sick. There was no mistaking that breathy, querulous voice: Aunt Winifred was below.

What had she come for? Richard had written saying he could not continue the allowance his father had paid her. No answer had come to this letter – and now it had come in the most catastrophic form imaginable.

Clare looked desperately at her window. Could she climb out and rush to the Swan? Cook and

Edith would aid any fugitive from Aunt Winifred. But no friendly creeper offered a foothold and the ground was at least twelve feet below. She was trapped and at any moment Richard would call her down.

The wave of sickness passed and she told herself not to be a fool. She was grown-up now, not the bullied sixteen-year-old she had been during Aunt Winifred's regime. She would sail downstairs and support Richard. But first she would try to glean what was happening. She opened her door a crack and listened.

Richard was saying, 'But you're far better off than we are, Aunt Winifred. You have a fixed income – and you own your house.'

'But I've let the house, Richard. I intended to spend the winter in a guest house.'

'Well, that seems a good idea–'

'It's an impossible idea, without the allowance your father always paid me. Good guest houses are expensive.'

'Surely with the rent you're getting from your house–'

'Only nominal – to make sure it isn't left empty. If you can't continue my allowance I must come back here.'

'But I've already told you what's happening,' said Richard. 'There'll be no one to wait on you.'

'You say Clare's still here.'

Quietly Clare closed her door and without a second's hesitation opened the suitcase and tipped out its contents. Then, with a speed of which she would not have believed herself capable, she set about packing clothes. Her technique was to open drawer after drawer and take out some of the contents, without wasting time on being selective. *Some* handkerchiefs, *some* stockings, *some* underwear ... everything was merely tossed in. Often she had seen this kind of packing done in films, by characters staging getaways, and thought that no one could ever pack like that. She had been wrong.

She scarcely hoped to get away without meeting Aunt Winifred. The great thing was to be ready to go the minute she got the chance. The suitcase, not large, was nearly full and she had not yet opened her wardrobe. Perhaps kind Jane would send some clothes after her. She crammed in her black chiffon dinner dress. Idiotic to pack like this – when she wasn't even quite sure Richard would give in. Again she listened at her door.

He was now saying, 'But you can't have your old room. Miss Minton's paying a good rent for it. You'll have to make do with the small spare room.'

'I can't spend the winter in that bandbox. I'd better use your father's room.'

'But his clothes are still in it.'

'They can be moved. Clare can do it. Please take my case upstairs and then send her to me. No, tell her to make me some tea while I wash. I'm extremely tired, after travelling all yesterday and a wretched night in a London hotel. Please tell Clare to hurry with the tea. The dear girl will be glad to see me.'

Again Clare closed her door. A wild hope had now awakened that she might avoid even meeting her aunt. She shoved the suitcase out of sight and looked around for a hiding place. By the time Richard knocked on her door she had rolled under the bed.

He called her name, knocked louder and called louder. Then she heard him open the door and close it again. She waited several seconds before rolling out from under the bed and changing, in barely half a minute, into a fairly new grey woollen dress. Now for her coat ... disaster! Last year's winter coat was at the cleaners, her new one not yet delivered. Frantically she hunted through her wardrobe, though knowing she would find no substitute. She was about to make do with a summer coat when she remembered: in the box-room was the black coat misguidedly bought in the spring. It was unbecoming but reasonably warm.

Could she get it? Richard would be looking for her in the kitchen and the garden. Aunt Winifred would now be washing. Stepping out of her shoes, she raced to the box-room.

But where was the black coat – or the check skirt and turtlenecked sweater bought with it? A second later, she knew – when she discovered Merry's school uniform. She might have guessed Merry would escape in disguise. Well, she too would do so. The only thing connected with school she had ever liked was the blue cloth cape worn in winter; it was circular, three-quarter length – but on her, Merry's would be full-length, which was all to the good. She dragged it from its hanger and dashed back to her room.

Here she forced herself to think coherently. Had she forgotten anything vital? Money! She had a five-pound note in her jewel box. As she got it she regretted that her diamond wristwatch, once her mother's, was away having its clasp mended. Her father had taken it for her – where? She had no idea. Anyway, perhaps he'd sold it, to help his escape. She wouldn't grudge that; but it was a pity not, like Merry, to have something pawnable.

She gave a last look around the room and saw her discarded apron with the address of Jane's Miss Gifford protruding from the pocket. She snatched it out, put it in her handbag, flung on the blue cloak and picked up her suitcase. Now nothing should stop her, not even if Aunt Winifred stood at the top of the stairs with a flaming sword.

But there was no sign of her aunt or Richard. She tiptoed along the gallery, went cautiously downstairs, then made a dash for the front door, flung it open and left it open behind her. She intended to run full tilt to the village and she did run down the drive and for fifty yards or so, with the suitcase thumping against her. Then she slowed to an exhausted walk. Please heaven the village taxi would be available!

It was, and she was soon on her way to the station, thankful that the driver, partially deaf and wholly unsociable, showed no desire to talk. She could sit back, regain her breath and think.

But thinking proved not altogether pleasurable. She was proud of escaping but ashamed of leaving Richard in the lurch – and without even a farewell note. She could telephone from the station, but suppose Aunt Winifred answered the telephone? A telegram would be better but what could she say in it? Only that she'd gone – and he'd know that soon enough. The untidy state of her usually tidy room would reveal her frantic packing and he'd have no difficulty in guessing the reason. It then occurred to her that her departure might actually help him, for if their aunt had no one to wait on her she might leave. This idea was most cheering, as was the thought of Aunt Winifred fending for herself in a stone-cold house. If Richard had any sense he'd die of cold rather than turn on the heating.

She now counted her money. The ten-mile taxi fare would be ruinous but she could manage it, and her fare to London, without breaking into her five-pound note. She would have to spend the night at some cheap hotel. How cheap were cheap hotels and where were they to be found? And suppose she didn't get the job of reading to the old gentleman? But she wouldn't look ahead. Enough for now that she'd escaped – she who believed herself so lacking in initiative. Almost, she could bless Aunt Winifred. But not quite.

She spent the rest of the drive re-organizing her packing and (thank goodness she'd packed her nail-scissors) unpicking the school badge from Merry's cloak. Arrived at the station, she had to wait an hour for the slowest train of the day and did not get to London until after three o'clock. Though hungry, she was unwilling to waste time or money on a proper meal but a station sandwich proved filling. She then set out, bravely determined to reach Miss Gifford.

For Clare, London was always an indeterminate

whirl of buses, buildings and people. (She could never understand how Merry and Drew could be so happily at home there. Richard, like herself, got lost.) On sunny days, the indeterminate whirl was vaguely yellow; today it was vaguely grey. The worst days of all were when the whirl was seen through rain, but all London days were bewildering. This afternoon, after making the most careful inquiries, she actually got on the right bus, but it was the right bus going in the wrong direction. By the time she had got off, been swept past by many buses because she wasn't waiting at a bus stop, taken the wrong bus because she had forgotten which she wanted, changed buses again, got off at the wrong place and misunderstood a policeman's directions, it was a quarter to five and she finally reached Miss Gifford only to find her preparing to close her office.

It was a most unimpressive office, at the top of the steep stairs of an old house in a back street. And Miss Gifford was not Clare's idea of a business woman. She was elderly, her white hair was untidy, her black dress as dowdy as her office. But her voice had a high, bright authority and her manner was brisk.

On hearing who Clare was, she said: 'Enterprising of you to come to London so soon but you should have got to me earlier. Now it's too late for today – or is it? Mr Rowley won't see anyone after five but you might get there in time if I put you in a taxi. I must leave now, anyway; I've a train to catch. Here, take this...'

She scribbled an introduction on a card, handed it to Clare and whisked her out of the office and down the stairs before Clare had caught her breath from hurrying up them. She then raced after Miss Gifford along the back street and into a main thoroughfare, trying to catch information thrown over Miss Gifford's shoulder. All she heard clearly was that one had to be tactful with Mr Rowley's nurse. 'I always find her pleasant when we talk on the telephone but some girls have fallen foul of her. Oh, dear, you've barely ten minutes! Taxi!'

By dint of signalling to, and shouting at, every taxi empty or full, Miss Gifford eventually got one, got Clare into it, slammed the door and gave instructions to the driver. She then talked at the closed window. Clare hastily lowered it but by then the taxi was moving, so all she heard were instructions to try again tomorrow if she failed to get in tonight.

She sat back and sighed with relief, moment- arily only, for she then began worrying about the taxi fare. Would she have enough to pay it with- out changing her five-pound note? If not, would the driver change it? And if he wouldn't, then what? She counted what was in her purse, then searched her handbag for stray coins: net glean, one halfpenny. The taxi kept stopping in traffic blocks, during which time the taximeter always, most unfairly, ticked up. She glanced at her watch. Already it was five to five. She was just giving up all hope when the taxi put on a spurt of speed, turned a corner and drew up.

A smiling commissionaire opened the door, took her case and helped her out. She handed the entire contents of her purse to the driver and asked if it was enough. He counted the money carefully and offered, not very pushingly, to return a shilling. Reckless with relief, she said: 'Oh, that's for you,' then followed the commissionaire into the hotel – for a hotel it was and a very grand one and its ornate clock said three minutes to five.

The commissionaire looked at her inquiringly.

'Mr Rowley,' she said. 'Before five.'

An impressive hall-porter heard her and shook his head.

'You're too late, miss. No use sending you up now.'

'Oh, please!' She gave the porter an appealing look.

'Well, we'll try, anyway,' said the porter, his manner becoming fatherly. 'Page!' An extremely small page was suddenly by his side. 'Take this young lady up to Mr Rowley as fast as you can. Hurry, now!'

The lift was waiting. As they went up, the page and the lift man exchanged glances. 'Nurse won't let her in,' said the lift man. 'It's not five yet,' said the page, 'but we'll have to run for it.' Up and up – Clare lost count of the floors. Then the lift door opened and she was running after the page along a wide corridor. They stopped outside a mahogany door and the page pressed a bell. 'Well, I got the bell rung before five,' he said triumphantly.

Ought she to tip him? Well, not with her five-pound note. She said: 'Thank you so much. I'm sorry I gave my last shilling to the taxi-driver.'

The page gave her a look of heartfelt sympathy.

'Gee, miss,' he said, speaking what he fondly thought was American. 'I sure hope you get the job.'

She was about to explain that it wasn't that kind of last shilling when the door was opened by an elderly, uniformed nurse. At that moment, a clock with a silvery but penetrating chime began to strike.

'Hear that?' said the nurse to the page in an ominous tone.

'We had to wait for the lift,' said the page, untruthfully.

The nurse now turned her attention to Clare and after a long critical look said: 'Well, you can come in but he may be too tired to see you. Here you are, page.' She handed him a coin from a bowl that stood on a table in the little entrance hall.

'Thanks, Nurse.' He gave Clare a parting smile before the door was closed on him.

'Sit down, please,' said the nurse and then left Clare alone in the hall. She counted the doors that opened into it: five, including the front door, all closed and all somehow looking as if they would never open again. But in a few minutes one did and the nurse reappeared.

'Mr Rowley will see you.' She dropped her voice to a whisper. 'Just remember he's ninety, dear. And don't be surprised at anything.'

2

Mr Rowley

How would a gentleman of ninety be liable to surprise one? As she followed the nurse, Clare visualized him as frail, bloodless, emaciated, probably in bed. She must smile winningly, both out of kindness and because she wanted the job.

The sitting-room she was shown into was dimly gold. Yellow brocade curtains were drawn against the late afternoon sunlight and a bright fire was protected by a gilt fireguard. She took in cream panelling and formal French furniture. Then she was being presented to Mr Rowley, who rose to shake hands with her.

He was the largest man she had ever seen, tall, broad, with a massive head and a vast expanse of sallow-complexioned face. His hair, though she was later to see it was thickly streaked with grey, gave the impression of blackness. He wore a long, dark dressing-gown and as he stood there in the firelight he seemed to her a pillar of darkness. She had been feeling nervous. Now she experienced a tremor of fear.

He held her hand an unusually long time and relinquished it slowly, seeming to feel it with the tips of his fingers. He then apologized for receiving her in his dressing-gown, saying he had been about to take a nap. His voice was deep and he had a slight foreign accent. Having asked her to sit down, and sat down himself, he spoke to the nurse.

'Now, if you please.'

'This is a very pretty young lady, much the prettiest who has been to see us this week. She has soft, fair hair, very blue eyes and ... I'd call them *delicate* features. She is wearing a long blue cloak–'

'A blue cloak? That sounds delightful. What shade of blue?'

'I'd call it a dark shade of powder-blue, Mr Rowley. And she has on a pale grey dress and grey gloves. None of the other young ladies wore gloves.'

'I think I must *see* this young lady.'

'Yes, I think you should, Mr Rowley.'

Clare was bewildered. She had not yet got over the shock of deciding Mr Rowley was blind. Now he was changing one pair of spectacles for another and the nurse was plugging in a modern electric fitting which looked most out of place in the room. Then the powerful bulb was switched on and focused on Clare. Blinking, she saw Mr Rowley's face coming closer and closer until it, too, was lit by the dazzling light. It seemed the wrecked face of a giant, full of ravines, the skin coarse and pitted, the mouth a blackish wine-colour. Then the terrifying face retreated and Mr Rowley said: 'We're frightening her, Nurse. You should have warned her.'

'Mr Rowley can see just a little,' the nurse explained. 'But it's a great strain for him.'

'Anyway, I now know you are a very pretty

263

young lady indeed and I shall be able to picture your face while you read to me.'

Clare, who up to now had said nothing beyond, 'How do you do?' asked if he hadn't better see if she read well enough.

'Yes, perhaps I should. But I'm sure all will be well. You have such a quiet, pleasant voice – and I'm glad to say I'm not at all deaf. Nurse, please turn off that ugly, glaring light and let in the daylight. And give the young lady today's paper.'

The nurse drew back the curtains of the wide window, revealing tree tops against the sky.

'Just read what you like, my dear,' said Mr Rowley.

Clare liked little in newspapers except the woman's page and not always that. Feeling selection was beyond her, she began at what she felt was the beginning, the top left-hand column of the front page. As this dealt with world affairs it barely made sense to her but she managed to read half a column without stumbling. Mr Rowley then stopped her.

'Yes, you read charmingly. You make the news so much less menacing than it always is. But I mustn't let you go on or I may fall asleep and that would be rude – Nurse will tell you I always sleep from five to seven. I wonder if you would be willing to come back this evening to read to me – say at nine o'clock?'

'I'd like to,' said Clare. 'The only thing is, I haven't yet found anywhere to sleep.'

'Nowhere to sleep? That sounds most alarming. She had better sleep here tonight, Nurse. She can use Mr Charles's room. And ... yes, I think it would be pleasant if she stayed here with us indefinitely. Will you please arrange that – if she's willing?' He smiled unseeingly in Clare's direction.

'Oh, most willing,' said Clare, fervently.

'Good. Until nine o'clock, then.'

He rose. The nurse steered him to the sofa, switched off the lights, and led the way out into the hall.

'Now we must talk,' she said. 'Come into my room.'

The bedroom they entered was as formally luxurious as the sitting-room; the nurse's possessions looked oddly at variance with their surroundings. She settled Clare into a brocaded armchair and herself into another.

'He's taken to you,' she said, her manner both authoritative and conspiratorial. 'I thought he might – I know his type of girl; not that we've had one for years. The girls just lately – so untidy, hair like floor mops, and some of them not even clean. And very bad manners, most of them. He's a dear old gentleman and he won't be with us much longer. Are you prepared to put yourself out for him a bit?'

Clare said indeed she was and the nurse continued.

'What he wants is two hours in the morning, two in the afternoons, and two in the evenings. Most girls won't stand for it. Of course it is awkward, having your whole day broken up – I'll admit that.'

'I shouldn't mind at all,' said Clare. 'If I could find somewhere fairly close to stay.'

'Oh, he means you to stay here. Didn't you hear him say so?'

'But surely not for good?'

'Oh, yes, dear – all found, lap of luxury. It happened once before with a pretty, nicely spoken girl, though she wasn't really nice and I had my doubts about her from the first. With you, well I'm sure there'll be nothing like that. Now about money: Mr Rowley's solicitor sends someone every month or so to settle all bills. He's just been so you'll have quite a while to wait. But if you're short I can help you out of my petty cash.'

'I'm all right for now,' said Clare. 'How much do I get paid?'

'Didn't Miss Gifford tell you?'

'If she did, I didn't hear. We had such a rush.'

'Well, I'll ask her tomorrow when I ring up to say you're fixed. I don't know what the last girl got and anyhow you ought to get more as you're going to live in.'

'Don't you mean less?'

The nurse shook her head. 'Oh, I know you'll get your board and lodging, but there's no telling how long your hours will be if he's got you right here on the premises. Anyway, don't worry about the money. Mr Rowley's very generous and very rich. Now where are your things for the night, dear?'

Where, indeed? For a blank moment she thought she had left them in the taxi. Then she remembered with relief. 'The commissionaire took my suitcase.'

'I'll send down for it.' The nurse went to the telephone.

'Oh, your name, dear? I've forgotten what was on the card.'

'Clare Carrington. Please call me Clare.'

'Thank you, dear. I'm Nurse Brown. Just call me Nurse.' She gave instructions for Clare's case to be sent up, then went into the hall and opened the door of the suite. 'Mustn't let them ring the bell and disturb Mr Rowley. They know not to, between five and seven, but some of them forget, especially the pages. That reminds me: we tip for everything that's brought up. If you're on your own, just hand out a coin from the bowl, here – I call it the Beggars' Bowl. And Mr Rowley never gives less than half-a-crown, even if it's just a page with the evening paper. That won't come up till after seven, when Mr Rowley's awake.'

When the suitcase had been delivered, Nurse Brown took a key from the drawer of the hall table and conducted Clare to a room next door to the suite, explaining it was always kept for Mr Rowley's grandson, Mr Charles Rowley. 'Mr Charles, he's always called, to differentiate between them. He's abroad now. You'll find a few of his things here but there'll be plenty of room for yours. Take your time over your unpacking, there's no need to come back to me till eight o'clock. Mr Rowley will have had his dinner by then and the night nurse will be putting him to bed. You and I can have our meal together and then you'll be ready to read to him at nine. Have you a dinner dress with you?'

'Yes, but it'll be a bit creased,' said Clare, open-ing her suitcase.

'Never mind, he'll like to know you changed

into it and I can leave out the creases when I describe it. Now I'll be off.'

Left alone, Clare looked around, enchanted. She much admired the grey and gold panelling, the green brocade curtains, the wide, convoluted brass bedstead. The only indications of Mr Charles were some silk pyjamas in a drawer, a dressing-gown in the room-sized cupboard, and some shaving tackle and expensive toilet accessories in the large bathroom off the little entrance hall. There was, as in Mr Rowley's suite, an atmosphere of formal luxury exactly to her taste, as was the idea of doling out half-crowns to pages who merely brought up evening papers. This was undoubtedly the life.

She unpacked and then decided to pass the time by having a bath. This proved an unnerving experience as the gleaming porcelain bath, the largest she had ever seen, was extremely slippery. Every attempt to lie back in it ended in a slide and frantic clutchings. (Bells on the wall beside it were marked 'Maid' and 'Valet'. Would one, if about to drown, have the delicacy to summon a rescuer of the right sex?) She was easily capable of spending an hour in a bath but not if she had to sit bolt-upright. This bath, she felt as she clambered out, was strictly for washing in, not dreaming in.

She dressed, and praised herself for having packed her evening shoes. But there were many things she had forgotten, notably her dressing-gown. She must send a list to Jane and also let Richard know where she was. But not yet. She would write to no one, boast to no one of the marvellous good fortune that had come her way. To do so would be ... unlucky? She only knew that for the present she must keep this, the first adventure of her life, entirely to herself.

It was now seven o'clock. Still with time to waste, she sat down intending to bask in a sense of achievement. But instead, she found herself remembering the moment when Mr Rowley's face had come closer and closer, lit by the Clare of the brilliant lamp. Such an old, old, terribly ugly man! She rebuked herself. No one could help age or ugliness and he was obviously generous and kind. She would overcome her repugnance and do all she could to please him.

The telephone bell startled her. Surely no one could be ringing her up?

It was Nurse Brown, sounding pleased and important. 'Mr Rowley would like you to dine with him. Are you dressed yet? The dinner will be up any minute.'

Clare said she would come at once and hurried to the suite. The nurse, admitting her, said how nice she looked and then announced her with as much pride as if she had invented her.

'Here she is, Mr Rowley, and wearing such a pretty dress – black chiffon.'

'Chiffon? Yes, I remember chiffon. Allow me to feel it.'

Clare handed him a fold. He fingered it gently.

'A delightful material. And black should suit such a fair young lady. Nurse tells me your name is Clare. I may call you that?'

'Oh, yes – please.'

'Thank you. Ah, here is dinner.'

269

It arrived with considerable clatter. One waiter wheeled in a laden trolley, another waiter followed with what looked like a portable oven. Silver dishes flashed. A vast amount of paraphernalia seemed needed to bring in clear soup, chicken and ice cream. Clare was supplied with lemonade; Mr Rowley drank water. Eventually the waiters left and Nurse Brown, declining Clare's help, managed on her own, serving the meal (which she did not share) and cutting up Mr Rowley's chicken. It was obvious that he could not see his plate clearly and Clare found it painful to see his occasional jabs at the tablecloth. She was thankful when dinner was over and the waiters had removed the table, oven, trolley and themselves.

Mr Rowley then said: 'Tonight I shall sit up for a while and Clare shall tell us something of herself. Are your parents alive, my dear? How do you come to be on your own in London?'

Oh, she should have anticipated this! She should have had some story ready! But she knew that even given time she could not have invented a convincing one – as Merry could have done even at a moment's notice. Clare often thought Merry's imagination was another name for plain lying. She herself was extremely truthful, partly because not being truthful entailed a mental effort that was beyond her. Now, after a dismayed silence, she simply described the catastrophe that had hit the Carrington family – and saw Nurse Brown's benign smile of sponsorship replaced by a look of alarm. Then the smile returned as Mr Rowley said: 'And this happened only last week?

My poor child! And now you are bravely facing the world alone? How fortunate you came to us! We must take good care of her, mustn't we, Nurse?'

'Yes, indeed, Mr Rowley.'

'You must tell me more of this later, my dear. Now I must go to bed so that Nurse can go off duty. My night nurse will be waiting. Oh, if only there were two Nurse Browns in the world!'

Nurse Brown escorted him from the room and then returned.

'He never likes his night nurse,' she told Clare, complacently. 'I'm always having to try a new one. Of course, they don't have to do much – just help him to bed and look in on him every hour or so. They know to call me if he doesn't seem himself in any way.' She sighed. 'My great fear is that he'll pass on in the night when I'm not there. Oh, I want him to go in his sleep, when the end comes; it'd be easiest for him. But I'd like to be with him, even if he didn't know I was. I've looked after him for ten years and I can't remember when I last took a day off. Never feel right if I'm away from him.'

She picked up a menu, preparatory to ordering her own dinner; then said she didn't really fancy anything. 'Wonderful food, but you get tired of it. I'll have bacon and eggs and a pot of tea in my room, later – they won't serve that until they've finished serving proper dinners. My word, that's a sad thing about your father, dear, but it makes a new interest for Mr Rowley. You tell him all you can.'

Before long, Clare was sent for. She followed

the night nurse into an over-warm, closely cur-
tained bedroom where the ornate French
furniture seemed unsuitable for a heavy old man.
Mr Rowley was sitting up in bed in a black bed-
jacket of curious shape which managed to look
both Chinese and military. Above its high collar,
his dark skin looked darker than ever against the
white pillow, his face more lined and ravaged. He
had taken his spectacles off and Clare doubted if
he could see at all, but his hooded eyes never
looked sightless. Indeed, sometimes they flickered with a surprising liveliness.

She had brought the evening paper with her.
She asked if she should read it to him.

But Mr Rowley did not want to be read to. He
wanted to talk – or rather, to listen. Gently but
inexorably he extracted information about herself and her family; no detail seemed too small to
interest him. She had to describe every room in
Dome House, the garden, the village, the surrounding country. She guessed that he was trying
to enter her world as an escape from his own and
she felt sympathetic, but after an hour or so she
found it very hard to go on. She seldom talked
much (oh, for Merry's volubility!) and she had
for some time been so dissatisfied with her daily
life that she took no pleasure in describing it. But
she persevered... By eleven o'clock she was conducting Mr Rowley through her schooldays.
Then, to her relief, Nurse Brown arrived to
reinforce the night nurse who had come in
several times and been waved away. Mr Rowley
must go to sleep. He submitted, and thanked
Clare for her company.

'You shall have her back tomorrow,' Nurse Brown assured him, whisking her out of the room.

Clare was now yawning uncontrollably.

Nurse Brown told her she could sleep late. 'Mr Rowley won't need you before eleven o'clock. You can have your breakfast in bed – just ring for the floor waiter. Better take some half-crowns out of the Beggar's Bowl so you can tip; don't go handing out your own money. Got the key of your room, have you? Well, good night, dear. And thank you.'

Clare, making her way along the silent corridor, felt triumphant. It was amazing to think she would actually have earned money by just talking. Not that it hadn't been exhausting; seldom had she longed for sleep as she longed for it now. She let herself into her beautiful room and got ready for bed as quickly as possible. She was about to turn out all the lights except her bedside lamp when every light in the room went out of its own accord.

The darkness was intense for the heavy curtains excluded every glimmer from the street lamps outside. She groped her way to the door onto the corridor and opened it. There was nothing wrong with the corridor lights and as they shone into her little entrance hall she noticed a small wooden fuse box. That would be the source of the trouble. Well, nothing could be done about it tonight. She closed the door and felt her way to the bed. The smooth linen sheets were as cold as a waterfall but wonderfully luxurious, and almost as she slid between them she slid into sleep.

3

Homage to Dumas

The dream, she afterwards remembered, seemed to go on and on, and throughout its long length she suspected it was a dream. But she could not wake and her efforts to do so increased her distress. Although the memory of that distress remained with her for days she could never recall what the dream itself had been about, except for its culmination, when she saw Mr Rowley's ravaged face, brilliantly lit, close to her own. Then the brilliance was replaced by a tiny flame, flickering in darkness – but now she was awake! Desperately she tried to believe she was still dreaming but it was no use. This was reality, a reality far worse than her nightmare. The tiny flame came from a cigarette lighter, beyond which was Mr Rowley's face. He had followed her here. The tiny flame went out and from the total darkness came a voice that certainly wasn't Mr Rowley's.

'For God's sake don't scream. I'm not going to hurt you. What are you doing in my bed? Damn this lighter.'

Again the flame sprang into life. Clare, always a quick waker, was now in full possession of her senses and she saw at once that the man by the bed, though like Mr Rowley, was younger. He was, however, still pretty old – too old, she'd have said, to be anyone's grandson, but Mr Rowley's grandson he must be, come back from abroad. She felt furious with him but she did not feel frightened – perhaps because she was so relieved that he wasn't his grandfather.

'I have no intention of screaming,' she said haughtily. 'And I've every right to be here. I'm employed by Mr Rowley. You, I suppose, are Mr Charles. I'm sorry no one warned you I was in your room but it's not my fault. Now please go away.'

A snort came from the face beyond the flickering flame. 'Very sure of yourself, aren't you?'

She thought this abominably rude. Glaring, she spoke with cold indignation. 'Go away *at once* – unless you want me to ring for help.'

'You dont *need* help. Oh, blast!' Again the lighter had gone out.

She heard him stumble over something and hoped he was leaving, but he had only gone to the window to draw back the curtains. A moment later she saw him in the light from the street lamps. Apart from being tall, dark, heavily built and heavily featured, he was less like Mr Rowley than she had thought – ugly in his own right she decided, greatly disliking the bags under his eyes. She took him to be quite fifty.

He turned to her. 'Listen, please – just for a minute.'

She had sat up while he was moving to the window. Now, conscious of the thinness of her nightgown, she clasped herself.

'Here, put this round you.' He picked up her

275

cloak from a chair and tossed it to her, then sank into the chair. 'I really am very sorry I burst in on you. It must have been frightening. Not that you seemed frightened.'

'Of course I was – until I saw it was you.'

'What? Well, I'm glad I look so innocuous.'

She wasn't going to explain. Instead, she said severely:

'Why didn't you let someone know you were coming back?'

'I didn't know it myself less than half an hour ago. It was a sudden emergency.'

'But if you were abroad–'

'I wasn't.'

'Well, Nurse Brown thinks you were.'

'She thinks no such thing. We telephone each other almost every day. It's just that my grandfather has to believe I'm abroad. Do you understand?'

'No,' said Clare.

'Well, you needn't. All I ask is that you won't tell him you've seen me and that you'll let me sit here quietly till morning.'

She said indignantly, 'Of course you can't. You'll have to ask for another bedroom.'

'If I go downstairs and say I found you in my bed it'll be all over the hotel by tomorrow. Do you like the idea?'

'I like it better than having you here. Besides, it's bound to be known. Somebody must have seen you come in. Isn't there a night porter?'

'There is, but he wasn't around. I had my key and simply walked upstairs. Anyway, I don't want the trouble of getting another room – if there is one; the hotel's usually full. I'm all in, and I've a very important day ahead of me.' He yawned. 'You can see I'm half asleep already. Do let me rest. I'll slip down the back stairs as soon as it's light.'

She found the yawn infectious and failed to stifle one of her own. 'But it won't be light for hours and hours.'

'Of course it will.' He lit his cigarette lighter again and looked at his wristwatch. 'It's six-fifteen already.'

'Goodness! I thought it was the middle of the night.'

'Well, it isn't. Now if you ask me, you're as sleepy as I am. Just take a little nap – and when you wake up I shall be gone. And if you're a wise girl, you'll tell no one I've been here.'

'I won't tell Mr Rowley. But I must tell Nurse Brown.'

'I wouldn't. It's most unfair but I think she might count it against you. She can't know you very well yet and she knows me rather too well. Some of my shocking character might ... well, brush off on you. Still, please yourself.'

Clare felt obscurely blackmailed. *Would* Nurse Brown count it against her?

'That's right,' said Mr Charles. 'You just think things over quietly. And I promise you no harm will come of it – if you play it my way.' He pulled up the dressing-table stool and put his feet on it.

She was still far from sure she ought to let him stay – but how could she get rid of him, short of ringing for help and creating a scene? And if the night was nearly over...

A loud snore from Mr Charles decided her. She

would let this sleeping dog lie till daylight – and dress in the bathroom before waking him. Then, if he refused to go, she could go herself. She slid down in the bed, longing for sleep but sure that the snoring would keep her awake. How did the wives of snoring husbands ever get to sleep? She had never before listened to a man snoring, a very strange noise indeed...

She was suddenly aware that she had dropped off – but not for long; it was still night. The snoring had stopped. She looked towards the armchair, which was silhouetted against the window. Surely ... yes: the chair was now empty. Where, then, was Mr Charles?

The next instant, she knew. He was lying beside her, jacket off, sleeping most peacefully. The quilt was over both of them and, though he lay on the blankets and she between the sheets, they looked exactly as if they were in bed together. Barely had she taken this in when a distant clock began to chime. She counted the strokes: unmistakably, five. Then he had lied to her about the time! She had no idea when he had arrived – or how long he had been beside her.

Furious, she sat up intending to shake him. Then her rage was replaced by caution. Judging by some of her favourite novels, men were apt to find angry women provocative – and he had admitted to a shocking character. She must be icily calm, and she must still wait for daylight. On no account must she fall asleep again; but she would not, as long as she remained sitting upright.

Her cloak had slithered to the floor but she was not cold – she was far too ... exhilarated. How extraordinary! And it was even more extra-ordinary that she had never, once she'd escaped from the nightmare, felt frightened. She was not introspective, finding attempts to understand herself both boring and baffling; indeed, she could never concentrate on them. But for once she was interested in her own reactions. He had said she was sure of herself, and that was exactly how she felt. Why? When as a rule she was so drearily tentative, so conscious of inferiority?

But as usual, her thoughts slid away from herself and she was soon reviewing the whole incident impersonally and objectively. London, dead of night, the great hotel, silent corridors, closed doors, a sleeping girl suddenly awakened: it was exciting enough to be in a book – and it *reminded* her of some book. The pitch-dark room ... yes, in *The Three Musketeers,* when D'Artagnan passes himself off as Milady's lover. 'At Night all Cats are Grey' – fascinating title of a fascinating, if unconvincing chapter; surely his voice would have given him away? Not for the first time Clare considered the matter very thoroughly, living so intensely in Milady's dark bedroom that she only returned to her own when the darkness was yielding to dawn. Her complete absorption had kept her very still; back in the present she found it hard not to fidget. And it was now light enough to get up.

But first she peered closely at Mr Charles. Had she overestimated his age? Yes, he might not be more than forty-five. But she hadn't over-estimated his ugliness ... those bags under his eyes, that heavy nose, the deep lines from the nose to the mouth – which wasn't too bad and he slept with it firmly closed, even though he was lying on his back. No doubt those snores had been histrionic – what a trick to play on her! But she no longer felt furious; merely elated, faintly amused and – most astonishing of all – just a little sorry for him. Lost in deep sleep he looked so ... helpless. But she told herself briskly that he wouldn't look it once he awoke.

Cautiously she slid out of bed and picked up her cloak. He stirred slightly. She was instantly still but it was too late; the next second, he had opened his eyes. She hardly had time to fling the cloak around her before he was saying, 'Hey, wait, you silly girl! What's the point of rushing out, now?'

'I'm not rushing out,' she told him. 'It's just that I have to use this cloak as a dressing-gown. I forgot mine.'

'There's one of mine here you're welcome to – though of course it'll swamp you. Good gracious!' Fully awake now, he gave her a long look. 'No wonder you were so sure of yourself.'

After a blank instant, she guessed that he meant she was pretty. Ignoring both his speech and his eyes, she said coldly, 'What time was it really, when you arrived?'

He grinned. 'Around two-thirty. Now don't look so indignant. This is my room – and I was dead beat. And you weren't in the least afraid of me. If you had been, you wouldn't have gone to sleep.'

'I happened to be dead beat too,' said Clare.

'Poor child! You're much younger than I

realized. My grandfather's readers are usually older, more experienced and a great deal more friendly.' He threw back the quilt and got up.

'Please go now,' said Clare.

'I will as soon as I've had a bath and a shave. All right?'

'Certainly not! Get out!' She had a strong desire to hit him.

He looked at her admiringly. 'I've always had a special fondness for angry kittens. Now listen: I *must* freshen up before I go out. Surely I've made it clear that I mean you no harm? Why not co-operate a bit? Here's an idea: you order a large breakfast while I bath and shave – and then we'll share it.'

'You're not going to bath and shave.'

'Well, come in and stop me,' said Mr Charles. 'I'll leave the door open.'

She followed him across the entrance hall and slammed the bathroom door on him, then went back to the bedroom. Infuriating man! Such arrogance! But somehow ... as well as wanting to hit him, she wanted to laugh.

She went to the dressing-table and had a good look at herself. As a rule she thought her pretti-ness insipid and old fashioned. This morning she felt fairly pleased with her face – well, consider-ing it was entirely devoid of make-up. Should she put on powder and lipstick? She decided it would be unwise to pay him any such compliment and merely combed her hair; then sat down and waited.

He was back sooner than she expected, looking fresher if no less ugly.

'What, no breakfast? Well, my hopes weren't exactly high. I *could* just ring for the waiter and order it myself.'

She surveyed him calmly. 'And I *could* tell your grandfather you've been here.'

'What a despicable threat!' He sounded shocked. 'But you win, of course. It's rather heartbreaking that anyone so young should be so unscrupulous. Do you know the corners of your mouth are twitching? Is it a nervous trick or an incipient sense of humour? Ah, that's better! What nice white teeth!'

She switched off her smile but found herself saying, 'Perhaps I might order you some breakfast – if you hide in the bathroom while the waiter brings it in.'

He shook his head. 'Here's where my true nobility comes out. It's time I went, if I'm to avoid being seen. I'd rather go starving into the storm than blemish your spotless reputation.' He turned up the collar of his jacket.

'The sun's shining,' said Clare.

'Is it? My mistake. Well, come and see me off. You'd better make sure there's no one in the corridor.'

They went into the entrance hall, where she opened the door and looked out, then turned and nodded to him.

'All clear? Dear me, that is a comic cloak – suggests some kind of holy order. Don't forget you can use my dressing-gown. Tell me, are you an actress?'

'Me? No. Do I look like one?' The idea pleased her.

'Frankly, no. It was just that I shouldn't have thought any girl who wasn't *acting* innocence could look quite as innocent as you do – not in these days.' He smiled down on her. 'Are you fooling me?'

'Well, I'd hardly tell you if I were,' said Clare, trying now to look enigmatic. She considered it shaming for a girl of twenty-one to be so abysmally innocent as she was.

'Excellent answer to an idiotic question,' said Mr Charles. 'Perhaps I will have some breakfast.'

'No, you won't, not now,' said Clare. 'But wait a second. I must take another look out.'

'Wise girl. You're obviously an old hand at this kind of thing.'

The corridor was still empty. 'Now go at once,' she told him sternly. 'Don't start another conversation.'

'*Of course* you're not an actress. You were born to be a schoolmistress.'

'Just *go.*' She held the door open for him.

He made a sudden dive and kissed her on the top of her head, which came well below his chin, then sprinted for the door leading to the backstairs. Reaching it, he looked back and smiled. She glared indignantly. He turned down the corners of his mouth lugubriously, then hurried down the stairs.

She closed her door and, for no reason she could possibly have explained, put the palm of her hand on the top of her head.

4

A Garden Enclosed

By five o'clock that afternoon, when Mr Rowley was left to take his nap, Clare had been on duty for eight hours. She had been sent for while finishing her breakfast (served by a fatherly floor waiter who had been much distressed to hear that her lights had fused. 'Such a thing to happen *here* – and to a young lady!') She had read the morning paper aloud for a short time and then been forced to talk until lunch arrived. It was a dull meal of steamed fish and rice pudding but at least it gave her a chance to stop talking as Nurse Brown was in attendance and Mr Rowley was eager to hand on much that Clare had said. Nurse Brown made such comments as 'Well, now, isn't that interesting? She must tell you more about that, mustn't she?' and beamed on Clare, who now felt she had nothing more to tell him about anything whatever.

After lunch she firmly suggested she should read.

'Lots of nice books on the table there,' said Nurse Brown. 'I expect Mr Rowley's in the middle of one of them.'

'I was, but my last young lady made it seem very dull. Anyway, Clare must start a new one or she won't enjoy it herself. Make your own choice, my dear.'

As all the books proved to be detective novels she felt her chance of enjoyment was small, but anything would be better than talking. Choosing the one with the most attractive jacket, she read as brightly as she could, even attempting to be dramatic. But it was no use. After a couple of chapters Mr Rowley stopped her.

'Even so splendidly read, this isn't interesting. Detective stories aren't what they used to be.'

To the best of Clare's belief, what they now lacked they had never had. She asked if he ever read historical novels. 'Oh, not modern ones; they're usually dull – or horrid. I mean lovely romantic ones, like Dumas.'

Mr Rowley smiled reminiscently. 'Dumas? He gave me great pleasure when I was a boy. How delightful to meet a young lady who knows his work. Kindly ring for Nurse Brown. She will telephone my bookseller.'

When the nurse came he told her to order a complete set of Dumas. Clare, about to protest that even one Dumas novel would last them for weeks, restrained herself. If complete sets existed she was all for having one around. Nurse Brown soon reported that Dumas had written several hundred books, many not obtainable, but a fine set of novels was being sent by special messenger.

'Then we shall have plenty to read this evening,' said Mr Rowley. 'So, for the moment, we'll talk.'

Somehow Clare got through the afternoon. Tea, with Nurse Brown present, made a break. And at last it was time for Mr Rowley's pre-dinner nap – before settling down to which, he made sure Clare would dine with him.

'It won't be like this every day,' Nurse Brown assured her, when they had closed the door on him. 'It's just – well, you're a novelty. Anyway, Miss Gifford's going to see that you get a good salary – I've told her what a fancy the dear old gentleman's taken to you. Now you'd better get some exercise. You can walk in the park.'

Clare hurried out, eager for fresh air and for a chance to think; not that she could make much of her thoughts. She was troubled by a sense of flatness – well, who wouldn't be, after having to talk so much? But there seemed more to it than that.

Walking in the autumnal park she took herself to task. She should be feeling nothing but gratitude for having found a job she could actually do – and one which included most luxurious board and lodging. And she should also be grateful for having come through last night without disaster; if she had made a scene it might so easily have been counted against her. She had kept her head. Surely most girls would have panicked? Really, she could be a little proud of herself. And now, presumably, Mr Charles had gone back 'abroad' and would trouble her no more. An elderly, ugly, arrogant man...

She turned to face the hotel and wondered which was the window of her room; then remembered it looked onto the street, not the park. She had a vivid memory of Mr Charles's tall, heavy figure as he drew back the curtains. What an adventure to have on her first day away from home! Considered as an adventure it seemed somehow valuable, to be recalled with pleasure, and she would recall it in fullest detail while taking a pre-dinner bath. She had that morning evolved a technique of lying back supported by one foot on the bath-rack

Re-entering the hotel, she was conscious of welcome. The commissionaire saluted, the hall porter smiled. Was that her special page? Yes! She responded to his wide grin. The lift man knew her floor, which was more than she did. Barely twenty-five hours ago she had arrived scarcely daring to hope. Now she was an accepted resident. Everything was wonderful. But she still felt flat.

A moment later, the flatness was replaced by dismay. As she approached her room she saw her suitcase being carried out by a chambermaid. Was she being evicted? Then Nurse Brown, at the door of Mr Rowley's suite, beckoned her in.

'The girl's moving your things for you, dear – I've had to get you another room. Mr Charles is coming back.'

For a second, Clare's thoughts whirled. She then implored herself to keep calm. Having taken Mr Charles's advice and said nothing about their meeting, she must now proceed with extreme caution. 'From abroad?' she asked, histrionically.

'Well, dear … come in to my room for a minute. Quietly – Mr Rowley's still asleep. Of course I'm always happy to see Mr Charles but I must say this is a bit sudden. I rang him up to tell him we'd found a young lady, and bless me if he didn't say he'd be back this very night. And before you meet him, dear, well, I do have to warn you of one or two things.'

'Oh?' said Clare, trying to sound only casually interested.

'To begin with, don't ask him questions about having been abroad. Oh, he'll make up some story to satisfy Mr Rowley but the least said about it the better. You see, dear, we sometimes *pretend* Mr Charles is abroad; otherwise his grandfather wants him to live at the hotel. Naturally Mr Charles can't do that all the time but he hates hurting the old gentleman's feelings. So he says he has to go abroad on business – which is true enough sometimes but more often he just goes off to his flat.'

'And Mr Rowley doesn't know about the flat?'

'Well, he does in a way, dear, but he thinks Mr Charles only visits a lady friend there.'

'Oh, *I* see,' said Clare. 'My father has that kind of lady friend in a flat. I mean he had before he bolted.'

'Really, dear? I thought it had rather gone out of fashion. Of course it was all the thing for gentlemen when Mr Rowley was young and he thinks it's the right thing for Mr Charles and likes hearing all about it. But the truth is that Mr Charles hardly ever has ladies to stay at his flat and anyway he hates telling Mr Rowley about his private life, so he's had to invent a lady. She's foreign and dashing, with a violent temper – he makes her sound ever so real. And now... But I mustn't tell you.'

'Oh, go on,' said Clare, coaxingly.

'Well, it's only fair you should know the kind of gentleman he is. And you'll see the funny side of

288

it. The truth is, he *has* had a lady staying at the flat for once, and she *is* foreign. "Nurse," he says to me just now on the phone, "it's a case of life imitating fiction." It seems they had a row yesterday before he went off to business, and, when he came back, in the small hours, she'd bolted the door against him. Short of breaking the door down, there was nothing he could do. No doubt she expected him to, but he wasn't having any. "I needed a night's *rest,* Nurse," he says, "and a kind friend let me have one." My word, it's a mercy he didn't come back here!' She laughed heartily.

Clare hastened to laugh too.

'Not that you'd have had any trouble. Mr Charles is a gentleman. Still, you will need to be careful, dear, because you're the type he most admires – quite a bit like the last girl who lived in, only you're much prettier.'

'Did she have trouble?'

The nurse chuckled. 'Her trouble was that she *didn't* have it – he changed his mind. He soon found out she wasn't as refined as she looked. But he was very generous to her. And you mustn't think he isn't nice. It's just that he has to have distractions, what with Mr Rowley on his hands and lots of business worries – property deals, if you know what they are; his name's often in the papers. It's a wonder he can ever spare time to stay here.'

Clare asked how long he would be staying.

'Well, he's completed some big business deal today, and got rid of the foreign lady – I mean the real one, not the one he tells Mr Rowley about.' Again the nurse chuckled. 'So he might stay quite a while. I hope so, anyway; life's quite different when Mr Charles is with us. Now you'd better get changed for dinner.'

'Will Mr Charles be here for it?' Clare's tone betrayed her nervousness.

Nurse Brown gave her a kind look. 'No, dear. He said he'd be very late and not see any of us till tomorrow. And you mustn't worry. Everything will be all right as long as ... well, I've given you the hint. Your new room's only a few doors away, across the corridor. The key's on the hall table.'

The room proved to be pleasant but less luxurious than Mr Charles's. Clare rather resented that he had ousted her; but other aspects of his return worried her far more.

All her usual self-distrust was back. Now that she knew more about him she felt sure her behaviour had been dangerously silly. She should have forced him to go or gone herself, to Nurse Brown. No wonder he had kissed her – not that the top of one's head really counted, but still, what impertinence! Like an eighteenth-century rake casually kissing a chambermaid. And she had conspired with him, deceived Nurse Brown. If that ever came out...

She must treat him with the greatest coldness. No, he might resent that and so might Nurse Brown who obviously adored him, and they might do her out of her job. She must be pleasant, but firm. He must be made to see the kind of girl she really was. And perhaps she was flattering herself in thinking she might have 'trouble' as Nurse Brown called it. And anyway, one could hardly have *serious* trouble unless one was to some extent willing – which one never would be, with such an ugly, elderly man. Still, she must be wary, both of 'trouble' and of losing her job. And she must be particularly wary of herself; that sense of confidence she had experienced last night was most dangerous, and just a form of conceit, really. She wasn't usually conceited. As a rule she did realize what a fool she was – and heaven help her if she forgot it! And now she couldn't bear thinking about it one moment longer. Anyway, she must dress.

She had barely finished when the telephone rang: 'These books you wanted have been sent up, dear. Could you come in and arrange them while Mr Rowley gets ready for dinner?'

She found a very large set of Dumas stacked on the sitting-room floor. The volumes were old but perfectly preserved, their edges gilt, their spines and corners bound in green leather, their sides in green and grey marbled paper. There were many titles of which she had never even heard. What treasure! She arranged the whole collection along the white marble mantel, wondering if she would ever get time to read some of it on her own. She liked to lose herself in books, live in them – as she never could do when reading aloud.

Nurse Brown steered Mr Rowley in. He was particularly cheerful and talked with pleasure of his grandson's return. 'He's a dear fellow. We've always been very close since his father died when Charles was eight. You'll like him, Clare – and he'll like you. I think, Nurse, we must see that Clare is carefully chaperoned.'

He and Nurse Brown seemed to think this a

very good joke. Dinner was served: again clear soup, chicken and ice cream; Clare gathered it was a standing order. She also gathered that Mr Rowley had very little sense of taste left. She was realizing more and more how extremely old he was. His height and breadth gave an illusion of virility which was indeed an illusion.

After dinner she had half an hour on her own while he was put to bed. She again began to worry about Mr Charles; even the beautifully engraved illustrations to the Dumas novels failed to distract her and she was glad when at last she was sent for. She took half a dozen of the novels with her and gave Mr Rowley his choice. But she found he wanted not to listen to Dumas but to her talking about Dumas. Would she describe the novels, tell him which were her own favourites and why? Well, if she had to talk, this gave her plenty to talk about, and if her powers of invention were weak, her memory was excellent. She said her favourite of all was *Louise de la Vallière* and launched into a description of it.

She had reached the night scene under the royal oak when she interrupted the story to say: 'Goodness, how excited I was when I first read that – I was only fourteen. You see, Louis Quatorze overhears Louise declare her love for him, so of course one gets afraid for her.'

'In case she loses her honour?' queried Mr Rowley, gravely.

'No, in case it puts him off. But it works just the other way and she becomes his mistress – but not for ages and she makes a terrible fuss about it. She's really rather dull and pious. Nell Gwynne was far more fun – and darling Charles II was *much* more exciting than Louis Quatorze. Still, it was reading about Louise that made me want to be a king's mistress.'

'My dear Clare! Surely you're not serious?'

She looked at him quickly. Was he shocked? He certainly had no right to be, if he liked his own grandson to keep a lady in a flat. Anyway, it was hard enough to think of things to tell him without having to censor her conversation. And perhaps he'd quite enjoy being a little bit shocked.

'I am, indeed,' she said gaily. 'It's a standing joke against me. Being a king's mistress is the only job I've ever fancied.'

'How very astonishing! Tell me how you ... er, visualize the job.'

He was smiling now, interested. No, he hadn't been shocked. And she was glad of another subject to talk about. Unearthing a memory of some old Ruritanian novel, she said: 'Well, I'd live in a secluded house on the outskirts of the capital city.'

'A villa, with a walled garden,' said Mr Rowley.

'Oh, *yes*, a walled garden would be lovely. His Majesty would arrive in the early evening, very much incognito...'

'And unlock the door in the garden wall,' said Mr Rowley. 'And you would be standing by the lily pond in a long white dress.'

'I could be,' said Clare eagerly. It was wonderful that he was really sharing a conversation, instead of merely prodding her with questions. 'Yes, of course there should be a lily pond.'

'And lilac blooming. What else?'

293

What did bloom with lilac? 'Laburnum, perhaps? And could there be lights streaming from
the windows?'

'No. The shutters would be closed. But the
door might be open and one might see across the
hall to a lighted room.'

'Would there be supper there?'

'Not in that room but there would certainly be
supper.'

'Champagne and caviar. And after supper?' He
was not smiling now but staring at her intently
with his dark, almost sightless eyes.

Suddenly embarrassed, she said: 'I'm afraid I
can't think of any more.'

He smiled again. 'Perhaps that's as well. Dear
child, I should like to *see* you again.'

'Tonight?' she said, dreading the ordeal by
lamp.

'No, perhaps not till tomorrow. I'm a little tired.
Indeed, I think I shall let you go now. Please send
my night nurse to me. Good night, my dear, and
thank you for reviving a very happy memory.'

A memory – of course! No doubt of some
foreign place; the walled garden suggested that,
as did his slightly foreign accent. No longer embarrassed, she experienced for the first time a
feeling approaching tenderness for him. Smilingly she said good night and hoped he would
sleep well.

He said he thought he would. 'But I shall not
mind if I lie awake for a while. You have left me
with such a pleasant subject for thought.'

She wondered if the very old were like the very
young in needing a bedtime story.

When she had summoned the night nurse, she went to replace the Dumas novels and to find *Louise de la Vallière* which she had not taken to Mr Rowley as it was the sequel to earlier books. Talking of it had made her want to re-read it and she would have done so by the sitting-room fire had not Nurse Brown chivvied her away. 'You get an early night while you can, dear.'

Well, she could read in bed. She undressed quickly, regretting the loss of Mr Charles's dressing-gown. She had tried it on that morning and, though the shoulders had come nearer to her elbows and the sleeves needed to be rolled up six inches, she had greatly liked the feel of the heavy silk. Boring of him to deprive her of it. But she no longer felt seriously worried about his return. Mr Rowley was so obviously pleased with her; surely he would not let her be dismissed even if she did have to repel his precious grandson – from whom she was now prepared to stand no nonsense whatever.

Having got into bed, she read absorbedly until not long before midnight, when she was disturbed by a quiet buzz. Was it the bell outside her door? More likely that of the next door which she had several times heard. The buzz came again and lasted longer and now she was sure it was her bell. Perhaps Nurse Brown or the night nurse wanted her. She flung on her cloak, hurried to the door, and was opening it before she remembered they could have summoned her by telephone.

Mr Charles, carrying a large parcel, stood outside smiling down on her.

'Go away!' she said instantly.

'Nonsense,' said Mr Charles, coming in and closing the door.

She gave him a stoney look. 'You won't get away with it this time. If you don't go I'll ring *all* the bells. I'll call the waiter, the valet, the chambermaid, the lot!'

'As late as this you'll only get the night waiter. He's a Frenchman I've known for years and certain to be on my side. Still, he might be embarrassed, so we won't have him in.' Mr Charles had adroitly got between her and the stand of bells on the bedside table. 'Now stop being silly. We have to talk before we meet officially tomorrow. Need I go on standing guard over these bells?'

'Oh, I suppose not if you'll say what you have to say quickly.' She certainly didn't want to summon an embarrassed French waiter.

Mr Charles frowned. 'What's the matter with you? Last night – and this morning – you behaved with such superb good sense.'

'I didn't. I behaved idiotically. And you got quite the wrong impression of me.'

He looked delighted. 'Really? How splendid. I do so much prefer disreputable women.'

'But I'm not–'

He cut her short. 'Oh, relax, you absurd girl. I know what's happened. Nurse Brown's been warning you against me.'

'Not at all,' said Clare, determined not to give the nurse away. 'Nurse Brown's devoted to you.'

'She is indeed. And she'd serve you up to me minced on toast if I wanted her to. After ten years with my grandfather and me she's lost every vestige of moral sense. Be nice to her, won't you? She's starved for someone to gossip to, poor dear. I do my best for her in that line, with vast indiscretion. But she must not, for your sake, know about last night.'

'Not now, I agree,' said Clare. 'I ought to have told her at once.'

'You ought not. And all you have to do now is to go on keeping your head, especially when we first meet.'

'I'll probably go scarlet.'

'I doubt it. And if you do, it will just be put down to girlish nervousness. Little does she know that you have nerves of iron.'

'Me?' She stared in astonishment.

'You had, last night.'

'That was ... peculiar,' said Clare. 'Anyway, I haven't as a rule and I'm hopeless at lying or even acting a lie.'

'I'm superb at both – after years of practice with my grandfather. So say as little as possible and let me carry things off. Well, that settles tomorrow. Here's a present for you.' He put his parcel on the bed and got a penknife from his pocket to cut the string.

Now she really would be firm. 'No, thank you. I don't want a present.'

'Well, you *need* this one. It's a dressing-gown.' He took the lid off the box. 'I bought the smallest size. Let's see how it fits.'

Clare, eyeing the box with interest, said: 'Sorry, but I'm not going to accept it.'

He sat down on the edge of the bed and addressed her in a matter-of-fact tone. 'Now stop pretending to be conventional. It *is* only pretence. No really conventional girl would have behaved so cleverly last night. I intend to give you quite a lot of presents, both because I enjoy giving presents and because I want to make your job bearable. Otherwise you won't stay with my grandfather; girls never stand him for long. Suppose we clear the ground a bit. I understand from Nurse Brown that you're twenty-one. Well, I'm forty-two.' He noted her surprised expression with amusement. 'Yes, I know I look older. That's due to the three D's: drink, drugs and dissipation, only one of which I actually allow myself. The first two affect one's wits and I have to live by mine.'

'Doesn't dissipation affect them?'

'Well, I've thrived on it so far. But what I want to make clear is that, in spite of anything dear Nurse Brown may have told you about me, I do have quite strict standards of ... let's say suitability. A girl of exactly half my age wouldn't measure up – or, rather, down to them, apart from the fact that I never lay siege to the innocent. So you would appear to be doubly safe. Now go and put your dressing-gown on in the bathroom. You really can't go on wearing that cloak. I can see your legs.'

She looked down hastily. 'Only to the knees – and you could do that if I wore a dress.'

'But legs seen through a nightgown are a different matter.' He took the dressing-gown out of its wrappings and handed it to her. 'Now off with you, and come back looking decent.'

She went.

It was the most luxurious garment she had ever

put on, of white cashmere lined and trimmed with white satin. She tied the satin sash and then returned to Mr Charles, who had now settled himself in her armchair.

He regarded her critically. 'Very becoming. You're a girl who should be dressed very simply, at enormous expense. Does it fit?'

'Marvellously. It's even the right length. Most ready-made things are too long for me.'

'They shortened it a little. I said it was for a girl whose head came below my chin. I happened to remember.'

She was busy admiring herself in the long looking-glass. 'You certainly have good taste in dressing-gowns. But I looked jolly funny in yours.'

'You wore it?' He sounded surprised.

'Well, you said I could.'

'Of course. But judging by that last angry glare you gave me, I shouldn't have thought you'd have felt friendly enough.'

'I think I was more startled than angry.'

'As a matter of fact, I was quite angry with myself – for succumbing to sudden temptation.'

She came towards him and sat on the bed. 'Good heavens, being kissed on the top of the head isn't the end of the world. Just forget it. Well, if I'm going to accept this lovely present I ought to be more gracious about it. Thank you *very* much.'

She smiled at him sweetly.

'That was charmingly said. And you won't distrust me any more?'

'I never did, really– I only felt I ought to. It's most extraordinary, but from the moment I woke up and saw you...' She found difficulty in putting it into words.

'Go on,' he said, watching her closely.

'Well, I was somehow so confident – brave as any lion. And that's terribly unlike me. Perhaps I knew instinctively that you'd be all right with the young and innocent. Not that I'm all that innocent.'

'Then I might not be all that all right. Don't worry; that was just a joke – still, I suggest you stop lolling on the bed. I begin to see you're a minx.'

She sat up straight. 'Not on purpose, truly. And haven't minxes gone out?'

'I was beginning to fear so.' He smiled at her speculatively. 'Perhaps you don't understand yourself.'

'There's no perhaps about it – I don't and I never have. And trying to always makes me feel demented.'

'Then don't try. Anyway, it's a mistake to know too much about oneself – does one out of exciting surprises.'

'My young sister says people who aren't introspective aren't fully alive.'

'She wouldn't be my type. Still, I do know what she means. And one mustn't *resist* self-knowledge. But I think the truest kind comes in flashes, not by taking thought.'

'Oh, I'm certain you're right,' said Clare, leaning forward with eager interest. 'Not that I've had any flashes yet. I sometimes think I'm mentally arrested.'

He threw his head back and laughed, and she

laughed too, then said through her laughter: 'No, really, I meant it. Oh, listen, that must be twelve o'clock striking. I think you should go.'

'I'm sure I should,' said Mr Charles, rising. 'Well, come and see me off. And this time I promise not to assault you. Though if you really didn't mind...'

They had reached the door. She gave him a quick smile and then obligingly bent her head.

'Thank you ... it's exactly like a chicken. And I speak from experience. At the age of six, mother-less and miserable, I did kiss a chicken. It hated it.'

'This chicken didn't,' said Clare looking up at him.

'This chicken is an out-and-out baggage – and in a certain amount of danger of being treated as one.'

She moved quickly away from him, then said seriously: 'I'm sorry, honestly. I keep doing and saying things without thinking. I suppose it's because I really do trust you now. You might be an uncle. Not that I ever had one.'

'And you haven't got one now,' said Mr Charles, laughing. 'Go right ahead. I don't mind your making fun of me.'

'But I'm not, I swear I'm not.'

For a silent second he looked down into her earnest eyes, his own eyes puzzled as well as amused. Then he said, 'I think I shall allow myself to believe you. Well, good night, and don't worry about tomorrow – or about absolutely anything.'

'I absolutely won't,' said Clare.

301

5

Mr Charles

Clare woke soon after eight feeling extremely cheerful. She bathed, dressed and ordered a large breakfast from her fatherly floor waiter, with whom she enjoyed a pleasant chat. He managed to combine a gentle playfulness with extreme respect, a manner she found admirably suited to the dignity of the hotel.

Soon after she began breakfast the telephone rang. She answered it eagerly and was sorry to learn that Nurse Brown was not summoning her. 'You won't be needed this morning, dear. Mr Rowley wants to talk to Mr Charles. But he says will you come in for lunch? Say, twelve-thirty. Now have your breakfast and go out for a walk. It's a lovely day.'

Clare, getting ready to go out, felt a lack of enthusiasm for her blue cloak over her grey dress, now worn for the third day running. If Mr Charles wanted to force a new outfit on her it would require a minimum of forcing.

She had been greatly struck with his view that she needed to be dressed 'very simply, at enormous expense'. Up to now she had taken little pleasure in her clothes. Ready-made ones neither fitted nor suited her; those achieved with the aid of the village dressmaker were usually

302

neat, sometimes pretty, but invariably un-distinguished. Clare, as usual, blamed herself for this; she could not create interesting designs or even choose the right ones to have copied. But this morning she had, anyway, a great desire to think about clothes. She would imagine herself possessed of unlimited money and go window shopping.

She did so, with waning enthusiasm, finally coming to the conclusion that the simple, enormously expensive clothes which now hovered before her mind's eye like some holy grail seldom came from firms which displayed their goods in windows, though one or two fur coats seemed tolerable.

By twelve o'clock she was back in her room getting ready to go to the suite, which she did on the dot of twelve-thirty. She felt extremely nervous when Nurse Brown took her into the sitting-room. Then she sighted Mr Charles and was suddenly confident.

He shook her warmly by the hand and said: 'I've heard so much about you that I feel I've already met you.'

'I feel just the same about you,' said Clare, her *sangfroid* fully equal to his; she wondered if he was as astonished by this as she was.

'I said you'd like each other, didn't I?' Mr Rowley beamed on them; then went on with ponderous playfulness. 'But don't forget she's mine, Charles. Nurse, I've promised myself to *see* her again. I think we've time before luncheon.'

Ordeal by lamp then proceeded and Clare was surprised to find that she now did not mind it at all. This was partly because she no longer found Mr Rowley frightening or even repulsive. It was also because she became interested in comparing his face with his grandson's. They stared at her and she smilingly stared back.

It struck her that, whereas Mr Rowley looked slightly foreign, Mr Charles looked completely English. And it was just possible to believe that Mr Rowley might once have been darkly hand-some, whereas Mr Charles could never have been anything but – rather less darkly – extremely ugly, in a humorous, sardonic way she found reassur-ing. She had no idea why she did and was content to have none; the reassurance was enough.

Meanwhile, the two Mr Rowleys were discuss-ing her freely. The elder asked for confirmation of his belief that her hair was the colour of ripe corn.

'Exactly,' said Mr Charles.

'And her eyes – look at me, child – a very deep blue?'

'Sapphire,' said Mr Charles.

'And the mouth unusually small?'

'A veritable rosebud,' said Mr Charles, winking at Clare. Her hair was a very pale shade of gold, her eyes a pale, though vivid, shade of blue, her mouth as unlike a rosebud as Nature and a lipstick could make it. But she interpreted the wink to mean that Mr Rowley should be allowed to 'see' her as he wished to, and she was content to let him.

The lamp was then put away and lunch, already ordered by Mr Charles, was served. It was the most interesting meal Clare had ever eaten and even Mr Rowley admitted that he could taste far more than he usually could, possibly because Mr Charles, who had insisted that Nurse Brown should eat with them, himself helped the old gentleman to eat and described exactly what was being eaten. Everyone was gay; even the waiters seemed to be enjoying themselves. Nurse Brown had indeed been right in saying: 'Life's quite different when Mr Charles is with us.'

The gaiety continued after lunch, when Mr Charles gave some amusing descriptions of recent adventures 'abroad'. Clare was quite unable to distinguish fact from fiction. Her guess was that he did go abroad very frequently for short periods and thus had material to draw on and embroider. In mentioning a few days spent in Switzerland, he broke off to say to her, 'Oh, my grandfather has told me whose daughter you are. I should think it's more than probable that your father's in Switzerland. If so, I might be able to get news of him. Would you like me to try?'

She considered, then said: 'He could let us know where he is if he wanted to. Perhaps he's as anxious to get away from his family as from the police. And I can understand it. I love my family – I really do – and yet I don't want to let them know where I am. But perhaps that's because Aunt Winifred's there.'

'Ah, the terrible Aunt Winifred,' said Mr Rowley, smiling.

'To whom we owe the pleasure of your company. But I wonder how much she really had to do with it. I think, Charles, this is a very unconventional young lady who wishes to lead her own life unencumbered by family ties.'

'My family wouldn't want to tie me. They'll be only too happy if I can earn a living – not to mention surprised. I've always been the family fool.'

'Now you mustn't ask us to believe that, dear,' said Nurse Brown.

'But it's true. Anyway, I'm a fool compared with my brothers and sister. They're really clever. No one could accuse me of that.'

'How clever of you to use the word "accuse",' said Mr Charles.

'All really clever women conceal their cleverness,' said Mr Rowley.

'I've never had to do any concealing,' said Clare.

Judging by their laughter, none of them believed her. And she suddenly did not quite believe herself. Perhaps she wasn't such a fool, after all. How kind they all were – and how *very* happy she was! She gave a little sigh of pure pleasure.

When Mr Rowley, not very willingly, had allowed them to leave him alone for his nap, Mr Charles said he would take her for a walk.

'That's right,' said Nurse Brown. 'And mind you look after her well.'

'I *was* thinking of abducting her,' said Mr Charles. 'Nurse, you will dress for dinner tonight, please. Your wine velvet.'

'He gave it to me,' Nurse Brown informed Clare, with satisfaction. 'Now hurry up and get your cloak, dear. Looks as though there might be a good sunset. It'll be ever so nice, walking in the park.'

But they went to no park. As soon as they left the hotel Mr Charles said: 'Let's buy something. I'm happy and that always gives me an appetite for spending. What do you want? Say the first thing that comes into your mind.'

'Toothpaste,' said Clare. 'I really do need some.'

'Well, you're not getting any. We've hardly any time before the shops shut.'

He took her first to a florist; never had she seen such superb flowers. He asked if she had any special favourites.

'No, I love them all, though I'm very bad at arranging them.'

'How original of you. Most women think they're good at it – and seldom are. These are *my* favourites.'

He bought three dozen roses of a kind she had never seen before, deep pink with a golden heart.

'And now let's make a dash for Bond Street.' He took her by the arm and hurried her along.

In Bond Street he bought chocolates, a round box as big as a car wheel. 'We can *roll* that back if we can't pick up a taxi. What next? Scent? No, we must have more time when we choose that.'

'Would that very grand shop over there sell toothpaste?' said Clare.

'Oh, bother your toothpaste – use soap. I want to get you to a jeweller's.'

'No,' said Clare. 'No jewellery.'

'I thought we'd decided you weren't con-ventional.'

'Anyway, it's too late. All the shops are closing.'

'We may just get inside – and if we do, you can't shame me by refusing.'

'I wonder if I would,' said Clare, with genuine speculation. 'Well, we shall never know. Look!'

The jeweller's he was hurrying her to was noticeably closed.

'Then we'll look in the window and you shall tell me what you'd like.'

'Oh, just the largest tiara.'

'Take care, you might get it tomorrow – and it really wouldn't suit you. Seriously, tell me what you admire. I'll promise not to force it on you.'

She gave the matter some consideration and then said, 'There's nothing I *terribly* like. I suppose that sounds silly.'

'It sounds as if you've very good taste. All the workmanship's excellent but the designs are dull. Those pearls are good. I fancy pearls are your jewels – orientals, of course, not cultured.'

'Well, naturally,' said Clare, laughing. 'Can one really tell the difference?'

'I can. Anyway, the difference in value is of the utmost significance. Without value, jewels mean nothing; and their meaning is an integral part of their beauty. They're as symbolic as a religious symbol.'

He hailed a passing taxi and, once inside, surveyed his purchases ruefully. 'I've nowhere near assuaged my spending appetite. And how strictly conventional we've been – flowers, chocolates, I wonder I didn't buy you a pair of gloves; even in my grandfather's youth, young ladies could accept those.'

'Well, so could I,' said Clare.

'And a dress to go with the gloves and a coat to go with the dress? Not that I haven't affectionate memories of that most peculiar cloak.'

'All right,' said Clare.

He laughed at her cheerful acceptance. 'But you're still adamant about jewellery? Is there anything else you draw the line at?'

'Well, furs, probably. And money, of course. Except my wages. Not that I've come by any yet.'

'You could have a loan against your salary.'

She opened her handbag and showed him her unchanged five-pound note.

'Plutocrat! Well, we'll go shopping again tomorrow, won't we?'

'Yes, please,' said Clare.

She enjoyed every minute of the short taxi drive. The home-going crowds on the pavements, the bright shop windows beyond them, the western sky glimpsed at cross streets, all gave her enormous pleasure. She tore the wrapping off the roses so that she could smell them, then turned to Mr Charles and said: 'Thank you.'

He smiled. 'You have a charming trick of being just a little late with your thanks and then completely making up for it.'

Back at the hotel he carried the roses and chocolates into her room, where a chambermaid was turning down the bed. He sent her for a vase.

'Won't she think it peculiar, your coming in here?' said Clare.

'My dear child, you must never give a thought to what servants think of you.'

She looked at him curiously. 'Every now and then you turn into a very arrogant person. *I* was brought up not to call servants "servants".'

'I wasn't. And until they quite die out – and

hotels like this are among the few places where they haven't – I shall go on calling them servants and treating them as servants.'

'But you were so nice to the waiters at lunch.'

'Of course. But I treated them as waiters. And so did you, by letting them wait on you.'

'I always feel a bit apologetic about it,' said Clare.

'How very shocking. Either wait on yourself or be waited on with a good grace, which means accepting servants as servants. Nowadays it's little more than an elaborate pretence – on both sides. But one must either pretend properly or completely rule out the idea of one human being waiting on another, as perhaps we ought. But I don't intend to until I have to. I must go. My grandfather will be awake.'

Clare, waiting for the vase to put her roses in, thought over what he had said and found she could accept his point of view; yet she also resented it. She was now on his side of the dividing line between master and servant but she had scarcely been that on their first meeting. She had been the chambermaid kissed by the rake. He had since apologized but only, presumably, because he had realized she was on his side of the line. Her feelings were extremely confused, as she was attracted by the arrogance she resented and incapable of understanding why. One direct result was that when the real chambermaid, a pretty Irish girl, returned she was given half a dozen roses and an apron-pocketful of chocolates.

She was touchingly grateful, especially for the roses; but her manner, Clare noted, underwent a

310

change Mr Charles would not have approved of. The word 'miss' disappeared from her vocabulary and, before leaving, she gave Clare a shrewd look and said: 'Good luck, dear.' Her meaning was obvious – and startling. Clare reminded herself, 'Never give a thought to what servants think.' Well, it would need practice.

When she had arranged her roses (if one had enough of them, they did the job for themselves) she dressed and went to the suite, feeling she need no longer wait to be summoned. Now for Nurse Brown in wine velvet! But she found the nurse still in her uniform and looking worried.

'Plans have been changed, dear. Mr Rowley's having his dinner in bed, with just Mr Charles there. Seems they've things to discuss – though, goodness knows they talked enough this morning. Funny, I thought the old gentleman was looking forward to a dinner party.'

'Perhaps he's feeling ill,' said Clare.

'Says not. But he didn't seem quite himself, after his nap. Anyway, he wanted just to be with Mr Charles. Their meal's gone in already. You're to have yours with me.'

Clare was disappointed, having hoped for a dinner as gay as lunch had been. She asked if they could wait a while. 'I'm not very hungry.'

'Oh, you will be when we start, dear, because Mr Charles has ordered dinner for us. He said I wasn't to fob you off with any old thing. The way he chooses food always gives me an appetite.'

Clare, too, found her appetite stimulated, as much by the fact that Mr Charles had taken the trouble to choose her dinner as by what he had

311

chosen. But it was not a cheerful meal as Nurse Brown was worried about Mr Rowley. When the waiters came to remove his dinner table, she left her coffee and went into his room with them. She came back more worried than ever.

'Something *is* wrong – he's eaten hardly anything. But I don't think he's ill, because Mr Charles is looking as cross as cross and he never would if the old gentleman wasn't well. Mr Charles is ever so sympathetic. Oh, dear, I do hope they haven't had a disagreement – so soon! And just when we've got you, and everything seemed so nice. You'd better wait a while, in case Mr Rowley wants you to read to him. I'll be in my room, having a word with the night nurse.'

Clare sat by the fire with volumes of Dumas beside her but found she had no desire to read. Usually reading was her means of escape from life. Now life had become more interesting than any book and she wanted its pages to go on turning.

Soon after nine o'clock Mr Charles came into the room. She asked if Mr Rowley was ready for her.

'He won't need you tonight,' said Mr Charles, closing the door.

As he came towards her she saw that he was looking unusually serious; indeed, his mouth was set quite grimly. She asked if Mr Rowley was ill.

'No, merely a little distressed because I must leave him so soon. Unfortunately, I have urgent business abroad.'

'Oh, goodness!' She stared at him in dismay. 'Really abroad – or will you just pretend again?'

He frowned. 'Did Nurse Brown tell you about that?'

'You did, too. On our first night together.'

His expression relaxed. 'How delightful you make that occasion sound. Yes, I remember now.' He sat silent for a moment, then said, 'No, not really abroad. But this time I was pretending to you, not my grandfather, to avoid explanations. And you mustn't ask me for any. I can only tell you that I expect shortly to leave the hotel. So I'm afraid this must be goodbye.'

'Do you mean for ever?'

'That does sound depressingly final. But I rather think it would be as well. I'm hardly a suitable friend for you.'

'*I* think you are. Still, just as you please, of course.' She tried and failed to sound casual.

'My dear child! Do you *want* to go on being friends with me?'

'I seem to,' said Clare.

'Why, exactly?'

'I suppose I must like you. And I so seldom do like anyone.'

He smiled. 'I hadn't realized you were such a misanthrope. Well, I like you, too, as you must have guessed. Dear me, I'd no idea I'd made such headway. When did you decide to like me?'

'I didn't decide – I've only just noticed it, really. Though I did decide I could let myself be friends with you, when you told me ... well, that it would be all right. You remember? Last night, in my room.'

'Of course I remember. I managed to make you believe you could trust me, and so you can.'

313

'And it's been such fun all today – going shopping and everything.'

'That reminds me: as I shan't be available for our shopping expedition tomorrow, I'll have some clothes sent in for you to choose from, and a fitter to make any alterations you need.'

She shook her head. 'I should choose the wrong ones. I always do. And it'd be no fun without you. Besides, I can't accept any more presents – from someone who doesn't like me enough to see me again.'

'Of course I like you enough. I may be able to arrange something later. No, I mustn't undertake that. The whole situation's become impossible, and the damnable thing is that I can't tell you why.'

'Perhaps I can guess,' said Clare. 'Is it that you find it a bore, being friendly with anyone as ... as innocuous as I am?'

He looked amused. 'You still think of me as a ravening wolf. No, my child, it would never be a bore – though I'll admit it just might become a *strain*. I doubt if I'm really cut out to remain an everlasting uncle. But that's not the trouble now. What can I say to stop you from jumping to wrong conclusions? This room's unbearably hot.'

He went to a window, flung it open and stood looking out. After a moment, she joined him and waited silently. The autumn night was misty, the trees in the park motionless, the air damply cold by contrast with that of the overheated room.

At last, without turning to her, he said: 'You'd get a plausible lie if I could think of one but as I can't you must have a portion of the truth. My

314

grandfather wants me to do something which is quite out of the question. I've told him so but he's determined to undermine me – and if I let him, I should never forgive myself. So I must clear out at once and stay away indefinitely.'

'But surely that will upset him terribly? It might even make him ill.'

'If so, I can't help it. I wouldn't give into him now even to save his life.'

She was shocked by the harshness of his tone. Very tentatively she said, 'But mightn't you be sorry later? He's so old and frail. Couldn't you possibly do what he wants?' Her voice became coaxing. 'Then we could all go on being happy.'

He turned towards her so suddenly that she backed a step.

'Do you *know* what he wants?'

'Me? How could I?'

He looked at her searchingly. 'You might conceivably guess.'

'Do you mean it's something to do with me?'

'I can't tell you any more, Clare. But it's just possible my grandfather might, after I've gone. If so, will you promise not to walk out on him – anyway, without giving me the chance to persuade you not to? Nurse Brown will always know where to find me.'

'Well, of course I'll promise. But can't you *please* tell me what the trouble is?' She looked at him miserably. 'If it is to do with me, if I'm to blame in some way…'

'It's abominable to bewilder you like this. Go back to the fire. You're shivering. Give me a moment to think.'

After a few seconds he closed the window and followed her.

'If I tell you the whole truth, will you try not to count it against him? You mean so much to him, Clare, and I'm so desperately afraid you'll leave him.'

'I won't, truly I won't,' she assured him earnestly.

'I must risk it, anyway. I can't leave you in the dark. Now listen, my dear. You said something to him, in all innocence I'm almost sure...'

He broke off as the door was opened by Nurse Brown.

'Mr Rowley's asking for you, Mr Charles.'

After a second's hesitation he said he would come at once, then turned to Clare. 'You should go to bed. We've no right to let you work such late hours.'

'I haven't done any work today,' said Clare. 'And it's too early for bed.'

'Well, go off duty, anyway. You can read in your room.'

He looked at her very directly and then gave her the suspicion of a wink, which she instantly took to mean he would come and visit her. She flashed him a smile and said she would go at once.

'Good night, then.'

'Good night. And please say good night to Mr Rowley for me.'

'I'll remember to.'

She hurried to her room and sat down to wait – and to think. What could she possibly have said to cause trouble? She cast her mind back over the hours she had been forced to talk to Mr Rowley – about her home, her family, her childhood, her schooldays, books, the house in the walled garden... She could disinter nothing which could have led to his asking Mr Charles to do something unreasonable. Perhaps the whole thing was nonsense, two men being obstinate and proud. Mr Rowley at least had the excuse of old age. Mr Charles ought to give in, and once he had told her the truth, surely she could persuade him to? Of course she could; she was suddenly confident of it.

By eleven o'clock she was less confident. Suppose he hadn't really meant to come and see her? Or suppose he had changed his mind? Suppose he actually went without seeing her? He had shown he didn't *want* to explain...

The telephone rang. She rushed to answer it and heard his voice.

'Clare? I'm speaking to you from my room. I'd hoped to come to you but now my grandfather has sent for me again.'

She said eagerly, 'I don't mind how late you come.'

'Well, I do. I shan't come now. It's possible that he's decided to see reason; if so, I shall be here in the morning. If not, I'll get in touch with you – that's a promise. Now go to sleep. Good night, my dear.'

'But please...'

He had rung off. For a moment she considered ringing him back – or should she intercept him on his way to Mr Rowley? It wasn't fair to leave her in suspense... She opened her door and looked along the quiet corridor, only to see Mr Charles enter the suite and close the door behind him.

Well, at least she had his promise. And his tone when he said, 'Good night, my dear,' had been very kind – even if he had hung up on her. She went to bed and to sleep.

At eight o'clock next morning the telephone woke her. She answered it sleepily.

Mr Charles, in a voice she scarcely recognized, said: 'Clare, I have bad news for you. My grandfather is dead.'

6

The Keys

After a few gasped words of dismay she had said
she would come at once. But Mt Charles had
told her not to, saying there was nothing she
could do.

'But I'd like to come – really! You must be
dreadfully upset.'

'Of course. But you can't help me. Stay where
you are. I've rung up to make sure you do.'

'But–'

'Don't argue, Clare. Just give me your word you
won't leave your room until you're sent for.'

She had done as he asked. Now, having
dressed, she waited miserably. Sorry as she was
about Mr Rowley she was even more distressed
by the harshness of Mr Charles's tone. She tried
to believe his own distress accounted for it but
could not help fearing he might, in remorse for
quarrelling with Mr Rowley, blame her for –
somehow – having had a share in it. And how
awful that she had warned him he might be sorry
later!

Around nine-thirty Nurse Brown telephoned.

'You can come in now, dear. They've taken Mr
Rowley away.'

Clare found the door of the suite open, as was
every door within and most of the windows. It

seemed to her that even the memory of Mr Rowley was being driven out.

'Couldn't he have stayed here in peace until the funeral?' she said, unhappily.

'Not in a hotel, dear. You couldn't expect it. Mr Charles is seeing to everything.'

Clare had now realized that Mr Charles was not in the suite. She asked when he would be back.

'Not for a day or two, he said; no doubt he'll be ringing me up. I shall be staying on here for a while and he hoped you'd be kind enough to keep me company. I told him you'd be entitled to a month's salary and, of course, he agreed. And he said how very sorry he was this should have happened so soon after you came to us.'

'I still can't take it in,' said Clare. 'It was so terribly sudden.'

'Death's never sudden when a man's ninety,' said Nurse Brown.

Clare was surprised to find how calm and almost cheerful the nurse seemed. Perhaps her professional acceptance of death ruled out personal regrets; or, rather, any display of them, for there was no doubt of the tenderness in her voice when she told Clare Mr Rowley had died in his sleep: 'Just as I always hoped he might. But I wasn't able to be with him, like I wanted. Well, that's my loss, not his. He couldn't have looked more peaceful.'

The night nurse had found Mr Rowley dead just before dawn. She had summoned Nurse Brown, who had waked Mr Charles. 'Poor soul, he was shattered. But I'm thankful he was here

320

when it happened.'

'Were they – was everything all right between them?' Clare's voice dwindled as she saw the nurse look at her quickly.

'How do you mean, dear?'

Clare thankfully remembered a justification for her question. 'Well, last night you were worried about them.'

Nurse Brown looked away. 'Oh, that was just my imagination. I'm sure they had ever such a happy evening together.

'Mr Charles didn't go to bed until nearly midnight. Now, have you had your breakfast?'

Clare said she didn't want any.

'I know how you feel, dear, but you must eat. And frankly I'll be glad of something myself. Just ring for the waiter, will you? And after breakfast perhaps you'll help me to pack Mr Rowley's belongings. I must send for his trunks.'

The trunks, when they were eventually brought to the suite, proved to be old-fashioned, luxurious and huge, capable of holding far more than there was to be packed in them. Clare was astonished that Mr Rowley had retained so few clothes.

'You see, he never went out,' Nurse Brown explained. 'That is, not for the last three years. Lots of things were sent to charities – refugees and the like.'

'One would have thought he'd have had more personal possessions, photographs, souvenirs.'

'There were never any here – not since I came, anyway. Of course he couldn't see very much. By the way, dear, you're to have those books you were going to read to him. I asked Mr Charles if I should send them back but he said his grandfather would have wished you to have them.'

Clare's spirits, already low, sank lower. Though delightful in itself, the set of Dumas seemed so like a farewell present – along with a month's salary.

'I suppose I'll have to look for another job,' she said gloomily.

'Whenever you like, unless I have to be out. One of us must be here in case Mr Charles rings up.'

'I don't know where to go, except Miss Gifford's. I could telephone her. But she won't be there this morning as it's Saturday.'

In any case, Clare would not have telephoned. She felt incapable of it until she had been in touch with Mr Charles; though what she hoped of him she had no idea. Even if he had not turned against her, he was unlikely to know of a job she was suited for – as hardly any such jobs existed. Already she had been overtaken by her old sense of spineless inadequacy.

The day dragged on, punctuated by meals served by the fatherly floor waiter, now positively motherly in his desire to sympathize. Clare was left much alone as Nurse Brown, after lunch, went to write letters and after dinner decided to get an early night. By then Clare realized that the nurse no longer wanted to talk and that her manner, when she could not avoid talking, had become guarded. While helping to pack Mr Rowleys clothes, Clare had asked various questions about him and Mr Charles, only to be gently stonewalled again and again by a vague 'I couldn't say, I'm sure, dear'. The nurse had spoken fairly freely about her own plans: she was going to retire and live with a widowed sister in Birmingham. 'I've saved quite a bit, and Mr Charles told me this morning that I'd never need to worry.' But as regards anything approaching gossip her shutters were now up.

Clare spent the evening reading *Louise de la Vallière*. Ever after, she was to associate that book with these days of waiting.

There were three more of them ahead of her. On the Sunday Nurse Brown only appeared at meals; she spoke of having to write more letters and sort all her belongings before she began packing them. She had now discarded her uniform and looked smaller, older and less impressive. On the Monday she went shopping: 'You won't mind staying in, dear? There's so much I need to buy before I leave London.' On the Tuesday she shopped again. It rained all day, the fatherly floor waiter was off-duty, and by the late afternoon Clare's low-spirited lethargy had changed to such acute misery that she made one of her rare attempts at self-analysis. Surely her circumstances didn't warrant such utter wretchedness?

She would have a month's salary (not that she'd ever discovered what her salary was to have been); a set of Dumas (possibly valuable but she would never sell it); and a superb dressing-gown (which had put her off all the other clothes she possessed). Quite a lot to have achieved in less than a week ... and Mr Charles *might* know of some job for her. If only he would ring up. It was this waiting that was getting her down; this waiting, waiting, waiting for the telephone to ring! But it would be even better if he would walk in – while Nurse Brown was out.

Her longing to see him was so intense that she suddenly wondered if she had fallen in love with him. But she was instantly sure she hadn't. His age would not have worried her (the characters she admired in history or novels were usually pretty mature) but he really was very ugly and most unromantic (though she still thought their first meeting romantic in its own right). All she felt for him was a comfortable sort of liking. 'And that was very important to me,' she told herself and remembered he had called her a mis-anthrope. She treasured the word because he had used it.

Nurse Brown at last came in, laden with purchases and willing to talk about them. And she remained fairly sociable throughout dinner, during the course of which she said she hoped to leave London in about a week. 'My room won't be ready till then. My sister's having it done over for me.'

'Shall I have to leave here when you do?' asked Clare.

'I couldn't say, I'm sure, dear,' said Nurse Brown, and changed the subject.

Again Clare sat reading till midnight, vainly willing the telephone to ring. As if to spite her, it eventually rang the next morning before she entered the suite.

Nurse Brown told her Mr Charles had sounded more cheerful. 'I suppose we should call him "Mr

Rowley" now. He says the dear old gentleman was cremated yesterday and everything went off nicely.'

(Did cremations, Clare wondered, ever not go off nicely?)

The nurse was continuing: 'I'm to take Mr Rowley's clothes to an address Mr Charles has given me – some charity; I'll get a taxi this afternoon. And you're to wait in and be ready dressed to go out at three o'clock.'

'Out? Where?' said Clare eagerly.

'I couldn't say, I'm sure, dear. Mr Charles said he'd let you know later. He'll probably telephone you.'

'Do you think he might have some job in mind for me?'

But all she got was another 'I couldn't say, I'm sure, dear,' and Nurse Brown turned away to order breakfast.

For the first time since Mr Rowley's death Clare enjoyed her food. Her lethargy was replaced by pleasurable excitement; the telephone became her friend, though she resented the fact that at two-thirty it still had not rung. By then lunch was over and Nurse Brown was ready to go out.

'Get your outdoor things and wait here for your call,' she told Clare. 'I've got to go somewhere else after taking Mr Rowley's clothes so I want to be off.'

Clare got back to the suite as Nurse Brown was tipping porters for taking down Mr Rowley's trunks. 'That's almost cleared the Beggars' Bowl,' she said, 'and I'm nearly spent out. Mr Charles is posting me a cheque. Have you any money to spare, dear?'

Clare produced her still unchanged five-pound note.

'Thanks, dear. I'll get it changed downstairs, take a couple of pounds, and have the rest sent up to you. Put some of it in the Beggars' Bowl, will you? I'll straighten it all out when I get Mr Charles's cheque. Bye-bye, dear.'

Once more Clare was left staring at a silent telephone.

Just before three the door bell buzzed. She opened the door expecting the change from her five-pound note, but the page who stood outside only handed her a letter.

'For you, miss, and the car's waiting.'

It was the page who had first shown her to the suite, just a week ago. She remembered he had hoped she would get the job and that she hadn't been able to tip him. Now she gave him the last coin in the Beggars' Bowl before opening her letter.

The envelope contained two keys, one large, one small, and a note written in a heavy, black, strongly characterized writing which seemed to her particularly representative of Mr Charles.

My dear Clare,
I have sent my car for you. The driver knows where to go. Please don't ask him questions.

The two keys will, I think, speak for themselves. Use them. Look around. Do a little quiet considering. Wait until I join you.

Charles Rowley.

326

She read the letter twice, then dashed after the departing page, calling that he was to hold the lift for her. As they went down she remembered she hadn't had the change from her five-pound note; but no matter, as she would be meeting Mr Charles. Indeed, she rather liked the idea of venturing into the unknown without any money at all.

Bewildered, she was also enchanted; and the bewilderment was part of the enchantment. Getting into the large black car she smiled to think Mr Charles had imagined she might question the chauffeur. Not for worlds would she have known where she was going and she made no attempt to guess what was ahead of her. She merely gazed out at the sunny autumn afternoon and journeyed on in a haze of hope.

But she did wonder why those completely silent keys were supposed to speak for themselves.

The car took her up Bond Street; she recognized with pleasure the chocolate shop she had visited with Mr Charles. (Hardly any of her chocolates were eaten but her lovely roses had now begun to fall.) Was that the jeweller's where they had window-shopped? From then on, there were no more landmarks for her and she could not have said if she was being driven north, south, east or west. Vaguely she noticed wide, busy streets, then the entrance to a park and then a pleasant white church. Soon after this, they turned off the main road into a quiet residential district of old, well-kept houses; and here, in a narrow tree-lined street, the car drew up.

The chauffeur helped her out and she found herself facing a high garden wall with a green wooden door in it. And at last the keys spoke.

She took them from her handbag and fitted the largest into the keyhole of the green door. The chauffeur stood by until she had opened the door, then saluted and went back to the car. Soon after she passed through the doorway and closed the door she heard him drive away.

She stood quite still, looking around her. The moment she had seen the door in the wall she had remembered Mr Rowley's walled garden. So it was here in London, not outside some continental capital city. There was the lily pond, drained now, and two large bushes still retaining some shrivelled heads of lilac. Except for a scatter of recently fallen leaves the little enclosed garden was perfectly tidy, with the arid, minimum tidiness of a grave when its upkeep is paid for.

Ahead of her was the shuttered house. Walking towards it, she tried to remember what Mr Rowley had said about the interior ... something about a room seen across a lighted hall. She had a quick expectation of cobwebbed chandeliers, a setting for the Sleeping Beauty without any occupants – or would everything be shrouded in dustsheets? She turned the small key in the lock and opened the door.

The little hall was as tidy as the little garden. *Here* were no dust-sheets, no cobwebs – and no glass chandelier; the brass light-fitting hanging from the ceiling had three thick white globes and was a gaselier.

The doors opening onto the hall were festooned with maroon velvet draperies edged with a fringe of black, silk-covered balls. An empty brass *jardiniere* stood by a carved black oak hatstand of staggering ugliness. 'Well, at least it's a bearable floor,' she thought, looking down at the black and white tiles. 'I wonder they didn't cover it with lino.'

Opening the door nearest to her she peered into a room from which shutters excluded the daylight; but she had left the front door open and enough light came in from the hall to show her this was the dining-room. She noticed a yellow oak sideboard inlayed with copper panels, an elaborately draped mantel border of peacock blue wool which clashed with the blue china above it, and a copper gaselier with pink globes over the table. The idea of champagne and caviar consumed under gaslight struck her as ludicrous.

She closed the door on the setting of Mr Rowley's romantic suppers and opened the door opposite the front door. The room she now entered was shuttered like the dining-room and much larger; the daylight she let in only made a bright path down its length, leaving much of it dim. But she could see it was a drawing-room, beflounced in silk and satin, with chiffon and lace on the many cushions and the ruched shades of the wrought-iron standard lamps. Colours were even uglier than in the hall and dining-room; the upholstery was of embossed tobacco velvet, the draperies a dark yellow. There was too much detail to take in quickly but one problem was instantly solved for her: this was where Mr Rowley had kept his photographs – dozens of them, mainly in heavy silver frames of tortured design. She would look at them when she had explored the rest of the house.

The only other door from the hall opened into a passage leading to the kitchen. She disliked kitchens even when they were pleasant, and one quick glance into this highly unpleasant one's dim dankness sent her hurrying back to the daylight in the hall.

Now for the bedrooms – if she could see them. She was thankful to find, as she turned the bend of the little staircase, that there was a skylight above the square landing.

One bedroom door stood open. Through it could be seen a large double bed, canopied and side-curtained in some drab material suggestive of tapestry. Staring with distaste she had a vivid mental picture of Mr Rowley sitting up in his bed at the hotel, smilingly remembering this most depressing house. Her thoughts of Mr Rowley young and Mr Rowley old were a confusion of repulsion and pity, and it was, she vaguely knew, the thought of the young Mr Rowley which she found repulsive.

She would explore no further. On the landing was a circular red ottoman, buttoned and heavily fringed. She sat down on it under the skylight and tried to think clearly.

Why had Mr Charles sent her here? Obviously Mr Rowley must have told him of the talk about the house with the walled garden – which must have impressed the old gentleman far more than she'd realized; though she did remember his pleasure. But why had she to see the house? And why had Mr Charles told her to do a little quiet considering?

It then occurred to her he might mean to offer her the job of looking after the place. Certainly someone was looking after it now; it was scrupulously clean. She thought the cleanliness increased the ugliness; cobwebs might have been kinder, might have spun a merciful veil of romance. But nothing could have made that drably-curtained bed romantic. She looked at it again – and hastily looked away.

Should she go down and study the photographs? She found she had no desire to – nor, indeed, to do anything, even to move; though she did not at all care for being where she was, so close to that sinister bed. She no longer felt pleasurably enchanted but was weighed down, rendered inert, by depression which had in it an element of fear.

Her heart gave a leap. Surely that was the door in the garden wall opening – and closing? Footsteps now, on the flagged path...

Then, from the hall, Mr Charles called: 'Clare, where are you?'

'Here!' Springing up, she answered him gladly, instantly released from inertia, depression and fear.

7

Charles

She saw him as she reached the bend of the stairs and stopped dead, looking down on him. He was standing under the brass gaselier, wearing a long dark coat which made him seem even taller than usual. For days she had been steadily improving his looks. Now she had again to accept his true ugliness. It didn't make her any less glad to see him.

He was saying, 'I'm sorry you've had to find your way around in this gloom. The woman who looks after this place should have opened the shutters. She always used to, when I wrote to say I was coming.'

'It doesn't matter,' said Clare. She came down the last stairs slowly, noting that he was not smiling. Her own smile faded.

'We'll have some more light.' He went into the drawing-room and tried to open a shutter. Its small knob came off in his hand.

Clare, following him, told him not to bother. 'I'm used to the gloom now. And this house would be even sadder by the full light of day. Why did you send me here?'

'I'll explain later. Sit down. How are you?' He was smiling now but his tone lacked warmth. 'I trust Nurse Brown has been kind to you?'

'Perfectly kind but very unforthcoming. Did you tell her not to talk to me? I mean about you and Mr Rowley?'

He returned her direct gaze. 'I did. She probably overheard part of my quarrel with him. I don't think she'd have told you but it seemed wiser to give her a general warning. I hardly fancied your hearing the details from her.'

Clare nodded understandingly. 'You mean you'd rather tell me yourself: you were going to, that night, only you couldn't come and see me. Will you tell me now?'

'Not yet, anyway.' He was silent for a few seconds, then spoke as if determined to be businesslike. 'Well, now: you do realize what this house was? My grandfather told you about it.'

'Hardly that,' said Clare. 'Though ... yes, I did guess he was remembering some real house. But I thought it was somewhere abroad – not here in London. How long is it since he lived here?'

'I doubt if he ever actually lived here.'

'Well, visited.'

'His last visit was three years ago. Up till then, over a very long period, he paid a yearly visit, and after his sight began to fail I always accompanied him. But I first came here long before that, when I was sixteen and considered old enough to know the details of his highly disreputable life. I felt something of a dog, particularly as he more or less told me, "Go thou and do likewise," and shortly provided the occasion. Of course, the heyday of his visits here was in the eighteen-nineties. I suspect that was the kind of visit you were inquiring about.'

333

'It was, really. Tell me about his lady.'

'Her name was legion. She was usually an actress.'

Clare looked around. 'I suppose there are photographs?'

'Not dating from the nineties. He destroyed them all when the last lady was installed, in 1900. There are plenty of her – this was his favourite. That extremely ugly frame is solid gold and the stones set in it are rubies.'

Sitting in the shaft of daylight from the open front door, she had no difficulty in seeing the photograph he handed to her. It was of a young woman with a fair, frizzy fringe, a longish face with a heavy jaw, and a cruelly treated figure; a large bust was pushed up nearly to her shoulders and massive hips sprang out below a pinched waist.

'Well?' said Mr Charles. 'Do you see the resemblance to yourself?'

She looked at him in surprise. 'But I couldn't be less like her, surely?'

'Don't be too anxious to disclaim the likeness; she was considered a beauty.' His tone hardened. 'My dear Clare, you have fair hair and blue eyes as she had. That was enough for an almost blind old man – anyway, it was after you told him you wished to be a king's mistress. She, too, had that laudable ambition.'

'How extraordinary,' said Clare. 'Though it's not so very, really. Several girls at school with me fancied the idea; we used to pick our kings. But it must have seemed a great coincidence to Mr Rowley. No wonder he was amused.'

'Not amused. Enchanted – and completely

deceived. He believed you meant what you said and of course he had no idea you knew all about him. I was a fraction suspicious from the ... and so ashamed of myself for it.'

She was obviously being accused of something – but what? 'I haven't the faintest idea what you're talking about,' she said with hauteur.

'Please stop pretending, Clare. You knew perfectly well that my grandfather had been a king.'

Indignation almost swamped her astonishment. 'I did *not* know! How could I? Nurse Brown didn't tell me.'

'Nurse Brown doesn't know. But the woman who sent you for the job does; her mother supplied my grandfather with servants when he first came to London. I called on Miss Gifford this morning and she admitted she'd told Miss ... the woman you speak of as Jane.'

'That may be, but Jane didn't mention it to me. As if I would have said what I did if I'd known he'd been a king! You must think me crude!'

'That's not a word I should ever apply to you. I thought you a very clever little schemer, just trying to ingratiate yourself. Do you swear–?' He broke off. 'But I've no right to ask that. I can see you're telling the truth. My dear, I apologize most abjectly.'

Her indignation melted. 'You don't have to, really. I can understand why you thought what you did. But you might have asked me, instead of going to Miss Gifford.' She looked at him with mild reproach.

'Again I apologize. Owing to ... certain circumstances connected with my grandfather's death

I've been mentally confused these last days. And forgive me if I don't talk about that – for the moment.'

She nodded sympathetically and chose questions he could hardly mind answering. 'When was he a king? And of what country?'

'It no longer exists as a separate entity and I doubt if its old name would mean anything to you...'

It didn't, nor did what he said about its location. Geography was one of her many weak subjects and she was always apt to confuse the Balkans with the Baltic. But she was fascinated to hear that he had once visited his grandfather's palace as an ordinary tourist. 'The architecture's delightful but the furniture and decorations are beyond belief, not unlike what you see here but on a mammoth scale. Everything had been brought over from England. He'd been educated here and always spent much time here, particularly after his wife died. He was in London when he got slung off his throne – that was in 1903. He'd anticipated it and transferred vast sums of money; also brought my eight-year-old father with him. They both became British subjects.'

'Then "Rowley" was just an incognito?'

'Chosen to please the lady of that photograph. She said it was a nickname given to a great favourite of hers, Charles II.'

'*Old* Rowley,' said Clare, knowledgeably. 'After a stallion in the royal stables.'

'Good God, did they teach you that at school?'

She laughed. 'No, I picked it up from a novel. Oh dear, I actually mentioned Charles to Mr Rowley.'

'So he told me. And you can imagine how it pleased him as he liked to believe he had Stuart blood. I have my doubts about that but he did, when young, have a look of Charles II.'

He handed her a photograph of a dark young man in full Coronation regalia, then took from a cabinet a miniature of Charles II. 'There's a grim, dissolute face,' he said as he handed her the miniature.

Again she laughed. 'But he's absolutely sweet. I've always adored him. This is like the portrait I have in my bedroom – oh, just a postcard.' She found the young Mr Rowley disappointing. His crown was on at a very comic angle and he had a bristling moustache. Still, the resemblance was there; and it now occurred to her that– She took a quick look at Mr Charles and visualized his heavy features framed by the wig in the miniature. Delighted with the result, she opened her mouth to say his own resemblance was far stronger; then, remembering he had called the miniatured face grim and dissolute, said instead: 'What happened to the lady? I suppose she's dead now?'

'She died only a couple of years after my grandfather settled in England. She was, by the way, a well-educated girl of good family, quite unlike most of his lady friends. He cared for her very deeply.'

'And always remained faithful to her memory?'

'In his fashion. He kept this house as a shrine. No other woman was ever installed here.'

'But there were other women?'

'My dear Clare! He was only in his early thirties. There were dozens of other women, right

337

up to the time when his health and his sight began to fail. That was when I first joined him at the hotel. I can't remember a time when he didn't live there, except during the war years when I got him to go into the country.'

'Was there no one but you to look after him?'

'Not since he needed looking after,' said Mr Charles. He had been moving about restlessly; now he sat, and turned to her as if asking for understanding. 'I can't tell you what a problem it's been, Clare. When I was a boy he was my idol. There was something magnificent about him, a sort of aura of kingship. And he was immensely generous to me – and to everyone else he had any dealings with. He just poured money out, especially on his ladies – their flats, allowances, settlements; even *his* fortune couldn't stand up to it for ever. Luckily I'd money of my own, left to me by my mother, and was able to go into business soon after the war was over. I've been fortunate. So he never needed to know the true state of his finances.'

'Then he wasn't rich? It was all your money?'

'I wonder why I told you all that?' said Mr Charles gloomily. 'I'm probably patting myself on the back for treating him well – trying to get rid of the guilt of causing his death. Do you remember warning me I should be sorry?'

'But I didn't mean...! Of course you didn't cause his death! When a man's ninety–'

He interrupted her. 'When a man's ninety, one should humour him – as I had done for years, God knows. Well, let's not talk about it.'

'Yes, do let's,' said Clare firmly. 'I'm sure you'll

feel better if you do. Besides, I terribly want to know. I was somehow involved in it, wasn't I? What went wrong?'

'For the first time in my life I opposed what he wanted without even a hint of tactful deception. He was pathetically easy to deceive; one only had to temporize, do a bit of inventing ... I knew exactly how to handle him. But that night of all nights I stonewalled him completely. It seemed unthinkable not to. You see, my dear, he was absolutely determined I should persuade you to become my mistress.'

Her main reaction was one of pleasure, and though she felt she mustn't show this she wasn't going to pretend she was shocked. So she said quite lightly: 'Goodness, how awful for you! Though I'm sure he meant it kindly. Couldn't you just have said you'd think it over?'

Mr Charles was looking at her in surprise. 'How remarkably well you've taken that disclosure. Of course I ought to have done just what you suggest. Though he wouldn't have left it at that.'

'If he'd lived, perhaps we could have pretended ... well, to be interested in each other.'

'That flashed through my head when I decided to tell you what the trouble was. And on my part it wouldn't have been pretence, as I'm sure you know. But it wouldn't have satisfied him for long. He was obsessed by his delightful plan for us.'

'I can see why,' said Clare. 'He thought he'd ... somehow have a share in it. I suppose it'd have been a way of re-living his youth.'

'And that idea doesn't appall you?'

'No, why should it?'

339

'Well, I've always thought women have stronger stomachs than men,' said Mr Charles.

She looked puzzled. 'It's true I do have a very strong stomach but...'

'Oh, my dear child!' He laughed, then became serious again. 'Don't you really understand what he had in mind? You ought to, knowing how he'd made you talk to him, tried to live vicariously in your life. It was a sort of mental vampirism, due to the frustrations of old age.'

She said, after a second: 'I do understand what you mean. Nurse Brown said he expected you to ... tell him all the details of your life. But what had he to live on but the lives of others? And he must have known he hadn't much time left. That's why he tried to rush you into doing what he wanted.'

'It was indeed,' said Mr Charles. 'When he sent for me again – just before I telephoned you, remember? – he told me he'd awakened from his afternoon nap with a premonition of death. He asked me at least to see that, after his death, you were provided for financially. That I could willingly promise. And I also said that, if he'd be a little patient, I'd consider asking you what *you* felt about his wishes for us. By then I had the idea of some sort of a conspiracy with you. He said: "And if I die suddenly?" I said in that case I'd promise to ask you.'

She gave herself no time to think about this before saying, 'But that was marvellous. You did humour him. So you can't possibly blame your-self for his death.'

'It was my high-handed treatment of him

earlier that did the damage; he was extremely distressed. I shall always blame myself for that.'

'Nonsense,' said Clare briskly. 'He'd already had his premonition. You might as well blame *me*, for just happening.'

'I did blame you – for trying to intrigue him. No doubt I let myself suspect you in an effort to get rid of my own guilt.'

She said reflectively, 'I shall let myself believe that; then I shan't worry about your having such a wrong idea of me. Did you send me to this sad place as a punishment?'

'I wonder. No, I don't think so. But I did want you to get the implications of this house. And it seemed a good setting for ... a scene which isn't now going to be played here.' He smiled at her. 'It would have been suitable for the girl I mistook you for but not for the girl you are.'

'Then you shouldn't have mentioned it,' said Clare. 'Now I want to know what it was.'

'Well, you probably will, eventually – in less depressing surroundings. Though I really don't know, now...' He frowned and shook his head. 'I almost wish you were the girl I mistook you for. Of course, I should like you less but even that would make it easier. My dear, you're looking as enigmatic as the Mona Lisa and considerably prettier. Am I right in thinking you guess what I was planning to ask you?'

'No guesses,' said Clare blandly, barely permitting any to herself. She continued to sit quietly waiting, still holding the miniature of Charles II; she had long since put down the photographs of Mr Rowley and his lady. Frequently, but never when the living Charles was looking, she took a satisfying glance at the long dead Charles. She sneaked one now, then abandoned Mona Lisa quiescence and said cheerfully: 'Whatever it is, need you make quite such heavy weather of it?'

'It's just that I'm conscious of betraying a trust,' said Mr Charles, unhappily. 'You have, I think, a certain confidence in me – and I deliberately created it.'

She found herself wanting both to help him and to express something that was dawning on her. 'What matters most to me is the confidence you give me in *myself*. Usually I'm ... so utterly dim. But with you, from the very beginning, I've always felt...'

He waited, then prompted her. 'Well?'

'For the first time in my life, fully alive.'

'Thank you,' he said, gravely. 'Though I don't flatter myself that I, personally, have very much to do with it. I think you are the type of woman who only comes to life fully in the company of men who admire her. It's a type of infinite value – to men: and it becomes rarer and rarer as women acquire more and more interests. I'm a man who considers the proper study of woman-kind is man – provided I'm the man. Well, you've made it easier to say what I have to say – what's the matter?'

She had shivered uncontrollably. 'There's a draught – from the front door,' she said, untruthfully, knowing she had shivered from excitement, not cold.

He went into the hall and shut the door. Now daylight came in only through the fanlight, and

342

the skylight above the stairs. Rejoining her, he said: 'Good God, we can't sit here in the dark. Let's postpone this conversation. I'll take you out to tea.'

'I don't want tea,' said Clare, very decidedly. 'And there's quite a bit of light, really. Please go on with what you'd begun to say.'

'Well, I daresay the dark will be light enough for it – though I swear I have your happiness in view.'

He lit a cigarette and, as his lighter flickered, she was reminded of their first meeting in the pitch-dark hotel bedroom, and thought of it as the perfect prelude to this moment. The shuttered, secret house had become of great value to her; she even treasured the fear she had felt while, frozen into stillness, she had gazed at the sinister bed. And though almost breathless with excitement she was no longer troubled by suspense. Having become quite sure what he was going to say, she could await it blissfully.

'Very well, then,' he said at last. 'As I pointed out less than a week ago, I'm exactly twice your age.'

'But only for a month,' she said, sweetly.

'What?'

'I shall have a birthday then. Remember, when I was one year old, you were twenty-two times my age, but I've been catching up ever since. If you go on living until you're as old as Mr Rowley was, I shall be just on seven-ninths your age.'

He laughed. 'How magnificent you are at arithmetic.'

'Not usually,' said Clare, remembering hated housekeeping books. 'But I interrupted you.'

'And I think perhaps you shouldn't – helpful though I found that interruption.' He had become more at ease. 'Let me make the worst of myself first. And the worst includes worse than my age. I'm irrevocably married to a woman I haven't even seen for over ten years. Did you realize I was married?'

She said with complete truth, 'Do you know, I never even thought about it? Anyway, it couldn't matter less.'

'Should I take that for discouragement?'

'Good gracious, no,' she said in surprise.

Again he laughed. 'Well, it might denote a complete lack of interest. But hear me out. I've kept the worst till the last. I haven't, so far, had a talent for faithfulness; and whatever I may feel about the future, you should perhaps be warned by the past. And now ... I fear there's very little on the credit side, but I honestly believe I could make you happy. For one thing, you strike me as a girl who would thrive on luxury. Not that I'm implying that you're mercenary.'

'I never quite know what that means,' said Clare. 'I wouldn't – well, do anything I didn't want to do just for money. But I do find the idea of riches attractive.'

'So do most women,' said Mr Charles, dryly. 'But you're the only one I've met who was honest enough to admit it. Well, I'm rich enough. And, of course, I should make a settlement on you. But I can't offer that as an inducement as I shall make it whatever you decide.'

'Because you promised Mr Rowley?'

'As I told you, that was a willing promise. And

you couldn't refuse me the comfort of carrying out his wishes. Well, there it is. But you don't, of course, have to decide at once. The last time we met, you were kind enough to want me for a friend. Could you now accept me as ... a friend on probation for possible promotion? My dear, am I being unbearably stilted? It's largely due to guilt. I so well remember assuring you that I never laid siege to the innocent. Well, at least I offer you a safe conduct through the besieging forces – if you want it?' He waited, then went on. 'Might I now have – oh, not a definite answer, but your first reactions to what I've asked?'

'You haven't yet asked anything,' said Clare.

He frowned. 'How unlike you to be naive! You know exactly what I'm suggesting.'

'Still, I'd like it in plain English.'

'How brutal of you – when you've helped me out so kindly up to now. All right, then.' His tone became brusque. 'I'm asking you to become my mistress.'

She gave a little sigh of satisfaction. 'Thank you, Mr Charles. It's the first time anyone's ever asked me.'

'My God, I should hope so. And is this a moment to call me "Mr"?'

'Then, thank you – Charles. Thank you very much for asking me to be your mistress – such a beautiful, romantic word, don't you think?'

'I do not,' he said, grimly. 'And I detest the thought that it should ever describe you; so much so, that I doubt if I could ever have brought myself to ask you if I hadn't promised– What's the matter?'

345

She had gasped in sharp dismay. During the last few minutes she had been triumphantly happy, at last fully aware that she was in love. She had begun to realize it on seeing him standing in the hall. Since then, the fact of his royal descent, the resemblance to her old idol, Charles II, the growing sense of intimacy between them in this house of long-ago love, all these combined to make her more, and more sure until she had experienced a flash of complete certainty with the flash of the cigarette lighter. And now...!

In a whirling moment of confusion she remembered he had made no mention of caring for her. Presumably he was, at least, attracted – or could she not even presume as much as that, considering what he'd just said? A wave of her old sense of inferiority washed over her as she asked him, 'Is it *only* because you feel you must keep your promise?'

Little short of a declaration of love would have reassured her. Instead, he merely told her not to be absurd.

She assumed a high, bright voice intended to be sophisticated. 'Poor man, what an ordeal for you! But it's all right now. You've kept your promise – and I hereby let you off. Of course I can't be your mistress, Mr Charles.'

'Might I point out that if I had my rights I should be King Charles? I doubt if you'll get another chance to be a king's mistress.'

It was too dark to see his expression but she was quite sure his tone was bantering. It both comforted and infuriated her; no doubt he *was* attracted and that was something, but how dare he treat her as a joke?

She said icily: 'I'm sorry, but I had in mind a *reigning* king.' He gave a shout of laughter. She slammed down the miniature, snatched up her handbag and ran towards the door. He called after her, 'Clare, come back!'

'Not unless you make me,' she thought, walking briskly across the hall. Opening the front door, she dropped her handbag – and picking it up, remembered it hadn't so much as a penny in it. How was she to get from wherever she was to wherever she decided to go? She'd never return to the hotel. If he let her get through the garden door she would just walk and walk until she dropped – and died, if she could possibly manage it... Her pace along the garden path slowed. Surely, surely, he would come after her? But he didn't even call to her again. She reached the door in the wall and turned the handle–

To her unbounded relief the door was locked. And the keys? Heaven be praised, she had left them in the house.

She looked back. The afternoon sun was shining in through the front door, across the hall and into the dim drawing-room, where he now sat on the edge of the table on which she had put the keys. She saw him pick up the large one, then turn to her and smile.

Neither pride nor indignation any longer supported her; she was too utterly submerged in love. She looked back pleadingly, then thought: 'Oh, God, he'll think I'm pleading for the key.'

But she had, it appeared, underestimated his powers of perception.

Interlude Under the Dome

Jane

Walking towards the house after garaging her car, Jane saw that a good fire was burning in the hall; a cheerful sight had it not indicated that Miss Winifred Carrington would be in front of the fire and alone. Richard, Jane felt sure, would prefer to shiver in his music room rather than sit with his aunt.

She went a little way beyond the house so that she could see the barn. Yes, there was a light behind the drawn curtains; never before had she known him to draw them. She would have liked to go and talk to him but perhaps he was trying to work, in which case it would be kinder to join Miss Carrington and keep that most irritating woman from disturbing him.

Why, Jane asked herself, should one so dislike a small, quiet, really very pretty old lady? And how could an old lady so lacking in personality have such an effect on the atmosphere of Dome House? Though, to be fair, no doubt the absence of Merry, Drew, and Clare affected the atmosphere as adversely as did the presence of their aunt. *Great* aunt, of course: one always had to remember Miss Carrington was said to be in her middle seventies, in spite of her comparatively unlined face. Perhaps when one reached that age

348

one would be as selfish as she was. And one didn't, really, have to do so much for her; the main burden fell on Richard. Well, one would go in and behave pleasantly.

She opened the front door and smiled brightly. 'What a lovely welcoming fire!'

'I had a lot of trouble with it,' said Miss Carrington. 'Wood isn't what it used to be. And the logs are so heavy. I asked Richard to saw them all in half but he keeps forgetting. I expect you want your tea.'

This meant Miss Carrington wanted hers. Jane said she would put the kettle on.

The kitchen, these days, was cheerless and it was difficult to find what one wanted. As Miss Carrington frequently remarked, she was no longer equal to any household tasks, so Richard always had to cope with lunch *single-handed*. He combined tidyness with vagueness, putting everything away but seldom in the right place. However, Jane soon had a tray laid and bread and butter cut. The cake tin contained nothing but crumbs. This made her feel guilty as presumably she was still in charge of the housekeeping. But there had been plenty of cake yesterday. And really when one worked all day – and no one would co-operate... Nowadays the maids only brought home and cooked something for a pretty inadequate evening meal.

She carried the tea-tray into the hall.

'No cake,' said Miss Carrington resignedly. 'We finished it at luncheon as no one had provided us with a pudding. If only Clare were here! There's still no news of her.'

'She's probably too busy to write,' said Jane.

'But it's a whole week. I came the day she left, you know.'

Cause and effect, thought Jane, who had accepted Richard's view that Clare had bolted on hearing Miss Carrington's voice.

'She'd never have gone if she'd known I was coming. She owes so much to me. And I'm very fond of her. One can't help feeling anxious.'

'But I told you,' said Jane patiently. 'She's perfectly all right. I had that letter from my friend who runs an employment agency.'

'That's hardly the same as hearing from Clare. What did the letter say, exactly?'

Was the old lady becoming senile? Day after day this question had to be answered. 'It said Clare had found work, reading to an old gentleman, and would be staying with him and his nurse at one of the very best hotels.'

'And you're sure it didn't say which hotel? I could so easily go up to London...'

'Quite sure,' said Jane, firmly and untruthfully. Clare would want no visit from her aunt.

'If she knew I was here, she'd come back at once,' said Miss Carrington.

Jane looked at her curiously. Did she really not know that Clare detested her? And was her affection for Clare genuine or did she merely hanker for someone who had waited on her? Whatever the reason, she constantly spoke of Clare, whereas she seldom so much as mentioned Drew or Merry.

This was certainly fortunate as regards Merry. According to Richard, his aunt had unquestionably accepted his statement that the child was staying with relations on their mother's side of the family. All she said was, "Really? I never knew them." And then she went on bemoaning that Clare wasn't here. 'She's aged a lot, Jane, in the five years since she lived with us; that's really why I had to let her stay. Well, she's a poor exchange for Clare.'

She was indeed, thought Jane, handing her a second cup of tea. But one was glad the girl had escaped and was doing well, according to Miss Gifford, much liked by the old gentleman and his nurse. Drew, too, seemed to have found the right job. If only Merry would write! She had now been gone thirteen days and Jane was beginning to feel the maids had been right in wishing to inform the police.

She had felt it especially this afternoon, when two girls who were exact contemporaries of Merry's had sat in her office waiting to see Miss Willy. They had seemed such *children:* one would hardly have trusted them to be on their own in London even for a day, let alone all these nights. After seeing the head mistress they had barely restrained their giggles until out in the passage and running full tilt to ... their ponies or the playing fields or the swimming pool, and then to a very good tea. Their day's work was over except for an hour's 'prep' in the evening. What would Merry be doing in the evening?

'Don't you see the resemblance yourself?'

The direct question broke Jane's thoughts; she found she had no idea what Miss Carrington had been talking about. But the quiet, plaintive voice continued and supplied a clue. 'Before my hair went white it was the same pale gold as Clare's and our eyes are just the same shade of blue.'

'Yes, indeed,' said Jane heartily. Miss Carrington's eyes were now a very faded blue but there was, if one allowed for over fifty years difference in age, some faint resemblance between her and her great-niece. Their expressions, however, were very different. Clare's, when – as at most times – it lacked animation, was merely listless. Miss Carrington invariably looked peevishly discontented.

'And even now, our figures are similar.'

This was sheer nonsense. Clare's figure, on a miniature scale, was exquisite. Miss Carrington was now flat-chested and round-shouldered. But Jane hoped her smile would pass for agreement as she said: 'You must have been an unusually pretty girl.'

'Well, I always say "See Clare and you see me as I was",' said Miss Carrington, complacently.

A gruff bark outside announced that Burly and the maids were returning from the Swan.

'I'll just have a word with them,' said Jane, anxious to escape.

'They've become very slack. They need a tight rein. You should have known this household when *I* ran it.'

Jane couldn't resist saying, 'It was beautifully run when I first came here when there was money to run it.'

'If so, that was due to the way I trained Clare. Well, I shall take a nap before dinner – not that it'll deserve that name.'

And she won't be paying for it or raising a hand

to get it, thought Jane, carrying the tea-tray to the kitchen. One tried to be pleasant to the old girl but really...!

Cook, Edith and Burly had just come in. Burly showed more pleasure on sighting his basket than the maids did on sighting their kitchen. They looked tired.

'Any news?' they both asked together.

What they hoped for most was news of Merry but information about Drew or Clare would be welcomed. Jane had nothing to offer. They nodded resignedly and began preparations for the evening meal while Jane washed up the tea things.

'Miss C. her usual bright self?' Cook inquired.

'Yes, she seems quite well.' Jane always felt guilty when she discussed the old lady with the maids but could seldom resist it. 'She's been telling me how fond of Clare she is.'

Edith laughed satirically. 'That's a good one.'

'When she nearly worried the life out of the poor child,' said Cook.

'Just how?'

'She nagged – and she never praised.'

'It was the same with us,' said Edith. 'But we weren't as sensitive as Miss Clare was. She was only sixteen then. Mind you, there weren't any scenes. It was just pin-pricks, perpetual pin-pricks.'

And perpetual pin-pricks, Jane reflected, could amount to torture.

The telephone rang. Cook hastily answered it at the kitchen extension, hoping, Jane guessed, it would be Merry.

'It's for you, miss. A lady.'

Probably Miss Willy, always liable to ring up with some query. Jane said she would go into the study.

She settled herself at Rupert Carrington's desk and lifted the receiver. A click as the kitchen receiver was replaced followed her first 'hello'. Then, over a very bad line, she heard an irate voice so inaudible that it was a full minute before she realized she was listening to Miss Gifford, telephoning from London and accusing her of a breach of faith.

'But I did *not* tell Clare the old man was once a king,' said Jane indignantly. 'I didn't mention it to anyone.'

'Then how does Clare know?'

'She doesn't.'

'But she does. Mr Rowley says so. He came to see me this morning and was most annoyed. I can't think what my dear mother would have said. All these years we've been sending people to the old gentleman! And now he's dead.'

'Since this morning?'

'No, no–'

Jane eventually gathered that there were two Mr Rowleys, one dead and one annoyed. And the latter appeared to think Clare was 'a little adventuress'.

'Then he's a fathead,' said Jane.

'A what?'

'Oh, never mind. If the old man's dead I sup-pose Clare's lost her job?'

'Well, she was engaged for a month and she's to stay on for the present. And I'm not quite happy about that. Mr Charles Rowley's rather a man-about-town, if you know what I mean.'

'A man without what?'

'Not without about.'

'About what?'

'Town – oh, never mind. It's just that one girl I sent had an unfortunate experience with him – though she didn't, in the end. And it was all her own fault – I mean, that she nearly had it, not that she didn't. She was most disappointed.' A spinsterish giggle came over the crackling line.

Constance Gifford's ageing, thought Jane and then said slowly and loudly: 'Well, if this man's annoyed with Clare and thinks she's an adventuress he's hardly likely to–'

Miss Gifford interrupted. 'Oh, it was *me* he was annoyed with. He seemed still to like Clare. And he didn't actually call her an adventuress. I think his phrase was "a bit of a minx". And I thought that might make him all the more inclined... Still, I daresay it's all right. He's not staying at the hotel now and the nurse is. I'll write and tell him Clare couldn't have known – or shall I leave well alone? If it *is* well. I'm sure he wouldn't *force* his attentions on her. And she wouldn't encourage him, would she? After all, he's almost middle-aged and really rather an ugly man, though with a good deal of charm. If you could...'

The high, breathy voice continued amid crackles. Jane was advised to write Clare a word of warning but on no account to say it emanated from Miss Gifford. 'It might get back to Mr Charles Rowley, and after all these years...' Miss Gifford's mother was then mentioned again and there followed a history of the Gifford Emplacement Agency since its foundation in 1892. 'So you'll leave me out of it, won't you? Are you still there?'

'Yes, yes, all right,' said Jane. 'This call must be costing you a lot.'

'Oh, heavens, yes. Well, goodbye then. I'm sorry I misjudged you but it's really very puzzling–'

'Goodbye,' said Jane firmly, hanging up. Damn the woman, how could one warn Clare without saying where the warning came from? And anyway, it was all nonsense. Clare would never encourage an elderly, ugly man-about-town – of all the ridiculous phrases! Still, perhaps one should just mention it to Richard, though what he could do about it Jane couldn't imagine.

She went into the hall meaning to go and see him in his music room. But he had already come in and was standing by the fire beside a slim, dark, rather beautiful young woman with large appealing eyes. She wore a simple but very elegant black dress and carried a fur coat.

'Jane, this is Violet Vernon,' said Richard. 'This is Jane Minton, Violet, who's been so good to us.'

Violet Vernon smiled sweetly. 'He's told me so much about you.'

Jane thought the voice charming but found the accent over-refined, suggestive of Mayfair and high society. She shook hands while Richard amplified his introduction.

'Violet's a friend of my father's.'

'Well, *ectually*, we were engaged,' said Violet.

'What a difficult time this must be for you,' said Jane, sympathetically. A memory was stirring of an overheard snatch of conversation...

'She's coming to stay with us.' Richard avoided Jane's eyes.

'Ah, how nice!' said Jane, intending it to sound as if she meant it. The memory was now fully awake. She had stood by her bedroom door and heard Richard, below, say: 'Father didn't even say goodbye to her.' Clare had said: 'Oh, poor Violet!' Then there had been something about the rent of a flat...

So this was 'poor Violet'.

BOOK FIVE

Richard

1

A Tall, Red-haired Young Woman...

He closed the door of his music room and flung himself down on the divan. Just how long would it be before he went raving mad? An idiotic question, of course, as madness implied escape and he felt quite sure that, in no form, would escape come his way. His father had escaped. Merry, Drew and Clare had escaped. But he, Richard, was obviously doomed, as Jane so often and so cheerfully put it, to 'hold the fort'; the fort being a large and now very uncomfortable house which, it seemed, he had to maintain chiefly as a roof for five women.

Jane, Cook and Edith were contributing generously towards expenses. But their contributions did not enable him to settle outstanding bills, some of which could hardly remain outstanding much longer if the house was to be kept open. Then there were the bills looming ahead: rent, rates, electricity, telephone – the list was interminable. And already he had doled out half the money his father had left, just in order to 'keep the flag flying' – Jane again; recently she had taken to bucking him up with a fine line in military metaphors.

Aunt Winifred paid not one penny and had this morning borrowed a pound. According to her, she had been mainly dependent on her now non-existent allowance; and the rent paid to her for her house had already been spent. He doubted if all this was true but was inclined to think she believed it was, just as she now believed she and Clare had been devoted to each other. During his great-aunt's regime at Dome House he had several times stood up to her. But how could one stand up to this frail, slightly dotty old woman? She was now, he felt, more wispish than waspish.

Violet, of course, was a guest. She had offered to pay, saying she still had some money, but he had waved the suggestion aside. It was now just a week since she had arrived – without warning; he had answered the front-door bell to find her standing outside with two suitcases. She had said: 'Oh, Richard, I just had to see you!' Then he had taken her to his music room and listened to her story. She had felt so lost, so lonely, and something had gone wrong about the rent of her flat. Yes, she had thought it was paid, that day he had so kindly come to see her. He asked how much she needed. But she had let the flat go; it was a furnished flat, so expensive, she'd just have to take a room somewhere. And the idea had come to her that she might find one near Rupert's family so that if there should be any news of him... And anyway, she'd so much wanted to see Richard again. She'd felt that there was ... well, *ec*tually, a sort of sympathy between them.

Richard had felt this too, from their first meeting. Back in the summer he had gone up to London for a concert at the Albert Hall, taken a walk in Hyde Park and run into his father and Violet. She had suggested they should all have a drink at her flat. There was evidence there – possessions strewn about – that his father was staying at the flat; and afterwards his manner, when speaking of Violet as a charming woman he had known for a couple of years, made it clear that she was more than a casual friend – so clear, in fact, that Richard had not hesitated to call on her after his father's flight, to see if she needed help. And her behaviour then had confirmed all he had thought.

But now he was not so sure. Once invited to stay at Dome House she had turned into his father's fiancée and she sometimes gave the impression of having been a perfectly respectable fiancée. Also she'd recently, though very vaguely, mentioned her investments. Richard began to wonder if his father *had* been supporting her. She was certainly most unlike his own idea of a 'kept woman'. True, it had been implicitly accepted by them both that his father had paid her rent, but might not a man offer a little financial aid to his perfectly respectable fiancée? And anyway, did her exact status matter?

It mattered extremely. Because Violet had already made it clear to Richard that she was falling for him; and though he trusted he had *not* made it clear to Violet, he was undoubtedly falling for her. The idea of falling for one's father's ex-girl friend was distasteful, whereas falling for one's father's respectable fiancée was merely dis-honourable and far preferable. Hence he favoured a respectable Violet.

Not that he'd yet decided how far he would let himself fall. He was careful not to meet her half-way – quarter-way, rather, that being all she'd left room for. But he did freely admit to himself that having her around made life more interesting. And she pulled her weight in the house, helping him to make beds, cook, wash up; whenever he had a job to do she was ready to join him. Also she did quite a lot for Aunt Winifred and got on well with her. This morning, the two of them had gone to have their hair washed and set. Jane, before going to Miss Willy, had driven them the necessary ten miles and he was to bring them back in time for lunch. That gave him ... he reckoned he had two clear hours before he need start. Should he attempt to work?

He had absolutely no urge to. It might come if he forced himself to begin, but he felt incapable of forcing himself. Should he play the piano? But he played it so badly – and no other instrument any better. Drew had once said: 'You criticize yourself out of existence, Richard. Be more tender to your imperfections.' But could one lower one's stan-dards deliberately? And Richard disliked the word 'tender', equating it with sentimentality – anyway, as regards himself. Drew could be tender without being sentimental; some astringent quality in his nature stopped the rot.

He had heard from Drew that morning. He took the letter from his pocket and re-read it. Well, Drew certainly seemed dug in at Whitesea.

He'd now won the confidence of Miss White-cliff's solicitor. Her niece, described as a trying girl, had come and gone without upsetting the *ménage*. Miss Whitecliff and her two ancient maids were lambs. (Ghastly old crones, Richard felt sure.) Life at White Turrets was getting more and more comfortable...

Yet Drew was unable to work on his novel, missed the family, longed for news: 'I wrote to Clare but she hasn't answered. It's hard to imagine her on her own in London. You don't think she'll get run over or kidnapped? Such a dithery girl, and her kind of prettiness seems to demand a top-hatted, black-moustached villain. As for Merry, I wake in the night and worry about her. If I'd got this job before she bolted I could have asked her to stay...'

Richard, too, worried about Merry, but not about Clare. They knew where Clare was – in the lap of luxury, incidentally, though it seemed unlikely she'd be there much longer. Jane had come to him with some fantastic story about ... well, it sounded rather like Drew's top-hatted villain, but Jane herself had thought it was nonsense. Anyway, he'd at once written to Clare, saying how sorry he was that her old gentleman had died, suggesting she might come home for a few days when she was free, assuring her that Aunt Winifred was no longer a serious menace, and positively begging for even a postcard from her. Well, if she didn't want to write, that was that. She was twenty-one and not too much of a dithery girl to have pulled down a job. No, he wasn't worried about Clare.

But Merry! Had he and Drew been wrong in not notifying the police? In two days she would have been gone three weeks – a child of fourteen! Surely she could have sent one line of news? Just the words 'All's well' would have reassured him. But perhaps all wasn't well. Oh God, worrying would get him nowhere ... and he was frittering away his rare two hours of peace.

He would play his gramophone – a Beethoven quartet: the 9th, the Third Rasoumovsky, a particular favourite of his. Not as great as the Last Quartets, but he did not this morning feel entitled to any of the Last Quartets; he was not sufficiently in a state of grace. Perhaps he didn't even deserve the 9th ... but he found the record and put it on; then opened the door and looked down at the wreckage of the autumn garden. It needed to be decently put to bed for the winter but they had been without a gardener since the late summer and could not now consider employing one. He must do some tidying up; perhaps Violet would help him, though he doubted if she had any shoes with heels less than three inches high. Anyway, he wasn't going to think of Violet now or of anyone or anything else except the music.

He went back to the divan, lay down, and listened intently, more analytically than emotionally. But soon analysis and emotion fused for him. The music simply *was,* and while it was, nothing else was, not even himself.

He was brought back to earth, shortly before the end of the first movement, by a voice saying: 'Richard!' He looked quickly towards the door. A tall, red-haired young woman was standing there.

'Richard!' she said again. 'Oh, darling Richard!'

'Merry! My God!' He sprang up and dashed to her.

They hugged ecstatically.

'Merry, darling! Are you all right?' He hastily switched off the record-player.

'Well, I'm still a virgin, if that's what you want to know.'

'Of course you are,' he said heartily.

'There's no "of course" about it. Lots of girls my age aren't. And I needn't have stayed one – anyway, not much longer. If I hadn't run away last night I'd soon have been married – to an earl.'

He laughed appreciatively, so thankful to have her back that her nonsense amused him. Still, he hoped she wasn't going to be at her most inventive.

'That happens to be true,' she said, coldly. 'And it wasn't at all funny. I'll tell you about it later. Where are the others? I couldn't find anyone in the house. And what about Father? Any news of him?'

'Not a word.' Richard gave her a sketchy outline of what had happened during her absence but did not reach the arrival of Violet; mention of Aunt Winifred provoked an interrupting wail.

'Richard, how frightful! Aunt Winifred here – and Clare and Drew gone! And poor me come crawling home needing to be comforted!'

'Well, Jane will comfort you and so will Cook and Edith. And I'll do my best. What happened? Couldn't you get a job?'

She sat down, sighed heavily and pushed back

her preposterous copper hair. He asked if the dye would wash off.

'No, never. I could have my hair dyed back to its natural shade but I'm not sure I want to. Don't you like it as it is?'

'I do not,' said Richard. 'And it makes you look years older.'

'That's not only my hair. It's what I've been through. I'd better tell you.'

'Take your time," he said, kindly. 'And Merry, darling, let it be reasonably true – much as I always enjoy your inventions.'

'This time, truth is stranger than fiction.'

She gave him a world-weary look which struck him as slightly histrionic; but almost from the beginning he believed her story. Had she been inventing she would have told it much more dramatically, and also more coherently. As it was, he had some difficulty in following her. But she did gradually convey an impression of her life at Crestover (he had driven through the village once and seen the house across the park) and painted fairly vivid portraits of Lady Crestover and her brother. (The names, Donna and Desmond Deane, seemed familiar; had he seen them on one of Drew's old musical-comedy scores?) The blank in Merry's canvas was Lord Crestover. She did little more than state his age, say he had been very kind, had proposed and been accepted.

'Then were you in love with him?' Richard asked.

'Of course – or I wouldn't have accepted him.' She went on to describe her two days' engagement, her trip to London, what she had overheard in the library and her discovery that she couldn't legally marry until she was sixteen. 'After that, I just had to run away, hadn't I?'

'I think you should have told them the truth,' said Richard.

'You mean, to their faces? Yes, *I* thought that but only when it was too late. Anyway, I told it to them in my farewell letter. At least, it was the truth when I wrote it. Oh, Richard, such an awful thing happened. The bus I caught was just a local bus, and I needed one that would take me to some station where I could get a train to London. So I got off at the next village but one. The bus I needed wasn't due for twenty minutes so I went into the inn and had a drink – beer, quite beastly, I only like champagne – but there was some pork pie that wasn't bad; I was jolly hungry as I'd run away before dinner. Well, I was sitting there at the bar, wondering if I'd get to London that night and where I'd sleep if I did, and how long my money would last – of course I never got paid any of my hundred-guinea fee so all I had was six pounds, and I'd left my diamond brooch at Crestover to repay them a bit. Suddenly I heard Claude's voice, out in the passage. He'd driven after me and was asking which road my bus had taken. It was a marvellous moment. I thought: "He'll forgive me and wait till I'm sixteen – everything's going to come right, after all." I couldn't see him, the open door was in my way, so leaned a bit forward and then I could. He was standing just under a glaring electric light and, oh, Richard, it was as if I really saw him for the very first time. He had practically no chin, and his expression! He's exactly like a codfish – a caricature of a nobleman. I fell *instantaneously* out of love with him. It was ghastly.'

'Poor Merry! But isn't it just as well?'

'I suppose so, but it's heart-breaking, too. You see, while I was in love with him I could be miserable in an interesting sort of way. Now I'm miserable in a deadly dreary way. And it upsets me to think I let him kiss me. I can't even like him now, though I'm very sorry for him. His mother never let him have a dog, and his cat got in a trap – though that is a long time ago. Oh, dear! Anyway, after that awful moment – you could call it the moment of truth, really – I dodged back out of sight and heard him say good night, and drive off. I felt *sick*, Richard. I never finished my piece of pie. And I was in no spirits to arrive in London late at night so I asked if they'd a bed at the inn, and they had, if you could call it a bed; it felt like a gate with a sheet spread on it. I scarcely slept at all. And this morning I was a beaten woman – no courage left to conquer London. So here I am. Richard, he couldn't find me, could he?'

'You put no address on your letter?'

'Of course not. And he doesn't know my real name.'

'Then you should be safe enough. But ... Merry, did you tell him you were only fourteen?'

'Fourteen and nearly seven months. Yes, I told him that.'

'Then he must be very anxious about you. Let me write to him and say you're with your family again.'

She looked horrified. 'No, Richard! He might come after me. Even if you put no address, there'd be a postmark.'

'We could get the letter posted somewhere else.'

'I'd have to think out what you could say. Leave it for now – please, Richard!'

'It's pretty callous, Merry. Still...' He could see that the very thought of poor Lord Crestover was seriously distressing her. 'The thing we've got to decide now is what to do about you.'

'I suppose I'll have to go back to being a child and go to some dreary school – *and* face life with Aunt Winifred.'

And with Violet too, he thought. Not that Merry would mind that, but he would mind it for her and even more on his own account. He'd told Drew and Clare about Violet after his first meeting with her but they'd all agreed Merry shouldn't be told. He hated the thought of explaining Violet to her, and he positively loathed the thought that Merry would quickly spot Violet's interest in him – not to mention his in her. God, how awful! Desperation led to inspiration.

He said: 'Merry, I've had a wonderful idea. Don't ask me what it is yet. I must go in and telephone.'

'Telephone who? If it's about me–'

'Please, Merry. I'll discuss it with you the minute I know if my plan will work. Now you stay here till I come back. I want to be sure no one sees you yet.'

'Oh, all right. But ... Richard, you're not going to telephone the Crestovers?'

'No, I swear it. Just wait.'

He dashed out and ran into the house. Drew's letter contained the telephone number of Miss Whitecliff's solicitor, to be used in case of emergency as there was no telephone at White Turrets. But could one reach Drew quickly? Well, it was worth trying.

He got the number after only a short delay, gave his name and asked for Mr Cyril Severn, who was soon apologizing for keeping him waiting, and proving remarkably quick on the uptake.

'Drew's brother? Nothing wrong, I hope?'

'No, no,' said Richard. 'But could Drew telephone me – quickly?'

'If he's at home I could get him down here within half an hour. But he may be out shopping. Can *I* be of any help?'

Drew's letter had made it dear that Mr Severn's decisions governed the Whitecliff household. Richard plunged straight in. 'It's my younger sister. She's been away and now she's come home.'

'What, the missing teenager?' Mr Severn obviously knew about her. 'Is she all right?'

'Yes, quite. But I particularly want to get her away from here. Drew did mention he could have asked her to stay–'

'Of course he can,' said Mr Severn heartily. 'When do you want to send her?'

'Would this afternoon be too soon?'

'Not at all. There's a good train from London at 4.30. I'll arrange for Drew to meet her.'

'Drew's employer won't mind?'

'She'll be delighted. So am I. It'll help keep

Drew amused. He's a saint but he might get bored by being one – in which case my life would fall in ruins. Anything else?'

'Well, no, if you're sure... You did say 4.30?'

'That's right. She'll have to change trains but that won't worry her if she's been on her own all this time. Hope she *is* all right. Girls, nowadays...! Anyway, we'll take care of her.'

'I'm most awfully grateful to you,' said Richard.

'Be a pleasure Why not come and see us yourself?'

'I only wish I could,' said Richard, and meant it.

'Well, do when you can. Goodbye now, or you'll run into another three minutes.'

God, I wish that man was *my* solicitor, thought Richard, hanging up. He sat still for a moment, slightly dazed by Mr Severn's briskness; then he looked up the morning trains to London.

Now to break the news to Merry. As he hurried through the garden he heard the gramophone. She had started it again.

'This is the Third Rasoumovsky, isn't it?' she said, when he opened the door. 'Do you remember the lovely story I made up about the second movement? Oh, I know you don't approve of making music programmatic but you did like that story.'

'Did I?' He silenced the gramophone. 'Wonderful news, darling – it's all arranged! You're going straight to Drew.'

She looked dismayed. 'But I don't want to. You said he was working for a dreary old lady.'

'I didn't say she was dreary. According to Drew

370

she's sweet. And you and he can have a marvellous time together.'

'No, Richard! I want to stay here and sleep in my own room and write all my sorrows in my journal.' Her eyes brimmed with tears. 'I'm pretty miserable, Richard.' She began to gulp, loudly and painfully.

'Stop dramatizing yourself,' said Richard, firmly.

She gave him an outraged stare. 'Those were genuine tears, Richard.'

'They were, but the gulps weren't. The tears got impressed with themselves. Now listen: you can write your journal at Whitesea. And you may not have to go to school at once there, as you certainly would here. What's more, life here isn't what it used to be, with Cook and Edith out all day and Aunt Winifred in.'

Merry looked thoughtful. 'And we're a bit too close to the Crestovers. They sometimes drive past this house. Oh, Richard, it was awful that evening I drove past. I didn't tell you–'

'Tell me in the car,' said Richard.

'You can't want me to start at once. I'll have to re-pack, take some different clothes ... and I'm hungry.'

'Well, you can have twenty minutes for packing and I'll bring you some food. I've got to get you to the station before I pick up Aunt Winifred at the hairdresser's. Which reminds me: you'll have some time in London as your train doesn't leave till 4.30. Could you get your hair put right?'

'I might. But it would cost quite a bit.'

He took out his notecase. 'I'll give you five

pounds – if you'll promise to go straight to Drew and not run away again.'

'All right. I haven't the spirit to run away now.'

He handed her the notes, then hurried her out and through the garden. 'Not much peace for a girl,' she said as they reached the house.

'You'll get plenty of peace at Whitesea.'

He carried her suitcase up for her and then went to make her some very thick sandwiches out of the cold meat intended for lunch. When he took them, with a glass of milk, up to her room he found her wearing a schoolgirlish flannel suit which made her look years younger.

'Terribly juvenile,' she said gloomily. 'But Clare's coat will hide it. Could I call on her while I'm in London?'

'There won't be time if you're to get your hair done.'

She looked at herself in the glass and nodded resignedly. 'It *is* a bit much – for here. It looked all right at Crestover. I think it needs spacious surroundings.'

Somehow he got her to finish packing. She was still munching a sandwich when he hurried her into the car. 'Keep your head down while we drive through the village,' he told her. 'If you're seen I shall be asked awkward questions.'

'What a bore! I wanted to look at everything.'

'You can come up for air now,' he said at last.

'Need I duck when we pass my dear old school? No, it's too far from the road. Fancy Jane working for Weary Willy! That's practically treason. Shall you tell her I'm back?'

'Yes, and I shall tell Cook and Edith but ask

them all to keep it from Aunt Winifred. Duck again, will you? Here comes the Vicar's car.'

Later, she said: 'Richard, how brisk and … well, managerial you've become. You used to be so vague and wrapped up in your work.'

He said he'd had to snap out of that.

'But I admired you for it – for being so dedicated. Are you working at all?'

He shook his head. 'There's too much on my mind. And life's not easy now. In some ways I'd like to leave home and try for a job, teaching in a school. Handling a school orchestra would do me a world of good.'

'Well, why not do it?'

'I can't close the house, when Cook and Edith and Jane and Aunt Winifred want to live in it.' To say nothing of Violet. 'And you or Clare or Drew might want to come home.'

'To hell with the lot of us,' said Merry. 'Nothing should come in front of your work, not even good deeds. You'll get punished for it, Richard – just as I shall. Only in my case, it was bad deeds.'

'Such as, darling?'

'I stopped being dedicated. I thought I'd like to be a countess, and that it would help me to get parts without really working for them. That was blasphemy. I sinned against my own personal Holy Ghost.'

'But not for long. And you did fall in love with the man.'

She shuddered. 'I almost hate him now – and all the Crestovers. It's unjust of me but they were my stumbling blocks. And one does feel like kicking stumbling blocks.'

373

'Unwise, lovey. You just stub your toe a second time.' She laughed and relaxed. He wondered if he should ask her again to let him write to Lord Crestover, then decided not to worry her. Let her remain childishly callous about that if she could. He suspected she had more than enough on her conscience. Dramatize herself she might, but he was quite sure she was already genuinely and even maturely dedicated.

They had only just enough time to catch her train. He found her a seat, repeated instructions for her journey to Whitesea, begged her to enjoy herself and to write fully.

'Oh, I shall,' she said. 'And I shall nag you to stop sinning against your Holy Ghost.'

The other occupants of the compartment looked startled. Only when he watched her train leaving the station did he fully realize how sorry he was to let her go.

2

The Noble Lord

As Aunt Winifred held herself aloof from all household matters and Violet merely helped assemble what food there was, he did not have to account for the cold meat eaten by Merry. He simply announced there would only be eggs for lunch.

'How shall we have them?' he asked Violet, as she followed him into the kitchen. 'Not enough butter to scramble them and frying would mean cleaning the frying pan.'

'And poaching is very tricky. They'll be safest boiled.'

Even so, they cracked.

'Clare would have made us a delicious omelette,' said Aunt Winifred.

Richard doubted if Clare had ever even attempted to make an omelette. But no doubt Clare the good cook was now as real to the old lady as Clare the devoted niece.

After lunch and the subsequent washing-up, he decided to work, for the first time since catastrophe had struck; Merry had both stirred his conscience and stimulated him. But he made the mistake of telling Violet and she at once asked if she could come and listen. 'Oh, please! I'll keep very quiet. I do want to hear some of your music.'

He told her he was working on a sextet which would not make sense to her if he attempted to play it on the piano. But as she still begged to come, he let her, the truth being that he wanted to.

He rather expected her to insist on talking but she settled herself on the divan and seemed genuinely anxious both to listen and to understand. So he did his best to give her an impression of his first movement, indicating such melody as there was and explaining about the various instruments. He found her most attentive, and several times she asked him to repeat a phrase and expressed admiration for it. But after a while she seemed less alert and he didn't blame her. His music, whether good or bad, certainly wasn't simple. He decided she needed a rest from it. Leaving the piano, he wandered around the room, talking of music generally.

Very soon she said: 'How restless you are, dear Richard. Come and sit down.'

He sat, but not beside her. Instead, he placed a chair where he could face her. She was reclining against his cushions with her feet tucked under her, looking small and young. As almost always, she was wearing a black, clinging dress unsuitable for the country but very becoming to her. He wondered if it was usual for pale, black-haired women to look so well in black and he noticed, not for the first time, the beautiful line of her jaw and throat.

'What are you thinking about?' she asked, after a moment. He had no intention of telling her. Instead he commented on the lack of any news about his father. 'It must be so very worrying for you, Violet.'

She sighed. 'Yes, indeed. But I'm more worried on his account than on my own. You know, Richard, I doubt if he and I would ever have got married.'

Richard, too, doubted it.

She went on, 'For one thing, there was such a difference in our ages. After all, I'm only twenty-seven.'

Less than a week ago she'd mentioned that she was twenty-nine – or had he misheard her? Today she didn't even seem twenty-seven. 'You look like a little girl,' he told her. 'Sitting there with your feet tucked up.'

She raised her arms and clasped her hands behind her head – and stopped looking like a little girl. The movement tightened her already tight dress, and the way she now sank back against the cushions constituted an invitation hard to ignore. He ought to have known this would happen if he let her come to the music room. Perhaps he had known it.

He rose and came towards her, wondering how one took hold of a woman who had bunched herself into a lump and was protected on three sides by cushions. As if understanding his problem she instantly shot her feet from under her, reclined full length, and gave him a smile of comprehensive welcome. This offered more than he had bargained for – anyway, at present. So he said: 'Sit up like a good girl and I'll kiss you.'

She laughed delightedly and somehow managed to lie down even flatter.

He turned towards the door, uncertain whether to bolt it or merely bolt. It suddenly opened to admit an almost breathless Aunt Winifred.

'Richard, there's a man wants you on the telephone. And you should hurry as it's a trunk call and he said it was most urgent, and I'm afraid I've taken rather a long time to get here because I couldn't find my glasses.'

As she wore glasses only for reading he couldn't think why she needed them to walk through the garden. 'Well, sit down and get your breath back,' he told her as he hurried out.

Could the call be something to do with his father? Or was it Drew calling from Whitesea? He dashed into the study and heard, even before he reached the desk, shrill sounds coming from the receiver. That certainly wasn't Drew.

It proved to be the local doctor's wife ringing up the local laundry about a missing pillow slip; that at least had been her intention. 'But I've been hanging on for ages,' she wailed when Richard told her she had the wrong number. 'And she said it was the right number.'

'She's getting very deaf,' said Richard untruthfully. Hanging up, he wondered if his aunt had really thought she'd heard a male voice urgently calling him from a distance, or if she'd merely wanted to make a dramatic entrance. Anyway, she and Violet could now have a chat while he did some thinking.

Why, why, had he let himself tell Violet he would kiss her? Up to now it had been – just – possible to pretend he did not realize their interest in each other. From now on, that would be out of the question. And what was he going to do about it?

He had come nowhere near deciding when the front-door bell rang. He went to answer it.

Opening the door, he found himself facing a tall, very fair man whose features combined extreme distinction with just the faintest suggestion of half-wittedness. On seeing Richard, he swallowed nervously before saying: 'It's difficult to explain but I'm trying to find a Miss Merry le Jeune – though I believe her real name is Carrington.'

'Come in,' said Richard. 'And stop worrying. She's quite safe.'

'Thank God,' said Lord Crestover.

Richard took him to the study, hoping Violet and Aunt Winifred would stay out of the way. He explained that he was Merry's brother and had been told a good deal about her adventures. Lord Crestover, seeming slightly dazed, sank on to the proffered chair.

'I've been so anxious – we all have. Is she really only fourteen and a half?'

Richard nodded ruefully. 'It's her only excuse for such disgraceful behaviour.'

'Oh, we none of us count it against her, I assure you. Poor child! Though it's still hard to realize she *is* a child. Believe me, I never for one moment suspected–'

Richard interrupted hastily. 'Of course you didn't. She's a brilliant actress and she *looks* grown up with that hair. I thought so this morning.'

'She told me in her farewell letter – so honestly – that it was dyed. What colour is it really?'

'Just a light brown.'

'I shall like that,' said Lord Crestover, his eyes shining.

The poor devil's demented about her, thought Richard, and then asked: 'How did you trace her – and so quickly?'

Lord Crestover took Merry's diamond brooch from his pocket and handed it to Richard. 'The dear girl left this. We were all more touched than I can say. You'll notice the name of the jeweller engraved on the back; my mother's jeweller, incidentally. I drove up to London this morning and had no difficulty in finding out the brooch was originally sold to a Mr Rupert Carrington. And when the salesman happened to mention, well, certain things, I knew I was on the right track. You see, Merry's letter said her father was a fugitive from justice.'

'It never occurred to her – or me – that you could find her.' Richard handed the brooch back.

'She must keep this, of course. But I'll return it myself. May I see her now, please?'

'I'm afraid not,' said Richard. 'She's gone to stay with my younger brother at ... well, quite a long way off.'

'Can I reach her tonight?'

Richard wondered how to protect Merry without being brutal. At last he said: 'I think it would be a great mistake to see her, Lord Crestover. She feels you should forget her.'

'That's because she thinks I shall want to. I must see her at once – for her sake as well as mine; I must relieve her mind. Please give me the address and the telephone number. I'll ring her at once and say I'm coming.'

'There's no telephone. And I can't, I really can't give you her address – not until I have her permission. She made it so absolutely clear that ... that she *wants* you to forget her.'

'Then it's because she thinks it's for my own good. She can't want it on her own account – not after her letter. I'd better show it to you.' Lord Crestover took the letter from his pocket, gave it a reverently loving look and handed it over. 'I'm sure you'll be as moved by it as we all were.'

Richard was indeed moved. Poor Merry, confessing to her dyed hair and false figure. But an hour – no, it must have been less – after her 'dearest Claude' had read that she truly loved him she had seen him as a codfish. Really the comparison was too cruel!

Richard looked up from the letter. Lord Crestover was regarding him with anxious, wide-open eyes and a mouth even more widely open. Cruel the comparison might be but it was also apt. And if a girl had once seen a man as a codfish, could she ever in future fail to see him as one?

'Now you'll understand why I must go to her at once,' said Lord Crestover. 'And let me tell you our plans for her. My mother wishes to adopt her, either officially or unofficially, whichever seems best. We shall take a flat in London. I'm told that Merry, absurd though it seems, is still under school-leaving age. Well, of course she can go to classes or have private tuition before starting her career. Then everything can proceed just as we'd planned.'

'Not everything, surely?'

Lord Crestover flushed. 'Naturally, we shall consider her a child. You surely don't imagine that I...' The flush had now reached his shining fair hair.

'No, no!' Richard protested. 'I think you're behaving most admirably – really quite nobly. And I know you always would. But surely it would be difficult for you, feeling as you do about her?'

'Remember she feels the same way about me,' said Lord Crestover, emotionally.

'That would make things even worse. Do you realize she couldn't be married for years and years?'

'She could be legally married at sixteen. And she's unusually mature in her feelings. And she told me once that Juliet was married at fourteen.'

Juliet! That patron saint of the precocious! And remembering Merry's school performance of Juliet, Richard could well believe she might, thinking herself to be in love, have given an impression of maturity. But it wasn't genuine maturity. He said firmly: 'My father would never agree. And neither would I, if I had any say in the matter.'

'Well, that's all in the future. The great thing now is to let the dear child know that all is well. I have affectionate messages for her from my mother and sisters – and my uncle, for whom Merry has a special regard.'

'Mr Desmond Deane?' said Richard, remembering Merry's narrative. Wasn't he the one who had warned her off?

'He asked me to tell her he now likes her better than ever. Surely you can trust us?'

'Indeed I do,' said Richard, and meant it as regard Lord Crestover. He wasn't so sure about the mother who, according to Merry, merely wanted a reason for living in London. 'It's only that– Can I get you a drink or something? Perhaps you'd like some tea?'

'No, thank you. I'd just like to go to Merry,' said Lord Crestover, doggedly.

Should one hand over the address? Could one, in decency, refuse? Richard got up and walked to the window, thinking hard... There was now a light in his music room – well, thank God Violet and Aunt Winifred were staying put. If Merry rejoined the Crestovers there'd be such enormous advantages as regards her immediate future. And no one could *make* her marry. Anyway, she ought at least to *see* this extremely nice man. Could any girl fail to be moved by such devotion? Perhaps she'd have another change of heart... But not yet. And pursued in her present mood of revulsion, she might be brutal; one must withold the address as much for Lord Crestover's sake as for hers.

He turned (and now got his lordship in full profile ... that jutting nose, that receding chin – neither would have looked so bad without the other). 'Please consider this,' he said, persuasively. 'My sister will be extremely tired when she arrives. If she has to face an emotional scene tonight it could be very bad for her, after the mental strain she's recently been under. Suppose we both of us just write to her – now. I'll put your letter in mine and she'll get them both tomorrow morning – we can still catch the post. How would that be? And I'll promise to tell her how wonderful I think you're being.' He felt as if cajoling a child.

Lord Crestover seemed impressed. 'Perhaps she would be too tired to see me tonight. But I'm not a good letter writer.'

'Just tell her what you've told me – and I'll tell her, too. She'll understand.'

He settled Lord Crestover at the desk and said they would allow themselves twenty minutes. 'It's easier to think when one's alone so I'll leave you for the moment.' He took writing paper into the hall. Here he could, if necessary, head off Violet and Aunt Winifred.

In his own letter, he found himself coming out strongly for Lord Crestover. Well, one was so damn sorry for him. And Merry was no shrinking violet. (Nor was Violet... He dragged his thoughts back from his own problem.) It really wouldn't hurt his quite tough young sister to have a talk with a man who would undoubtedly behave most chivalrously. After all, she'd made her bed... He refrained from writing that but had no hesitation in telling her she'd incurred the responsibility of being both kind and tactful. He'd felt she was being a bit callous...

He remembered then that he'd also felt she'd better go on being callous, but that was before he'd met the poor codfish.

He wouldn't mention 'codfish' in his letter. Instead, he wrote of Lord Crestover's great distinction and good looks (well, he had large eyes and – most fortunately – good teeth). He pointed out the advantages of life with the Crestovers and concluded by saying, 'And do remember, he *loves* you.'

He had finished his letter in a quarter of an hour and was fairly pleased with it. He went back to the study.

Lord Crestover was working hard and breathing heavily — through his nose; for once his mouth was closed, in grim determination. He looked up and said: 'One feels inadequate. And it's difficult ... in the circumstances. Do you think – after all, she will want to know – do you think it's all right to tell her I love her?'

'Of course it is,' said Richard heartily. 'And I've said you do, too. Now we haven't much time left.'

Lord Crestover finished his letter and then Richard put it in an envelope with his own and addressed the envelope. 'Would you like to see this posted?' he asked.

'Yes, please. Let me drive you to the post office.'

They went out into the chilly late afternoon. 'Soon be winter,' said Lord Crestover. 'Merry wouldn't like Crestover in winter – such a cold house, much as I love it. But she won't mind coming back there for a few weeks while we find a London flat.'

If only he wasn't so optimistic, thought Richard, getting into the Daimler. To change the subject he said breezily:

'I suppose this is the car you dashed after her in?'

Lord Crestover looked astonished. 'How did you know I did?'

What a gaffe! Richard hastily amended it. 'Oh, I just guessed you would.'

'I did indeed. But when I caught up with her bus, she wasn't on it.'

'She had to change buses in order to get home.'

'Yes, I see. What a difference it'd have made if I could have found her last night!'

Depending on whether you found her before or after she saw you as a codfish, thought Richard. Oh, damn Merry! She should have seen that resemblance earlier – or never.

They posted the letter together, Richard feeling embarrassed at keeping the address turned downwards.

'Do you think she'll telephone tomorrow?' said Lord Crestover.

'I wouldn't count on it. As I said, there's no telephone where she's staying and she might not like to speak from a call box, on such an intimate matter.'

'*I* think she'll telephone,' said Lord Crestover, fondly. He got back into the car.

Richard had decided to stay where he was and intercept Jane on her way home. It would be his best chance to tell her privately about Merry's return. 'Well, goodbye,' he said. 'And thank you for being ... so chivalrous. And so wonderfully kind to my sister.'

'I keep thinking of how she must have felt when she wrote that letter last night, not realizing I'd go on caring for her. It harrows me.'

Richard, watching Lord Crestover drive into the dusk, felt harrowed too; but not on Merry's account.

3

Brothers in Arms

The evening had gone smoothly. He had returned to Dome House safely chaperoned by Jane; and told Aunt Winifred and Violet that he'd had to go out to post a business letter, the writing of which had been necessitated by the telephone call he'd gone in to answer. He had never realized how truthful he normally was until he found how much he disliked telling the lies he now so constantly had to tell.

He had, anyway, told Jane the full truth about Merry, but they'd decided Cook and Edith mustn't know it as they would be shocked if they heard that Merry had been involved in a love affair. So he told them she'd merely stayed in a quiet boarding house, failed to get work on the stage, and come home when her money ran out. They were overjoyed that she was unharmed and would soon be safely with Drew. For days Richard had thought they seemed tired and lacklustre; he was glad of this chance to cheer them up.

Not until Jane and Aunt Winifred had gone to bed did he find himself alone with Violet. (Jane threw him by going to bed earlier than usual.) Violet at once said: 'Richard, I want to have a quiet talk with you, and not here; we're so liable

387

to be overheard. Will you come to my room or shall I come to yours?'

'Neither,' said Richard. Whatever she meant by a quiet talk he wasn't having it so close to Jane and Aunt Winifred. 'Let's talk tomorrow.' He got up and moved towards the stairs.

'No, tonight – please, Richard! I shan't sleep unless we do. You see, I've let you make a dreadful mistake about me and it's on my conscience – because I know it's worrying you. I was going to explain this afternoon when your aunt came in.'

'Like hell you were,' said Richard.

'Well, I will now and it'll make all the difference. I'll tell you the whole truth.'

'Tomorrow, Violet dear,' he said firmly; then went upstairs and into his room as fast as he could without running.

Unfortunately he had to come out again to go to the bathroom. She was now lying full length on the hall sofa. Waving a languid hand, she called up that she was still around.

'So I noticed,' said Richard. 'Don't forget to put the lights out when you come up.'

Returning from the bathroom he was glad to see the hall was in darkness, but less glad when Violet opened her door. 'You knocked?' she said sweetly.

'No, I didn't and I hope *you* won't.' He went into his room wondering if it would be too like a nervous spinster if he locked his door. Well, he doubted if many spinsters were more nervous than he was. He turned the key.

He had just got into bed when he heard a gentle tap. Good God, he'd probably put the idea into her head. The tap came again, much louder; if she went on like that she'd rouse the house. Hurriedly he flung on his dressing-gown and opened the door.

Aunt Winifred stood outside.

'Richard, I'm extremely worried. That telephone call this afternoon, had it anything to do with Clare?'

He said patiently: 'No, Aunt Winifred. It was just a business matter. I told you, remember?'

'You weren't hiding anything? I suddenly wondered.'

She stared at him anxiously, a bunched, shrivelled old lady, her white hair flattened into what looked to him like a string bag. He said: 'I give you my word it had nothing to do with Clare. Now how about going back to bed?'

'It's so hard to sleep. Clare used to bring me hot milk.' And hated the job, he remembered, and his aunt's complaints about skim. Unwillingly, he offered to get her some hot milk himself.

'No, thank you!' Her tone implied grave doubts of any milk heated by Richard.

He steered her along to her room and gently pushed her in. As he closed the door he saw that Violet had come onto the gallery. With unwonted humour, she whispered: 'Now I know who my rival is.'

'Do go to bed,' he implored her.

'But Richard—!'

Jane came out of her bathroom, gave them one look and then scuttled into her bedroom.

'Please, Violet!' he said, then seized her by the shoulders and pushed her towards her room.

'But I'm on my way to the bathroom,' she wailed. He dived into his room recalling he'd once heard Jane tell Merry the hall was like the setting of some old French farce ... all those bedroom doors. But Aunt Winifred's mental state was scarcely funny; nor was his own situation much of a joke.

He woke next morning convinced that a difficult day lay ahead of him; not that he didn't quite look forward to it.

Violet, he suspected, would have renewed her attack during their shared washing-up after breakfast, had not Jane been around unusually late; she had been given the day off from work to drive up to London and do some shopping. By the time she left, after ten, he was safely settled with Aunt Winifred in the hall. Violet was there too, reading the morning paper. He had never before seen a woman read a paper lying flat on her back with the paper held above her.

The telephone rang and he went to the study to answer. The call proved to be from London; some woman wanted Jane, and wanted her badly. The agitated, hard-to-hear voice said: 'I know she'll be at the school where she works but I must please be given its telephone number. This is a matter of the utmost urgency.'

He explained the position about Jane. 'And when she gets to London I've no idea where she's going.'

'Oh, dear, this is dreadful. Are you one of Clare Carrington's brothers? I know she has some.'

'I'm her elder brother. Who is it speaking?'

'Miss Gifford, of the Gifford Emplacement

Bureau. I obtained a post for your sister – in the best possible faith, I assure you–'

He interrupted. 'Is something wrong?'

'I'm afraid so, Mr Carrington. And I fear it's serious.'

'Is Clare ill?'

'No, no...'

There was a silence so long that he asked if she was still there. Then she spoke again, sounding even more agitated.

'I'm wondering what I ought to do. I see no course but to speak frankly.'

He had never heard anyone speak less frankly, but some facts did gradually emerge. Hearing of a possible job for Clare, she had that morning tried to ring her up. 'She wasn't there, Mr Carrington, but I did have a word with the late Mr Rowley's nurse. Of course it's extremely difficult for her as she's being most generously pensioned by Mr Charles Rowley and she said she thought the world of him. And she likes Clare so much – though that was really her reason for speaking, not that she did speak, well, at all openly. Indeed, she said repeatedly how unwilling she was to say *anything* – just as I am, now...'

Richard thought this double unwillingness to communicate would have been completely successful but for the conversation he'd had with Jane a week before. As it was, he soon had no difficulty in guessing that the top-hatted, black-moustached menace had materialized. He then cut through Miss Gifford's monologue by saying satirically: 'Do I take it my sister's facing a fate worse than death?'

'Oh, come, that's a little old-fashioned, surely?'

Slightly irritated, he said: 'Anyway, I think you're imagining things. My sister's not the kind of girl–'

'But of course she's not – that's the whole point. And *I* thought I was imagining things, only a week ago. But one really must face facts. Clare shows no sign of wanting any more work. And she goes out with Mr Charles Rowley – to matinees, one understands, which is unobjectionable, and I'm glad to say she's in the hotel every night and Mr Charles Rowley isn't, so Nurse feels sure that up to now there hasn't been anything, well, *serious*. But she's leaving today, Mr Carrington. I mean, the nurse is.'

'I'll ring Clare up,' said Richard.

'She won't be back till six, the nurse said. After the matinee.'

'Well, I'll ring her then.'

'Couldn't you *see* her? Couldn't you be there when she gets back? I was going to ask Jane to, but a brother would have far more authority. The nurse, in spite of her loyalty for which I respect her, made it perfectly clear that once she was out of the way ... well...'

'Did she say so in so many words?' asked Richard.

'Oh, no, Mr Carrington. One couldn't expect it. And you mustn't, please, disclose that she said anything – or that I have. Indeed, I'm not at all sure my dear mother *would* have.'

Faced with another woman not saying anything, Richard hastily thanked Miss Gifford and undertook to give the matter serious thought.

'Well, it's in your hands now,' said Miss Gifford, almost gaily. 'That's a load off my mind. And if Clare does want another job... Not that I can fix her up with another king.'

'A what?' said Richard sharply.

'Oh, dear, this is my day for indiscretion. Still, I'd better tell you.' She gave him a brief sketch of the Rowley antecedents, concluding by saying: 'And Jane did tell me your sister fancied being a king's mistress. Really, all this would be funny, if it wasn't so serious. Now you must excuse me. I've people waiting.'

He excused her willingly. Good God, what did one do? At first, taking her for a silly old gossip, he had almost entirely discounted her suspicions but he had become more and more uneasy. Clare had been gone a fortnight without sending so much as a postcard. She had ignored letters from him and from Drew. And the very fact that she had got a job at all, and the first she had applied for, was ominous. Had this man had designs on her from the very beginning? And this ex-royalty nonsense, it was exactly the thing which would fetch his silly sister. Yes, Clare *was* silly. If Merry, at twenty-one, were involved in such a situation he'd hardly feel he had the right to attempt interference, but with Clare...

The telephone rang. What now?

It was Drew, his voice almost unrecognizable. Never before had Richard heard his brother really angry.

'Have you gone out of your senses, Richard? How could you do such a frightful thing? Letting this man loose on Merry!'

'What? Oh, God, has he managed to find her?'

'No, no. But you forwarded his indecent letter. And what about your own letter? Calmly wanting to hand your sister over to this atrocious man!'

'He's not atrocious!' said Richard, catching Drew's anger. 'And I don't believe his letter's indecent.'

'Of course it is. A man of his age telling a child he's in love with her and wants to marry her. And your letter backed him up!'

'Not as regards marrying him. I merely pointed out how the Crestovers could help her.'

'*And* tried to harrow her. Well, you've succeeded – and just when she was getting back to normal. I was seriously worried about her when she arrived yesterday; I wouldn't have put it past her to have a nervous breakdown. But the Severns came up in the evening and we all encouraged her and gradually she began to talk and get the whole wretched business out of her system. I must say she was terribly funny.'

'I bet she was,' said Richard, grimly.

'But it's not funny to think what she's been through. Still, she's pretty resilient and by the time she went to bed she was almost her old self. And then, this morning! She was utterly shattered, especially by *your* letter. I tell you, she was hysterical.'

'Ah, yes,' said Richard. 'Merry does very good hysterics.'

'Now listen,' said Drew, more angrily than ever. 'Just because you've been won over by this elderly roué...'

Richard laughed. 'Come out of the Edwardian

era – or shall I join you there and tell you Lord Crestover's the soul of honour?'

'No man who makes love to a child...'

'He didn't *know* she was a child.'

'But she *looks* one, Richard. Actually, she's looking even younger than usual – with that pretty fair hair.'

'That *what* hair? Oh, God! Well, she didn't look a child when she came home, with her hair flaming red and a false bust, though I didn't realize the bust was false till afterwards. Which reminds me, do you know about her farewell letter to Lord Crestover?'

'I think she did say she left one.'

'Well, I've read the letter. Now calm down, Drew, and take this in. She told him she truly loved him and would have married him if the law would let her. What's more, she meant it when she wrote it. You get her to tell you the whole story when she hasn't got such a large audience. Oh, she didn't deliberately lie to you all. She just got carried away.'

There was a silence. Then Drew said deflatedly: 'You could be right. Damn it, of course you are. But she's still got to be protected. She *is* only a child.'

'Well, she behaved like a grown-up for nearly three weeks and that needs imagination as well as acting ability. Tell her to use her imagination now and write the truth to Lord Crestover as kindly as she can. If she sends the letter to me, I'll forward it without letting him know where she is, and I'll see him again if necessary. I'll protect her all right, but she's got to behave decently. Believe me, he deserves it.'

Drew sighed heavily. 'She kept saying he was like a codfish – and we all laughed madly. Miss Whitecliff adores her and so do Mr and Mrs Severn.'

'Well, so do I,' said Richard. 'Even if I do want to kick her.'

'She's at a café with Miss Whitecliff now, eating ice-cream. I was so impressed by the brave way she'd perked up again, and all the more furious with you. I *am* sorry.'

'Oh, forget it,' said Richard. 'And forget Merry for the moment. For God's sake give me some advice about Clare.'

It took him no time at all to relay the few bare facts, shorn of Miss Gifford's verbiage. Indeed, facts were so few and bare that he was surprised Drew took them so seriously.

'Richard, how frightful! And exactly the kind of thing that could happen to Clare. You must go to her at once.'

'She won't be in till six. And of all the awful jobs! Suppose the man's with her? What do I do?'

'With Clare involved, there should be a duel by candlelight. Is King Rudolf of Ruritania expected to spring the instant the nurse leaves the hotel?'

'That seems to be the idea. And Clare's so silly she might not quite know what she was in for until – well, it had happened. Drew, could you possibly come up to London and see her with me?'

'Let me have a word with Mr Severn. Hold on, will you?' Richard waited, trying to visualize Drew in Mr Severn's office, and Merry eating

396

ice-cream – with *fair* hair now, damn her! But he couldn't feel really angry with her, for that or for anything else. He understood her too well.

Drew was back in little over a minute. 'I can come. Mr Severn says he has Merry for a hostage now.'

'You won't tell her what you're coming for?'

'No, I'll say I have to see Father's solicitor with you. Will you meet my train? Make a note of the time. You know how vague you are.'

Richard had just jotted down the time and the station when Aunt Winifred opened the door. 'Yes, Aunt Winifred?' he said loudly, for Drew's benefit.

'I heard that,' said Drew. 'You'll want to ring off. See you this afternoon.'

Richard replaced the receiver and looked nervously at his aunt. The walls of Dome House were thick and he had kept his voice low even when annoyed with Drew. Still, she might have overheard something. But she only said he had been talking a long time and she'd suddenly felt it might be about Clare.

He hoped she wasn't becoming psychic as well as crazy. 'Nothing whatever to do with her,' he said emphatically. 'Just Father's solicitor. I have to go to London to see him.' Drew's lie came in very handily. 'Excuse me, please. I've barely time to catch my train.'

He hurried past her, and past the still recumbent Violet, and dashed up to his room. A few minutes later there was a knock on his door followed by the instantaneous entrance of Violet, who closed the door behind her.

'Richard, your aunt says you're going to London. Will you be staying the night?'

He said he didn't expect to.

'Well, why don't you? And I'll come up with you and open the flat. Then we can have a quiet, uninterrupted talk.'

He stated at her in amazement. 'But you've let the flat go.'

'Well, not *exactly*, Richard. It's all part of what I have to tell you and you won't give me the chance to.'

'And I can't now,' said Richard, 'or I shall miss my train.'

'I don't want to, *now*. I want you to come to the flat tonight.'

He said with sudden anger: 'I'm not spending the night at a flat my father paid for.'

'But he didn't. Oh, dear!' She burst into tears and flung herself on the bed, face downwards.

'Well, he did in the past. Oh, for God's sake stop crying.'

'I'm trying to, but when once I start... I just don't understand how anyone as good as you are can be so cruel.'

'I wouldn't say I was either good or cruel.' He could see her tears were genuine and she seemed to be making a genuine effort to control them. Patting her on the shoulder, he added, 'I'm sorry – really, I am. We'll talk fully as soon as I'm home.'

She instantly rolled over on her back and put her arm round his neck.

'No, Violet – I *must* go!' He broke away and made for the door, then turned to say, 'If only you knew how much I have on my mind today.'

'All right, darling. Good luck!'

She spoke with sudden reasonableness, and smiled at him so sweetly that he nearly went back – but not quite.

Hurrying out to the car, he wondered if he really had time to catch his train; and then the car proved difficult to start. Driving faster than he cared to, he still reached the station five minutes too late and was faced with a long wait for the next train, a deadly slow one. Well, he'd drive all the way, though he disliked taking the car to London. He never knew where to park, was uncertain of his way and invariably got confused by traffic regulations. But he could take his time now and put in some thinking...

Had he been cruel to Violet? Damn it, he hadn't been holding out on her very long; it was only yesterday that he'd been sure of her intentions ... well, *quite* sure; he'd been pretty sure from the day she arrived. Had she no sense of decency? Obviously not his sense of it, or was his sense of it really conventionality? Anyway, he couldn't go on like this. Whisking himself out of Violet's clutches was so bloody coy. And what were all the disclosures she intended to make?

He rested his mind from Violet by thinking of Clare, rested it from Clare by thinking of Merry, then thought of Drew – with a certain amount of envy, though *he* wouldn't care to be the ewe lamb of even the most charming old lady. After that, he spared a few thoughts for his vanished father, gone nearly a month now. Then back to Violet again. It was a relief when the traffic in the London suburbs forced him to keep his whole mind on driving.

He parked the car near Regent's Park, had some sandwiches at a café – it was too late for lunch; then took himself to the Zoo until it was time to meet Drew's train.

4

Survivals

Drew, looking particularly slight, neat and reassuring, came hurrying towards him.

'Richard, how very glad I am to see you.'

'And I to see you,' said Richard.

'Sorry about this morning. You were right. Merry admits it. She says she knew she was behaving badly but somehow couldn't stop herself. And I gather she didn't lie, exactly – just left things out and gave the whole story a comic slant. Now she's swung to the opposite extreme and feels tragically guilty. I had to cheer her up. Anyway, she's sent Crestover a telegram saying: "Writing fully. Grateful love to all."'

'Hope he doesn't notice where it was handed in.'

'He's welcome to. Mr Severn got someone in Manchester to send it. She swears she'll write a long, kind letter tomorrow – says it'll be a mortification as she really wants to pour out her soul in her journal. Anyway, we can stop worrying about her for the moment. Let's concentrate on Clare.'

'I loathe spying on her.'

'Just *visiting* her,' said Drew. 'And you didn't exactly dress for it, did you?'

'I meant to change but ... circumstances were

401

against it.' Only when well on his way had he noticed he was wearing his oldest tweed jacket.

'Never mind. You look an honest, home-spun brother. I'm really a bit too dapper. By the way, Mr Severn has heard of the villainous Mr Charles Rowley. He's a property-deals tycoon and possibly a millionaire. So are you sure we're justified in forbidding the – what's the disreputable equivalent of the banns?'

'I gather you're not as worried as I am,' said Richard. 'I keep thinking how miserable she might feel ... well, afterwards.'

'I suppose so,' said Drew, more soberly. 'Though she just might be peeved at being rescued. No, I don't really believe that. The poor darling simply doesn't understand. Well, what do we do now?' They had made their way out of the station. 'It's not nearly six yet.'

'Let's get there early. It might be a good thing to meet her as she comes in.'

'Ah, in case he's waiting to pounce. Richard, why was Miss What's-her-name so sure he hasn't pounced already?'

'I told you. He doesn't stay at the hotel at night.'

'And is the daytime close season for pouncing? Anyway, it'll soon be dark. We'd better hurry.'

They got to the hotel at half-past five.

'What grandeur!' said Drew. 'Perhaps they'll chuck us out.'

'They might me. You do the inquiring.'

'Need I? Can't we just sit down and wait?'

'She might have come back earlier than was expected.'

They went to the desk. Drew's inquiry was received with great courtesy but Miss Carrington was thought not to be in. Then a very small page, standing by, said: 'Yes, she is. Came back ten minutes ago.'

Richard said firmly: 'We're her brothers. And she's expecting us. What number is her room?'

But they had to wait while Clare was informed by telephone. Suppose she refused to see them? He'd telephone her from a call-box... But she did not refuse and the small page was soon escorting them into a lift. As they went up, he informed the lift man that these were Miss Carrington's brothers. 'Well, isn't that nice?' said the lift man. 'It's been sad for her, the old gentleman dying so soon after she came.' Richard relaxed. The smiling page, the kindly lift man, the dignified luxury of the hotel, all tended to reassure him. He had panicked, been fooled by the gossip of a silly old woman – and he must be careful to hide this from Clare. He only hoped Drew would follow his lead.

The page, conducting them along a thickly carpeted corridor, said: 'Miss Carrington's my very favourite lady. I brought her up the first day she came here and wished her luck. There she is.'

She had opened a door at the far end of the corridor and now stood awaiting them, wearing a long white garment which Richard presumed was a negligé. As they drew nearer, she turned, took a coin from a bowl on a table behind her and had it ready for the page. He beamed on her, she beamed on him, then on Richard and Drew.

'How lovely to see you both! Come in.'

'Clare, you look wonderful,' said Drew.

'Do I? This is only a dressing-gown.'

'I wasn't referring to it,' said Drew.

She steered them into a large cream and gold sitting-room. Richard thought its luxury over-ornate but guessed it would very much appeal to Clare. A fire burned brightly and the warm air was scented by a vast bunch of particularly beautiful roses.

'Sorry the place is so untidy,' said Clare, glancing around at the litter of tissue paper, cardboard boxes and a great many expensive things which had been taken out of them. 'I've just come back from shopping.'

'For whom?' said Richard.

'Me, of course.' She looked at him very directly. 'Did you come for any special reason, Richard?'

He asked why she hadn't answered their letters.

'I've kept meaning to. Is that the only reason you came?'

He'd better tell her the truth. 'No, Clare. I heard ... some distressing rumours.'

'Who from? Oh, Miss Gifford, perhaps. She must think it's peculiar that I don't want another job. You couldn't have heard from Nurse Brown because we've kept everything from her. I've never even let myself go out shopping until to-day; she's gone now. You see, she'd have been upset. And so would my friends on the staff here, especially my floor waiter who's been quite a father to me. That's why we've been so careful to keep things respectable.'

'Well, thank God you have,' said Richard. 'Now listen, before it's too late...'

Drew interrupted him. 'You've misunderstood her, Richard. It *is* ... what you mean by too late. Isn't it, Clare, darling?'

'Yes, of course,' she said, smilingly. 'Are you shocked?'

'I'm not,' said Drew.

Richard, avoiding her questioning gaze, said: 'I'm partly to blame. I ought to have got in touch with you last week, when Miss Gifford first rang Jane.'

'What day was that?' Clare inquired.

'Let's see ... Wednesday. Yes, Wednesday evening.'

'Then you'd still have been too late, Richard.' She smiled reminiscently. 'Wednesday was the first day I went to my house.'

'The great thing is that you're happy,' said Drew. 'That's easy to see.'

'I'm a bit better looking, don't you think? Yes, I'm blissful. They say no one's ever a hundred per cent happy but I would be, if only Charles would be. He worries so. You see, he doesn't think it should have happened.'

'Then why did he let it?' said Richard.

'Well, he'd be much *less* happy if it hadn't. And anyway, it wasn't his fault. There were all sorts of complicated reasons – including the fact that I was positively dying of love. All right, Richard, I won't tell you any more. I can see you're embarrassed.'

'Not embarrassed, exactly.'

'Just plain horrified?'

Drew said suddenly: 'Clare, is that an original Renoir?'

She turned to him eagerly. 'Yes, Charles brought it from his flat – which I'm not allowed to visit; I fancy he thinks his disreputable past lingers on in it and might contaminate me. He was quite cross because I said he must have another mistress there. He thought I might like the Renoir for my house and so I would.'

'Tell me about your house,' said Drew.

'It's in St John's Wood. Old Mr Rowley kept *his* mistresses there – over sixty years ago, imagine! Oh, Drew, you should have seen the furniture – and now it's too late; everything went to be stored this morning. I actually cried when I said goodbye to it, yesterday afternoon. I've got so fond of it this last week, though at first I thought it was horrible, really frightening. Anyway, now the house is going to be done up and filled with really lovely things. We shall probably go away soon until it's ready. I can't live an un-respectable life at this hotel. My friends here wouldn't like it.'

'It's a good thing we've caught you before you leave,' said Drew.

'Well, I'd have written – I think; you know I'm not good at letters like you and Merry are. Oh, is there any news of her?'

Between them, they supplied her with a brief history of Merry's adventures and arrival at Whitesea.

'Goodness, she has had a time,' said Clare. 'And how lovely that she can be with you, Drew. What's happening at home, Richard?'

'Nothing,' said Richard.

'Must be dull for you. Would you like a job? I'm sure Charles could get you one. He seems able to

406

manage almost everything and he's very anxious to help our family.'

'No, thank you,' said Richard.

'Ah, darling, don't be stuffy. You'll feel differently when you've met him. No one could help liking him.'

'I don't think I want to meet him,' said Richard.

'Well, you'll have to – because I hear him, now.' She opened the door and called: 'Charles, my brothers are here.'

A voice from the entrance hall said: 'Oh, my God! Have they brought guns or will they settle for knocking me down?' Then Charles Rowley came into the room.

Drew said smilingly: 'Perhaps if you'd kneel – and we could both hit you together...'

Richard, who was only just under six foot, resented this remark. Still, he doubted if he could have knocked Charles Rowley down single-handed. And he had no desire to; his disapproval was cold, not violent. Clare said appealingly, 'Richard, please!'

'Give him time, my dear. For the moment, he's fully occupied in thinking me the ugliest man he's ever met and wondering what you see in me.'

Richard thought the sardonic, heavily featured face too well-proportioned for real ugliness, and he was instantly sure that Charles Rowley was likable. But he had no intention of selling out to the likability. Still unsmiling, he said: 'I'm sorry, but ... well, I do find this whole thing shocking – for Clare.'

'I should hope you did. Does it help at all that I'm moving heaven and earth to get a divorce?'

'A great waste of energy,' said Clare. 'Because even if you get it, I shan't marry you.'

'Then I shall turn you out.'

'You won't be able to. My house is to be legally mine. Did you go to the bank?'

'Yes. We'll talk about that later.'

'No, now,' said Clare, very decidedly. 'I want to show them. Are they in your overcoat pocket?'

He nodded, smiling as if at an importunate child. Then, as she hurried out into the hall, he said to Richard: 'Sorry about this.'

She came back with a leather case, saying blithely, 'Crown jewels. Did you know Charles was really a king?'

'I am not a king. My father wasn't a king. And my grandfather was only a king for a very few years and was delighted to stop being one. The whole silly business has been lived down.'

She had taken a double row of pearls from the leather case. 'Oh, Charles, they're lovely. And not large enough to be vulgar.'

'I *have* some vulgar ones.'

'You'd better let me see them. They may not be as vulgar as you think. Fasten these for me, please.'

He did so, remarking, 'My dear, this scene is in the worst possible taste.'

'I find it charming,' said Drew, benignly. 'And it's only with the greatest regret that I tear myself away. Unfortunately I have a train to catch.'

Richard looked at him in surprise. He had understood Drew's train did not leave until mid-evening. But he was glad enough to go. And he noticed that Clare made no effort to detain them.

408

Drew, taking a last look around the room, said: 'This is my ideal hotel.'

'I shall love it as long as I live,' said Clare. 'You will both come and see me at my house? And can Merry come? Or won't that be allowed? Charles is dubious about it. He's terribly square in spite of the life he's led.'

'I'm sure she'll insist on coming,' said Richard.

'Charles would like to help her finish her education, and then with her training for the stage.'

Richard, about to refuse, checked himself. He had no right to expect Merry to be governed by his own sense of fitness. 'That must be for her to decide.'

They had reached the door of the suite.

'Clare, darling, you *will* write?' said Drew.

'I promise. It'll be easier now. Give my love to Merry.' She turned to Richard. 'And to Jane and Cook and Edith. And even to Aunt Winifred, if you like. I couldn't hate anyone now.'

Charles Rowley looked at him earnestly. 'She is happy and I'll try to keep her happy. Incidentally, if I died tomorrow she'd be extremely rich.'

'Not for long,' said Clare. 'Because I should die, too.'

'I shall miss my train,' said Drew, urging Richard out.

At last they were on their way along the corridor. As they approached the corner Drew looked back and then said: 'Manage a smile, Richard.'

Richard turned. Clare and her king were still standing at the door of the suite. She had slipped her arm through his and was leaning her head against his shoulder. Richard managed the smile, but only just.

They turned the corner and heard the door of the suite close. 'Why were you suddenly anxious to get away?' said Richard, as they waited for the lift.

'Because I couldn't bear to go on keeping them out of each other's arms,' said Drew.

Going down in the lift, Richard wondered if Clare was right in thinking she had fooled her friends on the hotel staff. Probably they all knew, including the pleasant lift man, and thought it delightful that a pretty girl should be set up as the mistress of a rich man. In the hall the little page, scurrying on some errand, flashed a quick smile. Probably even he was in on it.

It was dark when they came out of the hotel; a chilly, faintly misty evening.

'Let's walk a while,' said Drew. 'Through the back streets – one can talk better.'

'All right, if you know your way. I'm apt to get lost even in the main streets.'

'I've made rather a study of London back streets. Well? You talk first.'

'You can say what you like, Drew, but it isn't pretty.'

'No, pretty's too small a word. Richard, can you really disapprove of such intense happiness?'

'I suppose I'm a prig,' said Richard.

'Just a puritan – which no doubt you should be, as a serious creative artist. I'm essentially frivolous – that's why anything so unfrivolous as what those two feel for each other strikes me as

410

positively holy.'

Richard had never thought Drew frivolous. He said so, adding: 'But I think that, for once, you're being sentimental.'

'If so, it's highly unsuitable for the occasion. I doubt if there's much sentimentality in Clare's formidable friend. And she's always been romantic, not sentimental; there's a world of difference. Your true romantic will accept things sentimentalists would run a mile from – including a certain amount of horror.'

Richard looked at his brother curiously. 'Then you admit the situation has its horror? I thought you found it holy.'

'So do I. But I feel in my bones there's some horror lurking in the background. That house of assignations – she spoke of it as frightening. It's fascinating to remember that St John's Wood once enjoyed a bad reputation because so many men kept their mistresses there. It was jocularly referred to as Jack's Forest.'

'The things you know! Clare seemed to take a particular pleasure in using the word "mistress".'

'True. No sentimentalist would. Impressive to see the dithery girl so sure of herself. I wish we knew how the affair started. She told us nothing. And I pine to have seen her house as it was, and know all about its past.'

'I know more than I care about its future,' said Richard. 'Where are we?'

'Back streets of St James's and Piccadilly. Surprising, aren't they? So small and at night so deserted.'

'Yet they don't look like business premises.'

Empty milk bottles stood outside many of the doors. Aspidistras graced several downstairs windows. A drowsy cat on a window-sill awaited admission.

'No, I think people live here,' said Drew. 'Club servants, perhaps; cleaners and the like. Strange that such streets should survive in a district where land's so fabulously valuable. Well, they won't survive much longer. Look!'

They had turned a corner. Not far ahead was a half demolished row of houses and, beyond it, a tall new block of offices.

'I wonder if Rowley had a hand in that,' said Richard. 'You know, I think I'd mind less if he wasn't so rich.'

'Really? Personally, I'm delighted the wages of sin are high.'

'So's Clare. She's so obviously proud of his wealth.'

'Well, it's inbred in women to be proud of capturing a rich man. Dear me, I hope Clare's tiny ego can assimilate so much food – adoration from rich ex-royalty. And you must admit he's charming.'

'Also dissipated,' said Richard grimly.

'I wouldn't put it past her to be proud of that, too.'

Richard chuckled. 'How worldly wise you are, Drew!'

'Well, it's wonderful what one can learn from literature, life being something one's rather remote from.'

Richard thought his brother's tone a trifle bleak. 'Are you tolerably happy at Whitesea?' he asked, seriously.

Drew was silent for several seconds: then he spoke with his usual cheerfulness. 'Oh, rather more than tolerably. There's quite a satisfaction in the job. But I've written to you about it pretty fully. Let's talk about you. Not a copious letter writer, are you?'

'Nothing to write about ... well, nothing much.' He hadn't so far written or spoken about Violet's arrival. Should he mention it now? But if he did, he would do more than mention it. And he did not fancy launching out about Violet so soon after his disapproval of Clare. If the Clare story wasn't pretty, neither was the Violet story... But he did want to tell it to Drew. They walked on in silence until Drew said: 'Well, let me know if you decide to tell me whatever it is you haven't yet decided to.'

Richard laughed. 'The famous Drew intuition! This is the Haymarket, isn't it? Did we come through Piccadilly Circus?'

'No, we skirted it. Even you, Richard, would surely have noticed Piccadilly Circus? Now let me see, between Haymarket and Leicester Square there used to be one or two nice little mean streets – but one always fears they'll be gone.'

Eventually he found one but was dissatisfied with it. 'Not very attractive now, so messy; though there is still the faintest suggestion of a street in a country town – such small, dim shops.'

Richard, only mildly interested, said: 'I suppose there'd have been prostitutes here, before the streets were cleared of them. And now the poor

413

dears have to sit at windows. There's one up there.'

'I think not, Richard. Look again – and you needn't mind staring.'

'What...? Good God!'

Leaning out of a brightly lit third floor window was a large collie dog. Its front paws flopped over the sill, its silky hair stirred gently, and it appeared to be regarding them most benignly down its long, pointed nose.

'The things one sees in London!' said Drew, happily. 'I shall never forget that. Now let's walk very fast across Leicester Square because I hate it. Well, not really. It can't help being like it is; still, lets hurry.'

'Where to?' said Richard, who had begun to feel hungry.

'Back of the Strand. The quiet streets there are very different ... sombre, dignified, some of them.'

'I find this depressing,' said Richard, a few minutes later.

'I know what you mean. But I do love Covent Garden. We might have a look around there.'

'I'd rather get a meal,' said Richard. 'I shall have to eat before I drive home. And my lunch was forgettable.'

'We'd better go into the Strand.'

'I'd like somewhere quiet.' Richard was now sure he would talk about Violet. 'And I'm not dressed for any decent restaurant.'

'I don't think they expect much of one nowadays. And you *are* wearing a tie – just. Still ... there's a café over there – or rather, a caff, and that's flattering it. Undoubtedly quiet.'

414

It was almost empty. Richard opted for it.

'Difficult to choose between twenty tables,' said Drew. They settled near the window, far away from the counter. 'Well, I gather one goes and gets what one wants.'

Sandwiches seemed safest, plus cups of tea, no pots being available. 'Sorry I let you in for this,' said Richard, as they went back to their table. 'You wouldn't think such places could survive – those archaic urns, in these days of dashing Espressos.'

'It's probably used by Covent Garden porters. Anyway, London's full of survivals, like the streets we've walked through. For that matter, all England is, as our family's proved these last weeks. Merry with the desiccated Crestovers – they're typical of hundreds of great families on their last legs. Me with Miss Whitecliff, though I don't say she's typical. I'm not sure I didn't create her out of my love of Edwardiana; perhaps she isn't there when I'm not.'

'And is Clare's man typical royal blood and all?'

'Perhaps *she* created him. But really he *is* typical and so's my Miss Whitecliff, in a curious, basic way. They're typical because of ... their unusualness, their eccentricity. I'm convinced England's overflowing with eccentric people, places, happenings. Indeed, you might say eccentricity's normal in England.'

'Only it just so happens that Rowley isn't of English descent.'

'Well, England not only breeds eccentrics, it plays host to them. How I long to have met that old dead king! Come to think of it, we're a bit freakish as a family, particularly Clare and I. Do you think that's why we've landed in such ... well, freakish circumstances? Perhaps like gravitates to like.'

It was the kind of discussion Drew could enjoy for hours. 'What interests me more,' said Richard, 'is that you've gravitated to such rich circumstances. Why haven't I that knack?'

'Probably because you belong to the future – not to the past, as individual wealth really does. Anyway, I never heard of a great composer who began life wealthy.'

'The idea of my becoming any kind of composer has begun to strike me as ludicrous,' said Richard gloomily.

'No work at all? Well, you've so much to worry about. I do wish you'd let me help with expenses at home.'

'I will when I need to.' Richard took a long drink of very nasty tea and decided it was now or never as regards mentioning Violet and it was going to be now. 'By the way, I don't think I've told you that Violet has arrived.'

Drew looked blank but only for a second. 'You mean Father's Violet? No, Richard, you haven't told me that.'

There was no sign of avid curiosity; merely a mild, encouraging interest. It was the usual Drew technique for eliciting a full confidence and Richard had no desire to resist it. He waded in without conscious reservations, and knew that Drew was liable to spot unconscious ones and trot them out for inspection. Incidentally, telling the story clarified certain points for himself and he was not surprised when Drew said: 'But, my dear Richard, she obviously came with just one idea in her head: you. Didn't she show any special interest in you when you called on her after Father bolted?'

'Looking back, I see that she may have done.'

'I, of course, knew of your interest in her from your very first meeting. I assure you I did.'

'Nonsense. You're just being wise after the event.'

'No, really. Clare knew, too.'

'Well, I didn't, anyway,' said Richard.

'Because you didn't let yourself. It would have been – what's the word you've just used repeatedly? Distasteful: a horrid word, sort of sour. Well, what are you going to do? Obviously you must let the girl have her head, I mean as regards having her say.'

'I'm convinced she'll just tell me a pack of lies.'

Drew looked at him searchingly. 'Richard, do you *like* her at all? I used the word advisedly.'

'Not much. Sometimes I actually dislike her.'

'Then I think you should turf her out. I don't feel at all strongly about your "distasteful" angle. It's a bore she was Father's girl friend but that barrier's not much more than conventional and if you were really in love I'd give you my blessing. I even would if you ... well, just felt fond of her. But to have an affair with a woman you actually dislike strikes me as sheer vice.'

'You're leaving out one trifling fact,' said Richard. 'At times I find her overpoweringly attractive.'

'You don't – if she hasn't overpowered you.'

'Well, she's only been on the job a week.' Richard was beginning to find Drew's paternal manner annoying. Really, his dear, intuitive but utterly innocent brother was out of his depth. 'Oh, I must just work it out for myself. And I ought to be able to – after all, I had two affairs when I was in Germany.'

Drew smilingly remembered. 'One with a near tart and one with a near virgin, you told me. An interesting selection, though I never believed in the latter; virgins, surely, are or aren't. Anyway, my advice is: go home, let poor Violet talk, then make up your mind what you really want. Don't just, well, oblige her. Would you like some more of this revolting tea?'

Richard shook his head.

'Then let's go. Peculiar place this – like a television set without enough people in it. Where did you leave your car?'

'Back of Regent's Park – vaguely.'

'I hope you don't *mean* "vaguely".'

'No, no, I memorized the name of the street. Only ... well, it'll come back to me.'

'It had better,' said Drew, ominously. 'Let's cut through to the Strand and get a taxi. I'll come with you. I've still got over an hour. Don't talk. Just try to remember.'

'I feel sure it was near the Zoo.'

'Well, that's something. We'll start there.'

As they got into the taxi Richard said: 'It was one of those streets which run *away* from the Zoo.'

'Run north?'

'If that *would* be north.'

Drew and the taxi driver worked out a plan of campaign which conveyed little to Richard. He sat looking out of the window and presently remarked that the Strand struck him as garish.

'Very. Don't waste your mind on it,' Drew told him. 'Just go on trying to remember.'

'I *am* sorry. And I'd have said I'd been better of late; nothing like as absent-minded as when I'm working.'

'I'm all *for* your being absent-minded when you're working. And you're really more single-minded than absent-minded. But you might have to spend hours looking for that car.'

They drove in silence until Richard suddenly said:

'Hello! This looks like the place.'

'This, Richard, is the south side of the park and quite a long way from the Zoo.'

'Oh. Well, I *am* sure about the Zoo, because I went there. Though it comes to me now that I parked before I had lunch and then walked to the Zoo.'

'Well, we'll start east of Primrose Hill and try every street.' They went for some distance up three streets. Richard gazed at the lighted windows of flats and houses with envy. So many people safely in for the night, and so aloof from him and his plight; slight resentment was added to the envy. After another street, Drew said: 'Are you sure you came in the car?'

Richard's eyes went blank; then light returned to them. 'Yes! Look, I've got the key!'

They tried more streets, with no better luck.

'You'll miss your train, Drew,' said Richard.

'I *shall* have to dash for it soon, as I promised to get back tonight.'

'And I'm sure we're too far from the Zoo. You take this taxi on to your station and I'll walk back and go a bit farther up each street, right from the beginning.'

'You wouldn't know where the beginning was,' said Drew. 'Anyway, let's do the job properly. There are only two more streets before the road where all the buses are. Even you couldn't have parked there.'

They found the car in St John's Wood High Street, close to the churchyard.

'Believe it or not,' said Drew, 'that building has nothing to do with the Zoo. It's St John's Wood Church – Clare's future parish church, incidentally. Not that she was ever by way of being religious.'

Richard apologized abjectly and offered to pay for the taxi. 'Well, at least let me drive you to the station,' he said, when Drew waved the money away.

'No, thank you,' said Drew. 'I want to get there.'

He saw Richard into the car, then stood by the open window.

'There's so much we still haven't talked about,' said Richard, regretting he hadn't done more to make Drew talk about himself.

'Well, we must meet again before long. Richard, I was intolerant about Violet. And I don't believe you do dislike her.'

Richard smiled. 'You couldn't be intolerant, Drew. And just because *you* never dislike anyone–'

'But I do. And I can be intolerant.'

Drew's tone was so cold that Richard looked at him in surprise and saw, by the light of a street lamp, that his brother's expression was rigidly implacable. Then the moment passed and their usual liveliness returned to voice and face.

'I *must* go, Richard. Do write.'

'You, too. And tell Merry to.'

Richard waited until Drew was back in the taxi and on his way; then looked around, none too sure of his route out of London. Strange that Drew and Merry could always find their way about here, when Clare and he were so hopeless at it.

He wasn't conscious of any other resemblance between Clare and himself – but then, how little he'd known her. Perhaps she was just a born bad lot. He doubted that, but if she was, it might be as well that she'd found it out.

Along the High Street came a small, white, lady poodle, out for a walk on a pale blue leash. Remembering Clare's radiant confidence at the hotel, it occurred to him that she might be like those ultra-feminine dogs who are scared of even their own shadows but bold as brass with interested males. Being fond of dogs, he found the idea pleasing and his disapproval of Clare dwindled. Good luck to her, anyway. He cast a beneficent glance in what he imagined was the direction of St John's Wood, then thought about Drew on his way back to Merry... Less than a month ago the four of them had been together every day, taking each other for granted, hardly aware of the pleasure they found in each other's company.

Starting the car and heading – he hoped – for home, he played with the pretence that the Dome House of those days would be waiting for him, with the others asleep in their rooms when he entered the dark hall. But his thoughts soon slid to the Dome House of the present, where there was more than a chance that Violet would be waiting up when he entered the hall. Did he hope she would be? He couldn't decide. But he did drive a little faster.

5

Two Views of the Dome

No one was waiting up for him. And when he woke, very late the next morning, and came down in a dressing-gown, he found the house deserted. Jane, of course, would have gone to Miss Willy; Cook and Edith would be at the Swan. But where were Violet and Aunt Winifred? He then discovered a note, addressed to himself, on the hall table. It said:

Darling Richard,
As you wouldn't take me to London, I've gone on my own and taken your aunt – the poor old dear needs a change. Back in a day or two. Lots of love,
Violet.

Had they left yesterday or this morning? If this morning, Violet might not have made her bed... He looked into her room. The bed was made. Otherwise the room was untidy; but it smelt very nice and all the things left lying about were charming, not to say expensive. When with her, however much attracted, he always felt it his duty to be antagonistic. He was conscious of no such duty now and felt positively tender towards her possessions. Annoying of her not to be here when he was so much in the mood to see her...

He dressed, breakfasted on milk and biscuits, then sat in the hall reading the morning paper. Could one be so obsessed by the little problems of one's inner world when the outer world was facing such gigantic problems? Unfortunately – or perhaps mercifully – one could. He put the paper aside and lay down, staring upwards and remembering that, in his childhood, this worm's eye view of the dome had always made him feel physically small. He had mentioned this to his grandmother who had offered the explanation that the little dome of their house carried his thoughts up to the vast dome above it. Well, his thoughts weren't likely to do any such soaring this morning.

This memory of his grandmother reminded him of how seldom he thought about her ... strange, in view of how much her upbringing must have conditioned him. But he had never felt emotionally tied to her, as he would have to his mother if she'd ever given him the chance. 'Grand' had just been a kind, encouraging woman who put the tools of one's trade within reach and made life at Dome House very comfortable. It was that life as a whole he thought of when he looked back over the years. Someone had once, with faint disparagement, referred to him and his brother and sisters as 'grandmother's children', but they were really more the children of a house. Well, the others were out from under the dome now. He continued to stare up at it. The brightness of the mid-morning sun showed that it needed cleaning...

He was suddenly aware of having been lost in one of his moods of abstraction. He had been subject to them since his boyhood, had no control over them and only knew of them when they were over. They were of two kinds: one, a vague daydream, dimly rememberable, which left him depleted and dissatisfied with himself; the other, far rarer, left him with no memory of its content, but in a state bordering on exaltation and certain that he would shortly be capable of creative work. Today the mood was of the second description and he came out of it astounded at such good fortune, also very hungry, and surprised to find it was long past lunch time. He grabbed some bread and cheese, grudging the time it took, then hurried out to his music room.

On entering it he had a sudden doubt if he really would be able to work. But there was nothing new about that; for years he'd always had to force himself into actually starting. And he *had* felt confident. He must hang on to that.

The first three movements of his sextet, though far from satisfying him, did at least exist. The finale did not, in any performable shape – and it must be made to. With a tremendous mental effort, he got going.

He had been working a good three hours when Jane opened the door.

'Do forgive me for disturbing you, Richard. If I wait until you come indoors Violet and Miss Carrington may have returned, or the maids maybe around. And I need to speak to you privately.'

Curbing his irritation, he welcomed her in and settled her in a chair. She looked around with distressed eyes.

'Oh, dear, this is the first time I've been in this room, since I talked to your father here! Well, now...' She became determinedly cheerful. 'I don't quite know how to begin.'

He smiled at her with great liking. Kind, reliable Jane, in her cashmere sweater, her well-cut tweed skirt and her admirable shoes. He had always thought she had a sweet face, a very girlish face for a woman nearly in her forties; he suspected there would still be something girlish about it if she lived into her nineties.

'Plunge right in,' he advised.

'It's just that I've been working on a scheme. Briefly...'

She wasn't at all brief and, from the beginning, he had to restrain himself from blowing her scheme sky-high. For what she had to suggest was that Miss Willy should take over as many rooms as possible at Dome House, for her overflow of teachers and a few senior pupils.

'You see, if we could use Drew's room and Clare's and Merry's – and if you could sleep in here, well, that would be four rooms. And if Violet and Miss Carrington would ... well, go, that would make six. The rent of six rooms would enable us to keep the maids at home. They'd rather work here for a minimum wage than go to the Swan.'

'Have you asked them?' said Richard.

'Well, yes – I needed to know their feelings before approaching you. They dislike working at the Swan and poor old Burly is having trouble with the young dog there who doesn't respect his seniority. But I ought to say at once that the scheme will only work if we can let six rooms.'

'Then it's out of the question,' said Richard, with relief. 'I can't turn my aunt out, and Violet's stay is ... well, indefinite.'

'But how can things go on as they are? The maids are too tired now to do any cleaning here. The food gets worse and worse. The winter's coming, already the house is insufficiently heated. And can you afford to cope with even the minimum expenses? Do forgive me if I'm being impertinent.'

'You're not,' he assured her. 'And, frankly, I can't cope much longer. I see no chance, even, of paying next quarter's rent. But damn it, what *can* I do? My aunt says she has no money. And she's let her house.'

'She informed me she'd merely closed it. Anyway, if she's hard up, why doesn't she claim an old-age pension? She had the nerve to tell me that's something no lady would ever do. She's victimizing you, Richard. As for Violet! You surely don't think she's poor?'

'I did think she was, when she came,' he said, uncomfortably.

'With a mink coat over her arm? A very good mink, incidentally, and almost new. And what about her jewellery? Not to mention her car.'

He looked at Jane blankly. 'Her car? Surely she hasn't...?'

'Of course she has. She keeps it garaged at the Swan.'

'But she arrived in a taxi. It drove off as I let her in.'

'Then she only took it from the village. I haven't seen the car myself but the maids have and they say it looks expensive. She's gone to London in it. My dear, dear Richard, Violet is victimizing you, too.'

He said firmly: 'No, Jane. She did offer to pay. But how could I let her? My father made no kind of provision for her.'

Jane flushed. 'We don't know your father's side of that matter. Anyhow, if she did pay it wouldn't get us anywhere now. Apart from the fact that Miss Willy needs six rooms, she won't send her teachers or pupils here while Violet remains. I'm sorry. That's made you angry.'

'Well, not with you. But I do think it's outrageous. What the hell does she know about Violet?'

'From me, only that Violet describes herself as your father's fiancée. I can't say why Miss Willy thinks otherwise but she does. Besides ... oh, Richard, do be reasonable!'

She had been avoiding his eyes. Now she looked at him very directly and it was he who looked away. Was she aware of the situation between himself and Violet? She'd seen them together so seldom, still... Anyway, apart from Miss Willy's prejudices, he and Violet couldn't conduct their skirmishes in front of the interested eyes of a bunch of school teachers and schoolgirls...

He was silent so long that Jane gave up waiting for an answer. 'Well, please think it over – fairly quickly; there is an empty house Miss Willy could rent. And do remember that if you're driven into closing the house, Violet and your aunt will have to go anyway.'

It made sense. He said without enthusiasm, 'I'd better write and see what Drew thinks. And suppose Merry wants to come home?'

'We could just manage that, by putting two beds in one room. Of course there's Clare, but one presumes she'll get more work.'

'She won't need to,' said Richard. 'You don't know that I saw her yesterday. I'd better tell you about it.'

He was soon to wish he had done no such thing for it became obvious that Jane was both shocked and indignant; indeed, her disapproval was so extreme that he found himself defending Clare.

'She's very deeply in love, Jane. She looked quite dazzlingly happy.'

'How can she be in love with an ugly, middle-aged man?'

'He didn't strike me as either.'

'Well, Miss Gifford told me he was. Oh, if only we'd done something when she warned me!'

'Clare said it wouldn't have made any difference. She *is* in love with him, Jane. And he obviously adores her.'

Jane's tone became withering. 'From what you say, they'd only known each other a week when – when this appalling thing began. Don't tell me it has anything to do with love. I'm not an intolerant woman. I don't think I'm even conventional...'

'You are, dear Jane,' he said gently.

'Perhaps what you call conventionality, I call decency. Anyway, I'm so shocked that I don't want to hear any more.'

She'd seemed quite unshocked by Merry's adventures; indeed, he thought she rather hoped that, after four or five years, Merry might reward a gallant, faithful earl by becoming his countess. *That* story was romantic, but Clare's – to herself the very essence of romance – was to Jane the most brutal reality.

'Well, I'm partly on your side,' he said appeasingly.

'I should hope so. Richard, you won't tell Cook and Edith?'

'No fear. And heaven help me if Aunt Winifred finds out. I must invent something.'

'You could say Clare has got a new job ... as a companion.'

'I could – with perfect truth.'

She did not return his smile. And he suddenly knew just why there would always be something girlish about her; and he knew, too, why such a sweet-faced, graceful and very kind woman had never married. Buried within her was a spinsterly core which had conditioned not only her outlook but also the events of her life. One gets, he thought, not what one wants but what one is.

'Well, it's time for tea.' She spoke with unusual briskness, as if dismissing Clare from her mind. 'Come in if you'd like some.'

'I would, thank you. I had rather a sketchy lunch.'

At once she became her kindest self. 'You need regular meals, Richard. Just think what it would be like to have this house properly run again.'

'It used to be so very comfortable. Not luxurious; just comfortable.'

430

'That's the best kind of luxury. I often look back to my first day here. That wonderful steak-and-kidney pudding's become a sort of *symbol* of comfort to me. We could surely achieve that again. And this could be made into an excellent bed-sitting-room; you could afford enough coke to keep your stove going.' She shivered. 'You can't go on working in this ice-house. However, I mustn't try to coerce you.'

After tea he scribbled a letter to Drew about Jane's scheme and caught the post with it. Then he worked on what he thought of as his counter-scheme. Suppose Drew contributed a little, Violet was allowed to pay, and something was extracted from Aunt Winifred? Alas, this couldn't compete with what Miss Willy was offering. A pity he couldn't ask Clare to toss him a few hundred-pound notes, which she could doubt-less get for the asking.

He tried to work again in the evening but Jane's mention of an ice-house had made him fully conscious of how cold his music room was, so he went to bed early. But next morning, after his usual difficulty in starting, he got on fairly well and came in to lunch feeling cheerful; as it was Saturday, he didn't have to get it himself. Simply because he wanted her to, he convinced himself Violet would return that afternoon. She did not, nor did she on the next day, when it rained incessantly. He got stuck with his work; obviously his impulse to create had no staying power. And when he went indoors Cook and Edith begged him to agree to Jane's scheme. He fobbed them off by saying he must wait for Drew's answer,

431

then persuaded them to come in and watch television. Burly was hoisted on the sofa between them and for a while, with the fire burning brightly, there was a semblance of cheerfulness. Then he saw that they had both fallen asleep, and small wonder as they had worked all weekend at cooking and cleaning, allowing themselves no leisure at all. He couldn't let them go on like this much longer.

On Monday he woke up in a temper. If Violet and Aunt Winifred did not return today, they could stay away for good. They couldn't just use his house as a hotel – and anyway, people paid in hotels. Incapable of even an attempt to work, he sat in the hall all morning, waiting. Would Violet this time arrive in her own car? Good God, no wonder his father had gone broke, if he'd paid for her car, mink coat and jewellery, not to mention that most expensive flat!

After a bread and cheese lunch he decided to go for a walk. He opened the front door and was just in time to see a most impressive car coming up the drive. Violet was at the wheel with his aunt beside her. As they got out, in remarkably good spirits, he noted that they both appeared to be wearing new clothes. Aunt Winifred was in pale grey, two pink roses pinned to her coat. Violet had achieved a most expensive-looking tweed and leather outfit. It was the first time he'd seen her in clothes suitable for the country and the fact that she was in them now struck him as ominous, as did the wardrobe trunk in the car. Violet was about to dig herself in. She greeted him with a happy, 'Richard, darling!'

'Excuse me, I have to go out,' he said curtly and brushed past them both. He heard Violet wail: 'Richard, is something wrong? Do come back!' But he strode along the drive at a terrific pace, turned away from the village and started to climb the hill. He was annoyed and hoped he'd made it plain.

By the time he reached the hill top, the annoyance was directed towards himself. What a ridiculous display of temper and without real justification! Why shouldn't they have taken a trip to London? His irritation was really due to the fact that he had been missing Violet. He would go back and make his peace with them... But not just yet.

He leaned against the signpost and looked down at his home. Under a heavily overcast sky, the dome was coldly grey; the surrounding trees were on their way towards wintry bareness. Whatever the time of year he liked this view. And as a rule, seeing the house from above made him feel pleasantly detached, even a little Godlike. He had no such feelings today and he knew they would not come to him. No view could engender any kind of philosophic peace in a mind as restless as his was now.

He would walk home along the field path, which meant sticking to the road for nearly a mile before turning into the fields behind Dome House. He remembered taking this walk with Merry on a very similar sunless afternoon when a mist – as now – was rising. It was then that she had told him about her 'programme' for the second movement of the Beethoven quartet he had been playing when she returned home with flaming hair and false bust. According to her, the music portrayed a lost traveller wandering through dense mist, conscious of surrounding menace. 'He's in a land of giants and enchanters, and castles where it would be safer not to shelter. But he never sees anything, just knows the menace is there, and sometimes he hears satiric laughter – only it's alluring laughter, too.' For Richard music never represented anything but itself and to invent stories about it was reprehensible, but she had created her menace-filled mist unforgettably and the memory of it haunted him as he walked across the fields.

Merry was so much in his mind that when he heard someone call his name he at first thought she must have come home. But when the voice called again he recognized it as Violet's. He called in answer and then left the path and climbed up on a nearby gate. From there he could see her crossing a stubble field. He called again and hurried towards her.

She came running to him. 'Oh, darling, I saw you from my window and came to meet you. And then the beastly mist came rolling at me, and I had a free fight getting through a hedge. And this stubble, if that's what it's called, is hell to walk on...'

'You should have stuck to the path,' he told her.

'I didn't find any path. Can we sit down and talk?'

'Well, it's pretty damp. Let's talk at home.'

'No, someone will interrupt there. And I must sit down. I'm exhausted, trying to walk in these

434

wretched low-heeled country shoes I bought – it's like running down a hill backwards.' She sat down just where she was, then looked resentfully at the stubble. 'Oh, I do hate the country.'

He sat down beside her. 'Then why did you come here?'

'You know why I came. You must by now, even if you didn't at first. Oh, darling, are you angry with me?'

He assured her he wasn't. 'And I'm sorry I was so rude just now, dashing away like that. I ought to have got your trunk out of the car for you.'

'Oh, that can wait till tomorrow. But *why* were you so cross?'

'It was just that... Oh, never mind. If you want to talk, talk.'

She looked at him reproachfully. 'I do think that's a putting-off thing to say. Why can't you be a better guesser?'

'Because there's too damn much to guess. Hadn't you better clear things up once and for all, Violet dear?'

'All right. I want to, really. I came because I liked you. I did the very first time we met. And I liked you much more when you came to see if your father had provided for me. That was sweet of you, Richard. And you'd have felt very snubbed if I'd told you he never had provided for me. I've never needed providing for. I've money of my own as well as a nice lump my first husband left me. Your father was ... well, just a good friend.'

'Do you mean there was never anything between you?'

435

She was silent for several seconds. Then she said loudly:

'Nothing whatever. You just imagined it.'

He felt sure she was lying. 'Then why was he staying at your flat that first time I came there?'

'He wasn't. Oh, well, he just may have been. Perhaps his own flat was being re-decorated or something. Anyway, I often ask people for weekends – it's my form of entertaining and, believe me, weekends in London can be much more fun than weekends in the boring country. You must try them. Darling, I'm sorry I told you lies, but if I'd let you know I was well-off how could I have come down here and asked you to take me in? And, oh, Richard, I'm so in love with you. There! Am I forgiven?'

He said: 'You would be, if you'd stop lying.'

'But I have, truly! I absolutely swear it.'

Well, why not let himself believe her, as he longed to? He had been stirred by her declaration. And never had he seen her look so beautiful. Against the dark green of her jacket, her pale skin had an almost snowy purity. Her silky black hair was less tidy than usual and particularly becoming. And her long legs, though stuck straight out in front of her most ungracefully, were such very nice legs; the fact that she had laddered both her superfine stockings – presumably when fighting the hedge – somehow added a touch of appeal.

He moved closer to her and put a comforting arm round her shoulders. Immediately, she executed an agile swivelling movement, at the same time flinging both her arms round his neck and pulling him downwards, with the net result that she was flat on her back and he was sprawling beside her.

'Stop it,' he said, disentangling himself. 'We're in full view of a public footpath.' He struggled to his feet and pulled her to hers.

She looked wistfully towards a ditch. 'We'd be out of sight down there.'

'We'd also be in a couple of feet of water. Anyway, when and if we do go to bed together, it's going to be in a bed.'

'Well, I've nothing against beds except that they're so often not around when needed. Let's make plans. Sit down again – just for a minute.'

'No,' he said firmly. 'You keep on your feet. The trouble with you is that you're far too conscious of the pull of gravity.'

She laughed. 'What a funny name for it.'

Richard laughed too, and began to feel cheerful. He could now have looked Drew in the face and said he liked her. 'You come on home,' he told her and steered her towards the path.

In a few minutes they were out of the dense patch of mist and Dome House was visible.

'Stop clinging to me,' said Richard. 'Someone may be looking out of a window.'

'No, they won't. Your aunt's taking a nap, and Jane and the maids won't be in yet.' Violet continued to cling. 'Has Jane told you she wants to fill your house with schoolteachers?'

'Yes, but who told you?' he said, astonished.

'I heard the maids talking. Well, why not let her? Just hand the house over and come to London with me. You can't live with a pack of giggling females. They'll accuse you of assaulting them. And we can have such fun in London.'

He stopped dead, in the lane outside the back garden. 'Violet, are you seriously suggesting that I come and live with you?'

'Why not? We might even get married. I'd just have to divorce my second husband but it wouldn't take long. Let's go to your music room and talk it all out.'

'Not now,' said Richard. 'You've got to let me do some thinking. And I'm sorry if I seem brutal but could you, from now on, leave the initiative to me?'

'Well, of course I'd adore to – if you'll promise to take it.'

'All I promise is that I *won't* take it if you don't lay off for a while. Now pull yourself together. Here are the maids coming home. Hello, Burly boy!'

'Oh, blast Burly boy!' said Violet. She opened the garden gate, banged it behind her and ran towards the house.

Richard waited for the maids. Surely they were back earlier than usual? He saw that Burly's ear was bleeding.

'That black brute at the Swan bit him,' said Edith. 'So we downed tools and brought him home.'

'Always shut up, that dog was, when Burly went there as a paying customer,' said Cook. 'Oh, Mr Richard, have you heard from Drew yet – if he thinks it would be all right for you to let the rooms?'

He noted that, though he was 'Mr Richard', Drew was still 'Drew', and would remain so until

438

he was twenty-one, when the maids would insist on using the prefix.

'Not yet,' he told them. 'But there may be something by the afternoon post. Cheer up, Burly.'

'He's a tired old dog,' said Cook.

'And we're tired old women,' said Edith.

He put his arm through theirs and walked them back to the house.

6

The Best Brains in the Family

He found two letters waiting for him: one from Drew and one, a very bulky one, from Merry. He opened Merry's first, thinking it might contain an enclosure for Lord Crestover, but saw only a wad of closely written pages which he set aside to read later. Drew, in quite a short letter, gave full approval of Jane's scheme, said he saw no likelihood of needing his own room and would be able to keep Merry with him. 'Everyone loves her and she has agreed to try a school run by Mrs Severn's cousin.' He advised Richard to evict Aunt Winifred. 'I don't believe she's broke – and at worst, it would pay you to send her a few pounds a week out of the rent Miss Willy pays. As for Violet, it would be impertinent to advise you, but as your letter mentions her mink coat and car (how like you not to know about them until told by Jane!) she can hardly be in need of a roof. And the Willy money does seem too good to turn down. I'll write again when I can. Now I have to escort Miss Whitecliff to the pictures. I hope they won't prove too much for her; she hasn't been since talkies came in.'

He had barely finished reading Drew's letter when Aunt Winifred, in a new sky-blue dress, with the pink roses – now slightly wilted – pinned against her shoulder, came downstairs.

'Richard,' she said, importantly. 'I must speak to you at once and very privately. Not here – it's far too public.'

She led the way into the drawing-room where they sat on two dust-sheeted chairs.

'Such a pretty room this used to be when *I* took charge of the house.' She looked around disapprovingly. 'Always full of flowers, so beautifully arranged by Clare. Well, now: I'm sure the dear child won't have told you quite all she told me but I gather you know the main outline of the situation. And I want to impress on you the necessity for the utmost discretion.'

He looked at her blankly. 'Are you talking of Clare? Do you mean you've seen her?'

'Yesterday. It was my main reason for going to London, though I spent some time on very necessary shopping before I began my inquiries. It was quite easy to find her as Jane Minton told me she was staying at one of the very best hotels. I asked first at the one I like most – where I've often been for tea. And there she was and simply delighted to see me. She told me the whole story at once. Poor child, she expected me to be shocked!'

'And you weren't?' said Richard dazedly.

'Of course not. But some people would be. That's why I urge complete discretion. Nothing must be known in the village; be careful not to talk in front of the maids. I've said nothing to Violet. And I strongly advise you not to tell Jane Minton. She's a good creature but her standards are essentially middle class. An affair like this needs the aristocratic approach.'

'Oh, quite,' said Richard, tickled to hear his aunt dissociate herself from the middle class.

'A king, whether reigning or not, is always above petty conventions. Perhaps Clare will assist him to regain his throne.'

'I don't fancy he wants to,' said Richard.

'He may now, on Clare's account. Perhaps we shall see her a queen – for of course he wishes to marry her. Unfortunately I was not able to meet him as he's abroad for a few days. He now reigns over what I believe is called a Business Empire. Clare hopes to present me later.'

She continued to chatter happily, stressing Clare's affection for her. 'The dear girl pinned these roses to my coat. A perfect setting for her, that lovely room, but no doubt her own house will be even more delightful. Our tastes, of course, have always been similar.' And gradually it dawned on him that she was partly identifying herself with Clare. Perhaps her past treatment of Clare, at times amounting to persecution, had been an effort to re-create Clare in her own image and she was now replacing this by re-creating herself in Clare's image, in order to enjoy a longed-for romance. He was more and more sure she was a little mad but her madness seemed harmless – indeed benign, for it emerged that she had decided to leave Dome House and live in London, to be near to Clare.

'But can you afford to?' he asked involuntarily.

'With economy, at some quiet hotel. I shall let my house.' No point in reminding her she'd told him it was already let, also that she was practically penniless; he doubted if she now knew the difference between fact and fiction. She might be inventing Clare's pleasure at seeing her, or had Clare, out of the largesse of her happiness, found some affection to spare for her once-hated old aunt? He thought it possible. Had not Clare said: 'I couldn't hate anyone now'?

'When do you plan to leave us?' he inquired politely.

'Almost at once. I came here as soon as I saw your father's name in the papers, to do all I could to help; at such times, family solidarity counts for so much. But you're over the first shock now and Clare's need of me is greater.'

How revelatory they were, those words 'name in the papers'! For her they had indicated not a reprehensible notoriety but a romantic celebrity, something it would increase her self-importance to share in; that was why she had come. And now her ego was feeding on thoughts of sharing far more romantic circumstances – he noted the visionary look in her faded blue eyes. He also noted something else: a faint but indubitable resemblance to Clare. And it occurred to him that there, but for the grace of God, went Clare in her old age, finding in some hazy cloud cuckoo land a refuge from a lifetime of repression. Though it seemed a bit blasphemous to equate the grace of God with Charles Rowley.

Incidentally, he wondered just how long his aunt's new dream world would last. For would Clare, however kind her present mood, be willing to see much of a half-dotty old woman? Pleased though he was that Aunt Winifred would soon be on her way, he felt a little sorry for her.

Edith, looking worried, opened the drawing-room door. 'Will you come and see Burly, Mr Richard? We're wondering if we ought to telephone the Vet.'

Richard rose at once, saying, 'You go back to the fire, Aunt Winifred.'

'That dog should be put down, Richard. It's not pleasant having an ailing old dog around the house.'

How swiftly she had lost his sympathy! Seeing Edith's outraged expression he whispered to her as they crossed the hall. 'Never mind. She's going.'

'Thank God for a bit of good news,' said Edith.

Cook was kneeling beside Burly who lay with his heavy golden head flopping over the edge of the basket, every line of his obese body indicating exhaustion. His wide-open old eyes stoically faced his fast-approaching death; they had been capable of that expression since puppyhood.

'Is his ear still bleeding?' asked Richard.

'Not now, but he won't eat,' said Cook.

Richard knelt, studied the selection of food which had already been offered, then festooned Burly's greying muzzle with a thin strip of boiled ham. In an effort to dislodge this, Burly got a bit inside his mouth and failed to disguise interest. After that, he accepted all there was for him and seemed to want more. Cook went happily to the refrigerator and no more was said about the Vet.

'Still, we won't take him to the Swan tomorrow,' said Edith. 'It upsets his pride. And one of us must stay at home with him. Mr Richard, *was* there a letter from Drew?'

He admitted there had been and that Drew had

nothing against letting rooms to Miss Willy. 'All the same, I can't decide yet.' He hurried out of the kitchen. Damn it, even Burly was now rooting for Jane's scheme. Finding Violet, horizontal in black lace, alone in the hall, he went to his bedroom until supper was ready. It proved to be a sparse meal only nominally liver and bacon, Burly having been given much of the liver.

After supper, Richard said: 'I have an important piece of work to finish and I shall be most grateful not to be disturbed unless it is absolutely necessary.'

This remark was greeted with such a stunned silence that he guessed he must have sounded pompous. But Jane did eventually manage a kind 'We quite understand.'

He went to his music room and locked himself in. If Violet arrived he would tell her to go to hell. He was not coming out until he had made up his mind.

But had it not been made up for him by Jane, Cook, Edith, Drew and even old basket-loving Burly? What opposition was there, now Aunt Winifred was going and Violet would surely leave willingly provided he accepted her invitation for London weekends? (He wasn't going to consider her suggestion that he should *live* in London... Well, he wasn't going to consider *yet*.) Why shouldn't he sit back, accept the Willy contingent, live peacefully here in his music room and work, say, five days a week?

He only knew that he loathed the idea of it. Well, that was just too bad as there was no alternative.

He looked around the room, trying to see it as a warm, comfortable bed-sitting-room. It was not only cold now; it was beginning to feel damp. His books would soon be mildewed and his piano would be affected. His eyes travelled from it to his gramophone. The Third Rasoumovsky Quartet was still on the record-player. Should he listen to it now? Certainly not. *He must make up his mind.*

Thinking of the quartet reminded him of Merry and her still unread letter. Well, he would allow himself that. He took it from his pocket and began to read, admiring the pretty, already formed hand which she could write with surprising speed.

Darling Richard,
I have written direct to Claude and told him where I am. If he wants to come here he must – it will be my cross and I deserve to bear it for my disgusting behaviour. Oh, Richard, I am deep in sin! I sinned against myself, as I told you, and now I have sinned against Claude and it is all due to vanity. Why do I lust to show off? I shall never achieve anything unless I cure myself of it. I may have a bit of talent (false humility – I'm convinced I've quite a lot) but it won't get me anywhere if I have a cheap, vain little soul.

Anyway, I haven't shown off in my letter to Claude. I've told him the plain truth – that I made a mistake through being young and foolish. And if he does come here I won't show off then – though I may act a bit and seem even younger than I am; I think that will cure him more than anything. I hear you say: 'Don't overdo it.' All right, I'll resist the temptation to be playing with my tiny bucket and spade on the sands (only shingle here). I'll be young in the dullest way, gawky and flat-chested – perhaps I can hire a brace to put on my teeth.

Poor Claude! It will be terrible for him to find he loves a girl who doesn't really exist. One might write a play about it – very good part for me. I truly do feel sorry for him and I'm ashamed that I called him a codfish. It was a cliché, anyway – but he does have a cliché face.

Now about Clare. Drew says you were shocked. Oh, Richard, you shouldn't be. What's happened is a miracle of rightness – for her. She'd never have married some nice young man, as one expects a pretty, rather colourless girl to. The truth is, she was only colourless because she was so bored with life – I can see it so clearly now. Somehow one expects anyone who looks so angelic to be angelic, anyway conventional, and dote on children, domesticity, arranging flowers and the like. I never knew Clare to dote on anything and thought she wasn't capable of it. Now I realize there was simply nothing at home she found dote-worthy. Why did we never guess she was too romantic for everyday life? Drew has a theory she's somehow invented the life that's right for her. And Charles Rowley sounds to me ravishing (suitable word, now I come to think of it, but perhaps that shocks you). Handsome men are dead out – oh, sorry, darling Richard; anyway, you're not handsome in a conventional way.

I wish I felt as happy about Drew as I feel about Clare. I can't help thinking he will become a

447

prisoner here, imprisoned by Miss Whitecliff's need of him. She's an absolute pet, somehow like an old lady and a very bright child rolled into one. I don't mean that she's the least bit crazy. It's just that, for her, it's 'O brave new world, that has such people in't' – the people being Drew and the world being brave because he's showing it to her. I'm sure he finds it rewarding work but will he always? Anyway, he'll one day be rich because she's left him half her money. She told me, with glee, that she'd changed her will just before her niece last came here, so that she could promise the niece she never would change it if the niece would leave her alone. I found Drew didn't know about this, though he can see now that it fits with her behaviour the day the niece came. He was grateful but seemed a bit upset too. Perhaps it makes him feel all the more tied. Oh, I expect things will work out. She gets more independent every day – and is avid for modernity, rather fancies flying! And in a way, I can see it's right for Drew. Anyhow, he's so good and good people are usually happy. But do happy things happen to the good, or can the good make happiness out of unhappiness?

And now about you. Drew's said so little and he wouldn't let me read the letter that came yesterday, only gave me the gist of it, so I suspect he's hiding something. If so, you probably told him to and I won't worry you by questions. But I want to say, in the loudest possible shout, that I utterly disapprove of the Weary Willy invasion idea. And if I rank as a voting member of the family, I vote NO, in outsize capitals.

Richard, you would loathe it. Remember, I know Weary Willy's teachers. You'd die of embarrassment when you came in for meals (not to mention baths) and probably end by being rude to them. And you can't live your whole life in that dreary music room. There's something wrong with that room, Richard. I felt it again when I was in there last week, playing the Third Rasouniovsky. I don't mean it's haunted – nothing so exciting – but it's somehow lifeless, like a church that's never been prayed in.

He broke off, staggered by her insight, which had revealed something he had never before admitted. At no time on entering the room had he felt a hopeful excitement, an eager readiness to work. He had experienced it in various other rooms: an attic in Germany, a practice room at school, the drawing-room at Dome House where he had first learned to play the piano. But here he had to chum up eagerness, kick himself into working – even when, as so recently, he had felt eagerly ready up to the very moment of opening the door. He looked around at his musical instruments, his library of scores, critical studies, books on composition – could one ask for a better equipped work room? Why, then, was it so hard to work in?

And it was no use blaming some inimical psychic emanation from the old barn, because he had loved the barn when it was a barn, often jotted down work here; indeed, his love of it was one of his reasons for converting it. But now...

He went back to Merry's letter.

Please forgive me if I seem impertinent, but I don't think you are ready yet for a peaceful, creative life – and therefore what should be the peace in your room is a kind of false peace, rather like death. Things would have come right if Father hadn't bolted. You wouldn't always have stayed put at home and gradually you'd have – well, caught up with your music room.

Did she mean that his room was pretentious, suitable for a talent more proved than his? If so, she was right. As well might one furnish a room with dictionaries and hope to turn into a poet. And he had always known he should have stayed in Germany longer; his father would have gone on financing him instead of footing the bill for converting the barn. But he'd missed his family and the comfort of his home – a womb-like comfort, no doubt... What more had Merry to say?

People who act, or perform in any way, can count on already created work to learn their job on. But creators have nothing but themselves, they just have to be – and surely it's very hard to be without doing a bit of living first? (Unless one's a Mozart and I always think he'd carried forward some living from a previous life.) It's most unfair that Clare and Drew and I have put in quite a lot of living this last month, while you've been tied to a niggling, worrying life which is most unnatural to you. And you still feel tied. It's utterly wrong, darling Richard. So I have done something which may annoy you. I won't say what it is, because nothing may come of it; besides, this letter must end now, if I'm to catch the post. But if anything does happen, please try to see some way. You could do it; however impossible it seems. Anyway, please don't be angry with me.

Your most loving sister, admirer and well-wisher

Merry.

Well, whatever she'd done, he wouldn't be angry with her; he was too grateful for her letter, all the more so because she had written it at a time when her own affairs might have been expected to fill her mind. And how astonishing that anyone of her age should be so shrewdly clear-sighted! Well, he'd always thought she had the best brains in the family. Still, he didn't see how she could have found any way of helping him.

He went to his record-player and started it at the Andante of the Third Rasoumovsky, telling himself he would play it as a tribute to Merry ... and also to get away from the thoughts her letter had provoked. He lay down on his divan and listened.

But the music did not as usual take over. Instead, he found himself thinking of Merry's menace-filled mist ... and then of Violet calling through the mist that afternoon, Violet sitting on the stubble with her long legs in laddered stockings thrust out in front of her. No other woman had ever told him she was in love with him. Suppose he did go and stay with her? At least that would be – in Merry's phrase – 'a bit of living'. Pretty luxurious living, he suspected, amused that like his brother and sisters he was gravitating towards riches. According to a theory of Drew's, one got from life what one subconsciously expected. Well, perhaps early security had conditioned them all to expect its continuance. And there were precedents for young composers having rich patrons. Violet, dear horizontal Violet, would make a charming patron. He found his mental stress driven away by a relaxing surge of emotion...

But he was incapable of sustaining such a mood for long and he soon felt annoyed with himself for using the music as a mere background for it. He got up and turned off the record-player. And as he did so, there was a knock on the door.

It would be Violet, of course. He was instantly furious with her, yet some of the tenderness of his banished mood remained. And the fury and the tenderness combined in a curiously pleasing manner. For once, Violet had chosen her moment well. He unlocked the door and flung it open.

Jane stood outside.

'Richard, I *am* sorry, but there's a personal call for you – from somewhere in Yorkshire.'

'There can't be. I don't know anyone in Yorkshire.' Perhaps it was one of Aunt Winifred's myths. 'Did my aunt take the call?'

'No, I did, and I'm quite sure about Yorkshire, though I didn't hear the name of the place clearly. It sounded like...'

But he barely waited to hear. He had suddenly remembered that he did indeed know someone in Yorkshire. So that was what Merry had been up to...

Epilogue Under the Dome

Jane

Unwisely, she'd let herself sit down in the music room after Richard went to the telephone, and had at once begun thinking of Rupert Carrington. She would always associate the room with their last meeting. When in there talking to Richard, a few days before, she'd held such thoughts at bay; but, left alone, she didn't even attempt to and was soon extremely depressed. For some while now she had given up hair-splitting as to the exact nature of her feeling for Rupert and simply accepted the fact that he mattered greatly to her; but her work, her plans, and an only occasionally lifted embargo on what she thought of as 'sentimental wallowing', had kept her cheerful. The music room provided an irresistible background for wallowing and it was a good ten minutes – Richard hadn't come back – before she returned to the house. She had found the hall deserted, had her bath and gone to bed.

Now, lying awake, she tried to overcome her depression by plans for the future and started worrying in case Richard would not agree to her scheme. She then thought uncomfortably about Richard and Violet. One simply couldn't believe that he ... but unfortunately one could. Perhaps even at this very moment... The house seemed unnaturally quiet. Miss Carrington might have gone to bed but surely not the other two, not so early. Her guess was that they'd slipped out to the music room while she was in her bath. Perhaps she'd hear them return ... or perhaps she wouldn't.

She then thought of Clare, accused herself of intolerance and exonerated herself. One was *not* narrow-minded; one hadn't been shocked that Rupert Carrington had a mistress. But for a lonely widower to find consolation (temporarily) with a woman no one could expect him to marry was a different matter from Clare's ugly affair. Clare must be mercenary.

She turned her thoughts to Drew in that cluttered Edwardian drawing-room at Whitesea. She was glad she could remember it and picture him there. And now Merry was with him. A pity one hadn't seen the dear child and heard her full story; Richard's version had been brief. It was pleasant to imagine Merry growing up and falling in love with Lord Crestover... But, oh dear, was one going to lie awake all night?

Waking suddenly, her first thought was: 'Well, I did get to sleep.' Then she wondered why she was so completely, alertly awake. Had something disturbed her? At that moment, she heard a definite sound outside – surely a car door closing? She got up, parted her heavy curtains and found it was just beginning to get light, but she could not yet see as far as the lane beyond the garden. Then she heard the click of the gate. A few seconds later she was able to make out the figure of a man who was coming towards the house. Although she could not see his features she had no doubt

454

whatever who it was.

Swiftly she got into her dressing-gown and bed-room slippers, grabbed a torch from her handbag and lit herself along the gallery, down the stairs and to the back door. She had it unbolted and open when he was still some little way off. Shining her torch towards him she saw him dazzled by it before she turned the beam downwards.

'Who is it?' he asked as he came nearer.

'Jane Minton. I thought you might like to be let in.'

He laughed quietly. 'Efficiency can go no further. You'll tell me next you were expecting me.'

'No. Your car woke me and I looked out.'

He was in the house now. She let him into the hall and said, 'In case you want to rest in your room I must tell you Miss Winifred Carrington's in it.'

'Oh Lord, is she? I couldn't need a chat with her less. Keep quiet a minute and don't let's switch a light on. And put that torch out, do you mind?'

No sound came from any room. After a moment, he said: 'Well, I don't seem to have disturbed anyone. We can talk a little if we keep our voices low. Let's sit down.'

They sat together on the sofa. The dome above them and the two tall windows were grey with dawn.

'Are you back for good, Mr Carrington?'

'In England, yes – but not here. I must go to London when I've seen Richard.' He looked towards the gallery as if thinking of going up to Richard's room.

She doubted if Richard was in it, then reminded herself it was only a guess on her part that he and Violet had gone to the music room; and, even if they had, they might have come back while she was asleep ... though she hadn't slept till long after midnight. Anyway she wanted to keep Rupert Carrington a little longer. 'Perhaps you'd like the latest news of them all,' she suggested; then wondered how she would relay the news of Clare.

'I've a fair idea of what's been happening – in outline, that is; Clare's no letter writer.'

Jane looked at him in astonishment. 'Clare wrote to you?'

'She jotted down some information for Charles Rowley to bring. But perhaps you don't know about him.'

'I do,' said Jane.

'One wouldn't have thought that two such small words could convey so much disapproval.' He sounded amused.

Her standards reeled. 'Surely *you* don't approve of him?'

'At present I'm too stunned by his kindness to feel anything but gratitude towards him. He flew out to Switzerland, found me and brought me back. I'm driving his car – or one of them; he probably has a fleet.'

'But was it wise for you to come?'

'I think so. With his backing I just may keep out of the law's clutches. There's never been a warrant for my arrest. There probably would have been, once I'd been questioned, and there may be now; if so, I'm almost certain to land in jail. But Rowley will lay on a first-rate counsel, and there

456

are some extenuating circumstances. I might get off with a light sentence.'

'But prison!' said Jane, in horror.

'I felt like that when I skipped the country. But, as Rowley pointed out, the stigma isn't what it used to be and the company's quite good. There are plenty of men in jail for offences similar to mine. Anyway, I couldn't have gone on where I was. Rowley would have financed me when my money ran out but he thought, as I did, that I'd find life unbearable. So here I am – hoping for the best but fairly cheerful about the very possible worst.'

He was talking with bravado but such bravado struck her as extremely brave. 'Well, there must be some good in Mr Rowley,' she conceded. 'And he's said to be devoted to Clare.'

'Oh, completely. But don't imagine he's helping me because she wants him to; judging by her letter, all she cared about was getting him back quickly. No, I really believe he has a fellow feeling for me; he's taken plenty of risks. But he's all right now, and how! I feel like a very minor and inefficient warlock befriended by the Prince of Darkness himself.'

She asked if he thought Clare would be happy. He said he hoped so and that Clare was temperamentally like both him and her mother, capable of utter absorption in one person only. 'That's why we neglected our children. I'd say all will be well – unless Rowley gets his divorce. Once married to her, he'd probably be unfaithful. The way things are, he'll go on adoring her – largely because she's given him something he never had before: a sense of sin. Anyway, I doubt if he'll get any divorce; his wife's a Catholic. Well, how are things here?'

She told him of her scheme and he approved of it: 'If Richard can stand it. I shan't be coming down, even if I keep out of jail.'

'There are still some difficulties. Miss Carrington's occupying a room and...' Now she must tell him. 'There's a friend of yours here – Violet Vernon.'

'What? *Why* is she here?'

Embarrassed, Jane said: 'She arrived unexpectedly. And Richard ... felt an obligation to let her stay.'

'But, good God, why?'

There was enough light now to see his bewildered expression. Jane found herself apologizing. 'I'm so sorry but ... I'm afraid he thought you'd been ... supporting her.'

'What, single-handed? It'd be a job for a syndicate. Mercifully, she doesn't need supporting. Violet, my dear Jane Minton, is a wealthy near-nymphomaniac, also a kind-hearted, generous and really very charming girl – or rather, woman; I'd say she's quite thirty. She must have come here after Richard – I knew he'd made an impression. Well, has he succumbed?'

'I don't know,' said Jane. 'Was she, then, merely a friend of yours?'

He said smilingly: 'Violet has no mere men friends. I was occasionally entertained for an illicit and highly luxurious weekend, but I'm afraid she thought me rather elderly. At the risk of shocking you past forgiveness I'd say she might

458

make an excellent un-mere friend for Richard. Well, I'd better wake him now.' He got up and snapped a light on.

So it didn't really matter if Richard was with Violet. And as Rupert Carrington could do no wrong, Jane's standards now prepared to accept their final knock-out. One had been ... well, un-sophisticated. And yet ... it wasn't, after all, a knock-out; instead, she found herself a formula: 'Judge not...'

Anyway, she only wanted to think about Rupert. With the light on she saw him, for an instant, as older and less handsome than she had remembered. Then his present self became the one that existed for her and was infinitely more appealing than his absent, idealized self.

He had picked up a letter from the hall table. 'This is for you,' he said, handing it to her. 'It's Richard's writing.'

'Good gracious!' She tore open the envelope and read hastily.

Dear, kind Jane,
I've run away – just as the others did. The trunk call was from a friend whose father runs a rather progressive school. Merry wrote and told him I wanted a job – she knew him because he stayed here once, after he and I came back from Germany. (I met him there.) It so happens they need someone at once, to teach music and handle their quite good little orchestra.

Please go ahead with your scheme – if you feel you can, on your own. It should be possible now as my aunt has decided to go; also Violet, who assures me she will be off tomorrow – or rather, today, as it's now four in the morning. I'd be grateful if you could spare a little coke for my music room – you can let that, too, if you like; it's been sacrosanct too long. If you need money, you know where I keep it in the study. I've left most of what I still have in hand. Anyway, I'll telephone very soon. And I hope to be in London for the weekend fairly often and could come and see you on my way.

Forgive me for writing instead of talking. You were in your bath when I went back to the barn and when I finally came in it was much too late to disturb you. And I'm just about to start – I promised I'd get there early to meet my friend's father before he leaves for some conference. Besides, running away is obviously a family habit – inherited from Father.

Much love and many, many thanks,
                    Richard.

There was an address and a telephone number at the foot of the letter. Handing it over, Jane regretted Rupert would see the reference to himself. He smiled when he reached it, then said: 'Well, I'm delighted for him. I'll write and wish him luck.' He copied the address and telephone number into his pocket book before handing the letter back to Jane. 'And now, as he's not here, I shall – true to family form – run away again.'

'Can't I get you some breakfast first?'

'No, thanks. I don't want to risk meeting my aunt – or dear Violet or even the maids. Are you willing to run this house, as Richard suggests? If not, it can be closed.'

'I'd like to try,' said Jane. 'Perhaps one day you'll all be here together again.' She had never ceased to long for the life she had once hoped to share with them.

He shook his head. 'I shall never live here again. Some of my children may, but I rather doubt that. Perhaps I did them a good turn by boosting them out into the world. Well, I shall be in touch with you once I know my plans – or the plans others have for me. At present I don't even know where I'm staying; I'm leaving all that to Charles Rowley. Try to feel kindly towards him. Believe me, I've cause to.'

'Then I will, too,' she said, smiling. And after all, he wanted to marry Clare, and it did sound as if they really loved each other. 'I'm afraid you should leave at once if you don't want to see the maids. They get up very early.'

He nodded. 'I'll go the back way.'

She went with him and quietly opened the door. Standing there, in the chill grey early morning, he said: 'Do you know it's just a month today since you saw me off before? I knew then that I was walking out on the perfect secretary – and a very good friend. If ever I get on my feet in business again, would you consider joining me? Though perhaps I shouldn't suggest it until I know if I can keep out of jail.'

'Why not?' She tried and failed to speak lightly. 'Even if you don't keep out you'll one day *get* out. And I shall be waiting.'

'At the prison gates? Don't promise or I might count on it.'

'You can,' said Jane.

'Then I shall. Well, goodbye – what was it Richard called you? Goodbye, dear, kind Jane.'

She blushed with pleasure but spoke calmly. 'Goodbye and good luck, Mr Carrington.'

'Am I rebuked for calling you Jane?'

'Of course not. It's just that secretaries rarely call their bosses by their Christian names.'

'But you're a very rare secretary.'

From high above their heads came the shrilling of an alarm clock. He shook hands warmly and hastily, then hurried through the garden. After closing the gate he turned and waved; an instant later he was out of sight. She waited while he started the car and drove off into the distance, then she went back to the hall and re-read Richard's letter. Everything would work out. She would run Dome House until such time as Rupert sent for her.

She was confident he would send. He must have seen she was devoted to him and it obviously hadn't embarrassed him.

He'd probably guessed she would never hope for anything beyond the opportunity to serve him, and a man in his position was likely to value undemanding, efficient devotion... Also she did feel that he rather liked her. It was, of course, dreadful that he might have to serve a prison sentence. But, in spite of that, never in her entire life had she felt quite so happy.

This Large Print Book for the partially sighted, who cannot read normal print, is published under the auspices of

THE ULVERSCROFT FOUNDATION